They never shoul[d]
battled—never sho[uld]
had gone wrong with time itself, and in mending
such shredded silk, might their loves—
and their lives—be the final sacrifice?

Two people had never truly hailed from such
different worlds as those in Heather Graham's
groundbreaking *The Last Cavalier*.

"This *New York Times* bestselling author
combines mystery with sizzling romance."
—*Publishers Weekly*

The cries in the night acquainted Julie Kingsdon
with one ghost of Kingsdon Hall. But in the haunted
eyes of her mesmerizing brother-in-law,
she found another. Soon nothing could tear her away
from this man—not even the growing fear
that she and her child were in mortal danger....

A woman who returns to her
late husband's home to collect her inheritance
finds herself caught in a web of mystery,
murder and romance in Carla Cassidy's
compelling novel *Mystery Child*.

"Ms. Cassidy engages both our minds
and our hearts with a deftly fashioned tale
of romantic suspense."
—*Romantic Times Magazine* on *Imminent Danger*

HEATHER GRAHAM

considers herself lucky to live in Florida, where she can indulge her love of water sports, like swimming and boating, year round. Her background includes stints as a model, actress and bartender. She was once actually tied to the railroad tracks to garner publicity for the dinner theater where she was acting. Now she's a full-time wife, mother of five and, of course, a *New York Times* bestselling writer of historical and contemporary romances.

CARLA CASSIDY

is an award-winning author who has written over forty books for Silhouette. In 1995 she won Best Silhouette Romance from *Romantic Times Magazine* for *Anything for Danny*. In 1998 she was a finalist in the traditional category for the Romance Writers of America RITA Award. That same year she also won a Career Achievement Award for Best Innovative Series from *Romantic Times Magazine*.

Carla lives in the midwest with her husband and hero, Frank. She believes the only thing better than reading a good book is sitting down at the computer to create a good book.

HEATHER GRAHAM

CARLA CASSIDY

Beautiful Stranger

Silhouette Books

Published by Silhouette Books

America's Publisher of Contemporary Romance

SILHOUETTE BOOKS

ISBN 0-373-21722-6

by Request

BEAUTIFUL STRANGER

Copyright © 2001 by Harlequin Books S.A.

The publisher acknowledges the copyright holders of the individual works as follows:

THE LAST CAVALIER
Copyright © 1993 by Heather Graham Pozzessere

MYSTERY CHILD
Copyright © 1996 by Carla Bracale

Visit Silhouette at www.eHarlequin.com

Printed in U.S.A.

CONTENTS

Dear Reader,

Years ago, traveling up and down the east coast, my family and I began to go to Civil War reenactments. I thought they were so fascinating, with camps all set up, with so many people dedicated to making history come alive. There was something about seeing how horrible it must have been to fight that taught me more than any history book could. The reenactors cooked by campfires, knew the clothing, the insignias, the medicine of the time, and so much about the lives of the people involved. Going to reenactments was really like taking a step back in time.

Once, when we were in Culpeper, Virginia, we arrived at a scene that was truly as good as a painting from the past. The tents were pitched, fires were going, the hills stretched behind the camps and people were going about in antebellum clothing and the uniforms of the time. The scene was wonderful except, on turning, we noticed a concession to the change in centuries—a giant fast-food stand. And it was impossible not to wonder what a soldier of the past might have thought if he had walked into the world today.

That was the inspiration behind *The Last Cavalier*, originally written as the first of Silhouette's Shadows line. It remains a personal favorite of mine, and if you've read it before, I hope you'll remember it fondly as well, and if not, I certainly hope you enjoy. Thanks so much.

Heather Graham

THE LAST CAVALIER
Heather Graham

(originally published under the name Heather Graham Pozzessere)

PROLOGUE

Blackfield's Mountain
September, 1862

Before...

The Confederate cavalry officer stood staring down Blackfield's Mountain, his gloved hands upon his hips, his silver-gray eyes fixed on the field that stretched out below him. His uniform sat well upon his broad shoulders and tautly muscled physique. His plumed hat sat low over his brow, concealing from his waiting men any emotion written in his eyes. His looks were striking; his handsomely chiseled features, hardened perhaps by the endless months of war, but arresting nonetheless. They were features that gave a measure of the man—the silver-gray eyes always steady; his mouth generous; his smile quick. He knew how to command, how to be stern, how to be merciful. Best of all, he knew how to instill his men with courage, while also doing his damnedest to keep them all alive.

A spasm of unease suddenly crept along his spine. He commanded the crest of the mountain at the moment, but there was something he didn't like about the day. The air was dry and still, yet curious gray clouds were forming to the east. It was early morning, but already the battlefield was nearly black with the powder from Yankee mortar and Confederate Napoleons. A man could barely see two feet in front of his face.

But Jason Tarkenton had been given the order to charge, and so he would. Jackson was the commanding general, and Jason deeply respected the man. General Jackson made few mistakes.

Cavalry was most often used as reconnaissance, riding ahead, scouting out enemy positions. Then sometimes cavalry met cavalry ahead of the other troops.

Today, both the Yanks and the Rebs were forced to use their cavalry units to fight. They had done so before. Too many times, Jason thought.

For some reason, though, it seemed that this time it was a mistake. But if old "Stonewall" had ordered him to take his troops into the battle, then Jason would do so. Jackson had ordered them to hold the mountain. They would damned well try their very best to do so.

"Now, Jason?"

He arched a brow. His brother, John, anxiously asked him the question. Young, but a damned good military man for his tender age, John stood holding the reins to Jason's big black gelding. After two years of training at West Point, John had been pulled back from the Yankee stronghold to fight the war. His rank was captain and his duties were to serve Jason as aide-de-camp.

In times like this, he never remembered to address Jason in a proper military fashion. But today, Jason just smiled. It didn't seem like the right time to remind anyone about protocol or procedure. Jason gazed at John, then blinked painfully against the oppressive powder and the debilitating heat of the day.

Now. Yes, it should be now.

Still, he hesitated, and wondered if the awful days of endless fighting in Virginia were wearing him down at last. *He didn't dare hesitate! The battle could be lost through hesitation!* What was wrong? He didn't like the day. He just didn't like the day.

Didn't like the day? Since when did he get to choose when the Yankees would attack?

The enemy had been gathering in the valley, definitely preparing to attack. They had to take the initiative!

He gritted his teeth, determined that his brother would not see his unease or his hesitation. He was accustomed to the blinding properties of the black powder created by the cannon fire and the gun shot. He knew the shouts and cries of battle, the screams of dying men and horses. Damn it, he knew how to lead men, how to charge and how to retreat.

Today, things seemed worse. Different. Maybe it was the air, the damned air. It had a feel about it. As if it were charged with more than an earthly fire.

Maybe it was the sky. There seemed to be a promise of rain from the heavens above. The distant clouds that had grown as black as the powder of cannon fire, seemed to billow and roil in a constant, wild action. Yet here, where he stood, the day seemed unbelievably still.

A tempest was coming. A tempest deeper than battle, louder than any clash of steel. It seemed as if God Himself had grown angry with the fratricide, and was about to grumble out his wrath. There was something ethereal about the air. Something tense, something charged with a strange lightning…

Something ghostly…

Jesu! And he was supposed to be a military man!

He pulled down impatiently on his hat, stiffening, and standing very tall in his cavalry officer's yellow-trimmed gray. Hell, it was war! No matter that he faced half his old friends from West Point, no matter that he had once been *U.S.* cavalry himself. He'd been facing old friends on the battlefield since his troops had first entered the fray at Manassas. This was war. *War.* It was natural that a battlefield should be fraught with tension. That it should be *charged.* It was even natural that God should be angry, watching all the men, so many in the flower of youth, bleed, break and die.

Naturally! There was something ghostly about it all. Men were going to die.

And it was time to enter into the fray.

"Now, John," he said quietly, keeping his emotion from his voice.

But it sure did look like suicide. If the Yank shot didn't get them, they might well be gunned down by their own artillery. He turned slightly, looking out over the field of his men. Young and old. Graybeards and green young fellows, all of them a little lean in the face, since they had been with him quite some time now. Some leaned upon their rifles, some just standing by their mounts. With level eyes and infinite faith, they watched him. In silence, they awaited his command. And every man jack there would follow him without question. He lowered his head, smiling. Well, hell, they had their pride. They might all be as stupid as all get-out to go racing into forces that outnumbered them three to one, but it was the courageous thing to do, and that was one thing every Southerner liked to claim—wagonloads of courage. And honor. He mustn't forget that. Young men fell like flies for the honor of dying for their beloved cause.

He was no better!

Again he reminded himself firmly, *It was war!* They had no choice.

Taking the reins from John, he mounted Max, his huge black gelding. Mortar exploded nearby, uprooting a giant oak. A horse screamed, and the powder in the air thickened around them. Max, good old war-horse that he was, remained still, as accustomed to shot and fire as his master.

"Jackson's asked us to keep the mountain, boys!" he told them.

"Yessir!" cried back one of the men.

"Yessir!" was echoed all around.

He pulled down on his hat again. "I'll guess we'll keep the mountain, then!"

Looking back up the mountain, Jason could scarcely see their own artillery. There was a fallen body at his side. A man killed in the earlier fighting. Jason knew that the dead man was an artillery private only by the stripe of red that ran along the side of his uniform trousers. There was nothing else left that could distinguish his identity.

The smoke cleared somewhat. Jason drew his saber from the sheath at his side and raised it high. Some distant ray of sunshine broke through the clouds and powder to touch down upon the blade, and it glinted silver in the air. The Yanks were down there regrouping, Jason knew. They were ready to start their own charge up the mountain. It would be far better to meet them in the valley, and leave themselves the top of the mountain for their field of retreat. In the valley, there would be room to maneuver, room to beat back numbers far greater than their own.

Now.

"Charge!" Jason ordered.

"Yessir!" rose the voices of his men.

He nodded. His saber slashed through the air as he stretched low over his horse's neck, leading the advance.

He felt the hoofbeats pound beneath him, and the vibration of the earth as over a hundred mounts followed hard behind him. Ahead of him lay the enemy in blue. Men and boys. Some would fall, and some would die. And soon, somewhere, someplace in time, mothers would cry and widows would grieve. And that was what war was: death and despair. But a man was called upon to fight it and it was best not to dwell upon the pain and horror. Better to think about staying mounted, about avoiding the falling shrapnel, about fighting and surviving.

Yet, if he fell… Well, how much would it matter? Widows and sweethearts were supposed to weep, and soldiers were supposed to die.

But here he rode, alive and well, while Lydia lay in the cold darkness of the earth, beautiful even in death, so fragile in that beauty.

"Jesu!" Even above the hideous pounding on the earth and the roar of fire, he could hear his brother's cry to heaven as mortar exploded all around them. The earth came up in big chunks and rained back down upon them. Jason looked John's way. It must have been a hundred degrees, and their uniforms were made of wool. Sweat dripped down the lean planes of John's face.

A chorus of shouts rose up behind Jason, loud and strong. The Rebel yell, coming from each of the men who were riding hard down the mountain for their date with destiny and doom.

They charged into the fray.

Jason lost all track of himself. He met Union steel with his Richmond saber and fought and hacked and fought again. The cavalry troops began the battle; they were quickly joined on the field by the infantry, running behind with their own Rebel yell.

All around him, horses and men screamed. Men in blue and gray. Cannons continued to bellow, guns to roar.

Jason stared into faces. Young faces. Faces of boys still wet behind the ears. Faces that would never age enough to bear more than a pale wisp of peach fuzz. Faces that were gnarled with years, gray whiskered, leathered. He couldn't choose between the faces. Kind faces, hard faces, gentle faces. This was war, so he must battle. When a sword raised to his, he fought for his own life, and shoved back any thoughts of an easier, gentler time when he might have shared a whiskey with any one of these Yanks in some nameless tavern upon a nameless road.

The smoke was awful. The day grew grayer. Darker. What little light there was, reflected in the blood spilled upon the earth.

The Confederate troops gained an advantage, and a retreat was sounded for the Union soldiers.

"*Jason!* We've done it!" John shouted, waving his arm. His horse pranced at a small distance from Jason's. "They're skedaddling, those blue bellies!"

"Look at them run!" cried Henry Ostraw, another of his men.

Jason shook his head with both impatience and sorrow. *Let them go. Let's all live!* his heart cried. But he was an officer. He couldn't let the Yanks regroup and come after them again. "Give chase!" he commanded.

His bugler began to sound out the order on the dark and dusky air. Jason waved his sword in a circle, and cried the order again. "Give chase!" Then he nudged Max's thighs, and the animal sprang forward, lunging into a gallop, racing after the enemy who was already disappearing into the forest at the base of the valley.

Suddenly, there was a roar of cannon, and his brother screamed. Jason saw that John was no longer riding at his side. He raised a hand to Lieutenant Nigel Keefe, his second in command, indicating that he should lead the men on forward. Nigel and his troops obeyed, racing onward into the darkening day.

Jason reined in Max, carefully trotting back, scarcely able to see in the red-and-gray day. He heard a moan, and only then saw John on the ground before him. He hastily dismounted, falling to his knees beside his brother. It was John's arm that had been hit. Shrapnel. The arm was badly ripped up. The bone had been shattered.

The surgeons would amputate, and hell, it seemed that infection always set in after an amputation, and then…

And then a man died.

Not my brother, damn it all to hell! He looked to heaven, both fury and agony in his heart. He'd lost too damned much already. Not John. He wouldn't lose John, too!

John was bleeding, bleeding badly. Jason quickly pulled his mustard scarf from about his throat and applied it as a tourniquet to John's arm. "It's going to be all right," he assured his brother. "I've just got to get a surgeon and—"

"Hell, no!" John protested. "Ah, hell, Jason, it's bad, really bad, and I'm not any man's fool. I'm going to die. Let me go easy, Jason. Don't let those old sawbones chop me up before I go."

"Now, dammit, John. You aren't going to die. I'm not going to let you die." Brave words. He had to get help. Despite the tourniquet, John was still bleeding badly.

But men were bleeding all over the battlefield. Men were dying all over the battlefield. The surgeons, orderlies and nurses were already out, attending to the wounded. They weren't alone. Some wives and lovers, camp followers, even some of the braver local population, were out, too, doing their best to tend to the wounded, to sort the living from the dead.

And seeing to the fallen men in blue, as well as the men in gray.

Jason gritted his teeth. Someone would be along. He had always prided himself on being such a damn good military man. He should turn away from John and ride on to lead his men.

But in the midst of all this suffering, something had to matter. In all the sacrifice and horror—in the great quest for honor—something still had to matter.

John mattered.

"Listen to me, John. You aren't going to die. Hell, I can't fight this stinking war without you! Ma would be rolling over in her grave right now, crashing into Pa! I can't let you go, John. I can't. Don't you dare die on me. The two of them will haunt me the rest of my days!"

As he'd hoped, he drew a painful smile from his brother.

"Now, I'll be right back. You just lie there, nice and still. In case we should start to lose this ground again, shimmy your way under that rock. You don't want to wind up injured in a Yank camp, right?"

John nodded at him bleakly. "You gotta lead the war, Colonel," John reminded him.

"Oh, so you do know my rank?" He was still trying to keep his voice light. "Keefe knows what he's doing. The war will wait for me for just a few minutes, I'm certain."

John tried to give Jason a thumbs-up signal, but pain was naked in his glazed gray eyes. He was just a kid, Jason thought. Barely twenty. That was war. War killed dreams and slaughtered the future!

Sometimes Jason just wished to hell he could walk away from all of it. Just up and walk away. Disappear.

He whistled for Max, and Max obediently came. Quickly Jason mounted his horse again. "You're going to make it!" he told John. He swung Max around, dug his heels in and leaned low against the gelding's neck to race hard with the gray-and-crimson day once again, trying to catch up to his own lines this time.

Jason swore when another cannon shot exploded right in front of him. The air was so thick with the explosion of powder and earth that he couldn't see a damned thing. He blinked and spoke out loud to Max. "Fools! Can't they keep from shooting at their own damned side?"

He reined in, feeling Max's power beneath him as the gelding pranced, waiting for the powder to settle and for light to break through the darkness. A wind had risen with that burst of cannon. A strange wind. One that seemed to come from both the east and the west.

No, the wind didn't come from the east and the west, especially not when the day had been dead calm just a few minutes ago. Dead calm, with a leaden gray sky.

But despite the strange wind, the powder swirl that had filled the air did not settle. It seemed to grow. Odd. There was a loud crack in the sky, like the sound of a cannon, but distinctly *not* the sound of a cannon.

He stared skyward. Clouds, billowing black and gray, seemed to rush down toward him. He threw out an arm in defense—in defense against a *cloud?*—and watched in amazement. There was an arbor of large oaks just to his side. Huge trees that reached the clouds themselves, their branches forming an archway. The clouds billowed and roiled. They curled back into themselves, puffing and swirling there in the archway formed by the swaying branches of trees. He realized with amazement that a strange doorway had been created in the arbor, in the blowing clouds and mist.

All around him strange winds rose, and in their whistling gust he heard a mournful wail, a cry that seemed to echo from the very heart of the dark, twisting heavens. The lashing branches moved like gigantic bony arms, mocking him, beckoning him closer, into their skeletal embrace. And as he watched, an unearthly sensation swept over his body from head to toe, as if someone— or something—was touching him. Touching him with clammy fingers that marked a chilling path down the length of his spine.

The sounds of battle grew dim, as if the fighting were taking place in the far-off distance—as if he heard no more than a memory of those sounds.

Max snorted. "Easy boy," Jason assured him, but he got no farther. His well-trained mount reared and screamed in sudden panic.

As if Max, too, had felt those damp, icy fingers on his flesh....

"Max!" Jason said more firmly, keeping his seat. But then, to his astonishment, his well-trained war-horse bucked and reared again with the violence of a wild stallion. Unprepared for such behavior from Max and half-hypnotized by the strange clouds, Jason reacted too slowly. He was thrown clear and far from the horse, so far that he couldn't even see the animal.

"Max, you son of a mule!" Jason swore as his backside hit the earth. "Max, you get over here!"

The horse whinnied. It seemed as if the sound was coming from very far away.

Jason couldn't see a thing. He pushed up from the ground, rising. He stuck his arms out into the black mist, trying to feel something ahead. He started to walk care-

fully. John was back there somewhere, but Jason didn't
have the time to wait for whatever the hell this was to
blow off. He had to keep walking.

The trees! There they were, ahead of him. The trees
where the clouds had created a shadowy passage through
the darkness and the mist. He had to reach them.

The wind picked up violently. He didn't need to walk
toward the trees anymore; he was being swept there.

Fingers! he thought wildly for a moment. Yes, it was
as if the bony fingers of some huge, unnatural hand
reached for him, dragged him forward. He gritted his
teeth, trying with all his strength to push against the fun-
neling winds. But those fingers had captured him in their
damp, bone-chilling grip. It was like living a nightmare,
feeling himself suspended in time, trapped in the twisting
darkness of this unearthly tempest. The winds howled
around him like the mournful voices of lost souls, their
chill screams and babbling curses hanging in the air.

He was a soldier in Lee's great Army of Northern Virginia! he reminded himself, shaking off the feelings. He
had to be afraid of Yankee guns and sabers, and he had
to rage against any strange winds that stood in his way.

John. He had to help his brother.

Keep moving!

But even as he moved, the earth itself seemed to shift
beneath his feet. Then all of a sudden it was as if he'd
walked into a brick wall. He veered back, tripped and
started to roll.

"Damnation!" he muttered. Bony fingers be damned,
tempests be damned, with his luck, he'd tumble right into
a Yank troop. But he couldn't seem to stop himself. He
was rolling and rolling and rolling. Mist and clouds and
black winds surrounded him.

Wicked, damp, bony fingers seemed to push him right

along. He moved faster. The blackness swallowed him. He was a part of it now, he thought. He reached out desperately for a hold to stop himself.

His head hit a rock, and he saw stars. The trees! He had come between them; he was rolling beneath the arbor or the branches that touched the skies, they, too, with long, bleached white, bony fingers that seemed to reach and stroke and scratch at the sky.

Later, he opened his eyes. For a moment, he lay still, his fingers entwined in the rough grass on the earth. He was still on the mountaintop, he thought. He hadn't gone so very far.

And yet, things were different. The blackness was gone. All gone. As if he had blinked it away. He pushed up and looked at the grass and dirt his fingers clutched. The tall grass was deep green, the earth, brown. The air fresh and sweet smelling. He looked up. The sky was a vivid blue, and the sun was blazing golden, high above him. He could hear a whistling, but no eerie moans, no sounds of battle.

"What the bloody hell is going on?" he muttered aloud. Had he been unconscious so very long? He had thought that he'd barely blacked out, just seconds, from the pain.

He started to rise, but then he heard someone calling out, and he ducked low again. Staring downhill through the long grasses, he could see row after row of tents. Army issue, Union tents. Cooking fires blazed away between the tents and delicious aromas rose from the pots hanging over them.

Then there were clusters of tripods created by angled guns. And there were stacks of supplies piled high beside the tents—blankets, tack, burlap sacks.

And there were people. Men and women.

The women were in simple cotton dresses; few seemed to be wearing many petticoats. They were well dressed for army-camp life. The men were in blue. Yankee-issue blue.

Jason pressed his palm against his temple. Damn, there were lots of them! It seemed that he had stumbled into the main portion of the Union army!

Quickly Jason crawled behind a large boulder and leaned his back against it. He closed his eyes. How had he come here? And just where the hell *was* here? How could he have left the mist and blackness so very far away?

How could he have left the battle, the screams for this? The deep green and rich brown of the earth was fresh and sweet smelling. He looked up. The sky was a vivid blue, and the sun was glazing golden, high above him.

CHAPTER ONE

Blackfield's Mountain

Now...

"I tell you, it was very nearly the worst move old Stonewall made during the entire war!"

Liam Douglas's blue eyes were ablaze beneath his shocking white brows and his gnarled old fist made a startling smacking sound against the rough wood table.

Vickie poured more draft into Milt Mahoney's stein and watched a little anxiously as her grandfather drew breath for a reply to Liam. "Jackson was the best general the Confederacy ever had, and Lee damned well knew it!"

Gramps was just as vehement as Liam. His great fist thundered against the table and his eyes crackled with the same blue fire beneath brows as white and bushy as Liam's. The difference between the two octogenarians, Vickie decided, was that Liam had a few strands of hair left, while Gramps was as bald as a buzzard.

"I say that Jackson made one hell of a mistake here!" Liam insisted.

Vickie decided that it was time for her to step into the discussion. "Boys, boys, *boys,* now!" She swooped into the midst of them, giving both Gramps and Liam refills on their beer. She smiled sweetly at all six of the old men filling her grandfather's tiny establishment and reminded them, "The war ended quite some time ago, you know!

Well over a hundred years ago now! It was *1865*, remember?''

Liam grinned sheepishly; Gramps looked disgruntled. His kepi was askew on his bald head and despite the air-conditioning in the little tavern, he was sweating. This was a big week for the small Virginia farming town. Not only would the battle itself be reenacted on Saturday, but already, some of the largest reenactment encampments ever drawn together were being set up out in Miller's cornfield right alongside the mountain. Everyone in town was involved in the reenactment in some way. Even those bored by history were entranced by the money-making possibilities stretching before them.

Of course, Gramps had always been a major-league Civil War buff, just like Liam. And therefore, she thought, so was she.

Gramps had gleefully decided that with all the tourists in town, they should dress just like the reenactors. So there he sat, in a Virginia militia field-artillery uniform, while she was walking around serving coffee and beer, dressed in a long antebellum dress. Gramps wanted to get the folks into the spirit of the festivities when they came in for their sandwiches and drinks, and this was the way to do it, he had decided.

She had refused point-blank at first—Gramps's passions got to be a bit too much for her at times—but then he had looked at her so mournfully that she had changed her mind. Gramps's business included an artifacts shop as well as the tavern, and there were times when it felt as if she'd had the history of the place up to her teeth.

But she loved Gramps. He was her only living relative. He'd been there for her when Brad had been killed. Gramps had been her only strength. While she still had the dear old man in her life, she was going to do her best to cherish him. He had wanted her in the dress and petticoats, and she could handle that. But she'd drawn the line at the pantalets and corset. There was no way she was crawling into that part of the costume, and he'd better think good and hard about it! Who was ever going to know what she wore beneath the dress?

Gramps had conceded, but it seemed that she had gained a small victory now. Her russet hair was clumped into a net at her nape and she was dying to set it free, just as she was dying to rid herself of the hot layers of her calico gown.

Glancing up at the clock, she saw that the afternoon was gone. She had promised Karen and Steve that she would come down to the Union camp and see them for dinner. Had she told them six? It was almost six now.

The discussion among the old men had picked up again. They had moved on to the battle of Gettysburg. Vickie politely interrupted them. "Do you need me anymore, Gramps?"

"What? Uh, no, honey. You can run on out and see your friends." He hesitated and added gruffly, "You still going to the Yankee camp?"

She had to laugh, setting a kiss upon his bald head. "Gramps, once again! The war ended, remember?" She set her hands upon his shoulders, lowering her head to whisper in his ear. "And I hate like hell to tell you this, but they did win, you know!" She heard his grunt, then rose, winking at his comrades.

Liam snickered and Gramps offered her the ghost of a smile.

"If I were you, young lady," Milt warned her, "I'd take that little filly of yours rather than a car. They aren't letting any cars into the fields where the tents are pitched. Since they have a bunch of the historical-society types coming in with their cameramen and all, they're trying to make everything look just as authentic as possible. You'll have to park way down the road, and you'll have a long, long walk!''

"Thanks for the suggestion, Milt," Vickie told him, glad to receive the information. She wasn't really all that far from the encampments, and Arabesque could certainly use the exercise.

She kissed her grandfather again. "'Night, Gramps.''

"Don't you fraternize with them Yankees too long," Liam teased.

"I promise not to divulge any military secrets," she added with a grin.

Vickie passed from the taproom into the entryway of the old house. She intended to go up to her room and change, but then she paused at the stairway and shrugged. Karen and Steve were very taken up by the make-believe of the whole event. She would stay dressed just as she was.

Gramps's house was old, far older than the Civil War. The carved stairway had been there since the late 1700s, and a tall man could barely walk through some of the doorframes. The foundation for the house had been laid in the late 1600s. It had been a tavern on and off for almost three hundred years.

In the dim light in the entryway she caught sight of her reflection in the wavery hallway mirror. She realized she definitely looked the part that Gramps had asked her to play. Her hand was against her throat and her full skirts were standing out and a web of net still held the bulk of her nearly waist-length hair. Called a day dress, her simple cotton gown had a high-buttoned bodice and a small frill of lace along the wrists, neckline and hem. It was pretty, though, and the dark colors of the plaid went well with her deep auburn hair and bright blue eyes. Gramps had ordered the dress for her from a company that produced the historically accurate uniforms the "soldiers" wore for the reenactments.

She shrugged at her reflection, thinking that the full skirts were actually flattering to her long legs and slim waist. Maybe she'd been unfair to resent the costume all day. "Let's get into the spirit of this thing!" she chastised her mirror image.

Going out the front of the house, she walked around to the rear of the old barn outside and into the stables.

Of the ten stalls, only two were in use, one by Dundee, the other by Arabesque. Vickie had bought Arabesque when she had first come home. Arabesque was a beautiful Arabian mare with a deep "dish" nose, the most beautifully cream-colored mane and tail, and softest bay body that Vickie had ever seen. In the deep and painful confusion that had haunted her after Brad's death, Vickie had learned to appreciate her investment. She had once believed she would never be able to truly accept what had happened. But roaming the endless blue and green fields and forest of the Virginia countryside on the sweet, spirited creature had allowed Vickie to come to a certain peace. She loved the mare.

Vickie slipped a bridle over the horse's nose, led her from her stall, and decided that no one could possibly be looking and made a less-than-ladylike leap onto the mare's sleek, bare back.

Heading northward, she gave Arabesque free rein, delighting in the cooler air that was coming with the setting of the sun. Summer had been viciously hot. Only the evenings gave a slight respite.

She slowed to skirt a neighbor's cornfield, then raced across a barren plain again, climbed over the mountain,

and at last saw the endless rows of authentically repro-
duced Civil War tents that stretched all along the cornfields. Yanks to the west, Rebels to the east, and all manner of sutlers, or salesmen of various goods, were set up
in between. Vickie reined Arabesque to a standstill. There
was really something special about the scene. The giant
Coca-Cola truck—which had been parked there all
through the long, hot afternoon by the sutlers' stands—
was long gone, as was the big semi that had hauled in
Porky's Big Pit Barbecue. The sun was almost down. The
horizon gleamed gold and pink over the few sentries who
packed corncob pipes and leaned against wooden fences.
A lone fiddler, silhouetted in the waning light, played a
soft and mournful tune.

"It really is rather beautiful, Gramps," she said softly.

Vickie nudged Arabesque and picked her way down
the mountain and through the trails within the cornfields.
She came upon the fiddler who had been joined by a
young man with a harmonica. She smiled, listening to
them. "Pretty tune," she said at last.

The fiddler, a young man with warm brown eyes and
hair, smiled back. "Pretty lady," he replied softly.

Her smile deepened. "Thanks. Could you tell me
where I could find the 5th Pennsylvania Artillery, Company B?" she asked him then.

The soldier gave Arabesque a pat on her silky neck.
He saluted, tipping his kepi to her. "Straight on down
the line here," he advised her. "You can't miss them.
They've a big flag out with their insignia on it."

"Thanks again. And good night."

"G'night, ma'am."

She idly walked Arabesque down the line, then noticed
the flag for the 5th Pennsylvania Artillery just a few tents
up ahead.

"Victoria!"

"Steve!" she cried delightedly.

Vickie slid off Arabesque and ran forward to meet the tall slim man with the slightly graying beard who had called her name. He picked her up off her feet, twirled her around, and set her at arm's length from himself. "You're looking good, Vickie, real good! The country air must agree with you!"

She shrugged. "Coming home is always good for the spirit, I think."

He smiled at her warmly. "It's a really beautiful place to come home to. I'm enjoying it tremendously here."

"Vickie!" Karen, Steve's wife, came running around the tent, with her dimpled face aglow, green eyes flashing, and braided blond hair flying. Vickie hugged her friend enthusiastically, then pushed away from her. At first she had thought that Karen had put on a little weight. But the hug had allowed her to realize that Karen was pregnant!

"Oh, you didn't tell me!" Vickie chastised. Then she added quickly, "Congratulations! How very wonderful! Oh, Karen! Are you sure you should be out here like this in your condition?"

"Vickie! I'm pregnant, not sick!" Karen assured her with a laugh. "Besides, Steve has a phone in his car and I'm not due for over three months. I'm fine. Promise."

"Fine enough to sleep in a tent?" Vickie asked, looking from one to the other of the pair.

"I'd sleep anywhere with Steve," Karen assured her, taking her husband's arm affectionately.

"Sure! Make me the heavy!" he moaned, but his gaze upon his wife was very tender. For the first time in a long time, Vickie felt the jagged edge of pain and loss sweep through her. She gritted her teeth, forcing her smile to stay in place. She could remember love like that.

"Come on," Karen said, blissfully unaware of her friend's heartache. "Let me introduce you around."

A number of Steve's fellows from the company were already milling around, jockeying to be close to the newcomer. Vickie was complimented on her gown and her horse, and then on her eyes. At that point, Karen told them all to behave and led Vickie to the cooking pot where she looked down with a mournful expression at some very pathetic vegetables.

"Made from a historically accurate recipe—but not exactly gourmet," Karen warned her. Vickie laughed.

"I don't care what I eat, as long as I eat with friends!" she teased her.

Karen flashed her a quick smile. "Yes, well, thanks to that big lunch I had from Porky's Barbecue, I'm able to agree. Look at this stuff—yuck!"

"Well, I suppose it's authentic."

Karen shoved an onion around with a large wooden spoon. "Maybe it doesn't taste as bad as it looks," she suggested hopefully.

"Maybe... Then again, I should have had the two of you up to the tavern. Gramps makes the meanest chili you've ever tasted this side of the Rio Grande."

"Torture! Torture!" Karen said, shaking her head. "Odd, how I just have a craving for chili at this moment. Well, we'll survive."

Dinner really wasn't so bad. Steve was in with a nice group of guys. One of his friends, Jerry Svenson, told her that the company was made up of New Yorkers, Pennsylvanians and Ohioans. They came from all walks of life, and tried to meet at least three times a year to decide which reenactments, battles and encampments they were going to do each year. "We're actually an open lot," he told her. "Some of the companies—North and South—are made up of men who hail from the same town, and had ancestors in the exact same companies in the real war. Real bunches of good old boys! They fight the war over and over again, as if it were still real. Fanatics."

She smiled, enjoying the cool breeze. "My grandfather is one of those 'good old boys,'" she told him.

"Oh, sorry! I didn't mean—"

"It's all right. And it is funny sometimes. They all had ancestors who actually fought right here, and believe me, they almost come to blows over who made the mistakes!"

"It's easy to become overly involved!"

His words were no sooner out than voices rose around them. Someone was arguing that Ulysses S. Grant had been no better than his predecessors—he had just come around with more men and supplies when Lee's men had just been too decimated and dog-tired to fight anymore.

The reply was quick and furious. Grant had been a damned good general—at the very least, he'd quit retreating.

Vickie smiled. She realized that she was having a good time. She also realized that Steve and Karen were trying very hard to make sure that she had a good time, and that was why they had invited her here. There were a few other wives around like Karen, who had joined their husbands in the reenactment. But the company was mainly male, and Vickie was definitely receiving a fair share of masculine attention.

And Jerry was pleasant. He was a single stockbroker with nice brown eyes and a deep, rich baritone voice.

Vickie just wasn't in the market.

"Where did you meet Steve and Karen?" he asked her.

"My husband and Steve started off in school together. We've been friends for years."

He frowned at the word *husband*. Karen was calling her, and Vickie decided not to enlighten Jerry as to her widowed status. She grinned, excused herself and hurried to Karen. The marshmallows Karen had tried to roast had turned to charred globs of glue.

Vickie laughed, trying to get Karen started again. "I give up!" Karen moaned. She watched Vickie as Vickie reset the sticks to go over the fire. "So how do you like Jerry?"

"He's very nice." She handed the sticks to Karen. "Now toast them—don't melt them."

But Karen ignored the marshmallows.

"Vickie, I know how deeply in love you and Brad were. But he's been dead a long time now. And I'm beginning to think that you're burying yourself down here—"

"I'm not," Vickie assured her quickly, squeezing her friend's hand. "I don't intend to mourn forever and ever…honest. It's just that I had the right thing once. If the right thing comes around again, I'll know it."

"But, Vickie, you'll never know—"

"And honestly, Jerry is very nice. I enjoyed his company. And I'll be back. I'll see you tomorrow. Tomorrow the public is allowed in and visit the camps, right? I'll come and sit with you for a while." She wrinkled her nose and deepened her accent, addressing the group. "Besides, I promised Gramps that I wouldn't spend too much time with any damned Yanks!"

"Leave if you have to—but don't forget, you promised us chili, right?" Karen laughed, and let her go. Steve came along, leading Arabesque. Vickie thanked him and mounted the horse. Again she waved a cheerful good-night to all of Company B, and turned Arabesque around to retrace her steps back home.

Salutes and waves and the warmth of campfires followed her at first. But she hadn't gone very far before she realized that she had truly left the light of civilization behind her to ride into the darkness. Once she was away from the glow of those fires, the night seemed stygian.

She was well accustomed to the country, but this night seemed exceptionally dark. There was no moon above to light her way. She reined in on Arabesque and looked back to the camp, suddenly seized by an eerie feeling of impending danger.

"How can I be afraid here?" she mocked herself out loud. But it was dark. So damned dark.

And no matter what she told herself, a feeling of unease had taken root inside her.

Arabesque seemed uneasy, as well. She suddenly whinnied, and then reared high. A night breeze picked up, strong and wild. The horse reared again.

"What—" Vickie began.

There was a blur in the darkness. A figure leapt from behind a rock with such speed that it seemed to swoop down upon her like the wings of a giant bird.

Vickie shrieked in terror as Arabesque reared wildly again, nearly pitching over backward. Vickie was a good rider, but she was bareback in her ridiculous long gown. She lost her grip. Crying out again, she was catapulted to the ground. She hit it hard.

Dazed, she heard a voice. A deep, soft masculine voice with a definite Virginia slur to it. "Whoa, whoa, there!" the voice from the darkness said, soothing Arabesque. For a moment Vickie remained where she was, too

stunned to be frightened, but then she heard the tremor
of hoofbeats against the earth as Arabesque went racing
away in fear. She heard a mumbled intonation of fury
from the man, and then she tried to rise. Her head was
splitting. What was the idiot doing?

"You stupid fool!" she hissed irately, but she was
quickly silenced. Rough hands held her by the shoulders,
dragging her to her feet. Her head still spinning, she
stared up into a pair of fierce, blazing, silver-gray eyes
that loomed out of the darkness, and a face that was taut
with tension.

She knew that she should be afraid. But the fear didn't
sink in quite yet. She was staring at him, realizing that
he was very handsome. All the planes and angles of his
face were lean and strong and nicely sculpted. The nose
was straight and the mouth, full and sensual.

"Shush!" he warned her.

"Don't you dare shush me!" Vickie protested loudly.
She noticed his cavalry hat then, and the large sweeping
plume that protruded from it. His uniform was gray wool
with yellow trim. Southern cavalry. Damned authentic,
right down to the dust and gunpowder marks. She wasn't
sure about the insignias on his uniform. What was he? A
colonel?

What difference did it make? It was all pretend.

And he had just caused her to be thrown. In fact, she
could have been killed. "Why, you incredible lout!
You—" she lashed out again.

A hand clamped over her mouth again. She started to
struggle but she suddenly found herself held tightly in
his arms, and she felt the deep simmering fire of the silver
in his eyes as they stared warningly down into hers.
"Sorry, ma'am. But you aren't going to get me caught!"

Caught? Wasn't he taking this playacting just a bit too seriously? What kind of a lunatic was this man?

She twisted, kicking him in the shin. She was furious, but panic was beginning to seize hold of her and she knew she had to act quickly. He grunted in pain and she cast back her head to scream again.

But she never managed to do so. His reflexes were incredibly fast and his hand was over her mouth again so quickly that she didn't manage to emit a single sound. "Shush, and I do mean shush, this time!" he warned her sharply. "All that I wanted was your horse, but I've lost that now. I really don't mean you any harm but I will be damned before I'll let any Yankee-loving whore get me tossed into a prison camp for the duration of this war!"

Her eyes widened incredulously and she was suddenly fueled by her fury again.

Enough was enough. She jerked hard, freeing herself from his grasp. She cracked her hand across his face with all her fury, and opened her mouth, not sure if she meant to scream or tell him exactly what she thought of him.

But it didn't matter. She never managed to do either. Suddenly he had dipped low and butted her belly with his shoulder, throwing her over his back. The air was knocked clean from her. She couldn't even breathe.

Then he was running, with her weight bearing him down, up the mountain. Dazed, Vickie realized that if she managed to scream now, it wouldn't do her a single bit of good. She was too far away from the encampment and heading for the trees that rimmed the crest of the mountain. No one would hear her if she did scream.

The panic she had fought now swept violently through her and she clamped down hard on her jaw as she thudded against his shoulder and back. She desperately sought some logical reason or thought. This had to be some kind of a joke. Steve and Karen had put this man up to this and had arranged it with others in their company. They were probably roaring with laughter right now. She could just imagine Karen innocently teasing her tomorrow. "Well, we thought that maybe a *Rebel* soldier would do the trick, since we Yanks didn't seem to be quite what you wanted...."

Yes, it had to be a trick.

Because if it wasn't, a maniac was dragging her up a mountain, and into an endless trail of forest and deep green darkness.

High atop the mountain, her captor stopped at last. He dropped her down upon the grass and retreated a couple of steps. She could barely see him in the darkness, but at least he was gasping now. Gasping desperately for breath. With some satisfaction, Vickie realized that it had exhausted him to carry her straight uphill for all that distance.

Served him right.

She stood up. She was frightened, but she was still so angry that she only had to swallow once for the courage to speak.

"All right, all right!" she told him. "Cute. Fine. Fun. I'm laughing. It was great. What a performance. But now, if you'll just excuse me—"

"You're not going anywhere," he said, interrupting her softly. Yet despite the quiet tone of his words, she felt a shiver snake along her spine. He meant them.

"I'm going where I damned well please!" she informed him, desperately determined that bravado would get her out of this. She whirled around. "Watch me!"

She started walking in the direction from which they had come, her arms swinging, her strides long. But despite her speed, she had barely gotten anywhere before he was upon her. She hadn't heard him move! Hadn't heard a thing. There had just been the slightest whisper of air, and then she was flying. In his arms, and flying.

She landed hard on her backside with the handsome but maniacal stranger straddling over her.

"I told you, I really don't want to hurt you!" he said, catching her chin between his thumb and forefinger. "But you came out of the Union camp," he said, bending closer. She saw the startling tension in his strong features, the fire in his eyes. "I'll be damned a thousand times over before I'll be turned in by a little redheaded witch!"

She stared at him for a long moment, shaken, and yet still furious. What was going on? Who would carry out a joke like this for so long? Was he mad?

But he didn't look mad. He looked just like a soldier, one weary and accustomed to battle, strong and determined. Not cruel, but needing to survive.

There was no war now! It had ended well over a hundred years ago! He was striking, he was unique, but he was either halfway—or all the way!—insane, or else going way too far with this reenactment business.

She stared at him a long moment and then exploded. "I have had it! I mean, I have had it! Okay, okay, I know that some of you guys really get into this thing, but I have really had it. Enough is enough. Now you listen, and listen good. You let me up. You let me up right this second, or so help me God, I will press charges against you for kidnapping and battery!"

A tawny brow hiked up into a curious arch over one of his sizzling silver eyes. "Charges! Charges! Oh, ma'am, I think not! You may be cottonin' up to the Feds here, lady, but this is still the great state of Virginia, and you're addressing a colonel in the Army of Northern Virginia. If any charges are going to be levied, I'll be the one leading those charges!''

"You are an idiot!" she accused him. He seemed really amused now. He didn't trust her in the least but he didn't seem to like the look of her one bit. But with his hard thighs straddled around her hips and his fingers pinning her wrists to the ground, she had nothing to fight with but words. "A fool!" she cried. "Get off of me! If you want to file charges, file charges—"

"Not tonight, I'm afraid. Not tonight!" Once again, his voice was soft. It carried the same chilling determination. "I'm afraid that neither of us is going anywhere tonight."

She felt his silver eyes, pinning her to the ground as strongly as the powerful heat of his touch. "What do you think you're doing!" she cried.

"Surviving," he replied, his gaze steady. "I've got to make it back. I've got to. I've got an injured man waiting for me."

"Who's injured? Tell me, maybe I can—"

"No Yankee help!" he said angrily. He shifted his weight, and she tried with every ounce of her strength to escape him then, but it didn't matter. He rolled her to her stomach and caught her wrists behind her back. He held them there and she screamed aloud in an absolute panic when she heard the fabric at her hem ripping away.

"I'm not going to hurt you!" he reiterated impatiently. "If you would just please shut up!" Apparently he didn't intend to hurt her at the moment, but he didn't intend to let her go, either. He was binding her wrists together with the fabric from her own gown.

Tears stung her eyes. She tasted the dirt and grass from the mountaintop.

She began to seethe and swear furiously against him.

Whoever he was, he was the lowest form of life she'd ever encountered in all her years. "You are an incredible idiot, a madman—oh, my God, I can't think of anything ill enough to call you! Bastard, slime, fool, madman—"

His head lowered down to hers against the ground. She felt his husky whisper against her ear, and heard his words, deep, masculine, warning. "I'm going to ask you once, lady. Please quit."

"You're nothing but a petty criminal!" she cried. Oh, God, she hoped that he was petty! What did he intend? "A snake in the grass, the most incredible ass—!"

"Enough!" he warned her.

"No!" she shrieked. "It's not enough. You've got to let me go—"

She heard fabric ripping again. He rolled her back to face him again and she realized that he'd pulled off another good swatch of her hemline. "No!" she cried, staring into his eyes. And he stared back, with those haunting silver eyes, with his disturbingly handsome and set features, and shook his head slowly. The barest curve of a smile turned his lips. "I'm sorry. I've got to get through the night." For a moment she was still, staring into his face. It seemed that he was so very haggard, so very war weary. It seemed as if he really was sorry, as if he didn't want to hurt her. But it also seemed as if he would have his way.

"No—"

The swatch of cloth was bound around her mouth. She shook her head wildly, fighting his touch. She stared at him then, fighting the tears that stung the backs of her eyes. It seemed that he was real....

But he couldn't be. She had been bound and gagged by a madman on the mountain crest. She was nearly helpless. He would hurt her now....

But he didn't touch her again. He straddled over her without a hand on her. He stared back at her, watching her, maybe a little amused, definitely very exasperated. Once again, she thought that he seemed ridiculously real in his uniform. She'd seen so many of those that belonged to the reenactors, and this one was authentic to the last detail. He was so striking in his person with his neck-length tawny hair, silver glinting eyes, lean cheeks, square jaw and hard, set features.

"Woman," he said very softly, "do you ever shut up?" Obviously, he wasn't waiting for an answer. "Go to sleep now," he commanded.

He rose, a tall, tautly muscled man, a powerful figure, standing over her. A man with eyes that blazed a definite strength and warning.

Sleep!

He turned away, and left her.

Sleep!

Oh, no, she would never, never sleep. Never. She was alone on a mountaintop with a maniac, bound and gagged. Her heart was pounding mercilessly, and she was terrified.

He hadn't hurt her. Not yet!

He didn't hurt her. Time passed. He came nowhere near her. She began to shiver with fear and with the damp night chill that settled over the earth.

Suddenly, a warm woolen jacket was tossed over her. A soft, masculine whisper touched her ears. "Please, shut up for a while, and we'll dispose of the gag."

She swallowed hard and nodded. Screaming wasn't going to get her anywhere up here anyway.

He untied the gag. She breathed deeply. She felt him watching her in the darkness, waiting for whatever she might try to do. She lay still, then flinched as he moved toward her, but he was only adjusting his jacket over her shoulder.

"Is that any better, ma'am?" he asked.

It was insane, really insane. His voice was so deep and husky. Masculine. A sexy voice.

She was *going* insane. He was a madman, and she was thinking that he had an arresting voice, a sensual one....

"Please, try to understand," he continued. "I really don't want to hurt you. I don't even want to hold you here. I just can't take any chances."

Bewildered and exhausted, Vickie held silent. She felt him lie down beside her, stretching out, just inches away. She closed her eyes tightly. Was he dangerous? How did one deal with such a misguided, demented madman? Humor him? Keep fighting him? Stay still?

She'd always suspected she should have taken more psychology classes in college instead of music and art.

What did they say to do on all those news programs? Memory eluded her.

He was so close to her. Lying beside her. Warm, human, and masculine. He had to sleep. She would lie still; she would feign exhaustion and pretend to sleep herself. And in the darkness of night, when he was deeply sleeping, she would manage to stumble to her feet and slip away.

Vickie shrieked anew at his sudden motion in the night. "Sorry," he apologized abruptly, but he wasn't sorry enough to keep from tethering her bound wrists to one of his own with another long strip of her skirt. She heard it ripping, felt it pulled taut. Terror filled her again.

Now. Surely, he was determined on rape or something worse....

But he was not. He lay down beside her again. She felt his warmth again. Heard his breathing in the night.

She stared numbly at the velvet sky. Night had come in earnest. Ironically, it was beautiful. The night heavens were a deep, black velvet color, touched by a thousand tiny stars that seemed to dazzle in a sea of tranquillity. The moon had risen now and sat high above her, casting a gentle, golden light down upon them.

Then suddenly, a cloud came creeping slowly over the moon. Inch by inch, it stole away the gentle light. From somewhere, she heard the high, mournful cry of a wolf.

It couldn't be a wolf, it couldn't be. They hadn't had wolves in this area in years and years....

There it went again. Distant, dim. The night seemed to have grown very cold. Tremors seemed to dance down her spine. She shivered, feeling as if someone had walked over her grave.

What was she doing to herself? She knew this mountain, loved it...

And she was suddenly terrified of it! Shivering, watching a dark cloud, listening to the howl of the wind or...

Something.

He lay closer to her. She blinked back sudden tears, amazed to be grateful that he was near her. Yes, he was her kidnapper, but he was strong and solid against the dark clouds in the night....

It was his fault that she was here!

But it didn't matter. She inched closer to him. And oddly, he was the protection against the fear she couldn't grasp or see.

She should fear him! she warned herself.

And she stared up at the dark sky, teeth clenched tightly together as she wondered whether to pray for the break of day...

Or pray instead that the night might last forever.

CHAPTER TWO

She was shivering. Somewhere deep in the night, she had been dreaming about being kidnapped, about being tied up, and now she was cold and shivering. Her nightmare, however, was very deep, and she couldn't seem to wake from it. She kept shivering.

Then suddenly, she was warm. Something was around her shoulders, comforting her against the cold. She was held close, tenderly, and felt the sun-sweet warmth entering into her body, into the length of her. The dreams faded, then disappeared. She was wrapped in a curious fog of security and she slept very well.

Then she awoke. Slowly. She heard birds chirping. Light seemed to beat against her eyelids. She felt the tickle of dew-damp grass against her nose.

She opened her eyes. Slowly.

And she saw the mountain, saw the grass. And the sky. Very beautiful today. Blue, with just a few wisps of soft white clouds. Extraordinary. They seemed to sweep by at a very swift speed, gentle, intangible.

Her nose itched. She wanted to scratch it. She couldn't move her arms. They were cramped and stiff.

But she was still warm. Despite the mountain, despite the chill of night that the sun had yet to burn away.

And she realized with a strangled little gasp of fear that her nightmares had been the truth, and any sense of comfort had been the greatest lie. She had been kidnapped. She was still being held. No one had come to rescue her in the night.

And her false sense of security had come from the very man who had caused this horror. His wool cavalry jacket was over her shoulders, and since she had probably shivered through that anyway, he had used the length and curve of his own body against hers to give her warmth. And his arm had come around her, and he held her still.

She almost cried out loud, but choked back the sound. What could she do? Could she possibly escape him in any way now? Ease from his hold, work upon the bonds that he had created from her own skirt hem?

First, she had to rid herself of him! She clenched her teeth together hard, trying to shift out of the draping cover of his arm. She shimmied and inched until she was free from his weight and his touch, and a great sense of relief came sweeping over her. She could manage this.

She tried to lie still and work studiously with her wrists, desperate to ease them from the fabric, equally desperate to keep still. She managed to undo the strip of fabric that tied her to her abductor. But her wrists were still bound up tight. Determined, she kept up the effort, feeling the tiny little beads of sweat break out on her brow, even though it was still very early morning, and the sun had yet to make the day warm at all.

Ease it, ease it...

She worked forever, feeling the sun, listening to the birds. She was almost free, could almost taste the sweetness of freedom. And then she heard him, heard his slow deep drawl, his words laced with a certain amusement.

"Ma'am, just what *do* you think you're doing?"

She flung over on her back, staring at him, longing to strike him with all her strength. He was up on an elbow, completely relaxed, watching her efforts with grave humor. He had been awake all along, she was certain. He had been watching her all the while she had been struggling to free her wrists. There was a subtle curve to his lips, a striking light to his silver-gray eyes. For a moment, despite her renewed fury and fear, she was taken aback again by his appearance. Morning's light did all manner of good things for him. Despite the shadowed hint of stubble on his cheeks, the lines and planes of his face were even more arresting, clean, almost *noble!* The curve of his mouth was hauntingly sensual, the flash of his eyes and the tousled length of his hair were startlingly appealing.

This was the man who had kidnapped her.

Her wrists weren't quite free. Her feet were. She lashed out with them strongly, furiously, catching his shins with a vengeance. "You sly, mealymouthed—"

"Eh!" His interruption was swift and frightening. Her feet had landed hard against his legs, and now he was landing hard against her. With swift agility he pounced, straddling over her waist, her bound wrists caught in either of his hands. She gritted her teeth, wildly trying to roll and free herself again, and managing to go nowhere. "Stop it!" he commanded.

She went still, staring up at him. "This has gone too far!" she cried out, trying very hard to remain calm. "It has gone too far! Let me go!"

He shook his head slowly, and seemed unhappy, weary suddenly. So weary, and so very worn, that for a startling moment, she wanted to reach out and touch his cheek.

"I'm sorry," he told her. "I cannot."

"What are you going to do with me?" she demanded, losing her breath in the effort.

"Well, you know," he said very softly, "I've been trying to assure you that I don't intend you any harm. But I've got to find a doctor. And I've got to get back to John. And I can't be taken right now. I can't be. You've got to understand. It's a matter of life and death.''

She shook her head, feeling the prick of tears behind her eyelids. ''It's not real!''

One tawny brow flew up. He sat back on his haunches, still straddling over her but keeping his weight on his own legs, rubbing his stubbled chin as he looked down at her. ''Not real?'' he repeated. ''Well, hel—'' he began, but broke off abruptly. ''Not real, hmm? None of us ever thought it was going to be real. Not like this. Not the Yanks, not the Rebs. We each thought we could beat the other in a matter of weeks. Fooled ourselves, all of us. But it's real. And it's John who is dying somewhere, and I've got to go back. And you're going to help me. You're obviously in deep with the Yanks around here. I need to know their positions, and you're going to give them to me.''

She inhaled sharply. He wanted to know their positions? Well, they were posted all over town!

''That's it? You want to know where the Yanks are,'' she asked carefully, ''and then you'll let me go?''

She saw his jaw twist slightly. ''I may need you with me for a while.''

''Oh!'' she exclaimed, feeling a fresh wave of fury sweep through her. ''Damn you, you've got to let me up! My grandfather is going to be worried sick. People are going to be looking for me. They'll string you up like smoked bacon if you don't let me go and let me go *now!*''

''I'm sure that lots of people are looking for me,'' he replied wearily. ''They always are. But I'm not going to rot in any Yankee prison camp. Not now. So pay attention to me, and pay attention good. *I do not want to hurt you!* But the more you cross me, well, the more you're going to suffer, I'm afraid.''

"You're insane!" she cried out. "The Yanks aren't going to arrest you and put you in any prison camp! They've already won the damned war! They've—"

"What?"

Incredulous, he was leaning down, staring at her. She felt the tension and the fevered heat in his body and she was both suddenly very afraid and, at the same time, remarkably aware of him as a man.

Dear God. He was insane. She had to be insane, too. No, she had just been alone way too long. It had been so long since Brad had been killed, and he had been too wonderful when he had lived. She'd simply missed him too much, and so she was finding this lunatic sensual and oddly arresting.

"The Yanks have won the war!" she spat out.

"They haven't!" he cried out furiously, silver eyes flashing now. "I'd have known if it had been that bad! Stonewall would have never just turned all in, surrendered. I know damned well that the Yanks haven't won yet!"

"Fine!" she shrieked. "And it's just fine, too! They will put you in jail when they get their hands on you! They'll stuff you in a cell, and they'll throw away the key. It will be a nicely padded cell, and—"

She broke off suddenly because he had pulled away, instantly alert and aware, listening.

Someone was coming! she thought suddenly.

"Help!" she cried out. "Hel—"

His hand fell flat over her mouth, so firmly that she couldn't muffle out another sound. She stared at him with daggers in her eyes; she tried to bite. He ignored her, staring toward a clump of bushes.

A jackrabbit suddenly bounded out. It stared at them for a moment, its nose moving a million miles a minute in terror, then it leapt on by.

Great. She was screaming for help—from a rabbit.

His hand fell away. He sat back with a sigh of relief, but eyed her with a deep weariness and warning in his gaze. "For your sake, for my sake, behave."

"Behave! You've taken me as a prisoner! Prisoners do not *behave!* You must be—"

"Thirsty. Very thirsty. And the first thing that you're going to do for me is find a stream. I know we were camped on one for a while, but I seem to have lost my bearings."

She studied him, wishing suddenly and desperately that he wasn't a madman.

"I'll get you to a stream," she told him.

"A stream without Yanks!" he warned.

She lifted her hands toward him, silently imploring that he untie her.

He hesitated. She felt as if fingers closed around her heart. Dear God, it *seemed* real. It seemed so very, very real to him. He didn't want to hurt her. He was just a desperate man....

The war had been over now for more than a hundred and twenty-five years. It couldn't be real. He had to be a madman. Or a paid actor, and that would even be worse.

Yet, to her surprise, he untied her wrists, staring into her eyes all the while. "Don't make me hurt you. Please. Don't try to escape me. My situation is desperate, and I need your help. And if you try to cross me again…"

His voice trailed away. She felt a curious trembling, deep within.

"Then what?" she demanded.

"I'll have to remember that you're the enemy."

"What makes you think that I'm the enemy? I was born here, on this mountain," she said quickly.

He smiled again. A slow, wry smile. "Well, ma'am, you were mighty tight with the Yanks down there. And that usually only happens if you're on their side. Or making real good money from them."

To her amazement, that one took a moment to sink in to her. And the moment it hit was the moment that her hands were freed. She struck out at him wildly, heedless at that moment that he might be a madman. "How dare you, how dare you! How dare you make any such implication about me! You—"

"Whoa!" He had caught her wrists again. But she was really furious and twisting and wriggling with a burst of pent-up tension and they did go rolling, picking up speed as they flipped over and over one another in a rapid descent down the mountain. She cried out, suddenly frightened by the force that had seized them. She felt his hand cupping her head then, and his arm encircling her. His body was taking the brunt of their long fall, and he was doing his damnedest to protect her from danger and damage.

They rolled to a halt at last. For a moment they were both dead still. Vickie could hear his heavy breathing, and feel the length of him, his hand still cradling her skull, the bulk of his tightly muscled body very hard and vital against hers. She felt herself trembling, and close to tears. And there was a curious voice whispering in the back of her mind.... Why did he have to be crazy? Why couldn't he be someone sane, whom she'd met in the usual, sane way?

"Are you all right?"

She nodded jerkily, desperate for him to free her, to not touch her so…closely.

"I'll get you to the stream—" she began, but then she slammed her hands against his shoulders, pushing him from her, her own eyes flashing. "But no more! I don't know if you're a mental case, or if someone is paying you to do this to me, but if you make one more insinuation about me, I'll rot and die with you before I'll make a move, do you understand?"

He didn't answer right away. He stood up, and reached down, offering her his hand. She didn't take it. Her eyes narrowed. "Do you understand?"

He caught her hand, pulled her to her feet without her consent. She stood very close to him and he did not release her. "Then what were you doing with the Yanks?" he demanded softly. "You've got to be a whore or a spy," he said huskily.

He caught her wrist when she would have slapped him. "All right, I'm sorry!" he said, and she found herself drawn against him, as he held tightly to the hand with which she had tried to slap him. "I'm sorry, I'm sorry. But you still haven't answered my question."

"I went to see friends!" she cried out passionately.

Something in the truth of her words seemed to touch him. He was still for a long moment, then said softly, "Well, I can understand that. Seems like I meet a lot of my old friends at the end of a sword."

She lowered her eyes quickly. When he spoke, it was just the same. It was with such ardor, such emotion. He was mad, she thought. He had to be.

"I'll take you to the stream," she told him.

"And not to the Yanks?"

"And not to anyone, not now," she said. She turned, and started back up the way that they had come. The most beautiful little spring meandered alongside the little valley just on the other side of the slope. She had always loved to ride alongside it.

Her heart started to pound. Maybe someone would be there. Someone who knew that she was missing.

And then again, she thought woefully, maybe nobody even knew she was missing as yet! Maybe Gramps would think that she had stayed at the encampment. He would keep shaking his head—just like this madman—wondering how she could spend the night with the enemy. But he might not be worried. Unless Arabesque had returned home without her. But Arabesque might not have made it home. She might have been waylaid by one of the cavalrymen on either side, and the reenactors might be running around, trying to find out who the horse belonged to. And they wouldn't be worried about her at the encampment, because they would be certain that she, who knew the area like the back of her hand, would have made it home, safe and sound.

She swallowed hard, aware that he was following behind her.

Just over the crest of the mountain, she saw the deep valley below. She saw the silver trickle of the stream, and the deep lush field of forest and trees that sloped away on either side.

The Yanks were encamped far down to her left.

The Rebels were encamped way down to her right. Neither of the encampments was visible because of the dense forest of trees. In fact, no one was visible at all from here. No houses, no barns. Just forests and trees and cornfields.

She didn't look back. She kept walking, hurrying for the water. She was all right, she told herself. She was convinced that he didn't intend to hurt her. So what did that mean? He was insane, obviously insane. But he wasn't dangerous. So she just had to humor him. Humor him, and keep him at his distance....

He had stopped behind her, she realized. She paused herself and looked back. He was staring over the mountaintop, seeing the view. She felt a little tremor in her heart again. He was enjoying it. Tremendously. His eyes touched hers, deeply silver.

"It's very beautiful," he said softly. "And peaceful. Like Eden." His eyes left hers, running over the exquisite scenery once again. "It's amazing, isn't it? From here, you might think that we were alone in all the world. And even in summer, the colors are so radiant. Purple and green and blue, and all touched by the yellow of those wild daisies over there. You'd never know that there was war," he said, and voice was very husky, barely a breath. "Never. In a thousand years. It's like the most beautiful place on earth."

"It is the most beautiful place on earth," she heard herself reply softly. Then she was oddly embarrassed, and she turned and hurried downward now, anxious to reach the little stream that was fed from the fresh springs deep within the earth.

He followed her again, staying close. He had given her a certain freedom now. But she realized that if she were to make the slightest move, he could pounce on her in a second. He didn't trust her.

They were certainly even on that score.

She paused at the streambed, kneeling down. She was amazingly thirsty. It had been a long night. Heedless of him for a moment, she cupped her hands in the cool water and brought them to her lips and drank deeply.

He had gone a step farther, striding right into it, burying his face in it. He soaked his throat and his sleeves and half his shirt. Vickie sat back, watching him. Then she ripped off more of her hem, wet it and dripped the cool water around her throat and neck, lifting her hair, relishing the sweet feel of it. She closed her eyes, listening to the movement of the water and feeling the sun. Then she opened her eyes, and discovered him staring at her, and the expression in his silver eyes was a startling one, a *hungry* one.

But it was quickly gone. He blinked, and once again his gaze and expression revealed nothing to her—nothing except hardness and determination. She stood quickly, aware then that she had done a good job of soaking herself. Her calico day dress was glued to her breasts.

"What now?" he asked a little bit desperately.

She was startled when he suddenly walked over to her. He lifted her left hand. His eyes were like blades on hers as his fingers moved over the simple gold wedding band there.

"Husband?" he asked her.

She felt a rise of color flood to her cheeks. She wrenched her hand free. "Dead," she lashed out.

"The war?"

"Yes." Then she realized that he meant *this* war. "He was killed in Iraq," she said swiftly. And despite herself, she heard bitter words fall from her lips. *"Friendly fire."*

"His own artillery?" he demanded.

Her eyes widened. At least he understood that. She nodded.

"Iraq?" he queried.

She sighed. Oh, he was good. There hadn't been any such place known as *Iraq* during the Civil War. Or the War Between the States, as Gramps was determined to call it.

"Never mind," she said wearily.

"Which army was he fighting for?" he demanded.

With a groan, Vickie sank down on the damp stream embankment. She shook her head. "We just have one army now. Just one."

He knelt down before her. He touched her chin, lifting it so that he could see into her eyes. "Which army?"

"The United States Army," she said wearily. "You don't believe me." She shook her head again, trying desperately to understand how this attractive, masculine and appealing man could be a maniac. "You must be a business exec who has snapped," she said flatly. "Hey, I understand, the pressure today can do it. People do just snap."

"I haven't snapped," he said angrily. "And I don't believe you! We haven't surrendered. We fight better. It's our homeland. And Stonewall wouldn't surrender us."

"Stonewall is dead," she said flatly.

He wrenched her up suddenly by her shoulders. "What?" he demanded fiercely.

"Stonewall Jackson is dead. But then again, so is Lincoln. Lee is dead, Grant is dead! Heck, Jefferson Davis survived them all, but damn it, he's dead now, too!"

"Stop it! I don't believe you, I don't believe any of it—"

"We're in the midst of the 1990s—"

"It's 1862—"

"No, no! You're all pretending that it's 1862! Please, get a grip on it all!" Vickie pleaded. "I'm telling you that it's—"

"And I'm telling you to stop it! Stop it now!" he cried angrily, rising. "It's 1862. This battle is still going and I've got to find my brother! He's hurt, he's injured and he's going to die—"

"No one will let him die!" Vickie cried. "There are emergency vehicles all over—"

"If the Yanks take him, he will die!" he cried passionately, silver eyes raking her once again.

To her amazement, she felt tears stinging her eyes once again. Mad or not, he believed it. He believed every word that he was saying to her.

"I don't know how to convince you!" she whispered miserably. "No one will hurt your brother. They'll help him, I swear it."

He was silent for a moment, then he turned away. "I wish that I could believe you," he told her.

His hands were on his hips. Vickie saw a glint there. She didn't know why, but she was standing suddenly. She strode through the shallow water to where he was standing, heedless of her boots. She reached for his left hand. There was a plain gold band there, too.

"Wife?" she queried, feeling as if she had choked on the word just a little bit.

She felt him go tense, swallowing hard. "Dead," he said huskily. And he added quickly, "And I don't know where the fire came from, a Yank gun or a Rebel gun. We had a home out on the peninsula. An old place," he added in a rush. "Built before 1700." He turned around, squinting as he stared up the mountain. "Well, it's burned to the ground now. And my wife is buried nearby." His eyes touched upon Vickie's. "It isn't very friendly fire, is it?"

She shook her head. Then she realized that she was agreeing with this man. He had told her that his wife had been killed by stray fire in the middle of a battle, a *Civil War* battle, and she was agreeing that it was possible.

She hurried over to him suddenly. "Listen to me,

please listen to me. You've got to understand. You need help—''

"Oh, indeed! I need help, lots of it.''

"You believe all this, don't you?'' she whispered.

He was reaching into his pocket, pulling out something square and whitish. He broke it with a hard snap, offering her half. Hardtack. She'd seen the stuff in museums all her life, and Gramps even had a few scraps of it in his prized collection of Civil War memorabilia.

This was so very real....

Reenactors made it, she reminded herself. Just like they made clothing, and guns and swords. Just like they pitched tents, and sang songs.

"It's not much, but it's all I've got,'' he told her. He walked over to stand by one of the trees, looking out over the valley. He took a crunchy bite out of his hardtack. Vickie looked down at the chunk of supposedly digestible food she held. Her stomach rumbled. She was starving. She hadn't eaten much last night.

"Eat this...?'' she murmured. But just then, she thought that she saw something very tiny within it moving. Something the same whitish color. Something like a...

A weevil. A creature. A maggot. She didn't know what. Something completely horrible.

She shrieked and threw the piece of food high into the air, backing away from it.

Instantly he was at her side, taking her into his arms, and looking anxiously about. "What, what is it? Where?'' He held her close, protectively, against him, drawing a gun from the holster at his side. It was a repeater, Vickie realized. She didn't know guns that well, but she thought that it was one of the Colt repeating rifles. It was large by current-day standards for a handgun....

But then, once again, she'd seen the like in Gramps's precious glass-encased collection shelves before.

He stared at her hand. "What happened? Is there a snake? Have you been bitten? What is it?"

She shook her head wildly, staring at him. "A *thing,* a white thing. In that piece of food you gave me. It moved."

Now he was looking at her as if she were the one who had gone absolutely mad.

"What?"

She shook her head, feeling sick.

He walked across the grass and found the piece of hardtack. He stared at it, then turned to look at her, troubled.

"This is pretty good," he said, studying her with a puzzled frown. "Why, there's only a maggot or two in it."

"A maggot—or *two?*" she whispered. "Oh!" she said, turning around, clutching her stomach.

She closed her eyes tightly. His hands were on her shoulders and he spun her around. "I'm sorry!" he said gruffly. "It's all I've got. I'll catch you something later. But for the moment—"

She shook her head violently. "I'm not hungry anymore."

"I've got to find my troops," he told her softly.

A breeze stirred. His hands were still on her shoulders; he seemed incredibly tall, broad shouldered, strikingly handsome. His silver eyes were passionate, the lean hard planes of his face and the square of his jaw all spoke of determination and a curious valor. "I've got to find the Yanks, and I've got to find my own troops."

"And you've got to have me to do it?" she whispered.

He nodded gravely.

"I can't let you go. You have to see that."

"I wish you'd believe me," she said. She wished she could help him snap out of his delusion. She wished he would suddenly be quite normal and they could start all over again. She wished...

What *was* she thinking?'

"Come on," he said softly, "let's go." But his hands were still on her shoulders. And suddenly he brushed her cheek with his knuckles. The motion was infinitely tender, and she closed her eyes for a moment, savoring it.

Then she swallowed hard, pulling away from him, her eyes lowered.

Even if he wasn't a *complete* lunatic, he certainly wasn't all there. And he'd already accused her of enough things!

Her eyes raised to his, and she was ready with a quick retort. It died in her throat. There was that desperate emotion in his eyes! Pain, determination...tenderness. She shook her head, with no voice to speak.

"I don't even know your name," he told her huskily.

"Victoria," she murmured softly. "Vickie."

"Jason," he murmured.

"Not colonel?" she inquired.

"Only if you intend to follow orders," he said with a curious, almost wistful smile.

"Well, I don't follow orders," she informed him.

"Then," he said, bowing formally, "I suppose I'll have to ask you politely to help me find the enemy troops—and my own."

"And if I refuse?" she said.

"Then I'll have to order you around," he said, catching her arm. "It's time to move on," he insisted, "Victoria."

Her name was soft coming from his lips. So soft.
His hand on her arm was absolutely insistent.
And once again, they were moving over the mountain.

CHAPTER THREE

Vickie had always thought that she knew the mountain better than the back of her own hand; however, that day, she seemed to lose her own bearings, too.

Gramps's house should have been to the west and the encampments should have been down in the valley to her extreme south. When she walked toward what she thought should have been the Rebel encampments, she realized that she had led him down a trail that was way too far north.

And walking on these slopes and inclines was much harder than riding over them. She had led him around in silence for hours, it seemed, when she realized her mistake. And then, of course, he stared at her as if she had done it all on purpose, and was trying to get him captured or cause something even worse to happen to him.

The strangest thing about the afternoon was that she was beginning to believe him. What he was saying couldn't possibly be true, and yet he was incredibly sincere and passionate and he just...

He acted so different. He looked different. He talked different. He was different. From anyone she knew. And no matter how she fought against it, there was something so compelling because of those differences.

His hand suddenly fell upon her shoulder. He pulled her to a halt. She whirled around and looked at him. A trickle of sweat slipped down the handsome planes of his face. A deep sandy brow arched to her and those hard silver-gray eyes of his seemed to fix her where she stood.

"Where are you taking me?" he asked her.

She lifted her hands and shook her head, "I'm trying. I swear it, I'm trying."

"To get me where?"

"To the Rebel encampment."

A cloud fell over his eyes. One of suspicion. "Hmm. So it seems."

"Damn you! Damn you!" she cried to him suddenly, slamming her fists against his chest and actually pushing him back with her force. Taken by surprise, he caught her wrists, and she was pulled up flush against his body again, held there while their hearts hammered together, her head cast back, throat arched, eyes blazing into his. No matter how he held her, she was determined to speak. "I'm just dying to get you to the Rebel encampment— sir! I'm dying for someone else to tell you that you're a madman, that this war has been over—I'm dying for you to believe me!"

Something in his hold seemed to ease. Yet he didn't release her. But the way that he stared at her changed. And the way that he held her changed, too.

"And I'm dying for you to believe me," he said very softly.

She relaxed in his hold. There was a trembling beginning deep within her. Truly, she was the one not in her right senses. When he held her, she wanted him to continue to do so. She wanted to rest her head against his shoulder, test the texture of his cavalry shirt. She wanted his hands to fall upon the length of her hair and soothe her.

And then...

Then she wanted more.

She felt her cheeks begin to burn as she tried to keep her stare level with his. This was really madness. She knew so many nice young men. All the fine young fellows Gramps kept bringing around so persistently. Friends. Friends of friends. All of them so usual, normal—and sane.

But since she had lost her husband, she hadn't felt the first spark of desire....

Until now. Until she had come upon this silver-eyed madman. Now she was feeling a surge of responses she had thought long buried, along with a handsome young man in a very different soldier's uniform.

She opened her mouth to speak, trying to shake the startling sensation of warmth that had filled her. No words came at first. She struggled. "I—I must believe you in a way," she said. "I believe that you believe what you're saying, anyway." She spun around quickly, eyes suddenly, inexplicably, filled with tears. "Come on. I'll get us somewhere, I promise."

She had barely begun walking when the day seemed to darken. She looked up. The morning had been beautiful. It had suddenly turned gray. Dark, billowing clouds raced across the sky. She had never seen clouds move so rapidly before. They made her uneasy. Just like that strange cry in the night had made her uneasy. She gritted her teeth, fighting the strange—and ridiculous—sensation of fear.

"We're in for some weather," she cried. What was the matter with her? She felt so cold. The world seemed so strange. As if she was treading where she shouldn't be treading, walking through a graveyard at midnight. She had a strange intuition, telling her she'd crossed some forbidden line. She was seeing things she wasn't meant to see. But again, she tried to assure herself that she was being ridiculous.

But Jason, too, had been looking up at the wild, darkening sky. His eyes touched hers. There was a strange expression in them, as if he had seen this strange "weather" before, as if he, too, had felt cold slivers of ice in the pit of his stomach. But he nodded to her, a smile of reassurance quickly curving his lips as he read her expression.

"There are a few caves near here. Let's get to one!" she said.

He reached for her hand. Just as they touched, a tremendous bolt of lightning flashed down near them, so blindingly visible that it was like watching ancient Zeus cast down a jagged streak of fire. The thunder that rolled and clashed in its wake was instant and alarming.

Vickie looked up. The sky was nearly black. It had happened in a matter of minutes.

"Jason!"

"Come closer!"

His arm was around her, as if he could combat invisible dragons, yet she was delighted to be with him, glad of his arm, of the comfort and the security.

Oddly, against the tempest of the sky, the rain that started then was light. Almost a mist. Of course, it could be just heralding the real storm to come. Right now, it was soft, cool. Like the breeze, it seemed to wrap around her with invisible threads, a spider's web to hold and haunt her. Despite the softness of the rain, the look of the day was still wicked, the black sky churning and spinning.

"Let's go!" It was Jason who started moving.

The wind began to whip anew. Vickie realized that in the sudden darkness, they were running blindly once again. She didn't know where they were going.

The caves were...to their left?

"This way!" she cried out suddenly, certain of her

own direction. But was she? The trees were dipping and swaying, bowed down beneath the strength of the wind. They seemed to form a maze in the darkness.

The two ran through the lashing trees. A field of electricity snapped and crackled around them. It seemed that they ran forever, and then they burst into a clearing.

She could see. The wind still lashed at them, the day seemed stranger than ever. The sky roiled. But the blackness had somewhat abated, and she could see before her. Horsemen were coming. Relief filled her. Men were practicing for the reenactment battles still to come. They were riding toward her and Jason now. All she had to do was cry out and wave to them. They would get her home. She would bring Jason. Introduce him to Gramps, and Gramps would know what to do. All that she had to do was cry out, and she could get home. The danger had passed.

She slammed to a stop with Jason right behind her. She felt his fingers on her shoulders, digging in.

"Jason! They'll help us—" she began.

"Help us, my foot!" he cried. "Look at the uniform!"

Yankee. She tried to explain. "Jason, they're reenactors. They're not going to—"

She heard an explosion, then felt the heat as something whistled by her cheek. There was a flat, slamming sound behind her. She swirled around, white and stunned.

She could see where the bullet intended for her had embedded into a tree.

The men in the mist were really shooting at them. Real Civil War soldiers, shooting real bullets....

It couldn't be! Only ghosts could travel these mountains—ghosts and memories—and neither could shoot real guns. Perhaps they were reenactors after all, intent on murder.

Dully, she thought, no. No motive. Men didn't go crazy all in a group.

A second whistle caressed her cheek. Another bullet whizzed by, just missing her.

"Get behind me!"

"But they're not real—"

"The hell they're not!"

She was behind him, shoved there, with the bulk of his body protecting her.

"They wouldn't be shooting at me—" she protested weakly.

"They can't see a damn thing in this rain and mist!" he assured her. "They don't mean to be shooting at a woman. You're standing in the middle of their battle."

One of them suddenly broke from the pack and came riding down upon them. She heard the rip of the steel as Jason pulled his cavalry sword from his scabbard. The thunderous sound of the horse's hooves came bearing down upon them hard. She barely saw the man upon the horse. She did see the muted glint of his sword, raised and ready to strike. She cried out.

Jason deflected the blow that was coming their way with a hideous clash of steel. His return was so forceful that the horseman wavered on his mount and then came crashing down to the ground. He started to struggle to his feet.

"Get back!" Jason commanded Vickie. Stunned, disbelieving, she did so, backing away just a few feet. The breeze that touched her cheeks now seemed very cold indeed. She stared, numb, stunned, as the Yankee stood and approached Jason, his sword waving. He was young, a teenager.

She still couldn't believe what was happening right before her eyes. She couldn't believe that Jason and this boy were fighting with swords, that they would bleed, that one of them would kill the other, right in front of her, here and now....

It couldn't be real.

She had lost her own mind.

The boy approached. But Jason was good. His sword rose and fell, striking the boy's. The sword went flying.

"Oh, God, don't hurt him!" Vickie cried out.

Jason looked to her quickly. She could hear the pounding of horses' hooves again. Other Yankees were about to bear down on them.

He turned around and caught the young soldier with a good blow to his cheek. He fell quickly, but there were at least five or six horses pounding toward them now. A bullet flew. This one nearly caught Vickie in the arm. Startled, she cried out. His body was suddenly shoved up in front of hers again, protecting her from whatever might come. "Let's go. Get your head down!"

They started to run, back through the arbor. They ran until Vickie suddenly caught her foot on a tree root. She fell hard, dragging Jason down with her. And they were suddenly rolling again. Hard, slamming against the earth. And it seemed that they rolled and rolled forever until they came to a stopgap of a valley.

The sky above them was still black. The misty rain was still falling.

But the sound of battle was gone. Completely. Jason lay on top of Vickie, staring down at her. She looked up at him incredulously.

He smiled suddenly. "At least you're not a known spy."

"What?"

"If those Yanks hadn't fired at you, I would have been extremely worried."

What kind of a nightmare had she entered? Had she imagined what had happened, or had it been real? It had all happened so very, very fast. And now the soldiers were gone. All gone. There were just the two of them on the mountain again, staring at one another in a very fine mist of rain.

"They couldn't have been real," she said dully. "They were just reenactors, getting carried away." But things had been so real! She could remember that awful thunking sound of the bullet embedding in the tree. She could remember the feel of it, whizzing by her face, the hot metal so very nearly touching her....

She could also remember the way that the cold breeze had touched her. The deep, almost primal fear that had filled her when they had come to that strange place. She couldn't shake the feeling that she had walked into some forbidden place, that she had stumbled into some other dimension.

All that had kept her sane then, kept her from shrieking out, had been Jason—Jason's touch....

But Jason couldn't be sane.

Oh, God! She closed her eyes quickly, opened them again. It was over. The strange clouds were gone. The feelings of fear were gone. And he was eyeing her very speculatively again.

"You did bring me to the Yanks," he said thoughtfully, staring at her.

"You son of a—" she began, but cut off suddenly. He wouldn't be accustomed to such language. Young women of any breeding back then watched their tongues carefully. What would he think?

What was she thinking? "You son of a bi—sea serpent!" she strangled out. "This whole thing is insane, the world is insane and it all started since I had the ill fortune to wander into you! I wasn't—''

Another bolt of lightning flashed wildly in the sky, interrupting her tirade. Thunder cracked loudly in its wake.

''It's really going to rain now,'' he said brusquely. He leapt agilely to his feet and pulled her up to him. He seemed to hold her for a brief moment, weighing his options. Again, she felt absurdly protected, secure, content and somehow right in his arms.

No...

Vickie shivered. Everyone was gone indeed. Had the soldiers been reenactors? Had she imagined the whiz of the bullets?

Maybe Jason wasn't even real....

But he was. His fingers curled warmly around hers.

''The caves,'' she whispered. ''We need to get to the caves.''

''I think that I'll lead this time,'' he said softly, and proceeded to do so. He turned about and stared around for a moment, then started off. Lightning lit up the entire sky for an instant. The thunder that followed caused Vickie to jump. The rain was starting to come harder. He slipped his arm around her shoulders, and hurried onward.

She didn't watch where they were going. And she didn't know how he managed to find the caves, but he did. Leading in a southeasterly course downhill, he brought them to the few small caves she had known since she was a child. They came upon them just as the rain really started, bursting down suddenly as if floodgates had been opened. Vickie stood just inside the entryway, shivering. Jason stood just behind her.

A second later, lightning flared again. Vickie let out a

startled scream, for it struck so close that it hit one of the tall trees just across from the entrance to the cave. She watched with fascination as sparks flew from the tree.

Then it began to fall. Toward her.

"Jesu, Mary and Joseph!" Jason swore suddenly. Before she knew it, he was on top of her, the force of his body carrying them both down to the floor of the cave—and away from the heavy trunk section of tree that came slamming down where Vickie had been standing just seconds before.

She looked from the tree trunk to the man who now lay atop her once again. Her breath caught and she trembled suddenly. Who was he?

Did it matter?

He had taken her captive, yes.

He might well be a madman on a mountain.

But time and time again, he had protected her. He had set himself between her and any threat of danger. For so long, she had barely felt alive.

And when he touched her…

She wanted to live again. And feel again. Everything.

He didn't move. Not for the longest time. Silver-gray eyes touched hers, searching for something, seeing something.… She wasn't sure what.

Then his hand moved, just slightly, the knuckle of his forefinger moving gently over her cheek. She felt that sensual stroke as if it enveloped the length of her with a curious warmth and magic.

Then she watched with fascination as he slowly lowered his head, and touched her lips with his own.

She didn't protest. She couldn't have done so had she wanted to. Sheer fascination held her still, let her feel the surging warmth and slow demand of that touch. His mouth formed over hers, the masculine scent of him seemed to fill her senses, the vital strength and tension of his body seemed to encompass hers in the most arousing way. It had been so long. She shouldn't be doing this, shouldn't be feeling this. Her heart had lain dormant so very long....

This stirring wasn't her heart, she told herself.

But in a way, it was. For his manner, his eyes, his ways, all had touched her as surely as the lips that now formed around her own.

His mouth on hers had been warm; it was suddenly hot. It had been forming and molding and coercive....

Now it was demanding.

Searing with wet heat, the tip of his tongue explored the outline of her lips. Then pressed between them. Deep. Deeper. Moving, exploring, demanding.

Remember, remember the past...a voice whispered deep inside of her.

But she could suddenly let the past slip away. The sweetness, and the pain. The memories of the laughter and the love. She could not conjure up the picture of the face that had once been hers....

The present was upon her. The present, and a man with silver-gray eyes and a will of steel and the most cavalier way of protecting her from harm.

His tongue moved more deeply into her mouth. Stroked in a way that seemed to evoke every fire within her. The rain beat down around them. The floor of the cave was rough and hard. She wasn't aware of any of it, only of the feel of him, the hot rugged hardness of his body, the feel of his mouth upon hers. His tongue. Stroking now in a way that was suggestive of a thousand things to come....

His mouth lifted slowly from hers. His eyes touched

down upon hers once again. She stared at him in return, waiting.

His eyes never left hers. In a sudden frenzy, he began undoing the buttons of his cavalry shirt. In seconds it was stripped from his body, and he was balling it into a pillow that he set beneath her head. Her gaze slipped to his chest and it seemed that her heart began to beat harder. It was a nice chest. An incredibly nice chest. He had appeared tall and slim; he was walled with muscle, very broad shouldered, the breadth of him handsomely covered with crisp, sandy blond hair that tapered to a little trail that disappeared enticingly beneath the waistband of his pants.

She dragged her eyes back to his. He watched her still. Waiting for a protest? She didn't know.

But one wasn't coming.

He stood then, and she was watching still. Just as that silver-gray stare of both challenge and determination touched her so continually. Then swept over her. Causing a riot of heat to strike her, causing her to feel the most incredible sensations where he still had yet to touch.

It wasn't real, couldn't be real....

But it was wonderful. Like a strange, exotic dream. The world was filled with the roaring sound of the rain beyond the cave. And beyond that, it was filled with the man. With the muscle-riddled length of him, the warmth of him, the scent of him....

His boots fell on the hard-packed earth of the cave. His socks upon them.

Then he stripped off his cavalry pants. He was authentic to his beliefs, she thought briefly. There were no boxers or B.V.D.s beneath them. He was in long johns.

And they quickly fell upon his socks, and once they did, Vickie couldn't think of the past or the present or anything but the immediate future. Her madman was quite incredible, muscled and bronze from head to toe, trim in the hips with rock-hard thighs.

And boldly, flagrantly aroused. A violent shudder ripped through her at the sight of his raw nakedness. Her eyes shot back to his and she knew that her face was flaming with color.

And oddly, she knew, too, that if she were to protest, even now, the Southern cavalry commander's costume would go back on, piece by piece, long johns to scabbard and boots. But she didn't want to protest. Yet she was still afraid, as if she were about to embark on the wings of an eagle, when she hadn't flown in a long, long time.

He came down on his knees before her. He scooped her into his arms, and her eyes searched out his. Then his lips touched hers once again. Exploded upon them, fierce, demanding, the stroke and length of his tongue a wild pillage within her mouth. Her arms snaked around him, and she held tightly to him, feeling the sweet wildness fill and pervade her. She returned the kiss, fingers winding into the hair at his nape, stroking, caressing. Then he broke away, his eyes touching hers once again. "How can this be ill fortune?" he queried softly, his breath a husky whisper against her cheek.

How indeed?

She shook her head, at a loss for the moment.

"You cannot be real," she assured him.

He arched a brow.

"If you are, then I must surely be a horrible person. A woman who was any kind of lady—"

"Would still feel this!" he swore with a soft but vehement passion.

Maybe. And maybe it was wrong. It didn't matter. She

just might wake up and discover that it was all a dream. But until then...

Her fingertips cradled his head, drawing him back to her. With a sudden burst of sweet surrender she gave way to all the hunger that had arisen within her, the longing, the fascination. His flesh was hot beneath her fingers, vibrant, so electric with energy and the taut strength of the muscles beneath it. Her fingers inched against his nape, feeling the brush of his hair. She tasted his mouth again, eagerly, parting her lips to his, feeling the sensual roll and thrust of his tongue. And she felt his touch in return, too. The fluid movement of his fingers upon the buttons of her calico day gown. One, and then the next, his knuckles brushing her flesh with each motion, bringing new fire to awaken within her, new aches of longing, yearning to be touched. The garment fell away. She was barely aware of its leaving; she was keenly aware of his stroke and brush of his fingers.

Then she gasped raggedly as his lips broke from hers. She was so deeply involved in her sea of sensation that it took her several minutes to realize that he had gone dead still.

Then she realized that his fingers were set upon the fine lace strap of her rather elegant designer bra. And his eyes were open and incredulous. When he moved again, it was to stroke that strap. His eyes did not leave it. He seemed to have forgotten that he was naked, that she was completely disheveled, and that he'd had her at the brink of one of the rarest and most momentous occasions of her life.

She might have been embarrassed. She might have even been hurt enough to be angry and feel like a fool. The emotions did flash through her. But then she realized his absolute amazement and she closed her eyes.

Someone had really fired a gun at her. As if there was a strange time warp on the mountain. And if that was true, then he was just beginning to really believe it himself, seeing at long last something that did not belong to his world.

No, it couldn't be....

But he was still just staring. Her fingers curled around his. He started, and his eyes met hers. "My God," he murmured hoarsely. "What—is this?"

She hesitated. "A new type of corset," she said simply, watching his eyes. A streak of warmth like a bolt of the lightning that continued to light up the sky now and then seemed to course through her. Did she believe him? Could she believe him?

And how could she do anything else when he stared with such amazement as he did now?

His touch became more intimate than before, yet strangely distanced. With a sudden determination he thrust the calico down from her shoulders and his forefinger drew a line over the trim cut of the elegant little undergarment. Where he touched her, she felt as if she burned. She bit her lip, telling herself that he had become interested in the mechanics of clothing much more than he was interested in the woman wearing that clothing. She felt her cheeks redden.

But then his gaze met hers. And he seemed to realize what he had done, and his arms encompassed her, sweeping her back against him again. Her head rested against his naked chest, and he rocked with her, holding her tight.

"What did you say it is?" he whispered huskily.

"The nineties."

"Eighteen?" he said hopefully.

She eased from his hold to look up. She shook her head. "Nineteen-hundred-type nineties," she told him.

"God," he whispered. "Dear God." He shook his head. "It's impossible. It's impossible. And it can't be. We just came from the scene of a skirmish. How…?"

His voice trailed away. He was right, Vickie thought. *The skirmish had been real. The bullets had been real. So just where were they right now? His world, or her own?*

She closed her eyes tightly. Hers. It had to be her world. Had to be.

Once again, lightning tore across the sky. The thunder crack was loud, deafening. She started, and his arms tightened around her. She stared up into his eyes and stroked his cheek with sudden compassion. "I'm sorry," she murmured. "I'm really sorry." He didn't seem to hear her at first. She eased herself to her knees and took his face between both her hands. She touched his lips with her own, hesitantly, brushing them. Touching them once again with just the tip of her tongue, trying to bring comfort.

But it seemed she brought more. Much more. With that gentle stroke, she stoked the fires already kindling. He encompassed her into his arms, hungrily accepting the kiss, returning it with a fever. He held her for a moment, then began to thrust her unbuttoned dress down farther from her shoulders until she was completely freed from the sleeves and the garment fell unheeded to the dirt flooring beneath them.

He cushioned her fall as he pressed her back to the ground. His fingers were both demanding and tender, brushing her cheek, her throat, her ribs. His lips trailed from hers to press hotly to the pulse that beat so rampantly against her flesh at the hollow base of her collarbone. Then his mouth moved lower, to caress the rise of her breasts above the silk-and-lace confines of the bra.

He looked up at her. A wry smile touched his lips. "How do I free you from this thing?" he asked.

She felt her cheeks flood with color. His smile deepened and he touched her lips briefly with his own. "Never mind, I'll figure it out."

And before she could speak, he had done just that.

Maybe he'd known women who wore a very different kind of undergarment, but apparently, he had found his way around those quite easily.

His fingers had found the center hook of her bra and deftly released it, spilling her breasts free. Then he was still for a second, and she could hear ragged breathing, and she realized that it came from them both and that it mingled on the air.

Then he uttered a hoarse cry, and stretched out beside her, his hands upon her bare flesh, exploring at first, so filled with fascination, with demand, with tenderness. Stroking, cupping, caressing. His palm rotated slowly over her nipple and she felt a little cry escape her own lips. His mouth covered hers. Then left it. Touched her flesh again. At her throat. At the rise of her breasts. Then it covered the fullness of her nipple, the roughened center of his tongue rubbing over and over it. She gasped again, amazed at the surge of desire that swept through her. Liquid fire surged through her limbs, winding into a center where hunger leapt out again like sparks of the liquid blaze.

Her fingers tugged into his hair, streaking over it, through it. She raked her nails gently over the rippled muscles of his shoulders and back, then allowed them to dig in slightly for a moment as a blinding wave of sensation seized her once again. "Please," she whispered, and she had no idea at all what she was asking him for— if she wanted him to move or to stay.

His hand slid low over her abdomen, pushing down the bunched fabric of her dress. He found the long slip she was wearing, yet shoved it easily enough along with the dress, never missing a beat in his lovemaking. His lips trailed down the deep valley between her breasts and farther, touching her hip, her belly. She felt his fingers upon the lace of the sexy panties that matched her bra. And suddenly he was very still.

She squeezed her eyes closed, praying that he wouldn't stop, that he wouldn't force her to think. Then she opened her eyes, and met his gaze. A sweep of fire rose to her cheeks and fanned out through the length of her body in a giant flush.

"You're—" he began, and he shook his head. "You're beautiful," he told her quietly. His eyes swept the length of her, pausing at the bikini panties. Then his hands were on her once again, sweeping her hips toward him. He leaned his face against her belly and her breath caught. He touched her. Drawing imaginary lines over the design in the lace. His knuckles brushed her thighs. His breath was hot against very sensitive flesh. He teased the rim of the panties with the tip of his tongue, and she cried out suddenly, thinking that she couldn't bear such exquisite teasing one second more.

His fingers curled around the band of the panties, and they were suddenly stripped away. And she gasped again with sheer pleasure at the warmth of his body as she felt the fullness of it against her own. His fingers curled into hers, his gaze locked with hers. She felt his hair-roughened legs against her own, felt the angle of his hips, the tantalizing brush of his chest and the fascinating, hot, protruding thrust of his sex. Against her. Against her thighs. Against the acutely sensitive petals of her sex. He held there for a moment, watching her eyes. His right hand released hers and came between them. Brushed her thigh. Touched her. Lightly. More deeply. Entering her. Stoking, Coaxing. Urging her beyond the limits of sensations she'd ever known.

She cried out softly, closing her eyes, burying her face against his shoulder. She felt him shift his weight. His touch was gone. Then it was with her again. She shuddered fiercely as he swept into her with the fullness of himself, seeming to enter her like molten steel, filling every void, touching the very depths of her. Her hands fell upon his back and her fingers dug into his hard muscles. She felt the ripple of muscle as he began to move. Slowly. Just seeming to slip more incredibly deeply into her with each enticing thrust. She would split, she would die, she thought. She did neither. She felt the sweetest rush of fire begin. Bursting from an inner core, streaking like lightning to totally fill her.

Her arms tightened around his back. Her hands moved wildly against him. And in just moments, she felt enveloped in a tempest of unimaginable pleasure, of hunger and magic. Wild streaks of fire, more radiant than lightning, bolted through her again and again. She arched with the wonder of him, writhed to his rhythm.

Aware of the hard earth beneath her, she barely felt it. She knew only the certainty of the force and power of the man, the wild reckless energy that now ruled his desire. He had been so careful at first, so patient and arousing a lover. Yet now he was a hungry one, demanding in each movement, drawing her with him to new heights of magic, receding, lifting her once again. She forgot everything except for the need to rise with him to the sweet blinding pinnacle they both sought. She clung to him, and felt the ragged tension in him as his hands slipped about her hips, holding her tightly as he thrust hard and deeply and held himself within her. A swiftly simmering heat seemed to explode within her, bringing a burst of stars to sweep the streaks of lightning from her world. Diamonds seemed to lay against velvet black. Perhaps she lost touch with this plane of existence for a moment. But she came to, with the hot sweet nectar of release sweeping wildly through her. She felt him moving again, once, shuddering violently, and a greater heat seemed to fill her. Then they were both still.

Slowly, slowly, she felt the earth beneath her once again. Felt the hard ground, the pillow of his cavalry shirt.

Slowly she heard the wild cry of the wind.

Yet it, too, was dying down.

He was damp and slick, lying atop her, then easing his weight from her, but keeping her within the confines of his arms. His fingers moved tenderly over her hair. His lips brushed her forehead.

"Ill fortune," he mused softly. "Yet you are the best thing to happen to me in all these long and bitter months of war."

She moved slightly, amazed now that he could still be there, that he could be holding her. She gritted her teeth, suddenly fighting tears. She wasn't sorry in the least for what she had done. She was amazed once again that he still lay here, that he was not a dream.

Sated now, she took the time to covertly admire her lover, allowing her gaze a leisurely journey over the length of him. There were scars upon his shoulder and back, which she had missed. They caused her to swallow, but they were all that marred his perfection. He was lean, but very well and tightly muscled, his hips so trim, legs so long, thighs so hard.

He lifted her chin suddenly, determined to meet her

eyes. She found herself flushing again when she discovered that he was very aware of her scrutiny.

"Isn't it a little late to decide if I pass muster?" he asked lightly.

With a brief smile, she told him that he did. She liked his face even more now, the handsome planes, the gravity in his eyes. She liked the curve of his smile, the tone of his voice. And the tenderness with which he held her now.

"You are wall-to-wall scars," she whispered, her voice trembling. She drew a finger delicately over one of the pale white and jagged lines on his shoulder.

"As I said, it's been a long and bitter war," he murmured.

A long and bitter war....

No. Not this war. This war was just a game. It was history. It was something for Gramps and his cronies to hash over and argue into the wee hours of the night. It couldn't be real.

But to this man, it was.

His thumb and forefinger moved over her cheek. "You are nearly perfection," he said, studying her eyes. "I—"

He broke off suddenly, into a dead silence. His eyes narrowed at her. Then she heard something outside the cave. A rustling that wasn't the wind.

He thrust her from him suddenly and leapt to his feet. Naked and agile. Bronzed muscles flexed and tensed.

"You know where we are, eh?" he roughly demanded.

"What?" she murmured.

"You definitely know how to take a man off guard, Miss Victoria," he drawled in a whisper. His gray eyes, so warm moments ago, were now cold with suspicion.

"Off guard?" she repeated. Then she heard it again.

A sound that wasn't the storm, wasn't the wind. Something creeping up to the cave. Furtively.

She leapt up, heedless of her own state of undress. "Of all the nerve!" she whispered back to him, fingers clenching into fists at her side. Then she realized that she was undressed. She snatched up her gown, holding it in front of her. "How dare you! How dare you!"

"Shh!"

In seconds he was behind her, drawing her against him, clamping a hand over her mouth. And holding her so, he urged her along with him until he could slip his sword from his scabbard that lay on the earthen floor.

She saw the glistening steel held out inches from her face.

Raw panic filled her as the sound came again. Closer. Someone was out there; something was out there. She clenched her teeth together, trying not to let them chatter. She suddenly felt cold, as cold as ice, wondering. What was it, what strange forces had been borne upon the breeze, what unearthly power had touched her? And she knew, knew in her heart, that she had traveled through some strange void, perhaps a place where only God should tread himself. And now, no matter how she tried to deny these thoughts, she was so very terrified....

"Behind me!"

Her mouth was dry, she was frozen as he suddenly thrust her behind him again, ready to meet the danger that came their way.

Nearer, nearer, coming to the entrance of the cave.

Did he feel it? Had he known the same sensations? If he was afraid, he did not betray it, but stood ready, his sword glittering.

She braced behind him, and the rustling sound came louder.

Closer.

Louder...

CHAPTER FOUR

The sound stopped at last. They heard a dull clicking. She realized that it was the slow movement of a horse's hooves, the animal approaching with care.

Vickie started to tremble, feeling the tension of the man before her.

Then it eased. Quickly, suddenly, completely.

"It's Max," he said, starting forward.

"Max?" Who the hell was Max? And how could Jason be so sure?

"I'll just get him."

"Don't you dare bring anyone in here!" Vickie cried, scrambling to get back into her clothing. But he had already stepped out—still stark naked—and he whistled, and then began to return.

"Jason—" she cried in fury and dismay.

"It's just my *horse!*" he assured her at last.

She had stumbled into her undergarments and had her dress over her head. In a second, helping hands were there along with her own. As her head came through the top of her dress, the first thing she saw was a handsome bay cavalry horse staring straight at her.

Max appeared just as authentic as his master, from his bridle to saddle pack. She'd seen dozens of horses that looked just like this one, in Gramps's old pictures of the war. Max was the exact replica of a Confederate cavalry horse.

Or else, he actually was one.

It seemed that the ever-faithful mount with the keen

sense of smell had once again found his master—this time through time!

Which made her wonder again if she might be the one losing her mind. Was this her world—or his? Could there really be a difference?

She didn't realize how long she had been staring at the horse, pondering the question, until she saw that Jason was dressed. His boots were on, and he was just buckling his scabbard onto his hips. He was watching her so intently that she inadvertently took a step back.

He strode over to her, capturing her hands, sweeping her back into his arms. He kissed her with a deep passion so reminiscent of their lovemaking that she found herself shuddering again, and remembering. She barely knew him. Nine out of ten, he wasn't all there. And she had just made love with him. And she should be astounded with herself, horrified, and all she knew was that...

His kiss made her long to lie down with him all over again. The tension in his arms around her assured her that he longed for the same. But his eyes, when they rose over hers, were filled with pain.

"I have to find my brother," he said. "I have to."

She nodded. She refrained from telling him that it had already been some time since he had found her, and so it had been quite some time since he had left his brother. If the man had been caught in the fire of a battle, he had probably been discovered by someone else. Or—he was dead.

"The rain—" she murmured.

"Has all but stopped. There's a bit of mist, that's all," he said.

She nodded again. He caught her hand again and led her, along with Max, out of the cave. The rain was a mist again. Delightfully cool against her face, when the days had been so atrociously hot.

He paused just outside the entrance to the cave. He touched her chin with his thumb and forefinger, raising it gently. She met the steady, silver-gray light of his eyes. She trembled slightly, afraid to close her own, afraid to be overtaken by a vision of his supple power, when he had held her, when he had made love to her.

The subtle curl of his lips was rueful. "I took you prisoner. I accused you of all manner of things."

"Yes, you did," she murmured in return.

"I'm sorry."

"You should be."

"Well, you're free now, you know."

Free? To her amazement, her heart did a double take. She couldn't possibly leave him. He could...

He could get hurt, she determined.

He was watching her so intently once again. She took a breath. Then she tossed back her hair and stared him down. "I'll help you find your brother," she said.

He was starting to mount his horse. "I don't want you hurt."

"And I don't want you arrested!" she sharply replied. "If you go stumbling around on this mountain and run into a twentieth-century cop, you're going to be in trouble!"

He had mounted his horse and was looking down at her. And she realized suddenly that she was furious. She'd been such a fool! Falling for this man, and now, insane or not, he was leaving her in the middle of nowhere after he'd imprisoned her for the night and...

And even managed to capture her heart.

"Oh! Go to hell!" she cried. "Surely that is the same for all worlds!"

She started to turn, but was amazed at the speed with which he leapt down, amazed at the vehemence with which he turned her to face him. "No!" she cried, finding herself in his arms once again, ready to beat against his chest. "No!" But the protest suddenly died on her lips as he held her and met her eyes. There was humor in his, and more. A myriad emotions she couldn't begin to determine, but she realized at last that one was concern.

"I don't know what I was thinking. I just wanted you to know that I wasn't...forcing you into being with me. But you're right. I can't let you go. You could stumble into real trouble."

"Me?"

"Into the midst of skirmishing," he told her.

"But—" She wanted to tell him that it hadn't been real. But how could she tell him that? She didn't want to believe, couldn't believe, *but she had felt the whistle of that bullet passing her cheek. She had felt it!* And it hadn't been just the bullets. It had been the blackness, the mist, the awful sense of fear, of the unknown.

They couldn't walk in and out of time! It was impossible. She closed her eyes, trying to remember exactly where they had been. The wind had been so fierce....

All she could remember was a strangely bowed arbor of trees. And she couldn't quite remember where they had been.

No, they had stumbled upon reenactors, men taking the game just a bit too seriously.

His lips touched her forehead and he was setting her up on his horse, and leaping up behind her.

"Which way shall we try?" he murmured softly.

"South," she said, trying to rethink the battle. She should have known every phase of it. Blackfield's Mountain hadn't been nearly as big a battle as some of the others that the historians had really concentrated on—not like Gettysburg, Sharpsburg or Shiloh. And though the reenactment centered around the pasture where the main action had taken place, the battle had been in sets and maneuvers and skirmishes over a period of three days. She knew almost hourly day by day what had occurred. Gramps and his friends had written a guidebook for the interested tourist, and she had been enlisted to do much of the typing. The book was a very good one, she had heard from some of her military friends.

And if her memory wasn't failing her, there had been some troop movements south of the main mountain. There would be men displaying some cavalry skills today, women in costumes, all manner of activity.

Or else...

There might be a real battle.

"I think we should try straight south," she murmured. But the sky was still gray. She shook her head ruefully. "I really do have a sense of direction, and I do know this mountain, but—"

"South is that way," he said, pointing. He nudged Max. She rested her head back against his chest, and they started to ride. For a moment, neither of them spoke. There was a startling comfort in being together now, feeling the easy movement of Jason's horse carrying them down the mountain. There was warmth. A sense of belonging.

"So you say it's all over," he murmured suddenly. There was a light tone to his voice, but she was also convinced that there was deeper feeling there, too. Just as she was believing in him against all good sense, he was believing in her. His voice was suddenly pained and very husky. "And we lost, huh?"

She nodded, suddenly loath to say more.

"When does it end?"

"Well, there were still some troops in the field after, but most historians agree that it ended at Appomattox Courthouse, April of 1865."

"In 1865? Dear God, there's going to be that much more of this?"

The anguish in his voice touched her heart as nothing had before. There was so much else that would surely rip into his soul, once he knew the truth.

What was the truth?

"I wonder if I'll survive it," he mused suddenly. "And John. And so many others. Stonewall, Stuart, Lee—" He broke off suddenly. "You know, don't you?" he murmured.

"Lee comes through magnificently," she said quickly, loath to tell him about the others. "History has celebrated him as one of the greatest American generals—"

"Even though he lost?"

"Even though he lost. The children supposedly ran out into the streets to see him at Gettysburg. He was always a gentleman. He hated the bloodshed, and he was such an incredible military man, except for a very few mistakes. Pickett's Charge at Gettysburg—"

"Gettysburg?" he said, puzzled.

Of course. The action at Blackfield's Mountain had taken place in late summer, 1862. Gettysburg had taken place in July, 1863. To Jason, at this moment, Gettysburg was just an unknown tiny town in the North.

"Trust me. Lee remained deeply admired through all the decades," she murmured.

"And Stonewall?"

She didn't want to answer that question. And suddenly she didn't have to. They could hear shots, and a burst of fire. Jason reined in quickly, slipping down from Max. He haunched low, walking to the edge of the slope to look downward.

Vickie dismounted from Max in his wake. He turned back to her swiftly. "Stay there!"

She had no intention of doing so. She followed quickly to his side. She had barely reached him before he was shoving her behind him, and then down to the ground. They looked down the slope to the valley together.

Men in formation were marching toward one another. Yanks to the left, Rebs to the right. They were in nearly perfect, incredible lines, following orders. They marched, halted, loaded their weapons. Some men dropped to their knees while others shot above their heads from the ranks. Watching, Vickie felt the same amazement that she always did to watch such a battle. *How had anyone ever gotten men to stare at one another point-blank, so very close, and fire weapons? How had anyone ever gotten them to stand still when others were firing so closely at them?*

"They're so slow!" Jason murmured suddenly.

Another volley of fire burst out. Men in the Yankee ranks fell down.

Where were they? Were they real soldiers out there, fighting for their lives? Or was it the wonderfully accurate reenactment?

Then she saw *them*—the crowd lined up by the almost invisible wire fencing at the rear of the action. The viewers were on someone's cattle-grazing land, lined up at the fences to watch the spectacle.

She started to rise. His firm grasp was instantly upon her. "Get down!" he commanded her.

"It's all right!" she returned quickly. "They aren't real bullets."

"You might have said that before—"

"Look! Jason, look!" she implored him. Slow perhaps, but other than that, the reenactors looked so real. Seeing them, one could believe that it was really 1862.

But then there were the tourists at the fence. And there was the refreshment stand, painted bright red, with Coca-Cola emblazoned on it.

"There, Jason, look," she repeated softly.

And he did. He looked beyond the action to the crowd. To the drink stand. And he stared.

His gaze was completely stunned. If he had, indeed, come from a different world, she could easily understand his amazement. Things had changed. It was summer, and it was hot. Men were in T-shirts and cutoffs, women were in halter tops and shorts. Dozens of cars were parked in the field just behind the trees; someone beeped a horn and Jason winced. He kept staring.

More rifle fire went off. Men dropped on the Confederate side. The battle continued.

And Jason kept staring.

Then he turned away and sank back against the earth. Her eyes met his. He arched a brow to her, shaking his head slightly. "They aren't wearing any clothes."

She smiled. "Honest, they're dressed quite respectably by today's standards."

"Fashion has...progressed."

He was speaking lightly. He was dazed, of course. Then she realized his concern when he spoke with a hollow anguish. "How the hell do I get back? If I don't, John will die."

They hadn't been watching. Now there was a sudden burst of applause. The reenactment program for the day had ended. The "dead" men were rising. Friends were talking, some people were walking toward their cars and some were walking toward the hills that hid the encampments from view.

She reached out, slipping her hand into his. "If we can get down there for now, I can get us something to eat. And we can go home. And maybe Gramps will have something to say that will help you somehow."

His eyes caught hers. He shook his head, still fighting his amazement.

"It has to help to have a decent meal!" she encouraged him.

At last he stood, bringing her with him to her feet. She curled her fingers around his. They started down the slope, Max trailing behind them.

Vickie had forgotten just how hungry she was until she began to smell food. The scent drove her nearly to distraction, but some warning bell went off in her head before they reached the crowd. She stopped, turning quickly, placing a hand against Jason's chest.

"Wait."

"What?"

"You can't just go down there and tell people—you can't run around telling people that you're from the real battle."

His eyes narrowed sharply at her.

"They won't believe you!"

His jaw set firmly. "It's the truth."

"But you can't say that it is. Don't you understand? I know they had asylums in your day—do you want to wind up in one?"

He was still staring at her. She clutched his arm. "This is my world!" she hissed to him. "You have to behave in it, or they'll cart you away. They'll never believe you."

He stared out over her head, trying to take in the twentieth-century world.

Then his gaze riveted upon hers. "Do you believe me?"

She hesitated the briefest moment. She believed with her whole heart that he meant what he said. And though it now seemed something of a blur, she could easily enough convince herself that the fighting up on the mountain earlier had been real. It had been a real bullet to nearly graze her cheek.

"Yes," she said suddenly, and it was the first time she really admitted it to herself. "I believe you."

He blinked. His lips curled into a slow smile. He bowed to her. "Then I am yours to command, Victoria. I shall behave however you bid."

Her eyes locked with his. She smiled, too. "For the moment, just keep quiet and I'll get us some hot dogs."

"You folks eat dog?"

She shook her head vehemently. "Sausages! They're like sausages. Can't you smell them? Aren't you starving? Come on!"

He stared downward once again. Parking hadn't been allowed very near the soldiers' camps, but there were cars in the field behind the trucks, past the battle site. Vickie saw that he was dead still, studying them gravely.

"Cars. Horseless carriages."

His eyes shot to hers. "How do they run?"

"On gas. Fuel. I don't really understand it myself."

"They're new?"

"Invented right around the turn of the century," Vickie said.

He started walking.

"You can't go inspecting cars! I have one at home.

I'll try to explain it to you. Please, please act normally!'' Vickie beseeched Jason.

He sighed and looked down at her. "I'll try," he promised. "But don't you see? Nothing is normal."

She bit her lip and nodded. *"Try."*

She hurried forward. He lagged behind her. She realized that there were more new sights he was staring at. More than just the cars parked in the field. The power poles rising far down the road. The people all around them. The reenactor Yanks now laughing with the reenactor Rebs.

"Please be careful," she warned him again.

He nodded. She held his arm, more or less leading him through the crowd.

They reached the stand. There was a girl in front of Vickie who ordered a soda and a hot dog and moved on. Jason watched her with keen interest. Vickie's stomach growled with hunger, but then she remembered that she didn't have any money with her, not a cent.

She backed away suddenly. "What's the matter?" Jason asked. He was blending in perfectly, she thought. People were staring at him, but they were all smiling, assuming he was part of the show. In turn, he politely inclined his head.

"I don't have any money with me," she said. "We'll—"

"I have money," he said. He stepped around her. "Two of those, please. And two of the drinks." He reached into a small waistband pocket of his pants where he kept a small fold of bills.

Confederate bills, Vickie realized.

"No!" she cried suddenly. She caught hold of his hands, trying to lower them before the man could see them. "Let's not have hot dogs."

Now everyone was staring at her. The balding hot-dog vendor, the people around her, Jason. "They're really not very healthy. They're awful for your cholesterol level."

"Your *what?*" Jason demanded.

More people were gathering around them. "Vickie, will you let me buy the things?" he said with exasperation. "You ran down here, craving one so deeply."

"I've changed my mind." Her fingers tightened around his. "Besides, this is really highway robbery. They're two-fifty apiece. *Two-fifty in American money.* Greenbacks. U.S. money. Federal money."

"Highway robbery?" the vendor protested. "Lady, these are good dogs. Mile-long dogs, all-beef, and they're kosher, as well!"

"If you don't want a hot dog," a little boy behind them said eagerly, "I do."

"We don't," Vickie said quickly. She caught Jason's wrist, pulling him from the line. And once they were outside it, she tried to explain in a rushed whisper, "You can't use Confederate money."

"It's worthless?"

"Yes. Well, actually, people collect it now, so it might be worth a great deal. But you can't buy hot dogs with it."

"Because we lost," he said softly, silver-gray eyes level, enigmatic, upon her.

She nodded.

"Vickie! There you are!"

She whirled around. Steve, clad in his Yankee blue, was hurrying toward them. She felt Jason stiffen at her side.

"He's a friend! And the war is over!" she hissed to Jason. "Steve!" she greeted her friend. "I didn't know that you were taking part in this skirmishing."

"Well, it must be because you didn't ask," he told her. He flung an arm around her shoulders and gave her a hug.

She was startled to feel a firm hand on her arm. Jason's. Drawing her back against him. And he was staring at Steve with a silver fire in his eyes.

"Hello," Steve said curiously to him.

"Steve, this is Jason."

"Colonel Tarkenton," Jason said.

Vickie gritted her teeth. "Jason, this is a very good friend of mine, Steve Hanson. He and my late husband went to school together."

"Nice to meet you," Steve said, looking over Jason with obvious curiosity. It was all she needed at the moment. Steve taking on a big-brother attitude. Jason behaving as if...

As if she was his woman. Well, just what impression had she given him?

"Where do you hail from—Colonel Tarkenton?" Steve asked politely.

"Virginia, but pretty far southwest from here. A little place past Staunton."

"Nice country over there, too."

"Beautiful. Thanks."

"You didn't go to GWU, too, did you?"

"Pardon?"

"To school?"

"Oh. I attended West Point. That was before the current difficulty, of course."

"The current difficulty?" Steve said blankly.

"The war, sir, the war!"

"Always in character!" Vickie murmured. "That's what makes these things so wonderful. You're just all so very...involved."

"Oh, right—the current difficulty," Steve said, and then he laughed.

Maybe they were thawing a little.

And maybe Steve had some money to lend her.

"Steve! Can I borrow ten dollars?" she asked quickly.

Jason stiffened as if he had been slapped, but Vickie ignored him. She was too hungry to go through the whole money conversation again, and certainly couldn't argue with Jason over it in front of Steve.

"Ten dollars? Sure," Steve said, laughing. He reached into an inside pocket of the Federal-issue jacket he was wearing and produced his wallet. He pulled out a bill, but Jason's hand fell on his before he could pass it to her.

"She can't take that, sir," he said firmly.

"Yes, she can!" Vickie insisted. She could already taste a delicious, cholesterol-filled hot dog this very moment.

"It's just ten dollars—" Steve began.

"Nevertheless, she can't just take it."

"But she can—" Vickie began insistently, yet she never got the chance to finish. She found herself drawn somewhat behind Jason Tarkenton and he was producing his Confederate notes, out of the Bank of Virginia. "We can't spend these," Jason said. "But I understand they're worth something. Can we trade?"

Steve stared from the bills to Jason's face incredulously. Very tentatively, he took one. Then he shook his head, staring at Jason again. "These are real."

"Well, of course they're real, sir! I'm certainly no counterfeiter."

Vickie kicked him. "What?" Steve said, frowning.

"Boys, boys, you do take this all so seriously!" Vickie

piped up quickly. Jason cast her one of his warning silver-gray stares. But Steve smiled a little bit sheepishly.

"Yeah, sometimes we do." He studied the note he had taken from Jason with fascination. Then he handed it back. "I'm not a collector in this field, but this is definitely worth more than ten dollars. I can't take it from you."

"Then we can't take your ten, sir," Jason said with a ring of steel to his voice.

We! Where did this "we" come in? She could *gladly* take the darned ten dollars. She was just about ready to kill for a hot dog!

"Steve! Please take the bill for ten," she begged.

"But he can't be serious," Steve said.

"But he is! *Please?*" she implored him.

Steve finally shrugged. "I hate to think I've taken advantage of anyone—"

"You're not." She slipped the ten from Steve's fingers. Jason pressed his Confederate bill back into Steve's hand.

She was grateful to see that there was no line now at the hot-dog truck. "Two, please! And two Cokes."

The hot-dog vendor remembered her. "I wouldn't want to rip you off, lady," he said pointedly.

"Please! Give me a hot dog!"

The vendor shook his head, muttering to himself. He delivered her the two hot dogs and sodas. She paid him, juggled everything to bring the food and drinks back to Jason.

To her dismay, she saw that another friend had joined Steve. And the three of them had gotten into a discussion over the battle that had been fought here today.

"Hell, Steve, he's right. This battle was a Confederate victory. History may call it something of a stalemate, but think about it. The Yanks had two-thirds more men. They were well supplied. The Rebs were trying to reach their supply line, and they were outnumbered two to one. It should have been all over except that Stonewall did rally more troops in,'' Steve's friend was saying.

And Jason was just staring at the man, trying to comprehend how the fellow in the Yankee blue could be on his side in the argument.

"They lost nearly equal numbers—'' Steve began stubbornly.

"They routed the Yanks,'' his friend said.

"They were better horsemen,'' Jason said suddenly.

Everyone stopped and stared at him. He smiled ruefully. "We—'' He caught Vickie's eyes. "They, I mean, were simply much better horsemen. Southerners were raised to hunt, to ride, to race. In a situation like this, they were able to ride a few circles around the Yanks.''

"See? Exactly my point!'' Steve's friend said excitedly. "Oh, the Yanks did have some good fellows. Custer did damned well at Gettysburg—''

"Who?'' Jason inquired.

"George Armstrong Custer. He—''

"That cutup?'' Jason said incredulously.

"What?''

Vickie slammed down on Jason's foot. He shook his head, frowning at her. "Custer really was a wretched student. That's in the records—I imagine. Sorry, go on.''

"Custer sure held up Stuart at Gettysburg. But then again, it was the first real bad time that Lee had to work without Stonewall—''

"Without Stonewall?'' Jason said.

"Sure. He was dead before Gettysburg, you know. And as to Custer, well he met his unhappy end in 1877, right? Took a lot of men with him, but it seems lots of folks—all Yanks by that time—thought that he acted such a brazen fool he all but deserved it himself.''

Jason stared at him blankly.

"The Battle of the Little Bighorn," Vickie said briefly, smiling. But Jason wasn't thinking about Custer. He was still assimilating the fact that Stonewall Jackson had been killed.

Vickie thrust a hot dog and drink into Jason's hand and slipped a finally free hand around his arm. "We've got to go," she said, searching her mind for a reason. She found one. A real one. "I—er—I've been gone a lot longer than I intended. Gramps is going to be very worried. Come on, Jason. We've got to see him!"

He followed her lead, but she could see that his face had turned somewhat pale.

"Hey, nice horse, Tarkenton!" Steve called after him. "You've really done it all right!"

Vickie waved cheerily. She urged Jason along. "This way. I know where I am now. My home is right over the next rise."

The hot dogs she had wanted so badly were still in their hands, untouched. She had at least managed to steer him away from the crowd. But even as they started up the rise, he pulled back.

"Stonewall?" he demanded.

She hesitated. "He was killed by one of his own pickets. Well, mortally wounded." She hesitated, biting into her lower lip.

He sank to the ground, sitting, staring back at the milling people. "It's a game. It's nothing more than a game to them. All those people gave so much! Fought and bled and died, and it's nothing more than a game to them!"

She stared down at him, seeing for a moment the bewilderment on his features, and then the anger.

And then she felt a little anger of her own taking root.

"No! No, it's much, much more than a *game!* Don't you see that? It's *history*. It's remembering, it's keeping the heartache and the pain alive. It's a way of honoring all that happened then. You shouldn't be angry. You should be grateful. No man who fought died in vain. Not Yanks, not Rebels. You tested our nation. You broke it apart. You fought and died, and in the end, over time, you made it whole, you made it strong. What happened probably had to happen so that we could meet the twentieth century with the strength needed to survive, to arise a world power. There's so much that you don't know. How can you fairly judge us?"

He set his hot dog and soda down on the ground and stood with a sudden vehemence that frightened her. Maybe she had been wrong to forget that he might be a madman.

Maybe she had really been a fool to contradict him so bluntly.

He walked toward her with his silver eyes glittering. A soft cry escaped her and she started backing away. He reached toward her. Lifted the food from her hands and set it down with purpose.

"Keep your distance, now," she demanded. "I'm warning you—"

He paused for a minute, silver eyes searing as they touched upon hers. "Oh?" he said softly. "Warning me? And just what are you going to do?"

She clenched her teeth together for a moment, staring him down. "I'm going to eat my damned hot dog, that's what I'm going to do! I'll just leave you to wallow in your self-pity, and eat my hot dog, since you've managed to starve me rather nicely! Then I'm going home!"

He took another step toward her. "I'm sorry!" she

cried. "I'm sorry for the horrible things that you're learning. But I can't change them, and I can't stop everyone else from telling you the truth. I still can't even really believe that this can be the truth, but I do believe you and I—I care about you and...stop!"

But neither warnings nor threats seemed to mean anything to him. He caught her by the shoulders. Wrenched her into his arms. Kissed her. Deeply. With that same passion that had made her forget everything except how much she wanted him. She wanted to protest; she stiffened in his arms at first. But the liquid fire of his kiss was overwhelming, and her hands fell upon his arms when they should have been beating against him.

Then she found her head leaned against his chest, his hands stroking over her hair. "It is a world gone mad," he said softly. "A nightmare. Yet you are in it." And his eyes touched her. "Wild, brash, brave. A touch of magic." His knuckles moved over her cheek.

Magic. Yes, that was it. He was magic himself....

And she was suddenly afraid. Very afraid. Magic could vanish. And she was allowing herself to become so intensely involved. Touched. Loved...

"We have to go," she said breathlessly. "My grandfather will be frightfully worried. Please..."

"Let's go, then." He set her drink and her hot dog back in her hands. "Wherever you shall lead, I will follow," he told her, silver-gray eyes shimmering into hers. "For the moment," he added softly.

"For the moment?"

"Don't you see, Victoria? I'm lost. I've got to find my way back. To John."

"Your brother."

"Yes, my brother. I promised him that I'd come back to him, Vickie."

"But what if there isn't a way?"

He shook his head. "There has to be a way. I've lost so much, Vickie. John is all I have left. And I promised him."

She bit her lip, watching him with a sudden flicker of tears stinging her eyes. She understood that.

Gramps. He was the someone she had left.

"There's a secret locked in the mountain up there," he persisted. "There's an archway, between the trees. I know it's there—I just have to find it again. Max stumbled through it. We stumbled through it. And left it once again."

"You don't know that—"

"I know it. And you know it. No one involved in one of your *reenactments* would have been shooting real bullets at us, right? I have to go back. But I am exhausted and starving—and grateful to you." He hesitated a moment, then stroked her cheek once again. She felt the breeze touch them then, too. Against the heat of the sun, it was cool, light, as soft as that stroke of his flesh. "Grateful, and much, much more!" he murmured, his tone husky, and very low. Then he continued, the soldier, the man, his voice growing deeper. "I want to see you home, and accept your help. Maybe in this world of modern wonders, there is something that I could bring back to save my brother. So, please," he said very softly, "lead forward."

CHAPTER FIVE

Vickie decided it was best if she first saw Gramps alone, so Jason waited at the roadside. As she walked up to the house, her heart was pounding with a sudden ferocity. Gramps was so old now, he was all that she had and he was probably worried sick!

She burst into the house, calling his name. "Gramps? Gramps? Where are you?"

The door to the taproom stood to her right, and the curving hallway to the bedrooms just upstairs was in front of her. She didn't know which way to run first.

"Gramps!"

The taproom door burst open and he came through, blue eyes wild and anxious.

"Vickie! Victoria! Where in tarnation have you been, young woman? When your horse came back without you last night, I'd have died with worry if I hadn't been so afraid!"

"I'm sorry, Gramps, so very sorry!" She linked her arms around his neck, hugging him fiercely, kissing his weathered cheek and then hugging him again. Where had she been? What story was she going to give him?

And just how was she going to explain Jason Tarkenton?

"The weather, Gramps," she said quickly. "There were the strangest storms on the peaks. Arabesque threw me and I'm afraid that I became horribly disoriented walking in the dark last night and—"

She broke off. Her grandfather's hold on her had stiffened and he was looking over her shoulder.

He was looking at Jason. And Max.

Why hadn't he waited, as they'd agreed? She had left the front door open when she came in the house and now Jason stood just outside, one foot on the first step, his handsome cavalry mount behind him. Jason had heard every word that she'd said, and now he was coming up the steps.

"I thought you went to see Yankees, girl?" Gramps asked softly.

"Yes, well, I did go to see my Yank friends," she said lightly. "But I ran into a Rebel on my way home." Oh, dear God, get her through this! she thought. She pulled away from her grandfather, trying to smile broadly. "Gramps, this is an old friend. Jason Tarkenton. He hasn't been able to find any lodging so I've brought him home for the night. It will only take a minute to fix up one of the guest rooms. He's, umm, he's been looking after me, it seems, since—lately. I knew you'd be happy to have him here." Was that close to the truth? Not in the least. And Jason wasn't going to let it go by.

Damn him!

He was now standing in the doorway. "My deepest apologies, sir. That your granddaughter was waylaid was entirely my fault, and I do beg your pardon. I'm deeply sorry for all the anxiety I've put you through."

Gramps looked from Jason to Vickie, arching a brow slowly. He looked their visitor over with a deliberate curiosity. He cast Vickie a glance of pure suspicion. Then he extended a hand to Jason. "How do you do, sir? An old friend of my granddaughter's, eh?"

"Yes," Vickie said.

"That's not exactly true," Jason told him. "As I said,

the fact that she was waylaid was entirely my fault. But I swear to you, sir, that I mean to honor our relationship."

Vickie winced. *Honor* their relationship?

She wanted to strangle him. But Gramps was still staring at them both with wonder.

"I swear it, sir," Jason told Gramps.

"Mmm—that chili smells delicious!" Vickie cried out. She needed to have a talk with Jason. A long talk. But for now, she'd just have to try and distract Gramps. "Gramps, please tell me that we've some chili left. I'm absolutely starving."

Gramps was still staring at Jason. "You been eating hardtack, huh?" he said.

It didn't sound as if he were teasing.

"An awful lot of it sir. And I just tried a hot dog, too."

"Gramps, will you excuse me for a moment? I need to speak with Jason alone outside for just a minute."

"You waylaid her, eh?" Gramps said.

She shoved against Jason's chest. He wasn't moving. "Yes, sir. I needed help. But I swear to you as a gentleman that I mean to protect her honor and—"

"Jason, may I please speak with you outside?"

"There's been more to this than a walk in the woods," Gramps said to Jason.

"Yes, sir."

"Jason! Gramps, you will excuse me!" She pushed with all her power against Jason's chest. He still didn't move. He obviously believed that this discussion was between him and Gramps. He wasn't budging, and he was muscled like steel. And Gramps wasn't politely moving away, either.

She decided to talk anyway. "This is the twentieth

century! I'm not one of your long-ago *possession-type* females. I make my own decisions! I'm not dishonored in any way, shape or form, and you don't *owe* me anything. And quite frankly, I'd truly appreciate it if you could manage not to be so damned *honorable* for a while, here! I resent being *owed* whatever it is you think that you owe me."

"Possession types?" he said, eyes intense, his voice very low, and sounding something like a growl.

"Yes! As if women are automatically things that you have to take responsibility for—"

"Let him be responsible!" Gramps chimed in.

"My females, Victoria, are not *possessions!*" Jason informed her. "They think, they feel, they weigh matters and they make decisions. But, Jesu, lady, they know how to listen, too, how to be cherished, how to love and cherish in return. And they also respect and honor the men in their lives!"

Suddenly—and a little bit too late—it seemed that Gramps had heard what she had said before and was anxious that the two of them get something to eat. "Chili's on!" he announced jovially. "Come on into the taproom, you two, and we'll see if we can't cool down your tempers by heating up your appetites. This is an unexpected ripple in the day, by golly!"

Oh, it was a ripple, all right, Vickie thought. She tried to control both her temper and her nervousness, giving Jason a very stern stare.

He ignored her, of course.

They followed him in. Gramps walked around the counter to the kitchen area. "Pour your man an ale, Victoria," Gramps commanded.

She gritted her teeth. "He isn't *my man*, Gramps. He's a friend." She stared at Jason very hard. "And I'm trying very hard to help him!" She dropped her voice for Jason alone. "You're making it very difficult!" she rasped beneath her breath.

He returned her stare and spoke softly. "I can *try* to behave, Victoria, but I can't change what I am."

Gramps, pulling a microwave container out of the refrigerator and slipping it into the microwave, grinned back. "Sounds interesting, anyway. You scared me half to death, young lady. I was ready to call in the FBI."

Vickie pulled the tap down for a draft beer for Jason, and then decided to have one herself.

She needed one.

She walked around the bar and saw that Jason was staring at what Gramps was doing. She realized then that the microwave and the refrigerator must be absolute wonders to him—not to mention the electric lights.

She set a beer down before him, and narrowed her eyes at him, trying desperately to warn him that he must be careful.

"Here we are!" Gramps said.

Jason's brows arched. "That fast? Cooked food that fast?"

She didn't think that Gramps had heard. "The world has been in an age of invention, almost since the war ended," she said, speaking incredibly quickly. "That's a refrigerator and freezer. It runs off electricity and keeps things cold. That's a microwave oven. I don't know exactly how microwaves work, but it cooks food very, very fast."

Almost as fast as she had been speaking, she thought with a wince. Jason couldn't have grasped too much of what she had said. But it didn't matter; she couldn't repeat anything. Gramps was on his way over with the chili now. Setting it down before them with plates and utensils and napkins. "Thanks, Vickie, I'll just get my own beer," Gramps said reproachfully.

She cast him a hard gaze. "You didn't say that you wanted one!" she reminded him, and she quickly went to pour a third beer, trying to keep her eye on the two men.

"You've been out for a while," Gramps said. "Bet you could use a nice hot bath and a change of clothing. After keeping my granddaughter out all that time."

"Gramps!"

"Sir, I've told you—"

"May I see that sword you've got there, Mr. Tarkenton?" Gramps asked suddenly.

"Of course."

Jason stood instantly and Vickie bit into her lower lip. He'd lost his plumed hat along the way and was clad only in his cavalry shirt, breeches and boots, but he wore them so exceptionally well. He was as lean and hard as any fighter, striking and agile as he drew his sword from its scabbard. Her heart seemed to catapult and spread as she watched him, fascinated by his movement, by the unruly length of his tawny hair, by the silver fire in his eyes and the hard-set determination in every line and plane of his face.

He walked his sword around to Gramps, who took it far more reverently than it had been offered.

Gramps studied the sword and Vickie held her breath. He looked up at Jason at last. "It's real!" he said in a whisper. "This thing is a real Confederate cavalry officer's sword, out of Richmond. I've never seen such a fine example. And the scabbard. It's real, too?"

Jason unbuckled his scabbard and handed it over, too. Gramps looked into his eyes, then to the scabbard. After a moment he said with certain wonder, "My God. This thing is in excellent shape. There's some slashes in the leather—"

"That one was Manassas," Jason said, leaning over.

Vickie tried to kick him unobtrusively. She managed to get his shin. He stared at her hard, brows knitting into a frown.

"Gramps," she admonished, still staring at Jason, "quit being such a historian, huh? Let the poor man eat his chili."

"Right. Go ahead, young man. Dig in. It's just that I'm a collector, you know. And an armchair historian. Well, I used to reenact, too, but the old bones are getting a little sore for sleeping out in tents and such. This is one of the finest pieces I've ever seen, including any I've seen in the top museums!"

"Er…thank you," Jason murmured.

"Eat your chili, son."

Jason did. Vickie realized that he must have been starving by then—*really* starving—because he tried to start slowly, but in a matter of minutes, he was eating as fast as his hand could carry his spoon from the plate to his mouth. And of course, she was starving herself. She ate quickly, too. And Gramps was silent until their spoons clinked against their bowls.

"That was excellent," Jason said quietly. "Thank you very much. It was truly the best meal I've had in—" He broke off. "Ages," he finished limply, watching Vickie.

Gramps grunted, still studying him. "It was a bowl of chili. Good recipe, but just chili. You haven't been eating very well lately, have you, Mr. Tarkenton?"

Vickie felt a twinge of real unease. Gramps just didn't intend to let her get away with this. She wished she could just tell him the truth.

Or what she thought she believed to be the truth!

"Gramps, really! My guest's eating habits—"

"Are darned curious, darned curious," Gramps finished. "So, let's see now, did you and Victoria go to school together, too?"

"Yes," Vickie lied.

"No," Jason said simultaneously.

"No!" Vickie said quickly, but Jason was in the process of changing his response to an emphatic, "Yes, sir!"

"Right," Gramps said, nodding gravely. "Where do you come from, Mr. Tarkenton?"

Vickie opened her mouth to answer quickly for him.

Gramps was quicker.

"Now, Victoria, I asked Mr. Tarkenton."

Jason grinned. He liked Gramps a lot, she could see that. Gramps was going to get right to any point.

"I come from a little town just west of Staunton."

"And your folks have been from around there for a long time, I take it?"

"That's right, sir. Late 1700s."

"Which is it? You did or didn't go to school with Vickie?"

"Didn't, sir."

"You attended college?"

"West Point."

"Gramps, can we please play Twenty Questions later?" Vickie said. "Jason needs a bath and some sleep—"

"Why?" Gramps asked her, wide-eyed.

"We were up all night," she said. "Trying to get back."

"Oh, yeah, right," Gramps said. "Where are your things, Mr. Tarkenton? You didn't ride your horse all the way up here from the Staunton area, did you?"

"Of course he didn't!" Vickie exclaimed quickly.

"What, did you trailer him on in for the reenactment?"

"Yes," Vickie answered.

"Let Mr. Tarkenton answer himself. That is, if you don't mind, Mr. Tarkenton," Gramps said.

But Jason, it seemed, did mind something. His eyes were steady on Gramps, his jaw was set. "I'll answer whatever you like. But let's get this settled. It's either Jason, sir, or Colonel Tarkenton. *Colonel* Tarkenton."

Gramps's brows shot up. Vickie would have kicked Jason beneath the table again—really hard—except that he stood then, not allowing her to do so.

Then Gramps was on his feet himself. "All right, *Colonel* Tarkenton, just where do you really come from?"

"The Staunton area!" Jason said.

"Then just why is everything about you so damned different? And why is it that you've been staring at the lights and the refrigerator and microwave as if you just walked off a spaceship?"

"A spaceship?" Jason said. He looked at Vickie, frowning. "A spaceship?"

She smiled suddenly. She'd always known that Gramps was sharp as nails, but she'd never imagined that things could get this difficult.

One thing she knew for certain, though, and she should have realized it from the beginning. No matter what she told him—and whether he believed her or not—he wouldn't act against her in any way. She was going to have to put some faith in him.

Either that, or gag Jason. She wasn't sure that that was possible.

She felt like laughing hysterically. She actually smiled at Jason. "A spaceship. You know, flying around in outer space. Men have walked on the moon, you see."

He shook his head. *"Men have walked on the moon?"*

She nodded gravely, still smiling. This was so ridiculous. There were moments when she couldn't fathom the fact that she had decided to believe all this herself. She looked at her grandfather.

"He's from the war, Gramps. The real one."

Gramps sank into his chair quickly, staring up at Jason. "'The war. The real one,'" he repeated.

"Before God, sir, it's the truth," Jason said. He spoke softly, but there was a passion in his voice that rang sincere. Gramps stared at Vickie. She stared back.

He shook his bald head, at a loss. "How?" he said at last. "You know…that just can't be."

"But it is," Jason assured him. "And I don't know how, not exactly. I think that there is some kind of a doorway within the arch of a number of trees. I think that I've been through it twice, and I'm convinced that I can find it again. I don't think I really believe all of this myself, except that I've come from a raging battle to see dozens of *horseless* carriages lined up in a field. Now I've seen strange lights and that thing you call a refrigerator or freezer. It really can't be true. I don't believe any of it—except that it's happened to me."

Gramps was just staring at him. Vickie held her breath. Then Gramps began to speak slowly. "If such a thing were going to happen—and I'm not saying for a minute that it has—the time would be right. These are the exact same days in which the battle and skirmishes were fought all those years ago. They've even fallen the same—Sunday is Sunday, and so forth. The weather is the same, the place is the same," Gramps murmured. "And there were storms. Strange and powerful electrical storms, like we're having now. So maybe, if a door were to open, it would open now."

"So you believe him?" Vickie breathed.

"I didn't say that at all!" Gramps warned her. He stared at Jason, frowning. "By the saints!" he muttered suddenly. "If what you're telling me is true, then...to you, it has all just begun. Stonewall is yet to come in to fight here. He's yet to—"

"Die," Jason said flatly.

"And the war—"

"Is yet to be lost," Jason finished.

Gramps nodded. "I'm sorry, young fellow. Truly sorry."

"I'm going to go back," Jason said. "I'm going to find the passageway. It exists. I was there, I *know* I was there. But we were outnumbered, and Vickie was with me. I didn't dare stay. But I must go back."

Gramps was shaking his head suddenly, vehemently.

"No. The South loses. It would be foolish for you to go back. And maybe that passageway is gone now. Have you thought of that? It has to be an extraordinary happening. If such things do open, then they must close, too."

Vickie clenched her teeth suddenly, fighting the chill that had seized her. There were moments when she truly questioned her sanity and wondered if she had imagined the events on the mountainside. There couldn't really be Yankees; they couldn't really have been shooting at her.

But even that battlefield hadn't been as frightening as the feel of the wind. Gramps was right—if there was a passageway from one time to another, it certainly was extraordinary. And if it opened—it would close. It was filled with a strange, dangerous violence, with a wild wind, with a frightening, gripping chill. It had seemed to enclose her as if it wanted to hold her there, in the wind and wicked darkness, forever.

She stared at Jason and spoke very softly, "Gramps is right. The South loses. What is there for you to go back for? Think about it, Jason. There's nothing back there except for fear and horror and…maybe death."

"I have to go back," Jason said firmly.

Gramps arched a brow high. "You've got a wife?" he said suspiciously.

"My wife is dead."

"Don't go back," Gramps insisted.

"He's right!" Vickie cried. "What's back there for you? Loss and pain. You can't change things—"

"Maybe I can."

They were all silent for a minute. Maybe he *could* change things, with what he knew now.

And what would that mean?

"You can't—tamper—with history."

"I *have* to go back. My brother is caught on that mountain, somewhere back in time, dying."

"Wounded?" Gramps said.

Jason nodded. Gramps drummed his fingers on the table. Then he jumped up suddenly. "Maybe you can do something. Maybe you can't. It's darn sure, though, that you can't find your way back now. Dusk is almost here, and it goes black on the mountaintop after that. I've got to go out. Vickie, let him finish his beer. Draw him a nice hot bath. Give him some clean clothing to wear. I'll be back by the time you're both spruced up."

"Where are you going?" Vickie demanded.

"To the library. And now, you— Never mind! I'll see you soon. Real soon." He started out, but paused at the door, looking back. "I'm not saying I believe a word of this, you know!"

Then he was gone. Vickie stared after him, then hurried to catch up. She left the taproom, came back into the entry of the house and stood by the screen door.

There was Gramps, patting Max on the nose. She felt Jason behind her. They both watched while Gramps inspected Max's feet, then patted him on the nose again.

"What is he doing?" Vickie murmured softly.

"Looking at the way he's shod. Inspecting the saddle and the saddlebags. He's a smart old fellow," Jason said. He was quiet for a minute. "Imagine. He believed in me right away," he said softly.

Vickie swung around. He was standing so close behind her that she was less than an inch away from him when she faced him. His warmth seemed to flood over her. She could feel the magical energy of his strength, feel his heat. He was impossible, unerringly courteous, so damned protective, it was irritating. No, it wasn't really irritating. It was different. And if she admitted it, she had been loved like that once before. Maybe it had been the twentieth century, but Brad had loved her like that, the way in which he cast himself between her and danger at all times. She was a twentieth-century woman, but that feeling of being cherished was a good one.

And maybe it didn't matter, with a man, just what era he'd come from. Jason Tarkenton was stubborn, set and determined.

But she didn't want him to go away. It was incredible. He had become so very much to her so quickly.

She swallowed hard. He *was* going back, with first light. When he could find his archway through time. No matter how extraordinary—or frightening—it was. And she had to let him go. He came from a world where battle still roared. He had lived all of his life believing that honor and loyalty were everything. She couldn't stop him from going.

And neither could she be sorry that he had come.

"Gramps is very special," she said quietly. "I owe him everything. He has always been there for me." She was suddenly convinced that she would burst into the strangest outpouring of tears if she wasn't careful. She pushed against his chest, determined to get by him. "I'll get some clothes for you. Brad was about your size—"

"Brad?"

"My husband. There's a bathroom at the top of the stairs, towels are in the linen closet in the hallway. Go on up and I'll find you something. If you're going to go back, you can leave with a full stomach, a hot bath and a good night's sleep behind you. Maybe that will help you change history."

He was staring at her. He winced, and she saw the pain and worry in his eyes. She knew that he was feeling a certain guilt for having strayed so far from his brother.

But she knew, too, that he was also fascinated by the time that he was spending with her.

"Jason!" she murmured suddenly.

"Yes?"

"You've got to start—"

A tawny brow arched high. "I've got to start what?" he demanded.

"I'm not helpless. I can take care of myself. You have to start being—careful."

"Meaning?"

"You don't have to protect me so much, that's all."

He lifted her chin, staring into her blue eyes. "I can't change the truth, and I'm sorry. I found it impossible to lie to a man like your grandfather—and I'm sorry again. Where I come from, we honor our commitments."

"But you can't honor anything, don't you see?" Vickie whispered. "Because you're going back!"

He stepped away from her. Maybe that was a truth that he had never seen. "I have to," he murmured painfully.

No! Vickie's heart seemed to cry. There had to be a way for him *not* to go back.

He suddenly lifted a piece of hair from her face, smoothing his knuckles over her cheek.

"Then there's nothing to honor."

"Maybe there is."

"How—?"

"You could come back with me," he said.

"What?" she barely formed the word.

He smiled. "I guess not. I'm going back to a war— and a country that loses that war. And through…through that tunnel. You've got hot dogs and microwaves. It would be incredibly foolish, wouldn't it?" He paused a moment, then brushed her lips tenderly with his. "This bathroom of yours is at the top of the stairs?" he asked.

She nodded. He turned around then and silently followed the instructions she had given him before, walking up the stairs to the second floor of the house.

She let out a long breath, watched him go and then hurried up the stairs behind him.

Take care of things, she thought. Don't think!

She had given most of Brad's things to charities when he had been killed, but there were still a number of his jeans and shirts in the back bedroom. She didn't sleep there. She hadn't slept near anything of his once he had died, not since the night she had cried all night because she'd had one of his shirts in her hands. That had been a long time ago now. She could do this.

She found a comfortable worn pair of light blue jeans and a tailored cotton shirt in a soft warm maroon. She walked down the hall to the front bathroom and suddenly heard an oath explode.

"Jesu!"

There was a burst of water.

She knocked lightly and opened the door. He was stripped of his uniform with a white towel knotted around his waist and for a second it seemed that her heart stopped, then plummeted onward again. Bronzed and so taut-muscled. She felt a flare of color rushing to her cheeks. She itched to touch him. Longed to open her mouth and say that she was so very afraid that she had missed something before, could she please inspect him from head to toe.

He didn't seem to notice that she was staring at him. "How do you manage these damned things?" he inquired of the faucets.

She smiled, and turned them both down. "Bath or shower?" she asked him.

A spark touched his eyes. His lips curled up slowly. "Well, I don't know. That depends. Are you joining me or not?" His hands were upon her. Touching her shoulders. Drawing her near to him. And then his mouth was on hers. She could feel the fire burning his flesh, the strength in his fingers. She stroked his arms, his chest, felt the fever seep like lava into her body, warming her, with each liquid sweep and caress of his tongue.

Oh, yes…!

He drew her closer and closer, molding her to his length. She could feel the muscled pressure of his thighs against hers, despite the towel, despite her dress. She could feel more. Insinuative, explicit, exciting. The rise of his desire, hard and pressing, against her. Sweetness reaching around her, creating a stirring hunger. She returned his kiss, hungry, wanting more.…

She could feel the tension that suddenly gripped his

body. The shudder that seemed to shake him from head
to toe.

And he groaned, deep in his throat.

And then suddenly, he was pressing her away from
him.

"Oh," he breathed, eyes a silver fire that riddled her.

She shook her head.

"It's your grandfather's house," he said quietly.

She stepped back herself. Gramps would understand.
Probably. She was well over twenty-one. He knew that
she knew all about the birds and the bees. He'd known
that she'd been married....

And he'd been longing to find the right someone to
match her up with for ages.

But this was his house. And he might be back any
minute. And it was simply a matter of...

Respect. The kind of thing that meant so very much
to Jason Tarkenton.

A shudder ripped through her. No. She couldn't let him
leave without touching him again. Without being held in
his arms. Without creating another memory to hold fast
to through the lonely nights that stretched ahead.

She knotted her fingers into her palms at her sides. She
was not reaching out for him. She swung around. "I've
a shower in my room. I'll see you downstairs." She indicated the pile of Brad's clothing. "I hope these things
fit you. There's a one-hour cleaner in town. We can get
your things back tonight."

"A cleaner?"

She shook her head. "A laundry."

She closed the bathroom door thoughtfully. It was
good that he was going! They didn't even speak the same
language; they just thought that they did.

Vickie hurried down the hallway to her bedroom and

into her own bathroom. She stripped off her long dress and stepped blindly into the shower, jumping when a cold wall of water came down upon her.

The water was startling, cleansing.

It helped. A little.

Go back with him....

That was impossible. Absolutely. Blindly she found the soap. Mechanically she began to wash.

Impossible! He didn't understand, truly couldn't understand. This world had penicillin, pasteurized milk.

AIDS. Bombs that could kill a million people in one single explosion....

This world had Gramps in it, and that was all that mattered.

But maybe she could convince Jason to stay. Maybe Gramps had found some records. Maybe...

Maybe he could prove that John Tarkenton would live whether Jason went back or not. Could such a thing be?

She didn't know.

She stepped from the shower, toweling herself strenuously. She walked on into her bedroom, dug through her drawers and found soft old jeans and a pink knit shirt. She had barely crawled into the clothing when she heard something pelting against her window.

She walked to it, drawing back the drapes.

Jason was down there. She opened the window.

He had looked striking in his cavalry clothing, tall, commanding, assured.

Yet, in a way, he was more striking now. His tawny hair remained long and shaggy, just curling over the collar of the tailored shirt. The worn jeans hugged his form, trim hips, long hard legs. His hands were shoved into the pockets. The shirt was opened a button or two at his throat.

His eyes were alight, startlingly silver. And he was smiling. For once the incredible tension was gone. In the twilight below her, he could have easily been of her world, a part of it.

No, for the way that her heart leapt, it seemed that he was her world at the moment.

He smiled at her, his lips curling slowly, ruefully.

"I wouldn't feel right about the house," he said softly. "But I noticed a great barn out here. Clean, sweet-smelling hay. Good blankets."

She stared down at him blankly for a moment, wishing that she could freeze him there.

For all time.

"Well, all right," he continued, "maybe I'm being a little presumptuous. And then again..." He paused, and then his voice was deep and husky and passionate when he continued. "And then again, maybe I can't quite make myself care if I'm being presumptuous or not. There's the very good possibility that I might run back up the stairs and burst into your room. And carry you on out to see just how wonderful that old barn can be."

She inhaled sharply. Her knees were trembling. She closed her eyes for a moment. She should have been thinking that he was wearing Brad's clothes.

She had loved Brad so very much. She hadn't even managed a decent dinner with anyone else.

Until now.

And Brad, she thought, would be glad.

"Vickie!"

She moistened her lips.

He started to turn. "I'm coming up!" he warned her. Her fingers gripped the windowsill. "No! No!"

He paused.

She smiled, biting into her lip. "I'm coming down!" she called softly, and spun quickly away to do so.

CHAPTER SIX

There were wonderful, incredible things to this new world.

None of them was more wonderful than Vickie.

Jason saw her slow smile at the window, and he saw her turn. He turned his eyes to the door of the old house—old by either of their standards—and he waited for her to emerge.

In seconds, she did so, the wealth of her hair streaming behind her, catching the last drops of sun, shimmering with red lights. She was wearing pants now, the same manner of pants he was wearing himself, and they hugged her hips, outlining with a fascinating clarity their curve and shape, the length of her legs, the subtle slimness and agility of her.

Hmm. So that was progress. People had ceased to wear as much clothing.

On Vickie, it *was* progress, he determined.

And as she approached him, he discovered again that everything else faded, the reality of a war that disappeared, the numbing incredulity that he had stepped into a different time. Everything faded for those precious moments, everything but the uniqueness of the woman.

In seconds she was before him with her stunning clear blue eyes and fire-lit wealth of soft auburn hair. He reached out to cup the cheek of the beautiful face and it felt as if all the desires within the universe burst forward within him. God, yes, she could make him forget the horror. Make him forget all he had left behind.

Because she was so important to him. With her courage, her fire, her determination. And with her simple beauty.

He groaned softly, then swept her up into his arms. Her fingers laced around his neck. Her eyes met his. Her brow rose delicately and the husky query in her voice sent hot shivers racing down his back.

"You don't mind barns, hmm?"

The sweet clean scent of her was intoxicating.

"Actually, ma'am, I'm mighty partial to barns."

Her lips curled in a slow, lazy smile. Keeping his eyes laced with hers, he walked the distance into the old red barn. He had happened upon the perfect place out there. A clean stall filled with fresh, newly mown hay. There had been an old blanket there, frayed but sweetly clean, too, and he'd cast it down already in very high hopes.

He carried her there and laid her down, taking her lips, marveling at the sweetness of them, of the giving that lay within her. The delicate pink tip of her tongue met with his, parried, rimmed his mouth with heady sensuality, met and locked with his once again. He wondered if he would ever understand what was so different and wonderful about this woman. He didn't think that it was time that had really changed her. From what he had seen so far, things changed, people didn't. He had been lonely and bitter for aeons, it seemed. Loving his wife, hating her death. In all those months nothing and no one had managed to dispel his deep sadness. It had been war, and survival and responsibility, he tried to tell himself.

But battle was not continuous—though it had seemed so at times. There had been nights in new cities, there had been women, lots of them. Women who made their trade with the soldiers, and women who had simply been left lonely too long, their men fighting the war, or lost to it. Often enough he found someone to ease those bitter fires of need that continued to rage in his body. But never someone who could touch his very soul. To change things. To change him.

Never…

'Til now.

And this was wrong, he tried to tell himself. He lifted his lips from hers, staring down at her as she looked back at him with beautiful, crystal-clear blue eyes, trusting eyes…sensual eyes. And damp, parted lips. It was wrong. Because he had to leave. No matter how wonderful this world was. He couldn't abandon his brother, and so he shouldn't be tarrying here. Maybe he couldn't find the way back through the darkness. Maybe he did have to stay the night.

He shouldn't be spending it here, with her, making the ties of silk and fire between them all the tighter.

Her fingers rimmed the length of his back, soft pressure bringing him back to her. Her lips touched his again. Melded with them.

He didn't care about the future or the past.

Only glorious present.

He felt her fingers pluck at the buttons of his shirt, then they were moving over his naked flesh. Something scalding burst and swept around him. He felt her touch like laps of flame as her fingertips and nails stroked over the expanse of him, through the short, crisp hair on his chest. Over his collarbone, lower, against the ribs, lower, near his waistline. The shirt was nearly freed from him already and he sat up, almost ripping it from his body. Those beautiful blue eyes of hers were still upon him, the rich length of her hair was spread out in the hay like a cloud around her head, still catching tiny rays of light to gleam reddish-gold. Her breathing was fast now, her breasts rising, rising and falling. He lifted her slightly into his arms, enough to discard the very soft shirt she had been wearing and discover another of her very fascinating undergarments. This one was all lace, a creation that covered, yet didn't cover at all. Beneath the sheer fabric, the dark crest of her nipple was clearly visible. Just the sight of it sent waves of desire cascading and crashing over him. He linked his arms behind her, supporting her back, and set his mouth upon her breast, teasing the flesh through the lace, touching it lightly, then closing his mouth upon it. She arched back with a little cry, fingers digging into his arms. In seconds he was frustrated with even that brief barrier of lace and he worked his fingers against the hook that held it there. The garment fell free. He crushed her nakedness to his and felt the wealth of searing warmth, the hardened peaks of her breasts pressed so sensually to the wall of his own bared flesh. They were upon their knees, their lips melding again. His fingers ran down the supple length of her back, caressed her spine. Then they moved to her flat stomach and found the button at the waistband of her jeans. Then the metal closure that went up and down...down, at the moment.

He pressed her back against the hay, working upon her jeans, tugging them down against the length of her body. They fell free. In the dim twilight she lay against the old frayed blanket in the hay with an incredibly seductive beauty, the underthings she wore upon her hips very like that which had covered her breasts, all lace, something that covered, yet something that didn't cover at all. He found himself reacting the same way. Having to touch her with the lace, against the lace, between the lace.

He met her eyes for one fascinated instant, then leaned low against her, his tongue rimming the band of the elusive garment where it lay just below her hips. The sweet fragrance of soap on her skin seemed to pervade him as his tongue first touched flesh and lace. Her flesh was ivory, soft, taut, fascinating. She moaned and writhed and whispered something as the wet fire of his tongue first touched against her. He worked it lower, tasting her flesh through those wisps of lace. Lace, and lower still. Her fingers fell against his shoulders, kneading there. His name fell from her lips like soft raindrops upon him, again and again. She whispered a ''no,'' and he paused a moment. The exquisite shape of her lay against the hay, the beauty of her flesh, her slimness, her curves, the rise of her breasts. Her eyes were nearly closed, her head was tossing from side to side. He smiled and looked back to the lace. It had been the most sensuous stuff in the world. Now he was impatient with it, as well. He stripped it from her hips, down the shapely length of her legs. And he began to kiss and stroke her intimately again, sliding his tongue against secret places, feeling the writhe of her body grow wild and erotic, hearing her cries become reckless and gasped.

He rose above her but she came up with him, pressing against him once again, her lips burning hungrily into his shoulder, teeth grazing his flesh, fingers stroking erotically upon it. In seconds. Her lips found his, his throat, his collarbone, and then moved wildly down the length of his chest. He felt her fingers at his waistband.

At the metal thing that went up and down.

Down...now.

Her fingers were working against the material of his pants, shoving them low over his hips. Her hands curved over his buttocks and his breath caught while his heart thundered. Her hands moved and cupped around the bulging length of him and a hoarse cry tore from his own throat. He encircled her with his arms, lifting her chin, finding her lips. He kissed her with a hungry passion while she continued to stroke and caress him until he couldn't bear another moment of it. Pressing her back, he rid himself of the pants. Amazingly, he paused another brief moment, absorbing the beauty of the woman against the hay, the red glory of her hair, the perfection of her body.

All the wonder in those blue eyes that still gazed into his so openly and trustingly. He loved her face, loved the curve of her lips, the wonderful fire in her eyes.

His eyes fell. He loved so much more. The rise of her breasts, the curve of her hips.

A deep yearning groan escaped him. He was suddenly in agony; the pulse within him was so great. He rose over her, and then sank within her. Felt the feminine sheathing of her body, the sweet ecstasy of being inside her, one with her, knowing that his hunger would be eased. Their eyes met. He began to move and move. His arms wrapped around her. His lips found hers. Then nothing mattered but the movement, the beat the pulse, the hunger that increased in each tenfold, and then, again. She was liquid beneath him, liquid that molded, folded, met and matched his every thrust and need. He heard the sweet, crystalline cry that escaped her and shuddered deeply. A thrust again, and again, and he echoed the sound himself, raggedly, hoarsely, explosively. The world burst and shimmered. It had been so long. He didn't remember release like this, satisfaction so damned wonderful and sweet. He seemed to hold forever, loath to leave her, but then he eased himself to her side and swept her protectively into his arms.

The world had gone absolutely mad. Yet how could he regret it?

Even if John lay dying somewhere? If he had died already?

He closed his eyes, tightening his arms around Vickie. But she rose up on an elbow, looking down at him. "What is it?"

He stroked her cheek, shaking his head. "You are magic," he told her softly.

She smiled, her lashes fell, and she met his gaze again. "Mmm. But I've lost you again already."

He lifted a hand in the shadows of the barn. "Guilt," he said softly. "I'm here, with you. It's as if I've touched heaven. And somewhere out there…"

"'Somewhere out there,'" she repeated. "War rages. And maybe there is nothing you can do. Maybe we're not supposed to travel through time or change history. But you're here. Through the violence of that dark tunnel. Perhaps you're supposed to be here. Maybe you're not supposed to go back—"

He groaned hard, sweeping her back into his arms, then pressing her against the hay, his leg cast upon her. Her eyes were very wide and defiant at that moment and he felt both the sweet ache of sorrow and a new rise of passion.

"How can we know what is *supposed* to be? How can we even believe what *is?*" He kissed her again, feverishly. Time itself was the rarity between them. He suddenly didn't want to waste it. "I can't even try to judge it, I don't dare think about it. I have to go back!"

She sounded as if she was choking. "You don't have to go back! The damned war will be lost without you, men will die without you, time will go on—"

"But it's not so simple, or so grand!" he whispered. "My brother is back there, and whether the war is won or lost, whether the future is changed, cannot matter. I can't see through God's eyes. All I know is that I gave my younger brother a promise, and that I could not live anywhere with my sanity if I did not keep it!''

''You could be trapped in that tunnel. Trapped forever.''

''The tunnel is frightening. But I still have to face it. I still have to go back.''

She fell silent, watching him. He thought that he saw the glint of tears in her eyes, and he kissed her. Her arms wrapped around him.

They were silent for a long while. Then she murmured to him, ''Gramps will be back.''

He nodded, pulling away from her. He stood, collecting their clothing from the various places where pieces had landed. He was loath to watch her dress. Time had given her to him. Time would soon snatch her away.

His fingers knotted into his palms. With all of his heart, he wished that he could forget time altogether. Forget the war, forget the blood, the death, and the heartache. Forget it all and just stay here. There must be endless new treasures to see in this new world, so many places to go, and they must be so easy to get to in those horseless carriages. Surely medicine had advanced, life had advanced—bathing had definitely advanced. He could just stay here. He'd been so damned determined he was going to be honorable in this new affair of his, and honorable still surely meant marrying the woman he loved. He had friends married to Northern wives. Some of them had run home, returned to their fathers. Still wed, they lived in different states. Many times, they were still in love, despite the war. Despite the distance.

Different states, not different times, he reminded himself. He was falling in love with her. He wanted to marry her. Sleep with her anywhere, including her grandfather's house. Make love to her on clean sheets, against the softness of a bed.

It would be so damned easy to stay!

His fingers tightened, his nails digging into the flesh of his palms. He couldn't stay. John was back there. John was waiting. With the first light he was going back. He had to.

But her back was to him then. She was just buttoning the pink shirt that draped so sensual against her shoulders. He dropped his hands gently upon her shoulders, drawing her back to him. He kissed the top of her head, and a rush of tension swept through him. He had to leave her. He couldn't really ask her to come with him, ask her to leave a world of hot dogs and Coca-Cola and come back to a time when the fury of war raged and blood ran hot between two sides of a warring nation. She couldn't come back; he couldn't ask her to, and he wouldn't want to endanger her.

But leaving her now was already like leaving a piece of his heart. The best of it.

She spun around in his arms. She saw the sorrow in his eyes. Luckily, perhaps, she misinterpreted it. She stroked his cheek tenderly, studying his eyes. "So much must hurt you!" she whispered. "And I'm so sorry. And honestly, Jason, I am a Virginian, I love Virginia, but more important, I'm an American, and you can't imagine how important that has come to be over the years! What's gone on between America and other nations since your time, you can't possibly imagine. There have been wars. Horrible, devastating wars, wars with bombs that kill tens of thousands of people at a single hit." She shook her head. "I'm so sorry for what you're suffering, but the North had to win. Had to. It was necessary for the United

States to become the power that it did." She hesitated. "Jason, if you go back, you can't change things."

He caught her hands and kissed each of her palms. "Your grandfather was going to the library?"

She nodded.

"Can you take me there?"

She nodded again.

"Do we ride the horses?"

She smiled and shook her head. "I have something called a Jeep Cherokee out back. It will be much less noticeable parked at the library," she assured him.

She took his hand and led him back around the barn to the drive where her bright red little Cherokee waited. The key was under the mat and she opened her door, found it and slid into the driver's seat, indicating that Jason should sit next to her. He did, hands moving over the upholstery, eyes riveted upon the Jeep's panel. "What are all those?"

"Umm—that's for your speed, that tells you how much gas—fuel—you've got. Let's see…windshield wipers, radio—"

"Radio?"

Vickie geared the car into life. She switched the knob for the radio and laughed when he stiffened like timber when the music blasted on.

He stared at her. "Airwaves. I think something like the telegraph probably led to all this," she explained.

He nodded. "It's loud."

"It can be turned down," she said, and did so. She started to drive. He stared straight ahead as she eased the car down the mountain, heading for the center of town. Luckily the night was quiet. There was almost no traffic. Everyone was either at his or her encampment or motel. Or maybe people were worn out from the day's activities.

Or resting for tomorrow's. The hardest fighting of the real battle had taken place that third day, and it would be the same with the reenacting.

Gramps was still there, she saw, as she parked in a space next to his old Buick. Jason stepped out of the car, looking at the buildings in the center of town. Many of them were old, some even older than the days of the Civil War. But some of them were new. The newspaper building was sleekly made with glass panels everywhere. Very modern. Jason just stared at it. At that moment, she heard the distant rumble of a jet. She looked up as Jason did. His hands on his hips, he stared.

"Men have walked on the moon," he murmured wondrously.

"Well, those men—and women—are probably just flying from Washington to Memphis, or some like destination. That's an airplane, not a spaceship. Moon travel isn't commonplace. Although," she added thoughtfully, "they say that someday it might be."

"People can fly. They can just fly anywhere?"

"Almost anywhere."

Vickie watched him staring up at the sky, fascination in his handsome features. His hands were set upon his hips and she found herself watching them next, remembering the way that they felt against her, sensual, exciting, tender.

She was really, truly, falling in love with him. With his smile, with the flash of his eyes.

With the way that he made love.

And even with his determination to leave her. To go back.

She cleared her throat. "Let's go in. Maybe we can find out what Gramps is up to."

But as they started to walk into the library, Gramps

was coming out. He seemed distracted and walked past Vickie without noticing her.

"Gramps?" she said, touching his arm.

"Vickie—Jason! What are you two doing out here?"

"Jason wanted to come to the library," Vickie said, frowning. "What's the matter with you?"

He had two very old books clutched in his hands. She saw that one was a history of Virginia companies of the Civil War, and another was an old, and probably out-of-print, history of Blackfield's Mountain.

Gramps looked at the two of them, shaking his head. Then he sighed. "Let's go somewhere. We can't just stand here in the doorway." He peered at Jason, who was watching him with a keen interest. "You still hungry, young fellow? We got a great steak place just yonder and it's late enough now not to be too busy."

"I'm still hungry, sir. But I still haven't any money—"

"Don't friends invite friends to dinner in your time, Jason Tarkenton?"

"Yes, of course."

"Well, I'm asking. And if you're any kind of gentleman, you're accepting."

Jason bowed his head slightly, hiding a smile. "Thank you. I accept your invitation with great pleasure. And I even know what a steak is!"

"Thought you might," Gramps said, and he grinned, but Vickie saw that the humor wasn't really touching his eyes. He was worried.

They didn't take the vehicles. Hunter's Place for Steaks was just up the road and they walked the distance in a few minutes. They were soon seated in one of the booths. The waitress asked them for a drink order. Jason hesitated, looking at Vickie.

"Have a whiskey," Gramps suggested. "I sure intend to."

Jason nodded. Vickie started to order iced tea, but watching her grandfather, she decided she could use something stronger herself and ordered a rum and Coke. Gramps asked Jason if he might just order for them all and Jason nodded politely. It was going to be a simple meal. Three T-bones, three baked potatoes and three great house Caesar salads. The waitress left them, and Vickie finally exploded, managing to do so in a whisper.

"Gramps, *what* is it?"

He sighed. He drummed his fingers on the table. Then his blue eyes set upon Jason and then her, and Jason again. "I thought I could find something in the books that would keep you from going back. For instance, maybe the history books would say you had just disappeared in the middle of the battle. And some brilliant doctor picked up your brother and he went on to live a long and happy life and survive the war and have a half-dozen children."

"But that's not what happened," Jason said evenly.

Gramps shook his head unhappily.

"Well, what does happen?" Jason demanded.

Gramps sighed. "Your brother, John, had been in the middle of some medical training before the war started, right?"

Jason nodded. Vickie gasped. "How could you know that?"

"Vickie, you should know. The military tends to keep pretty good records. Even though a lot of the stuff pertaining to the Confederacy was lost, you forget, the Daughters of the Confederacy and all those veterans' organizations were strong, even back then. This book was written by a Virginian war widow back in the 1890s. And

it has a fair amount about a Colonel Tarkenton in it—
and a John Tarkenton, too.''

"Gramps, *please,* get to the point!" Vickie insisted.

He still stared at the two of them a long moment, with
Jason returning his stare. Gramps was very old and wrinkled and bald; Jason was in his prime, his tawny hair
thick and rich, his face lines clean and striking.

Still, somehow, they looked very much alike at that
moment.

"Your troops do very well in the battle, Jason. You
lose only three men, and two are reported missing. Neither of them is your brother. He's injured, but you get
him to a field hospital and you stay with him. The surgeons want to take off his arm, but you don't let them.
His arm heals.''

Jason's head was lowered. "Thank God," he murmured.

He looked up. He realized that they were both staring
at him, stricken.

"I always knew I had to go back!" he told Vickie
softly.

"There's more to it than that," Gramps said wearily.
"You save Lee's life right before Gettysburg, battling it
out with a sniper before he can get to the general. Everything could change if Lee died.''

"Maybe I can save others now—"

Gramps leaned toward him, shaking his head. "No,"
he said slowly. "Don't you see? You can't try. You can't
change history. You can't keep Stonewall alive, you can't
risk changing the outcome of the war in any way.''

"Then why the hell do you think this all happened?"
Jason demanded suddenly, passionately. "Why should all
this have happened, anyway? Maybe I *am supposed* to
change the outcome. Maybe that's why I'm here—"

"No. You're here to save your brother."

Jason fell silent, staring at Gramps. "What do you mean? If I hadn't been away from him so long, I would have done much better saving him. I can only believe in you now because I'm so desperate to do so."

Gramps tapped his fork against the table, then looked at Jason again.

"There's a museum down in Petersburg. A pretty good little Civil War museum.... Anyway, the big battle at Petersburg is yet to come for you. It's pretty close to the end there. But I always remember, there's a little piece of sponge there. And there's a comment that some of the Confederate surgeons knew ahead of the Yanks that it was dangerous to use the same sponges on different men. We know now, of course, that germs were spread that way, that half of those men died of diseases because of those dirty sponges. They didn't really know that back then—they didn't understand all that we do now about germs and bacteria and viruses. That's the point."

"What point!" Vickie cried out.

Jason was staring at Gramps. "I think I've got it now, sir. You think that I'm here so that I can go back and save John—so that he can go onward and start men on their road to discovery. With his injury, he'll be sent home. And he'll start to practice medicine—"

"And he'll get others to start using clean sponges. And he'll save any number of lives," Gramps finished. "And his work will also start others on the road to discovery." He hesitated a moment, then continued. "Dr. John Tarkenton is behind some of the first research done in the field."

"Excuse me?"

They all turned. The waitress was there. "Drinks!" she said cheerfully.

Vickie didn't wait for hers to be served. She plucked it off the waitress's tray and took a deep swallow.

Her heart was pounding. *She had known. She had known he was going back. He had said it again and again. But maybe she had believed like Gramps that there might have been a way to make him stay!*

But they all knew it now. He had to go back. There was no hope. There were no choices.

Warm, strong fingers curled around Vickie's beneath the table. His eyes were on hers. Dark, silver, intense.

She was searching lamely for something to say when they suddenly heard a strangled gasp. Then there was the loud—and close!—retort of a shotgun blast. All three of them spun around, as did the other dozen or so patrons remaining at the restaurant.

A tall, scar-faced man in a dirty brown leather jacket stood at the register, with a shotgun leveled at the pretty blond cashier.

''Not another word!'' he shouted out over the clientele. ''Not a sound from one of you, or the idiot queen here—'' he caught the girl behind the register by her hair, causing her to shriek again as he dragged her out before him ''—gets it, ladies and gents, right in the head. Brains and blood all over your dinners, folks, so just stay still. Real still.''

They were still. Everyone in the restaurant.

Everyone but Jason. Vickie could feel the tension in his body.

She squeezed his fingers, sending him a silent message. *Don't!*

Then someone let out a terrified little gasp and the man spun around, throwing the pretty young cashier forward as he did so. She tripped, and he slapped her hard across the head. ''I just came in because I needed a little quick cash. I didn't mean for anyone to get hurt, but I'll do whatever I have to. Understand me? Don't make me kill you, girlie.''

Vickie felt the horror constricting her throat. The girl didn't mean to be giving him any trouble—she was just so scared silly that she couldn't stand properly. He started to pull her and she fell again. He swung the shotgun around, ready to knock her across the temple with it. Vickie forgot that she had been willing Jason to silence. He was bounding up, but she barely noticed him because she hadn't been able to keep still herself. She had somehow heard an imaginary sound in the back of her head, a cracking sound, the sound they would have heard if the man had managed to send the butt of his shotgun crashing against the girl's head.

Victoria screamed out, "No!"

The man paused. The shotgun started to level at her. He shoved the blonde away. "No? Fine, then *you* can get over here and get the money out of the register.''

Everything happened so fast then. The blonde fell against the front counter. The thief crossed the few feet to their table and was reaching for Vickie. Gramps was up.

But Jason was behind her.

And before the man could close his fingers around her wrist, Jason was around her, flying at the thief, thrusting her far behind him, to safety.

He slammed against the man.

She heard the sharp retort of the gun once again. Jason and the thief fell hard to the floor together, rolling toward the front door of the restaurant.

She screamed, starting to leap for them, but Gramps was pulling her back. "Wait, Vickie, wait! Let me see—''

"No, no!"

He was moving! Jason was moving. Straddled over the thug, Jason delivered a solid punch to the man's left cheek, and then the right. In the center of the floor, in front of the sobbing cashier, the robber was stone-cold unconscious and Jason was trying to scramble to his feet.

Vickie heard the scream of a siren.

Then she heard a burst of applause. The men, the women, the children, all the people in the restaurant, the clients, the help, everyone was clapping.

Jason turned around, smiling sheepishly. His eyes immediately sought out Vickie. He started to walk toward her. "That awful screeching sound means that the law is on the way, right?"

"Right—" she started to say.

But even as she spoke, he suddenly pitched forward, falling against her.

Blood stained the tailored shirt she had given him to wear. It seeped onto her pink knit, into her hands as she clasped him.

"Gramps!" she shrieked.

And then Jason's weight dragged her down to the floor. She cradled his head against her, smoothing back his bloodied hair.

She cried out his name, and then began to sob it.

Over, and over, and over again.

CHAPTER SEVEN

The waiting was a nightmare.

They wouldn't let her in, not once the ambulance reached the hospital.

Then, of course, there was that horror that probably would have been as shocking to Jason as the stark white hospital walls and the emergency room staff and the heart monitor and everything else—

Paperwork. Jason might well be astounded to realize that people just didn't let you into hospitals anymore, not without insurance, not without pages and pages of information.

She and Gramps just stared at each other at first, then he nudged his leg against hers. "You've got the card, Vickie. Give the nice lady the card."

Vickie just stared at him for a moment. She was feeling so horribly numb to begin with. She felt like bursting into tears, like melting into the floor. He had left a war, to be shot in an armed-robbery attempt.

It didn't seem just.

She had fallen in love with him.

And now she was losing him. Not because of the wicked violence of the tunnel, or the war. Because of *her* world.

She was going to lose him no matter what.

Not this way.

"The card, Victoria!"

The only insurance card she had was in Brad's name.

She'd never bothered to change the name. "Give the lady Brad's card, Vickie, come on now."

She drew the card out of her wallet and handed it to the emergency room clerk. The woman was being very patient, and understanding.

"That's fine," the woman said. "I'll just take all the information off this and return it to you in the waiting room over there. I'm sure the doctor will be right out."

There were cops crawling around then, too. There were a few minutes when the waiting was broken up by the questions that were fired her way. They were easy to answer. The whole thing had happened in just a matter of minutes. She just had to remember to keep calling Jason Brad, just in case someone from inside the hospital was listening. And then she had to hope that no one she knew came in at that moment, and blew the whole thing. She'd given them Brad's card, so it was assumed now that she was Jason's wife.

"How are we ever going to get out of this?" she asked Gramps.

He shrugged. "Does it matter? As long as we got him admitted?"

She shook her head. She still felt so numb. Then a man clad in white walked out into the waiting room, obviously looking for someone.

She gasped, recognizing the man.

He was very tall and ebony black, a handsome man with striking, strong features. His height had always compelled attention.

He certainly had Vickie's card now.

She'd never gone on to medical school, but she and Sam Dooley had taken a number of courses together in their very first year of college. She had known that he had gone on staff here, but had just forgotten about it completely.

Now, of course, his eyes found her. And he stared at her hard. "Vickie. May I speak with you now?"

She leapt up and stared at Gramps. He started to rise, to come with her.

No, whatever it was, she could handle it, she could handle it. And maybe Gramps couldn't....

"I'm all right!" she promised quickly.

She rushed over to Sam Dooley. He nodded gravely to her grandfather, opening a door that led into a hallway with doors on either side.

He leaned back against a wall, a chart in his hands, suspicion in his eyes.

"Vickie," he said softly. Then, "Just what is going on here?"

She shook her head, her lips very dry. "Sam, how *is* he? Please, how is he? Oh, my God, he's not—"

"He's fine."

"He's what?"

"He's fine. The bullet grazed his head, nothing more. There was a ton of blood because of where it struck. Of course, there's always the danger of concussion, but really, he could probably walk right out of here tonight. I think it's better that he stay for observation, so I'm keeping him. But you can see him."

She started to turn, seeking a direction in which to go. Sam clamped a heavy hand down on her shoulder.

"Who is he, Vickie? He isn't Brad Ahearn, I know that."

She inhaled swiftly. "I had to use Brad's card—"

"To get him in here. I understand that."

"He's just a friend. I really don't—I don't know a great deal about his past. But I do know that he's a good man. He probably saved that little cashier's life. Sam, please, I wish I could explain—''

''It's like he walked out of another world.''

''What?'' Vickie gasped.

Sam kept watching her very curiously. ''Well, for one, at first he kept asking me for the real doctor. I told him I was the real doctor. Then he looked right at me and exclaimed, 'A *darkie* is a real doctor?' Well, now, Vickie, I always have been bright enough to know that I'm a black man, but in all my days, no one has ever called me a *darkie* before. Now, more than that, Vickie. The man in there is scarred. As if he'd been hit with something like a saber a number of times! Now, you put that with the way that he's talking, and gawking at everything, and you have one strange man!''

She stared at him blankly for a minute. ''Sam, he—he was just shot in the head. He's probably not feeling quite right.''

''Hmm… Is that it? Vickie, who is he really?''

She sighed. ''If I told you, Sam, you wouldn't believe me.''

''Try me.''

Oh, yes. Try him. She bit into her lower lip. She met his dark gaze. ''He's a real Civil War soldier, Sam. He stumbled into our world by some strange connection through time. Gramps seems to think that the reenactment has something to do with it.''

She got the exact response she had expected—sheer incredulity. He stared at her, speechless at last.

''I told you that you wouldn't believe me.''

''Have you told this to anyone else?'' he said dryly.

''Just my grandfather.''

Sam threw his hands up. ''I give up!''

She caught his hand, holding it as she stared up at him

imploringly. "Sam, please, I'm begging, keep quiet about him. He's going to have enough difficulty dealing with the police, with the media. Please—"

"He's not some kind of fugitive or criminal, is he, Vickie? That's not why he's been all cut up, is it?"

"No!" she cried quickly. "Sam, I swear to you, he's a good man. Please, just keep quiet. I beg you."

"I'm not sure it's ethical."

She shook her head wildly. "Sam! He saved a life. On my honor, I swear he's no criminal."

"He just stepped out of the Civil War to check out the reenactments, right? Is that it?"

"Sam—"

He freed his hand from her grasp and wagged a finger under her nose. "All right, Vickie. I won't say a word. For all I know, he might be another Brad Ahearn. I'll keep quiet—just so long as you get your fellow in there to quit calling me *'boy.'* That's what he went to after *'darkie.'*" He threw his hands up in the air again. "Eight years of school, two years in a residency. And all I get is *'boy'*!"

"*Dr.* Dooley, I think you're wonderful!" She gave him a quick kiss on the cheek. "I'll get him into line. I promise. Where is he?"

"Upstairs. Room 306. You better go quick and tell him what his name is supposed to be. The police want to question him."

Vickie thanked him again and fled to the elevator. In seconds, she was hurrying down a hallway to his room. Jason was sitting up in bed, hair tousled, eyes a bit wild, clad in a washed-out hospital gown. There was a bandage against his left temple, but nothing more.

"What is this damn thing?" he asked her irritably,

plucking at the material of the gown. "There's no back to it! I feel...naked!"

She smiled. He was fine. He was really fine. She hurried to him and threw her arms around him, kissing him warmly. She drew away, arms still around him. "It's a hospital gown. And you have to wear it or else really be naked until I get a chance to run home and get you something else. Oh, God, Jason! You're all right!"

He heard the trembling in her voice and took her very tenderly into his arms again. "I'm fine. Just fine. I'm sorry you had such a scare. I must have blacked out just a shade there. But it's just a scratch. I've been injured much worse before."

She'd known that. She'd seen all the scars that had awakened Sam Dooley's keen interest.

"You saved my life," she told him.

"I don't know if your life was ever at risk."

"He meant to take me with him."

"Well, I'm not sure what it means these days, but he was certainly no gentleman."

She smiled. "There really are gentlemen these days, still. My husband was one. Steve, the man you met, is full of honor and caring and all kinds of great things. But there are men like the one you brought down, too."

He stroked her cheek. "There always have been."

There was a knock on the door. "Oh!" She said quickly, "Listen, I had to use my husband's old insurance card to get you in here."

"What?"

"Never mind, I'll explain later. They only give you medical attention free these days if you're actually killed, and then the coroner gets his shot at cutting up your body. That's cynical, isn't it?"

"I don't know what you're talking about."

"Right, I know, and I don't have time to explain. Just remember, when they question you, you need to say that your name is Brad Ahearn. Just while you're here, all right?"

"What?"

"Brad Ahearn," she repeated. The knocking was more insistent. What could have been an absolutely horrible incident had been averted. The awful man could have held a restaurant full of tourists hostage. Or worse. He could have started shooting. As it happened, Jason had managed to subdue it all. The police had been handed over a downed perpetrator, everyone else had gone away alive and well and unscathed—except for the terrified blond cashier, and she had been tranquilized right on the scene—and now Jason was even proving to be alive and barely scratched in the hospital.

The police surely wanted to close things up. All they had to do was get a statement from Jason now.

They wouldn't knock politely much longer.

"What's your name?" she hissed to him.

He shrugged, shaking his head. "Brad Ahearn? If that's what you want."

She started to walk away to open the door to his hospital room, then she hurried back to him. "And be careful, will you? We almost had a real problem. I went to school with Sam Dooley, and he's a great guy and a great doctor, but he was also on the football team and if you call him *'boy'* one more time, he just might come out swinging!"

Jason winced and grinned. "I had forgotten," he said quickly. "The Yanks win, right? Slavery is abolished. Imagine! Well, you're right, Vick. He seems like a darned good doctor, too. I'll watch my words."

She swung around quickly, reaching the door just as it

opened. The two officers waiting impatiently there were from the county. She was relieved to see that she didn't know either of them.

Officers Hewlett and Macy looked a bit like clones of one another, both about an even six feet, dark haired, lean faced and in county gray uniforms. They addressed Jason as Mr. Ahearn, and never questioned his name.

"You came in from the Staunton area for the battle, sir, is that right?"

Jason stared at Vickie, a brow arched, a smile curving his lips.

"Yes, that's right. Darned right," he said.

Officer Hewlett asked him to describe what had happened in the restaurant. Jason did. The officers took notes, but it appeared that everything was in perfect order.

"Well, sir, we're mighty glad that you did come over for this one. You might have saved some lives tonight. The fellow holding up the place came out of a prison called Raiford, in Florida. He's been making his way north over the bodies of a few unwary travelers. I don't think he would have thought twice about killing a hostage in this situation. Not twice. You've done us quite a service."

Jason shrugged. "Me, or someone else. The restaurant was crowded. Too many of us there for him to think he could just corral us all. Someone would have stopped him."

The officers looked at each other. They definitely thought that Jason wasn't quite all there. Sane men didn't risk their lives.

"Well, I think that that's all we need for now," Macy said. He then added politely, "The doc said that you might be wanting to get a little sleep now. We'll need to get hold of you again, of course, but I believe we've gotten your address—it's the one you gave us downstairs, right, ma'am?''

Vickie nodded, swallowing quickly.

Hewlett and Macy started for the door. She walked along with them, ready to close it in their wake. Hewlett paused, looking back to Jason.

"That's quite an incredible man you got there, Mrs. Ahearn.''

"He's not my—'' she started to say. She bit off the words. Well, Jason was supposed to be Mr. Ahearn here in the hospital. But that wasn't what made her pause.

"Yes, I do have an incredible man there,'' she assured Hewlett, smiling. *Truly, you don't know the half of it! He's quite incredible,* she wanted to add.

She closed the door behind the officers firmly, and turned back to Jason. He was watching her, smiling. He slipped from the bed, then seemed to realize that the back of his nightgown was open all the way down. He tried to draw it together as he approached her. He couldn't quite grasp the sides of it.

"Oh, the hell with it!'' he murmured, taking her into his arms. His lips touched hers. "That's awful language to use around a lady.''

She smiled up at him. "I've heard it before. I've used it rather frequently, I'm afraid.''

He smiled, and kissed her again. "I have to get out of here,'' he told her then softly.

She shook her head. "You might have suffered a concussion. They don't want to let you out.''

He arched a brow, frowning. "I've gone back into battle with just a bandage around broken ribs. And they want me to stay in here because of a cut on my forehead? Vickie, you know I've got to get out.''

She pressed him back toward the bed. "Jason, you can't just go waltzing out of here. And it's still the middle of the night. You have to wait until morning. Doctors make their rounds very early. I'm sure they'll release you right after sunrise."

The door opened then, without a knock sounding. A nurse was walking in with a tray. There was a syringe on it and a little white paper cup of pills.

Jason stared at her, remembered his open hospital gown, and started grabbing for edges again, backing toward the bed. He stared at Vickie reproachfully, with warning eyes, as if she had allowed someone entry here when he was so ridiculously vulnerable.

She smiled. She couldn't help it.

The nurse, a slim, attractive brunette of about thirty, looked from Jason to Vickie with a little sigh that seemed to say, "Guys! Great big he-men types, but you show them a little needle and they just go to pieces."

"Hello, Mrs. Ahearn, Mr. Ahearn. My name is Sheila. Dr. Dooley has ordered a tetanus shot for you since you didn't seem to know when you last had one. He hasn't had one recently, has he, Mrs. Ahearn?"

Vickie smiled at Jason. "Not recently. I'm sure he needs one. I'm absolutely sure of it."

Jason's eyes narrowed her way.

"Come now, Mr. Ahearn, you need the shot," Sheila told him cheerfully. She walked around the bed, setting her tray down on his nightstand and flicking the needle carefully. She stared at Jason. "You need to roll over please, Mr. Ahearn."

"I need to what?" he demanded.

"Roll over, Mr. Ahearn. A tetanus shot is very important—you must know that, Mr. Ahearn. It protects you from infection."

"You need the shot, you need to roll over," Vickie stated.

"If I need the shot, you had best find another place to deliver it!" Jason insisted. "I'm not rolling over for any female nurse—"

"Mr. Ahearn!" Sheila protested, her eyes wide. "If you can't behave, I'm going to have to call for the doctor—"

"I'm not rolling over—"

"Yes, you are!" Vickie insisted. She caught his hands. He stared at her. Hard. As if he was going to really strangle her the minute he could get his hands on her. She smiled sweetly. "It's necessary. It's very customary. Brad, it keeps you from getting an infection. It's good. It lasts a long time!"

"He doesn't know about a tetanus shot?" Sheila said curiously.

"You know men," Vickie said, staring hard at Jason. She reached for his hand. His fingers curled hard around hers.

"It's not going to hurt."

"It's not pain that I mind."

He gritted his teeth. He returned her stare with a hard violence in his eyes.

"Mrs. Ahearn, really, can you give me a hand with your husband? I have to have some cooperation! If not—"

"Brad, shift over. *Please, my love!*"

He shifted. Still holding her hand. Still staring at her.

"That's good, I can get you from there!" Sheila assured him. She bathed a spot of flesh with an alcohol swab and quickly gave him the shot. Jason didn't blink. He kept staring at Vickie.

Sheila made a *tsk*ing sound. "It's a good thing God didn't decide to let them have the babies."

Vickie quickly lowered her eyes. Jason's fingers squeezed hers, but Nurse Sheila was moving around between the two of them with the little paper cup of pills in her hands. "These will help you sleep."

"They'll what?" Jason said suspiciously.

"Honestly!" she said, shaking her head to Vickie once again. "You've had a rather hectic evening, Mr. Ahearn. Just in case you have difficulty, these will help you sleep. Come on now, Mr. Ahearn."

Vickie thought that he took the pills. He crumpled the little paper cup in his hands and accepted the glass of water Sheila poured for him.

"All down now," Sheila said, flashing them a bright smile. "Mrs. Ahearn, that chair stretches out into a cot, if you want to stay with your husband. If you need anything, just hit the nurses' call button. Anything at all." She hesitated a minute. "It was a pleasure to meet you, Mr. Ahearn. That was quite a brave thing you did."

"Anyone would have done it," Jason said flatly. He felt Vickie's gaze. "But thank you," he added quickly.

Vickie smiled and followed Sheila to the door. "Don't forget, just press the call button if you need anything. Oh, my—I almost forgot. Your grandfather is still waiting downstairs, Mrs. Ahearn. We've assured him, of course, that Mr. Ahearn is going to be just fine. But he's waiting to have a few words with you, whenever you get a chance."

"Thank you. Thank you very much."

"Good night, Mrs. Ahearn. Call if you need me."

"Thank you. I will. Good night."

She closed the door, and started to walk slowly back to Jason. He seemed to be staring straight ahead of himself. He didn't even seem to realize that she was coming near.

Then he started suddenly and turned back to her. She remembered the way that he had stared at her when he'd gotten his shot, and she hesitated.

"Come here!" he growled.

"Not when you talk to me like that!" she protested.

"All right," he drawled broadly, stretching out sideways on the bed, supported by an elbow, "Come here, *my love,* my dear little wife!"

"Did you want to get into the hospital or not?" she demanded. "And you were terribly rude to the nurse. Now I know that you had women nurses in your hospitals, even if the idea of women acting in such a capacity was rather new!"

"She was walking around just as if she owned the place. As if she had the right to tell me what to do!"

"Nurses rather do in a hospital. Most of the time, they're nice and polite because their patients act like adults."

He made a snorting sound. "Women all over," he muttered. "Next thing you know, they'll have the vote!"

Vickie smiled knowingly, deciding that she would enlighten him when he wasn't so riled up.

"An educated black man for a doctor!" he mused.

Vickie took a step closer to him. "Do you own slaves?" she asked him softly.

He looked at her for a moment without speaking. Then he nodded. "But I'm going to free them when I go home," he told her softly. "Not because I know now that the war is lost. But because I've met you."

"Not to mention Dr. Dooley," she reminded him softly.

"Who seems a very fine man."

Vickie smiled. He leaned forward on his elbow, moving closer to where she was standing and, as she bent down, his lips brushed hers very tenderly. Well, at least he wasn't going anywhere tonight. And maybe the tetanus shot he'd had here would help him when he—when he went home.

She didn't have much longer with him, she thought, and the pain seemed to tear into her. Just tonight. And he was in a hospital bed, doped out, ready to sleep.

It didn't matter. She'd stay with him. At his side.

"This whole place is pretty amazing," he told her. "So very clean. So quiet, so well organized. The machines—the shots. Medicine has come an incredibly long way."

She inhaled and exhaled slowly. "Yes, that's true. But we've new diseases, too. Killer diseases. We've managed to do away with the old, but we've been deviled by the new."

"Imagine, though. A tetanus shot. Something that protects against infection." He rolled over suddenly, reaching out to her. "That's what John needs. That—and a clean sponge, like your grandfather was saying. If I could just get him one of these shots, I could keep him from getting gangrene."

Vickie nodded. "Maybe," she murmured. He didn't seem to notice that she was there again for a moment. "Well, we can talk about it in the morning. Those pills you took will make you drowsy very soon," she told him. "I'm not going anywhere, though. I'll be here with you. Gramps is still downstairs. I just want to say good-night to him so that he'll go on home, okay?"

Jason nodded. "Tell him thank you for me, will you?"

"You'll see him again."

He nodded. His answer took a minute to come. "Tell him thank you for me, anyway."

"I'll be right back," Vickie promised.

She hurried down in the elevator. Gramps was standing in the waiting room. Her heart surged out to him. Of all the strange things she had done to him over the years, this had to be the strangest!

Bringing home a time traveler, and expecting him to cope!

But Gramps did. Magnificently. Gramps always did.

"Gramps?"

He turned, tall and straight for all his great age, his blue eyes sharp.

"He's really all right?"

"Just fine. Ornery as all hell, but just fine!" Vickie assured him with a grin. "They'll probably release him in the morning. Can you bring us both some new clothes? These things have blood all over them."

"Sure thing. You're going to stay with him here, I take it?"

Vickie nodded. "Do you mind?"

He lifted her chin. "Victoria, I wouldn't expect any less from you, granddaughter. That's one of the reasons I love you so much."

"Gramps..."

"The other is that, of course, you look like me. Well, not now, but when I was young and good-looking."

She grinned. "Go home and get some sleep."

He nodded, but he still paused. "It's a shame, Vickie. A darned shame. Hold him a little bit longer. Then you're going to have to let him go. You know that."

"I know that."

Gramps left and she went back up in the elevator, wondering if Jason might have fallen asleep already.

But he was awake, sitting up in bed, flicking the channels on the television. He stared at the screen, then shook his head at her.

"There are so many amazing things!"

"I imagine," she said softly.

He patted the bed beside him. She hesitated, and then came over. His arm came around her, his lips brushed her forehead.

"Good movie?" she asked him.

"I don't know, but I'd like to see it with you. I'd like to do so many things with you."

She smiled. "Making love in a bed would be nice."

"The nicest."

"I'm going to get into the chair so that you can sleep—"

"I don't need to sleep."

"But the pills—"

"These?" He lifted the paper cup, crumpled up with the pills still inside it.

"Yes, those!" she said with flat reproach.

"I may need them later," he said softly.

"Nurse Sheila could come back."

"Let her," he said softly. "I just need…to hold you. That's all."

She eased her head down on his shoulder. She needed to be held. To feel his arms around her. To know the tenderness, and the caring. It was all such a wonderful feeling.

The comfort and security were so sweet that her eyes began to close. She nudged against him more closely.

"I love you, Vickie," she heard.

She tried to open her eyes. *I love you, Vickie.*

They were such wonderful words.

Her lips curled into a slow and wistful smile. "I love you, too, Jason. So very much."

"I will love you forever," he told her. "Forever."

His fingers smoothed over her hair.

It was the last thing she remembered. She slept deeply, dreamlessly, surrounded, encompassed, by feelings of comfort and warmth and tenderness....

But then she was curiously cold.

"Mrs. Ahearn?"

She awoke to find a nurse staring at her. Another nurse. A heavyset, buxom woman who looked very confused.

"I'm sorry, Mrs. Ahearn, but I understand your husband is the patient. Isn't he supposed to be in the bed?"

Vickie jumped up. She stared at the bed. She had grown cold, of course, because she had been alone.

Jason was gone.

The bathroom!

She tore into it. Jason wasn't there. He was gone.

"Mrs. Ahearn?" the nurse said, concerned.

Vickie spun around. He was gone. Really gone.

She looked out the window. It was first light.

And then she knew.

Yes, he was gone. Really gone. He hadn't wanted to say goodbye, but he had headed for the mountain.

"Mrs. Ahearn?" the nurse said again.

But Vickie didn't hear her. She was already running out of the room.

She didn't know what she was going to do herself. She only knew that she had to catch up to him before he reached his doorway to the past.

CHAPTER EIGHT

When Vickie first left the hospital, she was at a loss.

She had left her Jeep at the library, having ridden the few minutes to the hospital with Jason in the ambulance.

Now she needed a cab, and they weren't that common in this kind of a small town.

"Damn!" she cried out, her heart sinking. Then she saw a green Volvo pulling out from the doctors' lot. It was Sam driving.

"Sam!" she cried, running in front of him. He slammed on his brakes, then leaned his long frame out of the window. "Vickie, have you lost your mind completely? I might have killed you!"

"Sam, can you get me home? I know you've been on a long shift, I know how tired you are, but I have to get home quickly!"

"Is your grandfather all right?"

"Oh, yes, he's fine. I think. I just have to get home."

He stared at her, but leaned back into the car, pushing the passenger's door open. Vickie ran around and slid into the car.

Sam started to drive. She leaned back, closing her eyes. She felt him watching her, but she didn't know what to say.

"So where is my patient?" Sam demanded.

Her eyes sprang open and she stared at him.

"I imagine he's taken off, and that's why you're in such a hurry to get somewhere," Sam said. "Your house?"

She bit her lip, shaking her head. "No, I don't think that he's still there."

"But he went there?"

"Well, he needed his horse and his uniform—"

She broke off, realizing that Sam was watching her.

"His sword, his gun? His men? Are they all running around your house, too?"

"Sam, this is serious!"

Sam sighed. "All right, how did he get to your house?"

She shook her head. "I don't know. Oh, I know that you don't believe me, but you can just quit making fun of me, Sam Dooley."

"Vickie, have you considered that he may be a madman?" he asked her worriedly.

Vickie smiled, looking to her lap. "I thought of it. I thought of it a lot. But he isn't. He isn't mad at all. He's just rare—very, very rare. As rare as Brad!" she said softly.

Sam sighed. At that hour, they hadn't hit much traffic, and in just a matter of minutes, he was pulling up to her grandfather's driveway.

"Thank you, Sam. Thank you so much," she told him.

She started to open the door. He caught it for a moment, and met her eyes. "This just may tie into something, Vickie. Early this morning one of the nurses in Emergency was preparing a tetanus shot for one of those reenactors who had cut himself up on his own bayonet." He paused, and Vickie arched a brow to him. "The syringe disappeared, all ready to go."

"Oh," she said softly.

"Vickie, will you pay attention to me? He could be dangerous."

She shook her head. "You don't understand. He needs it. His brother was wounded up on the mountain."

"Then he should bring him to the hospital."

"I don't think that he can." She leaned over and kissed his cheek impulsively. "Thank you for the ride. And for everything. Sam, you know that I'm not crazy, and I swear to God, I'm telling you the truth!"

Sam sighed, sitting back. "I don't know where this man is going to lead you, Vickie!"

"It doesn't really matter," she said. "I—"

"You what?"

"I'm in love with him. I never thought that I could love anyone again."

"Vickie—"

"Sam, I've got to go. I have to find him. I can't just let him disappear without saying goodbye."

Sam let her go. Vickie ran up to the house, calling for Gramps. He burst out onto the porch just as she reached it.

"I tried to call you at the hospital, Vickie. But you'd run out just as I got through," Gramps said.

"So he was here? He came here?"

Gramps nodded. "Came back for Max, his uniform, his sword. I tried to hold him. He said that it was too hard to leave you as it was. Told me that he loved you." He hesitated a minute. "Told me that he'd love you through all time."

"Oh! How did he get here? How long ago did he leave?"

"Seems he managed to hitch a ride easy enough, down the highway. Walked the rest of the way. He's only been gone a few minutes. I've got the horses saddled out back."

"You've got the what?"

"The horses saddled. Your Arabesque and old Dundee."

He suddenly tossed her something. It was a clean white blouse. "Your shirt's got bloodstains on it. Come on, let's go."

He was out the door while Vickie was still struggling into the clean shirt. She followed him quickly enough. "Gramps! What do you think you're doing? You—you can't come with me. This ride is too hard—"

"Am I still living and breathing and in my own senses, Victoria?" he demanded.

"Living and breathing, yes, but I was never too certain that you were in your right senses!"

"Young lady, you keep at it and you'll get your mouth washed out with soap."

"Indeed?" Vickie said, but she was panting then to keep up with him.

"Do you think I'd let you go alone, Vickie?"

She shook her head. "Go? Gramps, I'm not *going*. I wouldn't leave you. I just have to—"

"To what?"

"To say goodbye. To tell him to come back if there's ever a way. To tell him—"

"That you love him, too."

She nodded.

He wagged a finger at her suddenly. "Don't you ever give anything up for me, Victoria Ahearn! Ever. I'm an old man. Not much time left."

"Don't you talk like that! I'd never leave you—" she started to say, and she knew that that was exactly what she was afraid of. "Gramps, it never, never occurred to me to go back! To a life without cars, without washing machines—my God, I'm still a young woman. I could conceivably have a half-dozen children. Could you imagine having to go back to a life without disposable diapers?'' She smiled brilliantly for him. ''Gramps, go home!''

He swung around to her. ''Not a chance, Victoria. You listen! I've studied it, my whole life! The Civil War. I've collected, I've lectured, I've sold. I'm taking you to that doorway, Vickie, and that's that!''

She sighed and threw up her hands.

''Besides,'' he said smugly, ''I actually know the mountain much better than you do. I know the exact places where all the skirmishing took place. Can you say that much?''

''I know them well enough.''

''Well, do we stand here arguing like stupid old asses, or do we ride?''

Vickie walked on past her grandfather, leaping up on Arabesque. He was one stubborn old coot.

And for all his years, he could still swing up easily enough on old Dundee. They started out, Vickie leading the way.

They came through the back, past the area where the reenactments had already taken place, where the landscape was still heavily trampled and an occasional paper cup still lay around. Then she hesitated, trying to remember where she had been. She pictured the place past the Yankee encampments where Jason had first accosted her. Then she tried to recall where it seemed they had traveled back in time for those few brief moments.

''May I?'' Gramps drawled.

She swung back in her saddle, looking at him. He rode on past her, spurring old Dundee into a canter.

''You're going to have a heart attack!'' she called to him, giving Arabesque free rein to catch up.

But it was the best she had seen Gramps look in years. He grinned back at her. "Who wants to live forever?"

She shook her head, riding hard beside him. And amazingly, it seemed that Gramps did know where to go. Vickie recognized all the terrain they covered. Even as they rode higher and higher.

The first indication that they had come to the right place was the sky.

Vickie reined in, feeling the hard gusts of wind swirling around her. "Gramps?" she murmured uneasily.

She looked up. The blue day had gone very gray suddenly. Dark clouds were massing above her, some of them nearly black. The wind picked up with a low, chilling moan. Gramps was near her. Old Dundee was backing up and prancing nervously. Beneath Vickie, Arabesque was doing the same thing, her hooves kicking up clumps of dirt and rock.

"There's sure as hell something going on out here! It's going to storm," Gramps cried. Then he looked at her, his eyes wide with amazement. "The wind is circling here like a cyclone! Feel it! It's not coming from the east or the west, it's circling!"

"I remember this!" she cried. *Yes, this was what it had been like. This was the area that surrounded the break, the doorway, in time.*

And she had *passed through it before!*

Yes, this was it, Vickie thought. They had come too late. Jason was gone. They had missed him.

She could hear the awful cry and whip of the wind. It seemed to be building. She tried to control Arabesque as she looked around the slope of the mountain. She reined in, her mouth feeling dry. Ahead of her, right ahead of her, barely visible against the darkness that had arisen around them, was an archway of trees. Huge, tall trees, old trees, nearly as old as time itself, bent over and arched into a perfect arbor. Hesitantly, she nudged Arabesque over to the opening of it. Her breath caught. There was movement. Far at the end of the archway, she could see shadowy movement. A horse! A horse and rider.

"Jason!" she cried his name.

But was it him? She couldn't tell. Whoever it was didn't seem to hear her. The rider didn't stop.

And sitting there, she began to feel the cold, clammy sensations of fear come creeping over her again. The place did exist; yes, it was real, it was a break in time, extraordinary, and not quite right. The wind wasn't right, the feel of it was more than odd—unearthly. She realized suddenly that in the tunnel, she wouldn't really be anywhere, not in her world, not in his, just captured in a dark swirling void between past and present.

She couldn't go forward. Couldn't feel those awful, clammy fingers of dark wind and chilly air touch down upon her, wrap around her.

She couldn't do it.... But if she didn't, she'd never see Jason again. She couldn't go through that dark, terrifying passageway. She had to go through.

She swung around, staring at Gramps. "Stay there! Just stay put! I'll be right back."

She nudged Arabesque hard with her heels then. The horse reared up, and she tightened her thighs to hold her seat. "Don't you dare go getting temperamental and overbred on me now, Arabesque. Don't you dare!"

Arabesque landed on all four hooves. Then she leapt forward, bunched her muscles and started to race.

As Vickie urged her horse forward, the wind whipped cruelly around them. She tried to rein in on the mare, crying out a "Whoa!" But Arabesque ignored her, snorting and galloping her way wildly into the swirling green-

and-black darkness. Vickie lay low against her neck, wincing, clinging hard to the horse lest she be killed in the violence of the fall she would take if she lost her seat. God, it was awful! A wild, reckless gallop that she couldn't control. It was terrifying. She could feel some kind of walls. Walls, yes, invisible walls, tightening around her. Cold, clammy. Touching her.

Dear Lord, she thought! It was growing smaller! Changing. The door in time, if that was exactly what it was, was beginning to close.

Of course, she thought bleakly, the battles were almost over.

Air rushed and shrieked by her. Terror filled her. She kept riding. Hard. She closed her eyes against the blinding forces of the wind and Arabesque's whipping mane. Then she screamed out again for it seemed that the mare came to a halt just like a well-trained barrel-horse, right on a dime. Arabesque reared high again. Vickie still clung to her. The mare landed hard.

And the world seemed to explode.

There were men everywhere. Men mounted, men afoot. Shots were being fired, saber duels were taking place in front of her.

Bodies lay all about the field. Bodies in blue, and bodies in gray.

For a moment she stared, disbelieving, even after all that she had come to believe.

There were so many things to see.

The mountain had changed little. Men changed. The earth, if let be, did not. The terrain was still deep green and brown; it was littered with the yellow and purple of wildflowers. Trees and clumps of rock lay strewn about naturally as always.

Yet covered with fallen, bleeding men.

So many were so different. The Yanks seemed fairly uniform, but some of the Rebs were in kepis and some in slouch hats.

Some wore gray, and some wore faded, tattered colors that were no longer really discernible.

Some still fought, and some were in retreat. While Arabesque pranced and Vickie fought to control her, she could see that the fighting was going bad for the Rebs. In good order, they were forming a retreat up the mountain. They couldn't come down any farther, but they were going to hold their ground. They fought all the way.

Horses were rearing, screaming.

Men were screaming, crying out. The Yankees were taking the field before her. Oh, God! Had Jason come through? If so, where was he now? What could she do? Try to reach him?

Leave. Turn around and leave. There was nothing that she could do here. Gramps was behind her, waiting for her.

"Ho! You there!" someone called out.

She turned around. She blinked. There was a great deal of powder in the air, adding to the grayness of the day. The wind was still whipping it around, causing her eyes to sting.

There was a Yankee officer on a horse trotting toward her. She tensed, suddenly wondering just what she had done, and wondering now if she wasn't the mad one, not Jason.

She was in the midst of the war. The real one. It was incredible.

It was true.

"Who are you!" the man demanded. "State your business."

"I live on the mountain," she said. He still stared at

her demandingly, a man of about forty with a beard and sideburns. "It's my home!" she told him.

A younger officer rode up behind him. A man with long blond curls and a slim face and watery blue eyes. "It's another one of those Southern spies, sir! Look at her, look at the way she's dressed, riding a horse like a man." He spit on the ground and Vickie gasped.

"Well, excuse me!" she cried furiously. "And just who the hell do you think you are? And what the hell do you think you're doing on my damned mountain!"

As soon as the words were out of her mouth, she realized her mistake.

Too late.

"Smart mouth on her, too. She's a Southern spy, I swear it, like that girl from Front Royal, Belle Boyd. Like that Mrs. Greenhow in Washington, the one who caused our boys to be mown down back at Manassas!"

"I'm not a spy. I'm just looking for someone!" she said.

"Who?"

"An officer. A—"

She broke off.

"A Reb!" the blond man proclaimed, as if he had caught her in the act of murder.

The older officer moved his horse closer to hers. "And just what is it that you intend to tell this man—this Reb— once you find him?"

"What could I tell him?" she asked with exasperation. "You've already met up with the Rebs, they know where you are, you know where they are! Just what could I possibly have spied upon that everyone involved here doesn't know already?"

"She's a clever one!" the blond man said.

The older man nodded slowly. "Maybe you know

something about Rebel reinforcements. Something that could keep the Rebs fighting harder and longer.''

"I don't know anything—'' she said, then she broke off. Yes, she did. She knew everything that happened here. Jubal Early was due to bring his troops in at any time. Stonewall Jackson had sent for him, putting out a cry for help. And when Jubal Early made it, the Yanks were going to be pushed back. They would still claim victory; losses would be nearly equal, but the Rebels would keep their hold on this little piece of Virginia until the end of the war.

"Jesu!'' the older man exclaimed. "She does know something!''

A third man rode up. He was older still, very weary looking, silver haired, sharp-eyed. "What's going on here, Lieutenant Granger?'' he asked the dark-haired man.

"I'm afraid we've found a local spy, sir, trying to reach a certain Reb, Colonel Bickford.''

The newcomer looked Vickie up and down with curiosity. "It's dangerous business, ma'am, stumbling around in the middle of a battlefield,'' he told her in a light tone that still carried a note of warning.

"I'm not a spy.''

"She sure is!''

"You sure she's even a Reb?'' the colonel asked.

"Ain't ever seen no Northern girl dressed like that,'' the nasty-tempered blond man said.

"That's enough from you, Captain Harper.''

Vickie gave her attention to the colonel. "I'm not carrying secrets or messages. I'm just looking for a man to say goodbye.''

"Your husband?'' the colonel asked.

She hesitated a second too long.

"Not her husband!" the blond Captain Harper said, pouncing once again. He rode his horse slowly around Vickie. "Not her!" he exclaimed softly. "She wouldn't have time these days to settle down, to be a lady. Who are you looking for? A man, but not your husband. Someone to just fill a few of the hours that might be long and lonely otherwise? Well, ma'am, we've lots of Yank soldiers where we're going. Maybe you'll find another one you like."

"Captain Harper, that's enough!" the colonel insisted.

But Captain Harper had seemed to quickly acquire a deep and hostile interest in her. "We're not going to lose this battle, sir, because of a snooty Southern spy."

"No!" Vickie cried. "You're going to lose it because of Northern idiots like yourself who can barely sit a saddle!"

"And the Southerners are so much better, right?" he demanded, very close to her, a fanatic's sizzle in his eyes.

"You bet!" she promised softly. And the second that he came just a step closer, she nudged her heels hard against Arabesque's side.

Her mare leapt forward. She leaned low over the mare's neck, becoming one with the animal. She wasn't at all sure where she was going, just away. She couldn't go back to the archway in the trees; she couldn't even see it anymore, the settling of the powder had obliterated it. She started across the mountain, climbing, praying....

And wondering, too, if there was really anywhere for her to run.

It wasn't possible....

It was.

They were thundering after her. Arabesque was a fine mare, no matter what frame of comparison was made, against horses of any time. She could run like the wind.

And she was outrunning the nasty blond captain so set on Vickie being a spy. But even as she raced forward, there was a whistle and cry.

She was besting the men behind her.

But a string of ten riders was circling around her now, riding down, having given up on their pursuit of the retreating Rebs.

She reined back. She tried to seek out a route of escape.

There was none. She urged Arabesque to try to break through the ring of riders.

She had paused too long. The angry blond captain, Harper, had caught up with her. He threw himself from his own horse to hers, catching her from the animal, sending her hurtling to the ground with him atop her. A sense of panic seized her. She tried to struggle free from him and she knew that some of her punches caught hold of him good, but though he was slim, he was strong. He was quickly straddled over her, pinning her wrists to the ground. His eyes touched upon hers and chilled her. They were filled with both hatred—and lust.

He was a Union officer! There were now dozens of soldiers around. He couldn't possible hurt her, not really.

And he couldn't. Not then. The colonel came trotting up. ''Captain Harper, I do believe that our prisoner is subdued. Let her up now, son.''

''She's dangerous, sir, surely you saw that!''

''Tie her hands. Set her up on her horse and lead her back to camp.''

Vickie stared at the colonel, clamping down on her jaw as her hands were wrenched forward and quickly tied with a red scarf someone supplied.

''I'm not a spy!'' she told the colonel. ''Call off this creature of yours!''

But despite her words, Captain Harper was lifting her and setting her upon Arabesque. His eyes really sizzled now. "Nice filly," he said, gazing into hers. "Good flanks. If you decide to look for a Yank this time instead of a Reb, I just might be available."

She spit at him. He stepped away neatly.

"Yep. Maybe I'll see you later," he told her, and then he grinned. "And then maybe I'll see you hang!"

He meant her, not the horse. She tried to kick him.

"Harper, get on your horse!" the colonel commanded. He reached for the reins to Arabesque. "Call in your company, Captain. I want an orderly formation back to camp!"

Wrists tied together, forced upon Arabesque, Vickie had no choice but to be led along. Chills started to race down her spine. The mountain looked the same! It was covered with grass, with trees, with wildflowers....

It wasn't the same at all. They broke through a section of forest and down an incline and there, in the valley, she could see the Yankee encampment. It seemed to stretch forever.

So many more tents than there were for a reenactment!

Huge tents, command tents. A-frame tents that stretched on and on forever....

And no hot-dog stands on the sidelines. None at all....

She bit her lip, fighting the chills. She closed her eyes, trying desperately to remember all the history Gramps had taught her over so many years.

The Yankees hadn't really hanged any female spies, had they? Rose Greenhow had died, but she had drowned when her ship had gone down, returning from Europe with gold for the Confederate cause.

Belle Boyd had lived a very long life, performing in the theater, lecturing, dying at an old age in the North.

Mrs. Surratt had been convicted of being part of the plot to assassinate Lincoln. She had been the first to be hanged, hadn't she?

The first that history had recorded.

But things had happened during the war that *didn't* make it into the history books. Innocent victims killed by stray fire. Rapes, plundering, robbery.

No…

She was going to be all right, she assured herself. The absolute worst thing that she would face was the lack of a proper bathroom.

Captain Harper was a son of a bitch in any age. But it seemed that the colonel was a decent man, and he was the one really in control. Surely he wouldn't let them hang her…would he?

She stared at the tents again. Soldiers were riding in— some were starting cooking fires, some carried around the wounded. Some were in full uniform, some in half dress. There were at least several regiments of the Union Army here. Old men, young men. Drummer boys who couldn't have been more than twelve. Graybeards who made Gramps look like a youngster.

And they all stopped now, stopped whatever they'd been doing. Stopped to stare at her as the colonel led Arabesque on into the camp, heading for one of the large tents in the center of the field canvas.

They were were dead silent at first. Then someone cheered, and someone else waved. Vickie stared back, eyes wide.

Then a young fellow called out, "Pity we haven't a few like her on our side, eh, Colonel?"

"I'm sure we do, son, I'm sure we do!" the Colonel called back.

But I'm not a spy! Vickie longed to call back. *I'm just looking for a man!*

Her heart thundered. Jason. What was going to happen now? He didn't know that she was there, didn't know that she had followed him. Maybe he had found his brother. Maybe he had already injected him with the life-saving tetanus shot. Maybe he was carrying the wounded man to a field hospital.

Maybe all that had been done, and Jason had returned to his men, a bone-weary soldier who knew that he had to keep fighting, to do his best—and lose a war.

A deep, searing pain seized her along with a new sense of panic. She had lost Jason. And she had ridden into a nightmare. She had left Gramps behind. Waiting for her.

God, she had to escape....

"Here we are, ma'am." The silver-haired colonel dismounted from his horse with the slow agility of a man who was accustomed to being in the saddle, and had grown tired of it, too. He reached up and plucked Vickie down from Arabesque. "What's your name, ma'am?" he asked her.

"Victoria Ahearn," she said.

"Well, now, Miz Ahearn," he said softly, "I'm sorry that I have to detain you, but I do. We don't know where the Rebel forces are around here, but I think that our rash young Captain Harper is right—you do know something. It's in your eyes. I'll have to keep you here until we move out. This is my command tent. There will be pickets around it, but you won't be disturbed. The general will make all the final decisions regarding you, but he's a good, decent man. When this is all over, I know that he'll let you go."

She shook her head slightly. She couldn't stay here while they battled away.

The passageway in the arbor of trees was growing tighter. She didn't know how long she had left to return before the passage closed—but it *would* close, she was certain. Every minute wasted in this camp put her return in graver jeopardy.

"Please, Colonel—" she began.

"Don't go wheedling me now!" he warned her. He reached for the tie on her wrists. "You better resign yourself to confinement. I truly wish you no harm."

Her wrists were free. She rubbed them, watching him still. What would he do if she told him that she didn't belong here at all, that the North was going to win the war, it didn't matter at all what messages she gave the South. Thousands and thousands more men were doomed to die; Lincoln was going to be assassinated—

God, no! They'd hang her for sure on grounds of treason if she even mentioned such a thing!

"Miz Ahearn, you get on in there now. I'll see that you're brought some water and something to eat, and we'll do our very best to see to your comfort, but make no mistake about it, you are our prisoner."

He turned away.

"Wait!" she cried out to him.

But the colonel was a busy man. He was already walking away. When Vickie would have followed, she was suddenly accosted by a uniformed man on either side, each catching one of her arms.

"If you will, please, ma'am," one of them said politely.

Vickie stared into his eyes. He was a young man. Achingly young. Probably not even eighteen.

"Please?" he said politely again. "None of us, none of us wants to hurt you, ma'am."

"But—" She fell silent, looking at him. Then her

lashes lowered quickly. "Fine," she said, allowing her shoulders to slump.

Let them all think that she was resigned.

It might be her only hope.

She was led into the tent.

It was large, pleasant and spacious. There was a field desk in the center of it, a neatly made cot to the side, and several trunks piled up opposite from that. There were several chairs, obviously set up so that men could meet there and confer upon their strategy.

There was a bar set up next to the desk, too, she noticed.

There were glass flasks and silver tumblers.

All the niceties of home.

Oh, God.

The soldiers left her there, the young one smiling and assuring her they would see to her welfare. Vickie stared around herself, then sank down to the foot of the bed, covering her face with her hands.

She had to get out.

She was surrounded by tents, and those tents were filled with Yankees. Her enemies. No, they weren't her enemies! The war was over.

No, it was being fought right now.

She groaned aloud. Escape, she had to escape. Trick one of those handsome young boys somehow....

How? She fell against the colonel's neatly made cot. Her eyes filled with tears. There had to be a way to do it!

But time passed, and she lay there. Then she wiped away the dampness on her cheek. She would get nowhere lying there. She had to watch and listen. She had to be alert for her chance. The major battle should be today.

Maybe the majority of the men would ride out. If she could just take advantage of the rise of confusion…

She strode over to the liquor flasks and found the bottle of whiskey. She wanted a shot, just one shot, for courage, to get her moving.

She poured it out into one of the silver cups. She tossed back her head and swallowed the liquor.

Then she heard a noise and she looked to the opening of the canvas tent.

Her heart seemed to shudder within her chest. Captain Harper was back.

Standing there, watching her, his hands rested on his hips and a slow smile curved his mouth. "Well, now," he said softly. "I wish I could join you. Can't, though, duty calls. But it's awful nice to know a shapely little spy like you likes both men and whiskey."

Vickie set the silver cup down, backing warily away from him.

"What are you doing here?" she demanded. "Shouldn't you be fighting Rebs? Maybe women are easier for you to best than taking on men your own size."

She saw the flash of anger that touched his eyes, but he kept smiling.

And he came closer. "I don't give a damn what you have to say, *Miz Ahearn*. In fact, keep it up and I'll gag you. I'll see that you can't have anything left to say to me at all."

"You'll gag me? The colonel—"

"The colonel is with the general now, trying to plot this battle. You see, you're not really too important around here. Not at all." He came closer, leaning against the tent post. "The lieutenant couldn't even come. Seems there are more Reb troops arriving, but then, you knew that, didn't you? What a shame. I'm all that's left. So I'll be moving you.''

"Where?"

"Back to the main body of the army, down the eastern side of the mountains. Seems we can't quite let you go. We may even have to take you all the way to Washington with us."

"You can't do this to me—"

"Ah, but we can. This is war—ma'am," he said mockingly.

God, no! He couldn't take her away! She'd never get back.

"Wait, please—" she murmured, backing away still farther. "Wait—"

But he had caught her. His hands were on her wrists. "You can come with me riding on your own or tied over a mule. Which is it to be?"

She forced herself to remain dead still. "I'll come along on my own," she informed him icily. "You don't have to tie me up."

"I don't think I'll need to, either," he told her. He flipped open the tent's closure flap and she saw why. She was to have an escort of at least ten men. And it seemed that she was to be given one of the army's bay geldings. Arabesque was out there, but she was now wearing a United States Cavalry saddle.

"Can I help you up on old Billie over there? He's a fine horse. He has two gaits—slow and stop. You won't be running away this time, Miz Ahearn."

"I don't need your help," she said, walking by him.

But he caught her by the arm and she nearly cried out when he pulled her back to him. "Just remember, ma'am, I'm the man in charge here. And I think that little tarts like you don't much deserve to be treated like ladies. Do you understand yet? You're at my mercy. And I'm not a bountiful man!''

She jerked free of him, feeling panic race up and down her spine again.

Surely he still wouldn't dare hurt her. There were other men around!

Yes, but…

They were his men. And this was a war.

The bay was a big one. She hoped she could leap up without difficulty, especially the way that she was shaking now….

She managed to do so.

Captain Harper walked on out with a very pleased smile curved into his lips.

There was no hope for her. No hope, no hope.

Gramps came through shaking. He had forced his horse all the way, and he had forced himself, as well.

The feeling of fear was so intense coming into the arbor! Like nothing he had ever known before. Like being…touched. Grabbed. Like hands winding around him, taking hold of him, trying to…

Trying to hold on to him, maybe. Hold him back in a strange, dark, whirling funnel—damp, dank, green, chilling to the bone. Not here, and not there, not anywhere, really, nowhere at all.

He'd felt a strange tightening all the while, too. And he sensed that the door was closing. Not quickly. But inexorably. Bit by bit. Closing in, the winds twisting tighter and tighter. His horse had felt it. He had felt it. Whatever unknown power had opened this strange passageway had now decided to close it once more.

Some force—perhaps something in the stars, in the moon, in time, in magic—had caused the tunnel to open.

Maybe the alignment of the planets and the sun. Maybe it was everything that had been so exact—the reenactments on the exact same days, the battles being fought in the exact places, even the temperature being just about exact—maybe all those things had caused it.

And now, all the planets and stars were shifting again. The battles and their mirror-image reruns were almost over. And so the gap in time would soon be closed.

He could quickly return the way he'd come—except that Vickie was here.

He couldn't leave her. Not when he didn't even know if she'd managed to find her Colonel Jason Tarkenton or not. There were just too many dangers here.

His heart was slamming. She was everything to him. He had to know she was safe. Then Gramps forgot about his granddaughter for a minute for he stepped out into the nineteenth century.

He reined in quickly, swallowing down hard at the horror of everything before him.

He'd fought in a war himself, the Great War, and so he knew a lot about it. He'd seen carnage before. But this was horrible. Men lay all about. Groaning.

Dying.

"Hurry up, there, eh!" someone shouted suddenly. Gramps quickly backed old Dundee against a tree so that he couldn't be seen. A Yankee orderly with a bloodstained apron was urging his helpers to rush some bleeding, broken bodies onto a wagon. "The Rebs will be coming back for their own."

A second orderly threw a body onto the wagon, wiped his hands down his front and nodded to the others. "Did you see the spy they picked up?" he asked, then whistled sharply. "We don't get many that pretty, eh, Willie?"

Willie snorted and laughed. "Sure don't. Fiery little

thing she were, too, riding circles around that Cap'n Harper the way that she were. Too bad there were so many of them. She might have given him the slip.''

"Yep, but if she had, we might be a-wailing in our own blood right now, my man. She's a spy, and a spy is a spy, no matter how good-looking!''

"What they gonna do with her?''

"Colonel wanted to give her to the general. But then all the bigwigs got caught up in their maps and calculations for the battle. She's been turned back to the cap'n to guard.'' The man sniggered. "They're supposed to get her down to the main army. But I'll bet you a gold dollar that pretty filly will never make it! The cap'n sure had his eye on her!''

Gramps realized that he was holding his breath and felt as if he'd probably explode in about another ten seconds. He exhaled, and looked down at his shaking old gnarled hands.

So this was what it had come to! How darned ironic. All his life he'd loved history, he'd longed to go back, to see it firsthand....

And now he was seeing it. And Vickie was at the mercy of some sadistic soldier.

He backed farther against a tree as another rider came rushing through, barely pausing.

"The Rebs are coming back. In force. We've got to clear out of here *now!*''

"Yessir!'' Both men saluted. The rider went on.

"Hey, the Yank over there is still alive,'' the second one said. "Maybe we should—''

"Leave him! Unless you want to be a corpse yourself.''

Both men hopped onto their wagon of dead, wounded and dying. The wagon began to lumber away.

Gramps edged old Dundee out from around the tree. He rode out into the field of fallen men, and when he looked down, he wanted to cry.

Well, this was the truth of it! This was authenticity!

He held still as a troop of gray-clad riders came bursting out onto the field. The leader saw him, called out, a hand in the air drawing the men behind him to a halt.

"Sir! Halt and identify yourself!" the young Reb officer demanded.

"I'm a Virginian," Gramps called out. "And a desperate one. I've got to find Colonel Tarkenton, out of Staunton, Virginia, cavalry. Can you help me?"

"Are you addled, old man? A battle is about to begin on this mountain any moment."

"I've got to find the colonel," Gramps insisted. "Is his company headed this way?"

Other men had drawn beside the officer. They looked from one to the other.

Then the officer looked back to Gramps. "Why are you looking for him?"

Gramps lifted his chin. It had to be good. He knew that it had to be good.

What the hell? He might as well go for the dramatic. He had to have their help. He loved Vickie, but there was no way he could rescue her from a Union Army escort by himself.

"My granddaughter's got some information for him. *Important* information. She, er, she learns things, you know what I mean? But the Yanks have gotten her. Colonel Tarkenton will move heaven and earth for this woman's safe return. I swear."

They would help him! Surely they would help him.

That was...if they could. If Jason Tarkenton had made it back. If he hadn't been shot down already.

"That's quite a tale, sir," the young officer said finally.

"Do you know Colonel Tarkenton?"

"He's my commanding officer, sir. He's at our command tent." The young officer paused. "I suppose I'd best take you to him now," he said finally.

Gramps grinned. Broadly. "Thank you, son."

He looked up at the heavens and whispered under his breath, "Dear Lord, this is mighty weird. Mighty, mighty weird. But I do thank you for the small favors!"

Then Gramps started to ride. And he grinned again. Darn, if he just weren't so awfully worried, this might be all right. He was actually riding with the Army of Northern Virginia.

If Liam could just see him now!

CHAPTER NINE

Jason leaned idly against the support of a gnarled old oak tree, trying hard to convince himself that the time he had spent with Vickie had been a fantastic dream, born from the simple confusion and horror of the war.

Maybe, in time, he would believe it had all been an illusion.

But it was awfully difficult to do at the moment.

Hurtling through the archway, he had landed right in the thick of battle again. Yet, in all the days that he had ridden and fought, he had never been quite so desperately determined to win, to break through, to escape the enemy, as he had just then.

He wouldn't die. He just wouldn't. He had come too far to fall prey to a Yankee saber before managing to return to John with help—and the tetanus shot he had stolen from the hospital. He winced a little at the thought. In all his life, he had never stolen anything.

But it was so insignificant when it meant saving John's life.

Well, he hadn't died. And he had found his brother. A company of his men had already stumbled upon him and carried him off the field. But John had insisted on waiting for his brother before being taken in to any field hospital. And so Jason had managed to return, slicing his way through the raging battle, to rejoin his troops in time to be with John, in time to slip the shot into him, in time to reach the field hospital and stand there like a furious mother hen, making damned sure that the surgeons used a clean sponge when sopping up his brother's wound. He wouldn't allow them to amputate, and he gave them a firm warning that they needed to use clean sponges on other men, too.

Most of the bone-weary surgeons merely stared at him, and Jason smiled, and surely looked like a madman. They just didn't know yet that they were spreading germs and killing men. If he tried to tell them how he knew, they would see that he was locked up somewhere, in a home for Confederate officers who had gone daft.

He left one of his privates, one of John's best friends, to stand guard overnight with his brother. But when he had last seen John, he had been sleeping peacefully, on his way to recovery.

Very peacefully. John would get in a full night of restful sleep. Jason had managed to get him to swallow the two little sleeping pills he had saved in the scrunched-up paper cup.

He brother was going to live.

And he was grateful, so damned grateful.

But at this moment, he wasn't so sure he cared if he himself lived or died.

No, he told himself firmly, *he wasn't the kind of coward to be so willing to die! He was going to fight the war, survive the war, hold on to end the war.*

It was just that he felt so damned weary and lost at this moment. He shouldn't feel that way, of course. Despite the carnage, he should be very glad for the small favors of life. His men had loyally cared for his brother. They had searched for Jason. They had readily believed that he had become separated from them by the battle, that he had climbed the mountain continually trying to get back to John. They believed him without question.

And they were ready to follow him again.

The action seemed to have reached a lull for the day, he thought. His men had been ordered back. Rebs and Yanks both had gone to retrieve their dead and wounded. The Yanks were worried about the Confederate strength, while the Confederates kept them guessing as they awaited reinforcements. Stonewall Jackson had directed General Jubal Early and his army to join them. Their troops, combined with Early's men, would push the Yanks on down the mountain and back north again. Hopefully....

He closed his eyes. They were going to take this battle. Hadn't Vickie told him so? Did it really matter? They were going to lose the war.

It was terrible to know too much.

And terrible not to care at the moment.

He would lead his men again. He would see it all out. At the moment, he was glad of the fleeting interlude of peace.

He hurt.

No saber wound, no grazing bullet, had ever hurt quite like this. Even losing his wife had been different. His grief had been swift, searing and painful, but somehow easier to accept. To understand. God had taken her. She was completely, irrevocably lost.

Time had taken Vickie. Time, and his own foolish sense of honor. No, it hadn't been foolish to love his brother. Hadn't Gramps said that he had to return and save John? John's knowledge would lead to medical breakthroughs in the future.

Now...now! He could go back.

But Gramps had also said that he was supposed to save Lee's life at some later date.

And that might be all-important, too. It might have

something to do with the binding up of the nation. He couldn't turn his back on such a fate.

He could only remember how she had felt beside him, remember the blue beauty of her eyes, the openness within them. Remember her courage, her determination, her independence, her laughter. Her anger, her passion. The way it had felt to make love to her.

She existed, she lived. And he had only to turn his back on whatever responsibilities lay in this world and return to hers. An incredible new world.

He'd hardly touched that world. There were so many places she might have taken him, so many things he might have seen and done.

Did it matter? No, none of those things mattered. Cars or horses, old values, new inventions. People mattered. One person, who provided a reason to live.

And had he really been living at all since Lydia died? Until he had crossed that unique barrier, and come upon Vickie Ahearn? She had given him back his life. Could he really go on here without her?

Anguish tore at him. The door was closing. The strange passageway he had stumbled upon was closing. He felt the peculiar barriers of it as he had come through, almost like a swirling funnel, twisting tighter and tighter. In a short time—maybe by now—it would be impossible to move from this one world to the next.

"Colonel!"

He looked up, startled from his thoughts. Lieutenant Nigel Keefe was returning from a scouting mission with the rest of Company B. He'd scarcely been out an hour, but then, the last of the skirmishing had barely ended, and Company B might well be in need of a few minutes' respite. But they were excellent men, battle-hardened men. The cavalry had always been the eyes and ears of any army. His men were accustomed to finding the enemy positions, and then joining in the action once the infantry and artillery were advised. They'd ridden tired before.

Something unusual must have happened to bring them back.

Keefe was coming in fast, his horse foaming, prancing, shaking off bits of sweat to glitter in the now-dropping sun.

Jason stiffened, eyes narrowing, as he saw that they had been joined by an unusual horseman.

It was Gramps. Riding an ancient old horse, looking a little peaked and scared, but as curious as all hell, too, as he stared out at everything around him with his shrewd blue eyes.

"Colonel!"

Nigel Keefe leapt down from his horse before it had come to a stop. "We found him right at the scene of some of the fighting, sir. He asked for you right off. Seems some woman was trying to bring you information, but the Yanks got her."

Jason's heart slammed like a cannonball against his chest. For a moment, he couldn't breathe. "*Some* woman," Keefe had said.

"Do you know the old man, sir?" Keefe demanded. "He swore to us you'd back up his story."

"Yes, yes! I know him."

Jason stepped forward, hurrying to Gramps's horse, looking up at the old man. "What's happened?" he demanded quickly. "What are you doing *here?*"

Gramps looked up at the men all around them, then back down to Jason with a look that clearly said he couldn't tell him everything. "She came looking for you. She was supposed to be right back. I followed her. I heard some of the Yanks who were picking up their wounded talking about how they had picked up a spy. They have her under guard and are taking her down to the main army camp.''

Jason backed away from Gramps, stunned. He closed his eyes quickly, stiffening, looking down to the ground, trying not to let his men see how close he was to losing control.

He looked up. ''Lieutenant Keefe, you're in charge here again.'' He pointed a finger at Gramps. ''You! Sir! You stay here, in my tent. Out of the way, and out of trouble.''

''I'm coming with you!'' Gramps insisted.

''That horse would slow us down—''

''Then I'll take another horse.''

''You can't—''

''I have to!'' Gramps insisted. *''Please!''*

Jason sighed with exasperation. He looked at the men in Company B, then turned and called over his shoulder. ''Sergeant Morrison!''

''Yessir!'' His staff sergeant, in charge of his personal welfare, came running out from the field of tents, saluting quickly.

''I need you to find something this gentleman can wear,'' Jason told him. ''Anything that resembles a uniform. And borrow someone's mount. A good horse, one that moves like lightning.''

''Right, sir!'' the officer said, saluting.

''A uniform?'' Gramps said.

''We're going into the enemy lines,'' Jason said quietly. ''They'll hang you for a spy if you aren't dressed in some uniform, and if you're with us, sir, you're a Reb at the moment.''

Gramps's crinkled old face lit into a smile. He saluted

sharply and leapt down from his old horse with a surprising agility. He quickly followed the staff sergeant toward the tents.

"Lieutenant Keefe," Jason said, "I'll need to hear everything you know about enemy positions." He looked out over the men of Company B again. There were eighteen of them. Their captain, Jim Hodges, had been killed some time back. Hodges hadn't been replaced. The men fought under Lieutenant Keefe, with First Sergeant Jack Johnson often giving the orders when it came down to gritty hand-to-hand combat. Every one of the men in the company had been with him since he had first commanded troops at Manassas. He could trust them now when he needed them so desperately.

But he couldn't order them into this mission.

"I know you've had a rough time of it here up on Blackfield's Mountain," he told them. "You deserve some rest, for there's sure to be more fighting. I'm riding out to find someone who helped me survive. None of you is beholden. I need volunteers, and that's what I want, volunteers only. Drop on out if you want to sit this one out."

Not a soul moved.

"We're going right into the enemy camp," he reminded them. And he looked around at a sea of stubborn faces. Jack Johnson, a square-jawed Irishman, probably somewhere around thirty years old. The Jenson twins, Stan and Ben, early twenties, blond, blue-eyed, quick to sing at night, never faltering in a fray. They were coming with him. They were all coming with him.

He looked down, wincing. He knew now that he had to stay. Even if he could find Vickie, wrest her from the Yanks and bring her to safety, she would pass back into her own world. He had to stay. It did go beyond his brother. *Somehow, he just wasn't really allowed to leave!*

"Thank you," Jason told the men quietly. "Lieutenant Keefe, let's take a quick look at the maps—" he began, but someone cleared his throat behind him.

It was Gramps.

And actually, he looked darned good in the Rebel cavalry garb. Tall, straight as an arrow. Very dignified.

"You don't need to look at the maps. I know where all the positions are."

"He can't possibly know more—" Keefe began.

"But he does," Jason said with a slow smile. "This is his mountain, you see. He knows it backward and forward."

"The mountain, maybe. But what about the Yanks?"

"He's been studying their—er—battle tactics for years," Jason assured him. "Lieutenant, I put my faith in him. You wait here for word about our next movement. If I'm not back, you'll lead the troops into battle again."

Moments later, Jason's horse, Max, was brought before him. He quickly mounted and looked over Company B— and Gramps. "Gentlemen, we ride in stealth. We've got to discover where she's been taken. And then we've got to discover just how in hell we're going to take her back!"

He lifted a hand and lowered it. And they began to ride.

Captain Harper didn't seem to be in any hurry to get her wherever they were going. The lowering afternoon sun was still beating down upon them as they left the gigantic field of Yankee tents behind, following a curving path farther down the rolling fields, heading for the depths of the valley.

They walked; they plodded along. She, Harper and an escort of ten men.

They had been riding for over an hour, weaving in and out through heavily treed trails and open fields, when Harper suddenly called a halt. "We'll rest here, men. There's a stream down through the foliage there." Vickie stayed on her horse, staring at him as he dismounted. Harper looked at her, smiling. Then he addressed one of his men, a tall, heavyset fellow with small dark eyes. "Sergeant Rieger, keep a lookout! A good one. Shout at the first sign of movement, shoot anyone who hasn't got a right to be here."

"You—" he pointed at Vickie, his lips curving into a deep smile "—you come with me."

"No," she told him quickly, her heart beating hard. His men were at ease, dismounting from their horses. But surely they wouldn't all let him drag her off!

"You can come down," he warned her softly, blue eyes narrowed with warning, "or I can come up and get you."

"No!" she insisted.

Then she cried out sharply because he meant it. His hands were reaching for her, dragging her down. She punched, slapped and scratched at him, screaming, protesting.

"Captain!"

One of his men cried out to him in dismay. She had been right! The Yanks were like any other men, some of them good, and some of them—like Harper—not so good.

But Harper knew how to handle the situation. He wrenched Vickie on down to the ground, his arm around her throat in a chokehold. She could barely breathe. He swung around and stared at the young soldier who had protested. "How can you forget Manassas?" he demanded. "The Rebs beat us back like a pack of fools—*and all because of a spy like this one!* Josh Miller, you hush up now. Your very own brother was slaughtered down in the valley because a *lady* spy like this warned the Rebs we were coming. How can you all be such fools! I took her, and I'm going to see that she pays!"

"But, sir!" the young solder exclaimed unhappily. "How will we explain what…happened?"

"She tried to escape, soldier. She tried to escape."

Harper whirled around with her. She gasped for air and feared she was going to faint. Her heart was pounding all the more fiercely.

Dear God, she realized with a growing, paralyzing panic, he meant to kill her! Rape her, kill her. He'd have to kill her, or she would tell everyone what he had done. He meant to have his revenge against her. So far in this war, the Rebs had sent the Yanks into retreat one time too many. Harper had been humiliated.

And there was surely no way to explain to this man that the Yankees were going to win the war, that the Rebs were going to be vanquished!

Captain Harper, she thought, wasn't just somewhat of a bad man. He was a lunatic, a fanatic.

And no matter how she fought and struggled, he was taking her away.

Away from his men, from the eyes of the world.

Down the cliff, and toward the water.

Gramps knew his business. He led them through the trails to a break in the forest that stood just above the valley field with its endless ripple of Yankee canvas.

They reined, he stopping his men effortlessly with a

lift of his hand. They stood silent upon the crest, watching the activity in the camp.

A cry suddenly rose on the air, loud enough to carry across the distance.

Jason bit into his lower lip. There was a Yankee hospital tent down there. The surgeons were busy seeing to their wounded, doing what they could to patch up their injured before transporting them to hospitals in Washington.

There was movement down there. Men cleaning their weapons, tending horses, trying to relax, still ready. They all knew the troops would be meeting again.

The camps weren't so different. Not at all. Boys were writing to their mothers. Men were writing to their wives. None of them knew if it would be his last communication home.

He couldn't think about the Yanks now; he couldn't even think about the war now.

They had Vickie.

"What do you think?" Jack Johnson asked him, gnawing slowly on a blade of grass as they stared down at the activity together.

Jason looked to Gramps. His face looked very old and haggard now. He had gotten them there, all right. But now he was staring down at the Yankee camp with dismay.

He just hadn't realized how many of them there would be.

Jason pointed across the field to another clump of trees. "They've got to have a sentry there."

Jack Johnson nodded, hazel eyes grave. "You and me?" he said to Jason.

"I can go it alone."

"Better two."

"Maybe," Jason agreed with a rueful grin.

He turned around, addressing the others. "Jack and I are going to take the left field over there."

His troops nodded with understanding. They would remain where they were, just like a pack of sentinels.

"What are you doing?" Gramps asked him anxiously.

"We're going to try to get our hands on one of their pickets."

"But they won't give her back because we've got one of their men—"

"The plan, sir, is to have the picket tell us where Vickie is," he said softly. "If they've brought in a woman, I can guarantee you every fellow in that camp knows it now."

"But—" Gramps began.

Jason raised a brow to him. Gramps fell silent, then said quietly, "It's your war, boy. You know what you're doing."

His war, his enemy.

And they had *his* woman.

"Jack," Jason said, indicating it was time they moved. He nudged Max, and headed off, Jack Johnson coming along behind him.

They were good horsemen. And they were Virginians, accustomed to the terrain here. They circled around the summits, keeping a careful eye to the valley and watching their distance. They had come to the group of trees surrounding the east side of the camp. Jason signaled to Jack to dismount, and they both did so, leaving their horses then to circle around into the foliage from separate directions, treading silently upon the soft ground.

Jason saw the Yankee picket first. The man had probably been there a long time; it might have been the end of his duty. He looked very tired, and very bored. Jason was glad. It made him an easy mark.

Jason waited a moment anyway, watching him cautiously. The man took a twenty-yard walk, his rifle over his shoulder. He stretched, looked about and yawned.

Then Jason was glad he had waited because he watched the Yank pull a mirror from his jacket and signal back to someone down in the camp below. The flashes of light were returned to him.

An *all-clear* sign had been given.

Jason saw that Jack had come around, too, and was hunkered down across the small clearing from him. He nodded to him, motioning that he would move in first.

They waited, both tensed.

Then the picket turned his back on Jason, and Jason leapt out of the bushes. He sprang at the man's back, catching him in a throathold from behind before he even knew something was about to hit him.

Jack sprang forward, smiling to the picket, placing a knife warningly at his throat.

"We need some help, Yank," Jason warned from behind. He eased up a bit on his hold.

The Yank spit, but he was young and scared.

"I ain't no traitor. I ain't helping no Rebs."

"Then you're going die," Jason assured him. "Say a prayer, if you would, son."

He nodded. Jack came at the man more menacingly with his knife.

"Now wait a minute!" the Yank said quickly. "What is it you want, Reb?"

Jason smiled behind his back. Jack eased up with the knife. "Want to hand your rifle over, boy?"

The Yank did so quickly, with Jason's arm still locked around his throat.

"We're looking for a woman," Jason said softly.

The Yank hesitated a minute. Jason tightened his hold again and Jack set the blade against his throat.

"You're too late."

"Too late!" Jason exclaimed.

The Yank really thought that he was going to die. "She's gone—she's gone!" he yelped quickly. "Captain Harper is taking her on down to the main camp. He rode out about an hour ago. He—*hey!*"

Jason had him lifted off his feet, whirling him around to face the clump of brush where they had left the horses.

"Sorry, boy, you're coming with us," Jason said.

"I sure as bejesus am not—"

"You can come with us alive, or we can leave you here with your throat slit."

"A ride sounds fine," the Yank said quickly. "A ride sounds mighty fine!"

With his arm around her throat, Harper lifted Vickie cleanly off the ground. She tried to kick and struggled but he was dragging her quickly through the trees and the brush. There was a stream just below them. She could hear the gentle rippling of the water, the soft cry of the birds. As Harper dragged her through the foliage, though, she could see little except a blur of green.

And then he suddenly stopped, throwing her down.

She landed hard, but she landed on soft earth. They were right by the water, and the bank here was sponging and covered with soft mosses. The trees were closing in all around them, but as she tried to rise, she saw that the sun was breaking through upon the water.

Harper stared down at her, his hands on his hips. She had never seen such hatred in any man's eyes.

"You're making a mistake. I'm not what you think!" she cried suddenly, fiercely.

Those eyes narrowed. "I know what you are. Your kind have killed more men than bullets!" he swore.

She tried to rise, desperate to get away from him. She had nearly found her footing when his hand crashed savagely against her face, sending her reeling back down again. He pounced, straddling over her. He leaned low, trying to capture her lips.

She bit him and kicked him with all her strength at the same time. He bellowed out in pain, easing back, clutching his mouth and crotch.

But his weight upon her legs still pinned her down.

She tried to twist to escape from beneath him, a wealth of tears springing to her eyes while terror ravaged her heart.

Gramps...

He would think that she had just left him.

And Jason...

He would never know. Never know that she had tried to touch him, just one more time.

She would just die here, up on this mountain. Almost a hundred years before she had been destined to be born upon it.

"Bitch!" Harper shrieked. He caught her arm, wrenched her back. He rose up on his knees, his fingers knotting into a fist, his arm pulled back, ready to strike. If he hit her with such violence, she would lose consciousness.

And nothing else would matter....

"Captain!"

A warning shriek gave him pause. He stared upward through the foliage, toward the spot where they had left his men and the horses.

His man, the heavyset Rieger, burst through the greenness and stared down at them.

"Rebels coming, Captain! Coming fast."

Harper was up instantly. "Rebs! How many?"

"Fifteen, eighteen, I'm not sure. But they're riding on us fast."

Suddenly they all heard a cry. It was wild, a sound that seemed to tear up the air and the day. It was a cry of wild, reckless courage and danger. A Rebel cry, high, tearing through the air.

"Get up!" Harper cried, dragging her to her feet suddenly. He wrenched her against him. "And when I do get a hold of you, *ma'am,* you will rue the day you and your Rebel lover were born, you hear? Jesu, lady, you will pay!"

"No!" Vickie promised. "You will pay!"

He caught her arm, wrenching her around, dragging her up the rugged terrain he had just dragged her down.

They reached the Yanks and the restless horses. Harper threw her up upon her mount with a violence. Then he leapt atop his own, and they heard the cry again, wild, violent...closer.

And then Vickie saw them herself. Perhaps twenty men on wonderful, powerful mounts. Men in gray and butternut, in ragged apparel, elegant nonetheless. They rode hard, one with their horses, handsome in their fluid movement.

Jason was at the forefront. Jason, his sword held high even as he rode, the silver catching the glint of the sun, shining with vengeance.

Behind them, there were others. Gramps! Gramps in a gray uniform. Gramps, with a sword waving, too.

It was incredible. Absolutely incredible. But, perhaps, no more incredible than anything else that had happened.

The cavalry was coming.
Coming to her rescue.
Gramps!
And Jason.
Dear God, Jason…!

CHAPTER TEN

"Get her moving!" Captain Harper cried furiously. Mounted, he brought his horse, Arabesque, around behind Vickie's, his eye on the surging force of Confederates.

"You plan to outrun them?" Sergeant Rieger demanded incredulously.

"They've come for the woman!" Harper called quickly to his men. "She's going to give them all our positions, she's going to see that they know their own reinforcements are coming. We've got to get her away. Or kill her!"

"Jesu, Captain Harper!" one of the men gasped.

"Let's run her out, then!" another man cried.

"Make for those rocks, yonder!" Harper ordered. "We'll shoot them down as they come, damn now, courage men!"

He smacked Vickie's horse on the rump and even then, the old boy barely moved. Vickie tugged on the reins quickly, trying to get the horse to hightail it toward the raging Confederates.

But Harper was too quick, and too determined. He had Arabesque turned around and cutting her off before she could move more than ten feet.

"You'll die first, I swear it!" Harper promised her heatedly. "It's a pity I didn't get to taste what this damned fool Reb is ready to die for!"

"You're the fool!" she promised him. "You—" But she was cut off. Harper wasn't going to be caught out in the open. She tried to strike at him, tried to fight him. But in a matter of seconds, he had lifted her from the tired old horse and over Arabesque's saddle, throwing her facedown over the horse's neck. Then he slammed the reins against Arabesque's haunches and the mare took flight, racing ahead of the Yankee troops.

Vickie thought that she would die before they reached the rocks, that she would go flying from the horse's neck to the ground, and be pummeled to death beneath the pounding hooves. It seemed forever that she was slammed about there, tasting the mare's salty coat. Then Arabesque was reined in hard, and Harper was dragging her off the horse again.

"Take cover!" Harper commanded his men. "Take cover!"

They all fell back behind the rocks. Vickie shook off Harper for a moment and ran. In seconds, he was pelting down upon her, slamming her hard against the earth. His evil leer rose above her. "You'll never escape me, you little witch, I swear it!" She was wrenched up again and over his shoulder. She kicked and beat against him and he swore furiously.

But he didn't release his hold.

He dragged her down beside him behind one of the rocks for a moment, and she watched with him as the Rebels advanced. She managed to forget Harper for a single moment as she saw the two men she loved most in life, tearing up grass and earth, riding like God's vengeance upon these men. Her heart swelled with pride for Gramps, and with a certain awe for Jason—he was magnificent; a horseman, a soldier, in his element now, calling his commands to his troops.

"Ready!" Harper called, and she realized that his men were loading their rifles, ripping open catridges, ramming balls down their barrels. They weren't repeaters, she thought fleetingly. These men, at least, weren't armed with repeaters. Not yet.

"Aim!" Harper cried.

"No!" she shrieked out, terrified of the volley of death that would follow.

"Fire!" Harper commanded.

The volley sounded, tearing apart the air. Vickie screamed again, her head ringing, certain that the world itself had exploded.

But the men were still coming. They hadn't missed a beat. In beautiful, elegant formation, they were coming. Then, even as she flattened against the rock, they were there, the Rebs, their horses' hooves sailing over the rocks, engaging in hard hand-to-hand combat with the Yanks.

For a moment, there were men everywhere, swords flying, fists swinging.

She saw Jason, just ten feet from her. He had dismounted from Max, and he was fighting a Yankee, their swords flashing. The tip of Jason's sword gleamed red with blood.

"Jason!" she shrieked.

He paused for a heartbeat. His eyes met hers.

"Watch out!" she cried, and in just seconds, he parried the man who had sprung at him. Vickie gasped with relief, then screamed as fingers suddenly and violently wrenched into her hair.

"Move!" Harper commanded her.

She braced herself against the pain and whirled, nails ripping down his cheek. He swore, howling out with pain.

But he was a determined man. He didn't lose his grasp. With his free hand he wrenched a knife from the sheath at his ankle and set it against her throat.

"Move!" he repeated.

And then she had no choice.

In minutes they were crashing through trees and bushes. She was blinded by dirt and branches and leaves. She gasped, coughing, struggling for breath. She tried to halt. Harper dragged her down.

Then, finally, they came to the water again. Harper paused, looked around. He gasped himself, pushing her away from him, doubling over to draw in air.

He turned his head toward her, smiling. "We've done it, *lady*. We've done it."

She shook her head. "You've done nothing!" she gasped out at him.

He stood slowly, smiling. "They're fairly evenly matched. Only a few men will survive to come for you. And they'll be searching this forest from now until eternity."

Vickie took a step away from him. "You know," she told him, "eventually, your own kind are going to hang you."

"It won't be until long after I'm done with you," he assured her. Then his blond brow arched and his smile deepened. "You must be something, for a troop of men to come after you. Even *gallant* Southern men. Cavaliers. You could live, you know. You could show me what you've got that's so special, lady. Maybe I'd be in such bliss, I'd be willing to die for you, too."

Vickie shook her head slowly. "I'd rather die."

His smile faded, his lean features went hard. "Fine. I'll help myself to what I want. And leave the rest for vultures!"

He lunged at her.

"No!" Vickie grated out, sidestepping to escape him. She did so and he teetered precariously on a rock for a moment. She turned to flee, praying that she had the breath to outrun him. He was on her again before she could move. She fought furiously but found herself borne down to the ground. He rose above her, eyes searing their triumph, lips curled in an evil smile. He leaned down toward her and Vickie felt her stomach rise in fear and repulsion.

Then suddenly, a shout stilled him.

"Get off her this instant, you bastard—or I'll pluck your eyes out while you're still living."

Harper's smile faded.

He leapt up because he had to, straddling the earth just above Vickie's head. She tried to struggle up and managed to do so.

There was Jason on Max, staring furiously at Harper from the center of the stream.

He dismounted, striding through the water toward Harper.

Harper drew his sword suddenly from its sheath. Before Vickie could leap away, he had the point aimed against her throat. She stared at Jason with dismay, biting her lip.

"You want to see her ripped from throat to gullet, Reb?"

Jason paused for a moment. He was at least ten feet away. His eyes met hers, glistening silver.

"Take him, Jason!" she cried.

"She'll die!" Harper swore.

Jason eased back. "All right, then, let's negotiate," he told Harper. "You can kill both of us, but my men have surrounded this part of the mountain. Most of yours are dead, or turned tail and ran. Let her go, and I'll give the order to let you pass."

In that instant, Harper eased back just a shade.

Vickie took the opportunity to thrust the blade aside and leap to her feet. Harper swore, and swung his sword.

But too late.

Jason had leapt forward, his sword swinging. Vickie heard the awful clang of steel as their weapons first clashed. Harper fell back. Jason raised his sword again, and his blade crashed down, driving Harper to his knees.

One more crack of Jason's blade, and Harper's blade had flown from his grasp.

"Jesu, mercy!" Harper screamed out suddenly.

Jason looked as if he hadn't heard him. As if his sword would fall upon Harper's head.

"Jason!" she cried his name softly. He held still for a moment, and then turned to her very slowly. He paused just a fraction of a second, and then he smiled and turned toward her.

"Look out! He's got a knife!" another voice from somewhere back in the woods thundered out.

Jason whirled around, dragging Vickie down to the ground as he did so. Harper was pulling his knife from his ankle sheath again, aiming it at them.

Jason was faster. He, too, carried a weapon at his ankle. A gleaming little blade. He had pulled it from the sheath and hurled it for Harper before Harper's blade had left his hand.

Vickie screamed as she watched the blade plunge into Harper's throat. She buried her face into Jason's chest. She heard the man groan, and his gurgling death choke as he fell to the ground.

"Vickie, Vickie!" Jason drawled softly, his fingers working through her hair. "Thank God you're all right."

She looked up at him, shaking her head. She couldn't look at Harper. She couldn't wish any man's death, but that man had meant to cost her her life.

"I'm sorry, Jason! You risked so much for me. He would have killed us both if it hadn't been for—"

She broke off, her eyes widening.

And then they both spoke suddenly, in unison, realizing who had called out the warning to them.

"Gramps!"

With an arm around Vickie, Jason started leading her through the water. Gramps had come there, cutting a very striking figure in his gray cavalry uniform. He had been joined by a number of Jason's men. Vickie looked at them all, smiling as they gravely nodded to her one by one.

Jason walked forward to Gramps. "You saved my life, sir."

Gramps grinned, but his face looked rather gray.

"You saved my granddaughter's life, son. We're even."

"You were fantastic!" Vickie assured him. "Fantastic!"

He nodded, looking at her. "I was, wasn't I? I rather like it here," he told her. Her heart quickened. Maybe they could stay. She could stay, if Gramps were to stay, too.

She stared at Jason. He returned her gaze, and he seemed to understand the message in it. His fingers curled around hers, and he pulled her close, searching out her eyes.

"Yes!" she said breathlessly. "I think…"

"Colonel, sir?" one of his men said, clearing his throat.

Jason looked quickly to the man who had spoken. "Is everyone here, Jack?"

"Not a man lost, Colonel. Henry back there caught a

graze in his thigh, but the bullet went right through. Two minor saber wounds.''

"The Yanks?''

Jack shrugged. "Once they lost their captain there, they skedaddled. Which means that we'd best move out, else they'll be all over us like horseflies in August heat. What do you say, sir?''

"Right,'' Jason agreed. He started for Max, then turned back to Vickie. "You'll ride with me. I guess the Yanks have your horse.''

"They don't deserve her,'' Vickie said softly. Then she looked to Jason's men again, all of them. "Thank you,'' she told them. "Thank you all so very much.''

The one named Jack laughed. "Why, ma'am, it was an honor and a pleasure.''

Vickie smiled and Jason set her quickly atop Max. "Well, then, the order is to skedaddle'—'' he began, but Vickie gasped, cutting him off.

"Gramps!'' she shrieked.

Her grandfather's ruddy cheeks had gone white. He clutched his heart, and pitched forward.

Jason leapt down from Max and hurried toward Gramps. He stared back to Vickie. "He's breathing, his heart is still beating.'' He stared at her, and then he swallowed hard. They both knew in those seconds that they had to get Gramps back to the twentieth century.

Either that…or watch him die.

Jason quickly gave orders to his men. They'd ride back partway together, then Jack would see the rest of the men back to their brigade.

"I have to get this man home—'' Jason began to explain.

Jack waved a hand in the air. "Sir, he led us right and proper, he did. We'll send him a prayer.''

Jason nodded. He leapt up with Gramps on Dundee.

They moved out in silence, a very solemn party.

Partway back, the company split off and continued their return to camp. Jason led the way to the strange arbor of trees.

"It's closing, you know," Vickie told him hollowly.

He nodded.

"I can take Gramps now," she told him.

He shook his head. "No."

"Jason, I can't let you go through! It's closing. We might not get back and you—" She broke off, feeling a fierce gust of wind tear at her. "Jason, you can't—"

"Vickie, I am coming with you! You can't possibly get your grandfather through this. You haven't the strength."

The wind ripped and tore again. She met his eyes, her own a tempest. "I'm afraid!" she admitted on a whisper, but he seemed to hear it. His horse drew close to hers. "Close your eyes and ride hard!" he commanded her.

There was a whack on Max's rump and she was suddenly flying into the storm.

More than ever, she could feel it. Feel the walls of time closing around her. The fierce wind swirled and funneled, drawing her into its terrifying, mercilessly dark center. As before, mingled with the sounds of the wind, Vickie heard the voices, the howls and chilling moans clearer and closer, more gut-wrenching than ever before. Strange, dark shadows that were humanlike forms, and yet horrifyingly unhuman, grasped and reached for her. She heard her name on the wind. They wanted her, wanted to embrace her and make her one of them, imprisoned in this horrid, nowhere place for all eternity. Vickie…stay. Vickie, come, stay….

They stroked her face, tore at her hair. If she opened

her eyes, she would see them. Creatures who were barely formed, with empty eyes and pain-filled faces. Neither dead nor living, neither born nor unborn. She could hear their cries on the wind, feel them touching her, closing in on her, grabbing her, clutching her so desperately with their damp, lifeless fingers....

"Ride!" Jason yelled. *"Ride!"*

Jason was at her side, slapping her horse's flanks once again, urging her through.

They burst out into a lighter wind. A keening remained in the trees, but they were through. Her horse reared, and screamed. She maintained her seat until his gait evened out. She gazed at Jason. His face was pale. Vickie couldn't help wondering if he, too, had heard and felt the demon spirits reach for him as he had ridden through.

Gramps hadn't seen or felt any of it. He was slumped over, near death.

"Jason—" she whispered miserably. She was about to lose him again. And maybe Gramps, too, and her heart was filled with desolation for them all.

"We've got to get him to the hospital," Jason said.

"You can't come with me. The passage is almost closed. You'll be trapped in there, Jason. Trapped with those lost souls...."

"Vickie, let's go."

"Then you can't go back."

"Vickie! Let's get moving!"

She lowered her eyes, fighting tears. He wouldn't leave her until Gramps was in the hospital. Then he'd try to go back.

She couldn't seem to fight him on this, to convince him that it was far safer for him to turn back now, while the passageway was still open. She turned and urged her horse forward. They rode down the mountain, heading west, and quickly covered the short distance to Gramps's house. But as Vickie helped Jason carry Gramps inside, she wondered if they had been quick enough.

While Jason made Gramps as comfortable as possible, Vickie called the hospital. An ambulance arrived in minutes. Gramps was swiftly and efficiently whisked away with an oxygen mask over his face and a portable heart monitor attached to his chest.

Vickie and Jason followed in her Jeep. Again, Vickie wished Jason would head back. But she didn't have a moment to spare now to argue with him.

While Gramps was tended to by a team of doctors, Vickie was once again stuck in the admissions office, filling out forms. She prayed under her breath. Poor Gramps. He had to be all right. He just had to.

When she'd finished with the admissions clerk, she joined Jason in the waiting room. He stared at her, not touching her. His eyes fell upon hers.

"I love you," he told her.

She nodded, feeling tears well up in her eyes.

She didn't get to say anything, because someone cleared his throat behind her. It was Sam Dooley, the doctor on call here once again. He looked at them both suspiciously, but didn't say anything—Vickie didn't give him a chance.

She ran to him. "Gramps—will he be all right? Oh, please, Sam! Tell me he's going to be all right!"

Sam smiled at her. "He's fine, Vickie."

"What?" she gasped.

"He's fine. Just a bit of exhaustion."

"No heart attack?"

Sam shook his head. "I'm not sure what he was up to—I'm not sure what any of you are up to!—but he's just got to calm down a bit. No more of this reenacting for him, or he *will* have a heart attack. But this was just a scare."

"Oh, God!" Vickie whispered. "Can I see him?"

"You can even take him home in an hour or so if you want. Just keep him calm, okay? No more running around as if he were really fighting a battle, hmm? He's too old for it, Vickie. Take this as a warning. Make him behave."

"Yes, yes!" Vickie promised. "Thank you again, Sam, thank you. So much." She started to rush through the emergency room doors, but paused, hurrying back to Jason. "Wait!" she begged him. "You just wait this time! Promise. I'll—I'll at least go with you to the... door."

Jason nodded, his eyes very dark. "I'll wait," he promised her softly. He added, "We haven't much time."

She nodded, then rushed on in to see Gramps. She cried out and hugged him. "You're okay, thank God! I was so scared, Gramps! But you're going to be all right.'

"It was wonderful, Vickie!" he told her, reaching for her hand. "I wanted to stay."

She swallowed hard for a minute. "But it isn't possible, Gramps. You can't—"

"I'm an old man, and I wouldn't live without modern medicine," he finished grumpily.

"That's right."

His fingers curled around her wrist and his blue eyes were intense. "But you can, honey. You're young. Everything is ahead of you."

There was a knot in her throat and she willed it away, determined to speak lightly. "Gramps, think of it! No movies, no shopping malls, no great rock music. If I had children, no disposable diapers! No, Gramps, you and I will do just fine where we are. But I do have to say goodbye to Jason. I can take you home very soon, so you just rest and I'll be back in an hour or so.''

He clutched her hand.

"Gramps—''

He sighed and his fingers eased slowly. "You take all the time that you can, Victoria, you hear? Make him come home with you first. Give him a taste of cold beer and hot chili one more time. You take your time. I'll be just fine.''

"The passageway is closing,'' she said very softly. She tried not to shiver, thinking of the feeling she had had while going through.

"Yes, I know that. But you've got a little time. Make the most of it.''

"You're great, Gramps,'' she said softly. They didn't really have *any* time, but Gramps didn't know that.

"How many old coots like me get a granddaughter like you?''

"Gramps—''

"Go! Time is passing!''

She nodded, and hurried on out again. Jason was waiting. She looked up at him. "I'll drive you back to the house so you can get Max.''

"Let's go, then,'' he said, a husky undertone in his voice.

Vickie's Jeep was parked just outside the emergency room entrance. They drove the short distance back to the house in silence.

At the house, Jason slipped quickly out of the passenger's side of the vehicle. "I never got to learn how to drive this thing. It's amazing. I've seen so many women on the streets with them!''

"We were driving before we got the vote,'' Vickie said, smiling.

His eyes widened. *"Women* got the vote?" he inquired.

She lowered her head, smiling. "You bet!" she told him softly. "Got something against it?"

He shrugged. "I think it's...remarkable."

She started to laugh, and then she was afraid that she was going to cry. They both started walking toward the house.

Max waited patiently in front of the old oak tree that had stood there huge and gnarled as long as Vickie could remember. She would be willing to bet that if Jason were ever to go by the old house back in his day, the oak tree would be there, drooping and gnarled, just the same.

She was thinking about that tree when they had so little time left together!

She stared at Jason. Felt his eyes on her. She fought the temptation to laugh and to cry again. She swallowed hard. She turned to him, bracing herself for the painful task of saying goodbye. But then Jason surprised her.

"I'd like to come in," he told her softly.

Her conscience told her she should have reminded him of the risk he took in lingering even a moment longer. But she couldn't say a word. Instead, she walked up the porch steps and into the entryway, knowing that he was behind her. She swung around. "This is dangerous. We're playing with your life."

He shook his head. "Damn that tunnel. Damn the war. I can't leave you yet." He was silent for a moment, watching her. "Of all the things that I didn't taste enough, drink deeply enough of, hold close enough...that thing is you. Of all the things I would remember through all time, you are the most incredibly precious."

She threw herself into his arms suddenly. She kissed his lips, and his cheek, and his chin. He returned her hunger, touch by touch, his mouth seeking hers, her throat, her forehead, her lips again.

"You need to go now, Jason. I'm so afraid. That last time, I could feel things holding me, touching me—"

"And I'm not going back until *I* touch you. Just one more time, Vickie, for all time."

She was suddenly lifted into his arms and she stared into his eyes while he carried her surely up the stairs. He knew the right door, and booted it open with his foot. In seconds she was set upon the bed. Fleetingly, she realized it was the first time they had made love on a bed. But comfort was the least of her concerns. She would have made love to Jason anywhere, anytime.

Time was so very precious. She worked upon his buttons while he tugged upon hers. In just seconds their clothes were strewn upon the floor. They knelt upon the bed together, their eyes locked with one another's. Together they reached out, touched one another's shoulders, lovingly, solemnly.

Vickie cried out softly, finding herself borne down to the softness of the mattress, the clean fragrance of the sheets. Next to the coolness of that cotton, his flesh was fire. She stroked and touched him, desperate to memorize the play of his muscles beneath the toned flesh. She ran her fingers down the length of his chest, curling them around the pulse of his flesh. He cried out hoarsely, burying his face against her throat, then kissing her there, rising, starting to kiss, lick and savor the length of her, his tongue trailing through the valley of her breasts, then laving them, one by one, until each nipple was hard and red and peaked and aching. Until the burning streaks of desire begun there reached out through the length of her.

His lips moved from her breasts, trailing over her flesh, teasing her belly, hesitating there, hands beneath her, his caress going lower still. Sweet tremors seized her then, and she reached for him, tugging him back to her, her fingers tense and hungry as they tugged upon his hair.

Her lips hungry as they found his. Savoring his kiss again. She pressed him down beneath her then, taking his lead, trying to cherish every taut inch of him, her kisses traveling over his torso, fingers running lightly over the fine crisp hairs there, her body shimmying even lower against his, until she had taken him in the most intimate of caresses and he raggedly cried out his desire and pleasure. Then, with determined power, he reached for her, brought her beneath him, sunk sweetly inside her.

Moving...

Arms and limbs entwined, they rocked together in a timeless embrace. She couldn't bear to be apart from him, yet he forced her a distance so that he could watch her eyes while the richness of desire and need raced through them both. His movement was rhythmic, slow at first, then more urgent. She arched and writhed, desperate to have more of him.

To remember him for all time.

Then even the pain was lost with the pulse that burst upon them both, the driving, blinding desire to find the ultimate crest of pleasure. Climax seized Vickie first, shooting through her like silver arrows. Seconds later, even as she drifted in its exotic sweetness, she felt the sensual explosion of the man above her, heard his cry, felt the tension of his embrace.

Endless time enwrapped them.

Downward, to earth, they came. To the ragged sound of their own breathing.

To the clean softness of the bed beneath them.

Jason eased his weight down beside her. "Sweet heavens above, I can't leave you."

Vickie closed her eyes tightly. The war would go on without him.

But history might change. And not for the better.

She bit her lip, afraid of the lives she might destroy if she did not make him go.

She started to rise. He pulled her back, silver eyes intense upon hers.

"I love you," she said, and kissed his lips. But she tugged upon his hand, and he released her. He watched her while she dressed.

Then he rose. He, too, reached for his clothing. He took her into his arms. "I even love you more for your strength," he told her softly. "I'm sure I forgive you for it."

"And I'm not sure you *would* forgive me if you stayed."

"You could come with me."

"I would—you know that. If it weren't for Gramps."

"Then I'll go alone now—"

"No! I'm coming with you until the very last step!" she swore forcefully.

He smiled. "No sense arguing with a woman these days. You can't win." He tried to speak lightly. They were both quiet as they left the house. He lifted her up on Max, then leapt up behind her.

They started toward the mountain peak where a thick, chilling mist hung like black smoke in the air and an arbor of trees bowed low in a strange arch. The wind rose, pulling at them, coming from all directions at once. The tempest had never been so wild. She had never felt such a sense of fear.

Vickie gasped suddenly as they neared the archway of trees. There, standing just out of the dark passage was Gramps.

"There's a stubborn old fellow for you!" Jason murmured. "I know where *you* get the streak now."

Vickie cast him a quick glare, and he eased her down from Max, dismounting himself. Vickie raced to Gramps. "How did you get here? What are you doing out of the hospital?"

"Dr. Sam Dooley gave me a clean bill of health, Victoria. He said I could go. I saw a friend in the waiting room and asked for a ride—"

"Wheedled some poor innocent into taking you here!" Vickie charged.

He shrugged. "Found Amos Clinton still down by the Yank encampment, and he lent me that old mule of his over there to get up here."

Vickie glanced past his shoulder. There was no mule there, just a tall buckskin horse.

"Sam told you that you had to be careful—"

"Oh, I'm being careful. I just came to say goodbye to Jason, too."

Jason was there now. Gramps reached out a hand. Jason took it tightly. Their eyes met. "You're a fine fellow, Colonel," Gramps told him.

"Thank you, sir. And so are you."

"You'd better say goodbye yourself, Vickie," Gramps warned her, stepping back. "I've been watching the winds and the trees—the whole damned feeling of this place is changing with the seconds now. The door is closing."

"It's closing quickly," Jason agreed, looking down at Vickie.

She swung around and hugged him. He tried to step back. "Vickie..."

She nodded, and hugged him more tightly to her. He took her shoulders and pressed her away from him at arm's length, looking into the tumult in her eyes. He was going to tell her something. He was going to tell her that he was afraid to tamper with the future, that someday he was supposed to save Robert E. Lee's life, and if Lee were to die, things might be worse still, just as they had been made so very bad by Lincoln's assassination. He wanted to try and explain so many things.

But the words didn't come.

"Oh, God, Vickie!"

He took her back into his arms again and kissed her passionately. The wind was rising to a wild peak, whipping around them, lashing at them with a wicked fury.

His fingers moved tenderly through her hair. "I love you, Vickie, I love you. I love you so very much. Come with me."

A sob caught in her throat. God, yes! She would give anything to do it. She would brave the those moaning, clasping fingers in the tunnel. What did she have before her? More of those years of loneliness. Some special years with Gramps, of course, but then...

She could live a long, long time. Alone.

"Vickie, I love you. I love you."

"I can't. Oh, God, I would, Jason. But Gramps, he can't live with the hardships of your world, Jason. We've seen that—" Her voice broke off on another sob. "Kiss me again. Just once more."

He kissed her. Long and deeply. While the howling gray wind tore around them, she tasted the heat and the fire and the passion within him in that kiss. She felt the searing warmth of the man, his strength, his tenderness, his love.

Then she broke away from him, tears flooding her eyes. She had to let him go. Quickly. Or perhaps cost him his life. "Goodbye, Jason."

He stood stiffly against the wind. Tall and straight, the ultimate officer. Then he turned, and mounted Max, and started into the arbor.

The voice...

Vickie choked down a sob, watching the tempest grip him, toss him. She shuddered, turning back. But suddenly other hands were on her, surprisingly strong hands. She looked up into Gramps's eyes, her own eyes filled with tears.

"What do you think that you're doing, Victoria? Follow him! Quickly, now!"

She shook her head. "I can't leave you—"

"Do I look like a dimwit who can't take care of himself to you? Oh, Vickie, Vickie! I've only so long left, you know."

"Gramps, don't say—"

"What the hell do you think I'm doing here! I had to come to give you a boot through, just in case you didn't see clearly that *you must go*. I'll be fine. It's been a full life, a good life! And yes, I've got a little of it left. Time to argue Liam into the ground. *But I'll be okay*."

"Gramps, I can't—"

"Vickie! Do you want me spending my days half wishing I were dead because I stood in the way of your happiness? Vickie, let me live out what I've got left, happy myself, knowing that you're loved, that you've found your place. Damn you, granddaughter, go!"

She hugged him tightly. "I can't!"

"You can!" He extracted himself from her. "I love you, Vickie. You've been the best part of my life. Now, go. Make a life for yourself. You won't find your young cavalier again. Go with him. Make him a good wife. And if there is ever any way to do it, you let me know that you're all right, Vickie—that damned thing is almost closed. Go now!''

Once again, Gramps gently pushed her from him. Her face was soaked with tears now.

"Go!" he ordered. "You'll both die if you don't move, and the whole thing will have been for nothing."

"I love you," she told him. "I love you so much."

"*It's closing,* Vickie!"

He walked her to the arborway in the trees. The wind was so strong now that they could barely stand.

"Jason! Jason Tarkenton!" Gramps shouted.

Then he gave Vickie a shove.

She hesitated, looking back, her heart breaking. "Go on!" he cried to her. "*I'll be all right!* Happy as a lark, knowing you're being…loved! Move, move quickly!"

She closed her eyes, wondering how she could be in such anguish—and yet suddenly very sure of what to do. Gramps was right. She had found her rightful place, with Jason. She couldn't let him go without her.

The world didn't matter. Then, or now. The things that revolved within it didn't matter. Where was the meaning, the light?

Except for love. Love gave life meaning. *Love* was right.

She ran back to Gramps, throwing her arms around him one more time. "You'll always be with me. In my heart, always."

"And you, too, sweetheart. You, too. God go with you!"

She nodded, and turned and started to run into the arborway. She paused for a moment, terrified.

The trees lashed in the wind all around her, their branches like spidery hands. Clammy, wet. So chilling. She felt that they wanted to close around her, stop her, cast her back. Hold her there in the limbo, the whirlpool of time, neither in the past nor the present.

"Oh, God!" she cried out. "I can't move!"

Faces seemed to whip around her in the clouds. Anguished faces, groaning, crying out. Arms reached out. They were holding her.

The wind! It was the wind, screaming all around her. The space within the arbor was black and circling like some cataclysmic deep-space storm. It was closing quickly. Her hair whipped around her face, blinding her. She could barely see.

"Jason!" She shrieked out his name. There was nothing, nothing!

And then she saw him, a dark shadow upon a dark horse, nothing more for a moment than a dashing silhouette....

"Vickie!" His cry encompassed her. *"Victoria!"* Love and anguish filled his voice.

Then he was before her, reaching down for her, sweeping her up to sit before him atop Max. His lips touched hers so briefly. For they could both feel them now. The hands...holding them. Clinging to them. Trying to keep them from passing through to the other side.

"Hold me! Tightly!" Jason roared. He slammed his heels to Max's haunches. The horse reared, and bolted. Vickie shrieked. The wind made a last tug at her. They were free. While the gray whirlwind tore all around behind them, Jason's gaze met hers with its searing silver, his lips curled into a tender smile, and touched down upon hers.

"We made it. But you shouldn't have come. You risked your life—and you can't go back."

"I couldn't live without you," she whispered.

"Do you think you can live without all those modern

inventions—hot dogs, microwaves, cars…?'' he whispered.

She smiled, leaning back into the crook of his arm. ''You'll have to make it up to me,'' she told him.

''Hmm,'' he murmured thoughtfully. Then his lips were on hers again, hungrily. ''I'll have to work on that, won't I?''

She nodded, still watching his face with wonder. She stroked the strong planes of his cheeks. ''There will be so very much time to work on it together.'' She paused and gazed deeply into his eyes. ''One thing is certain. I love you, Jason.''

''I love you, too. So much. For all time, for eternity.''

He nudged Max. It was incredibly painful to leave Gramps behind.

It was also wonderful to face the future.

The past.

Whichever.

It didn't matter which. She was facing all the days to come with Jason. Love was leading the way.

His fingers curled around hers as they rode away from the wind-tossed trees, out of the gray swirling mist and into a new life together.

Gramps had just seen them. Despite the whipping winds, despite the deadening gray.

Vickie had stood alone for a moment, slim yet strong, facing the whirling tempest. His head had suddenly grown heavy with fear. It had been too late. They wouldn't make it.

But then he had seen the soldier ride out of the thick shadows, and sweep Vickie up, and away. He had seen them, silhouettes of black against the gray. His granddaughter, held so tenderly in those strong arms, her beautiful face cast back.

And the Reb had kissed her. And for a moment, they had been locked there like that.

They had ridden on quickly. And the swirling mist had closed in their wake.

He closed his eyes for a moment. *Let them be happy. God, please let them be happy!* he prayed.

Then he opened his eyes.

The mist was gone. There was nothing there. Just an arbor of old oaks, the branches barely lifted by a breeze. Nothing more.

He'd let her go. What a stupid old fool. But he smiled suddenly.

He would remember that kiss Jason and Vickie had given each other all the remainder of his days. All of them. And he would be happy.

EPILOGUE

Gramps was climbing up the steps of the house when he saw a car pulling into the driveway. He shaded his eyes from the sun with a hand for a moment, then smiled. It was Vickie's friend, the doctor.

"Hello, there, sir!" the young man called out, stepping from the car.

"Dr. Dooley, nice to see you, nice to see you."

Sam Dooley walked across the yard, taking Gramps's hand, shaking it.

"Didn't know doctors were making house calls these days, though, but it's mighty nice."

Sam grinned. "Well, it's not exactly a house call, though it is good to see that you're looking hale and hearty."

"I feel fine," Gramps told him. "You're a great doc."

"I try," Sam said.

"Come on in, since you seem to be in a frame of mind to chat. Have some chili."

"Thanks."

Sam was slow about getting around to what was on his mind. He was seated with a soda and big bowl of chili before he finally asked the obvious.

"So, have you heard from Vickie?"

Gramps drummed his fingers on the table. "Can't say that I have."

"So she really just ran off with that stranger who came to town for the reenactment, huh?"

"The fellow's name was Jason Tarkenton. Said he

came from just past Staunton. I'm not sure where they went, though.''

Sam grinned broadly. "You're an old con man, sir."

Gramps shrugged.

"It's hard to believe that she wouldn't have contacted you by now."

"Maybe it's hard for her to get in touch."

Sam nodded. He set his spoon down. "Good chili."

"Thanks."

"There's nothing you can tell me, huh?"

Gramps arched his eyebrows and Sam grinned.

"You came by to question me? The story is pretty simple and…and an old one, too. Vickie went away because she fell in love. Are you suspicious, Doc? Suspecting foul play?"

"I do know better," Sam said softly. "I know you wouldn't harm a hair on that girl's head, and you'd give hell to anyone who dared to think of it." Sam paused. "But I did happen to see some mutual friends of mine and Vickie's recently. Karen and Steve. Do you know them?"

"The Yankees?" Gramps said.

Dooley nodded. "Well, they also told me the fellow's name. And I wound up doing some research in some of the old records down in Staunton."

"*Old* records? Why, the fellow didn't look so old to me. I'd guess he was in his early thirties."

Sam's grin deepened, his teeth strong and white against the handsome ebony planes of his face. "You're something, Gramps."

"I'm something? Since when did you become a historian?" Gramps asked.

"I went to medical school. I'm accustomed to reading the fine print," Sam said, laughing. "Besides, I didn't come to ask you anything. I came to let you know something.''

He stood up, reached into his jacket pocket, and produced some papers. Gramps saw that they were photocopies of pages from an old record book.

''Go ahead. They're for you.''

Gramps picked up the papers. They were church listings, he realized. He saw the name Tanner at the top of the page, and then read lower, coming to Tarkenton.

Tarkenton, Jason and Victoria. Born June 30, 1863, a son, Joseph John. Born April 15, 1865, a son, Axel James. Born September 18, 1868, a daughter, Jeannie Marie. Born May 20, 1872, a daughter, Anne Elizabeth. Born October 17, 1876, a son, Jeremy James.

The next name down the list was Taylor, Henry. He started over, rereading all the Tarkentons.

Gramps looked up at Sam Dooley.

''Thought you might like to see that. Strange coincidence about the name, isn't it?''

''Mighty strange,'' Gramps agreed. His knees felt a little wavery. Sam was heading for the door now. Gramps started to walk him out.

''Thanks, Dr. Dooley,'' he said on the porch. He extended his liver-spotted hand. ''Thanks. It was mighty kind of you to come by.''

Sam nodded. ''You take care of yourself. If you need anything, call me.''

''And if I can ever do anything for you, sir, you just let me know.''

Sam nodded and folded his long body back into the driver's seat of his car.

Gramps waved, smiling slowly as the car disappeared.

''*Five* of them, Vickie!'' he said aloud, and started to

laugh. "Five of them!" He shook his head. "And not a disposable diaper in sight."

He squeezed his eyes tightly shut. *Well, she must have been—must be?—happy. She's living a full, long life. With a fine man, one who loves her.*

And no matter where you were in time, wasn't that what mattered?

Yes. And it felt damned good to know that he had a whole passel of great-great-grandchildren. Somewhere.

He started to turn to go back into the house, but then his eyes were suddenly drawn by something that seemed to be wedged in the lawn under the old oak tree.

Slowly, curiously, he walked toward it.

There was just a glint of metal. But the metal was attached to something embedded much deeper.

Gramps got down on his knees, and he began to dig. The metal was wedged pretty deep and the digging took some effort. And, after all, he was an old man.

But a persistent old man.

He grew excited as the object began to emerge. A sword. A Confederate cavalry officer's sword. One of the handsomest examples he had ever seen.

Carefully, reverently, he began to wipe the dirt from it. His hands began to shake. He had seen this very sword before.

Only…it was a bit different now.

Right on the blade, near the hilt, it had been engraved. A single tear ran down his cheek. He wiped it away, and he smiled broadly.

"Love you, Gramps. Always, all times. Vickie Tarkenton, September, 1862."

Gramps stood up slowly. He looked to the mountain. "Love you, too, Vickie. Love you, too."

He cradled the old sword to his chest, and walked on into the house.

* * * * *

Dear Reader,

I've always enjoyed gothic mysteries and movies. There is nothing quite so scary as a young, beautiful woman finding herself in a mansion on a hill and encountering things that go bump in the night. And of course, along with the things that go bump, there is always a wildly handsome man with mysterious secrets in his eyes that whisper of a dark torment in his soul.

These are the elements I kept in mind in writing *Mystery Child*. Julie Kingsdon and her young son have come to her dead husband's ancestral home. There she meets Forest Kingsdon, a man who stirs in her a desire she's never known...a man who is somehow tied to the bone-chilling cries that ring through the mansion in the dead of night.

Happy reading!

Carla Cassidy

MYSTERY CHILD
Carla Cassidy

CHAPTER ONE

No lights of welcome lit the long, narrow road that led to the house on the hill. Fog blanketed the valley below; gray, dense clouds completely covered the small town of Kingsdon, Missouri.

Julie Kingsdon edged her car to the shoulder of the narrow road and shut off the engine. Checking to make certain Bobby was still sleeping soundly in the back seat, she got out of the car. Stretching, she tried to unkink the muscles that had tensed up during the last two days of driving.

She took a deep breath and released it slowly, then leaned against the front bumper of the car. She needed to collect her thoughts before advancing the rest of the way up the hill to the house that belonged to her dead husband's brother.

She pulled her sweater more tightly around her, unsure if the chill that danced up her spine was a result of the cool, autumn-evening air or the reality of facing the unknown.

The unknown. Her gaze once again went to Kingsdon Manor. It was an architectural anachronism. Its gray stones and turret rooms belonged to another place, another time, certainly not on a hilltop in southern Missouri.

A rooster weather vane, incongruent with the design of the house, clung to one of the roof steeples, spinning chaotically in the late-evening breeze. The windows yawned darkly, as if ready to swallow anyone who ventured near. Even the golden hues of twilight couldn't chase away the forbidding shadows that surrounded the house.

Julie had driven halfway across the country to get here and had no idea what she would find. The only thing she knew for certain was that she needed to be here. She and her son had nowhere else to go.

With another shiver, she got back into the car, wondering if coming had been a mistake. Perhaps she should have just stayed in New York City, continued the daily struggle to survive.

She gripped the steering wheel in grim determination. No, she'd had to come here. She needed to meet her late husband's brother. It was important that Bobby meet the only relative he had besides her. And in any case, this was Bobby's heritage. She had every right to claim it for him.

She looked over her shoulder, to where her son slept, his arms wrapped tightly around the scraggly stuffed dog that he'd slept with every night for the past seven years. Sweet Bobby. Her heart softened as she gazed at his mahogany hair tousled into disarray, his cheeks ruddy with color. The last year had been so difficult for him, for them both.

Now it was time to go. She started the engine. As she drove up the lane, her heart thudded in frenzied anticipation. What sort of welcome could they expect? She had written several letters to Forest Kingsdon, detailing her desire to come and introduce Bobby to him, but she'd received no reply. Not that she'd really expected any. Forest hadn't come to Jeffrey's funeral, nor had he sent any note of sympathy. Julie didn't know what had caused the rift years ago between Jeffrey and his younger brother, but whatever it was, even death hadn't breached it.

She shoved the memory of her husband out of her mind, thoughts of him spearing through her with a myriad of raw emotions—pain, loss and always the sharp stab of guilt.

Pulling the car up in front of the house, she shut off the engine and stared out the window. It was even more forbidding up close. The fog had made its way up the hill, consuming the first level of the house in ghostly breath. The pale glow from interior lights changed the fog to an eerie yellowish green.

Jeffrey hadn't prepared her for the decayed grandeur of his ancestral home. Nor had he mentioned the utter isolation. Julie opened her door, the misty night air embracing her once again as she slid out of the car. The house sat by itself, surrounded by thick woods. She stood for a moment, listening to the cacophony of insect songs. It was pleasant, almost lulling, and she felt a burst of optimism. Everything was going to be okay, she told herself firmly. It was right that she had come.

Opening the back door, she lifted Bobby in her arms, not surprised when he didn't waken. Instead he curled his little body into the contours of hers and wrapped his legs around her waist. His breathing remained deep, regular in the rhythm of slumber. The child could sleep through an atomic war, she thought with a smile. It wouldn't be long before he'd be too big for her to carry. She breathed in his little-boy scent, her heart once again expanding with love.

She was worried about her son, who'd had difficulty adjusting to life without his father. In the last couple of months he'd been too somber, too quiet, and he'd regressed, relinquishing his seven-year-old independence for the clinging stage he'd gone through when he was younger. The psychologist had suggested that what the boy needed was a sense of connection to something or someone other than Julie. She hoped this visit to Kingsdon Manor would fill the void left by Jeffrey's absence. She wished she had family of her own that could rally around, but there was nobody. Jeffrey and Bobby had been her family, and now Jeffrey was gone.

She walked up the steps onto the large front porch, the weathered wood creaking ominously beneath her weight. She didn't see a doorbell and so knocked on the massive door, the sound echoing in the stillness of the night. She shifted Bobby from one hip to the other, her nerves suddenly raw as she waited for the door to be answered. The optimism that had filled her only moments before seeped away, like helium from a pinpricked balloon.

Maybe this was all a big mistake, Julie thought. Maybe Jeffrey had shut his brother out of his life for a very good reason. Part of her had a sudden urge to turn and run. But she fought the impulse and knocked again on the door, this time more forcefully. She hadn't driven halfway across the United States to turn coward at the last minute. She couldn't have closure, couldn't move forward with her life until she resolved some of the issues Jeffrey's death had left behind. She hadn't realized how little she actually knew about Jeffrey until she'd had to go through his paperwork after his death. And they'd been married for a little over eight years. Despite everything, half of this house belonged to her, as Jeffrey's widow, and Bobby.

As the front door creaked open, she straightened her shoulders with determination. "What do you want?" A churlish masculine voice issued forth from the tall, dark form in the shadowed doorway.

"I'm—I'm here to see Forest Kingsdon." Julie took a step forward, trying not to be intimidated by the broad shoulders, the daunting height, the shrouded features of the man before her.

"What for?" There was no attempt at civility in his brusque voice, and yet there was an odd familiarity in the tone. He flipped on a dim porch light, and as the thin glow fell on his features, she knew she was face-to-face with her husband's brother.

For a brief moment a flash of pain exploded in her as she gazed at him. He looked so like Jeffrey had when she had first met him nine years ago. At that time she'd been full of eagerness, anxious for the intimacy of marriage to chase away her loneliness.

"What do you want?" he repeated, a tinge of impatience in his deep voice.

"I'm Julie, Jeffrey's wife. I wrote to you several times." She hesitated a moment, then continued, "You never answered my letters."

"No, I didn't." No apology. No regret colored his succinct words.

Julie shifted Bobby's weight, and she saw Forest's eyes narrow, as if he was noticing the boy for the first time. He released a weighty sigh and opened the door. "Come in," he said, his voice weary with resignation.

She followed him through a large hallway and into a room where a fire snapped and crackled, producing an inviting barrier against the chill of the night. "You can put him down there," he said, gesturing toward a richly colored brocade sofa.

Julie relinquished the sleeping child to the comfort of the couch, relieved to rest her tired arms. She stood uncertainly, watching as Forest settled into a chair near the fireplace, his gaze absorbed by the flames dancing on the grate.

With the light of the fire shining on his face, she saw

that his initial resemblance to Jeffrey had been merely an illusion. There was a certain likeness, but she remembered Jeffrey's face as being softer, as if a sculptor had practiced on him before perfecting the harsh beauty of the man before her.

Forest Kingsdon's hair was a dark shock hanging well over the collar of his denim shirt. The lower portion of his face was darkly shadowed with a growth of whiskers. Jeffrey had been attractive in a refined, dignified sort of way. But this man was devastating in an uncivilized, primitive fashion. There was a whisper of cruelty in his harsh features, and Julie found herself both repelled by and oddly drawn to him.

"Why are you here? Why have you come?" He didn't look at her, but continued staring at the fire.

She moved over to the wing chair opposite him and sat down. "There are several reasons why I've come," she finally hedged.

He turned and looked at her, his dark eyes reflecting the fire's blaze. There was no softness in his expression, no hint of welcome or acceptance. "Give me one good one."

Julie stiffened at the command in his tone. "As Jeffrey's widow, I inherited half of this house."

He nodded, his lips twisting into a bitter parody of a smile. "Ah, yes. Congratulations." The smile immediately dissipated. He stood up abruptly. "You've had a long journey. I'll take you to the rooms you and the boy can use for the night."

"His name is Bobby," she said pointedly as she stood up. She wasn't sure what she'd expected from Jeffrey's brother, but it certainly wasn't this cold bitterness. She'd hoped to find a home here for themselves. She'd hoped that Forest Kingsdon would be a loving uncle to Bobby and a friend to her.

Tears burned in her eyes and made her realize the extent of her exhaustion. She'd just driven twelve hours, after a restless night in a cheap motel. Surely things would look brighter in the morning after a good night's sleep.

She leaned down and picked up the sleeping child, comforted by his sweet warmth. She and Bobby would be fine...with or without Forest Kingsdon. At least for the time being they had a roof over their heads and half equity in this mausoleum. It wasn't much, but it was a beginning.

She followed Forest up a wide staircase to the second floor. He lead her silently, as if he didn't much care whether she followed him or not. The hallway upstairs was dark, but he moved with the assurance of a cat whose vision grew sharper in the darkness.

He opened a door on his right and flipped on a light switch, illuminating a large bedroom with a canopy bed. "There's a smaller room there where the boy can sleep." He pointed to an adjoining doorway. "And the bathroom is down the hallway on your left." He turned to leave.

"Forest?" His name felt odd coming from her lips. Everything about the scene was odd, like a picture slightly out of focus. He pivoted to face her, his eyes dark and enigmatic. "I hope we get an opportunity to talk...about Jeffrey. There are some things I'd like to know, need to know."

He stared at her for a long moment, then his gaze moved from her to the child sleeping in her arms. His features grew taut and his eyes narrowed once again. Julie felt a shiver of apprehension dance up her spine, and she tightened her grip on Bobby.

"You have a legal right to be here, but I'll be quite honest. I don't want you here, and as far as I'm concerned, the subject of my brother is off-limits. Let the dead rest in peace." He whirled around and disappeared into the darkness of the hallway.

Julie stared after him for a long moment, then shut the door of the bedroom, relieved to find that it locked. She gently placed Bobby on the canopied bed, then stood back and breathed deeply, fighting against the anger that swirled inside her.

Damn him, his behavior was beyond rude! Even though he obviously hadn't been expecting her, that wasn't an excuse for his discourteous conduct. He didn't want her here. He probably expected them to move on in the morning. Well, he'd be disappointed. Julie was here and she wasn't going anywhere, at least not before she got her life back together.

Perhaps he was displeased that she had come to claim her inheritance as Jeffrey's widow. After all, he'd lived here for the past nine years without interference from Jeffrey. Surely he would be more accommodating when he realized Julie wanted nothing from him except some time to stay here and heal, both emotionally and financially.

She let go of the anger and instead focused on her surroundings. It was a pleasant room, with plush navy carpeting and navy-and-cream wallpaper. The dark, wooden furniture was ornate and obviously antique. There was a masculine feel to it, and she wondered whose room it had been when Jeffrey lived here and his parents were alive.

She moved across the floor to the doorway that led to the smaller room. Turning on the light, she gasped with surprise and delight. It was as if the room had been dec-

orated specifically with Bobby in mind. A brown cor-
duroy bedspread covered the single bed and the sports-
motif wallpaper proclaimed it distinctly boy territory.

Julie sank down on the edge of the small bed and
rubbed the center of her forehead, where a headache had
blossomed with potent intensity. Nothing was as she'd
expected, not this house nor her brother-in-law.

Who had slept in this little boy's room? The wallpaper
and furnishings, although not new, didn't look old
enough to have been either Jeffrey's or Forest's.

What had happened that had torn the brothers apart to
such an extent that Forest had no desire to befriend her
or Jeffrey's son? Julie wondered. And what caused the
haunted, tormented look in Forest's eyes? For a moment,
as he'd stared at Bobby, he'd looked just like Jeffrey had
when one of his black moods had descended.

She shivered and went back into the large bedroom,
where Bobby remained sleeping peacefully on the bed.
She would let him stay here with her for the night. He
might be frightened if he awakened in the unfamiliar
room next-door.

It was then she realized she'd left their suitcases in the
car. Oh well, they could make do for tonight, and she
would get their things in the morning.

She pulled off Bobby's shoes and socks, then tucked
him beneath the blankets of the bed, grateful that he wore
comfortable jogging pants instead of jeans.

She kicked off her own jeans, then pulled off her
sweater. The T-shirt beneath would make an adequate,
though short nightgown. She reached beneath the shirt
and unsnapped her bra, then maneuvered the straps down
and pulled it through an armhole. She smiled, remembering how astonished Jeffrey had been the first time
she'd removed her bra in this unconventional way. That

had been early in their marriage, when she'd still believed he could fill all the dark corners of her heart. She hadn't yet known that he was incapable of the kind of emotional closeness, the intimacy she so desired. It had taken her years of marriage to realize he would never be able to give her what she wanted. There was a part of himself he always kept separate from her, a shield that guarded him and didn't allow her inside.

Shoving these painful thoughts aside, she turned out the light, then made her way to the bed. Sliding beneath the covers, she released a deep sigh, her mind filling with visions of Forest Kingsdon. She knew he was thirty-eight years old…six years younger than Jeffrey. She knew his birthday was October 20. She'd gleaned odd little details about him from Jeffrey over their years of marriage, but nothing substantial, nothing to tell her what kind of man he was in his heart.

What she hadn't expected was his overt masculinity, the dark attractiveness that had instantly caused heat to unfurl in her stomach.

She shivered as she remembered that momentary darkness in his eyes as he'd stared at Bobby. She had a sudden feeling that coming here had been a horrible mistake, but there was nothing she could do about it now. She and Bobby were here, and for at least a while, they would just have to make the best of things.

Forest Kingsdon gasped convulsively and swallowed back the yell that clogged his throat. He sat up, his body drenched in sweat. Oh, God. He'd had the nightmare…again. He ran his hands across his face, his heart filled with a bleak horror. He hadn't had one in months, had thought he'd finally left them behind. But this one had been just like all the others, tormenting him, tearing him apart.

Drawing in a deep breath, he threw the blankets aside and got out of bed. Padding to the window, he stared out at the thick woods, his heartbeat slowing to a more natural rhythm.

It was just after midnight, and the fog had thickened, like witches' soup poured over the landscape. He shivered, wishing—demanding—the last remnants of the dream to leave him, but they clung as tenaciously as did the fog to the base of the trees.

He knew why the dream had returned. The presence of Jeffrey's widow and child had stirred the remains of the past, allowed it to rise like death's breath from an open grave. And the past frightened Forest. It frightened him as nothing else could.

They should never have come here.

He leaned his head against the cool panes of the window. He knew from experience that sleep would remain distant for some time.

Julie Kingsdon...Jeffrey's wife. Jeffrey's widow, he reminded himself, pain spearing through him at the thought of his older brother. When he'd first received letters from Julie, telling him of her wish to come here, he'd thought he would discourage her through silence. He'd figured that if he didn't answer her letters, she wouldn't come.

She'd surprised him, first by coming, then by her physical appearance. Forest had expected somebody older, more sophisticated. With her cloud of long brown hair and the sprinkling of freckles on the bridge of her nose, Julie Kingsdon looked little more than a teenager.

And yet he'd sensed a streak of strength in her, a backbone of fortitude that would make forcing her to leave

difficult. But he had to make her go. She *had* to take her
son and leave, run from here as fast as she could. His
dream had been an omen…a forecast of danger. They
weren't safe here.

"Daddy. Daddy!"
The little boy's voice was filled with pain. It cut
through Julie's sleep, pulled her from her dreams. She
awakened and immediately turned toward Bobby. She
swallowed her words of comfort as she saw him sleeping
soundly.

She frowned and sat up, bewildered for a moment. Had
the voice been part of her dream? It had sounded so real,
seemed so vivid. She swung her legs over the side of the
bed and stood up. She walked to the window, where the
moonlight shimmered in, painting the room in streaks of
pale illumination.

The childish voice had been filled with fear, the cry
that of a terrified little boy. If it was a dream, what on
earth had made her conjure up such a thing? She looked
at Bobby once again, wondering if her worry over her
son had somehow manifested itself in her dream world.
It probably had.

She turned away from the window, knowing she
should go back to bed, but she felt too wired for sleep.
Her mouth was cotton dry. She needed a glass of water;
however, she didn't like the thought of wandering around
the strange house in the middle of the night looking for
the kitchen. Forest had said the bathroom was just down
the hallway to the left.

Cautiously, she unlocked the bedroom door and eased
it open. The hallway was pitch-black. The house was
profoundly silent. She ran her hand along the wall to
guide herself. She walked a short distance and her fingers

encountered a doorframe, then the cool brass of a knob. She opened the door and took a single step inside.

She stopped, her breath immediately caught in her chest as she saw Forest standing in the moonlight at the window. He was naked, and there was a primitive, stark beauty in the masculine lines of his back, the muscled strength of his legs. For a moment she was frozen by the sight. He didn't seem to feel her presence, for he stood still.

Although his back was in shadow, there was enough light in the room for her to see the perfect symmetry of his physique. The broad expanse of his shoulders was emphasized by the leanness of his waist and hips. His buttocks were taut and his legs were long and muscular.

Her breath pressed tightly against her rib cage as she stared at his magnificent nakedness. She backed out of the room and silently closed the door, then leaned against the wall and willed her breathing to come naturally.

She closed her eyes, trying to shut away the vision of his masculine beauty, but it seemed burned into her brain cells. His back had been firmly muscled, a dark expanse of flesh that had looked both warm and inviting. She swallowed hard, her mouth achingly dry. Her blood felt thick, hot as it flowed through her veins, and she knew that, as crazy as it was, the sight of Forest had reawakened heated thoughts and hormones long dormant.

She shook her head in an attempt to dispel the mental image. She opened her eyes and scoffed inwardly. She was acting like a sexually deprived woman. She started to move down the hallway, but froze as she heard the distinct sound of a child sobbing. It was louder now, echoing in the darkness of the hallway—a pitiful sound that mournfully wrapped itself around her heart.

She stifled a scream as Forest's door flew open and he

collided with her. He expelled a curse, steadying her with his hands. To her relief, he'd thrown on a pair of jeans, covering the nakedness that had so disturbed her moments before. However, she was all too aware of his chest, broad and naked save for the curling dark hair that matted the center, then trailed downward in a narrow path that disappeared into the low waist of his jeans.

He released her shoulders and reached back to flip on the bedroom light. "What in the hell are you doing out here wandering around?" he asked, his face a tight mask of anger.

"I...I heard something," she said. As his gaze traveled the length of her, she was embarrassingly conscious of the shortness of her T-shirt, the way the thin material stretched taut across her breasts. She folded her arms protectively.

"And what did you hear?" he asked, his eyes dark and enigmatic as they focused once again on her face.

"I heard someone crying...a little boy." She flushed, realizing how ridiculous it sounded.

His eyes flared in something like surprise and he grabbed hold of her arm, his grip hot, feeling almost fevered. "What exactly did you hear?"

He stood too close to her, his body radiating heat, his eyes emanating a near madness that frightened her. "I— I heard a boy crying for his daddy. It woke me up."

"Perhaps it was a dream." He spoke the words flatly, as if he didn't really expect her to believe them.

"That's what I thought at first, but I heard it again... just a minute ago. A little boy sobbing." A chill shivered up her back, and she twisted out of his grip and stepped away from him. "You heard it, too. Didn't you?" She stared at him. "Is that what brought you out of your room?"

He hesitated, then nodded. "I thought it might be your boy. I thought perhaps he'd woken up and was wandering around the house in the dark, afraid."

She shook her head. "Bobby is sound asleep." She licked her lips nervously, wishing he would step back from her. His nearness was disturbing. "Who is it? Do you have a child?"

A wave of bitterness suffused his face, and his eyes, haunted with shadows, grew darker. "No. There's no child here except your son."

"Then whom did I hear?" she asked softly.

A smile twisted his lips, a horrible, bloodless smile that caused Julie to take another step backward. "You just got your introduction to the ghost of Kingsdon Hill. Welcome to hell."

CHAPTER TWO

"Mom?" One of Julie's eyelids was pulled open by a little finger. "Are you awake? Mom?" She groaned, still unaccustomed to this method of greeting a new day. "Mom, is this Uncle Forest's house?"

Bobby's question drove the last of her sleep away as she remembered the strange events of the night before. She sat up and shoved her hair out of her eyes, smiling at the little boy sprawled on his stomach next to her.

"Good morning, champ," she said, reaching out to smooth a lock of his dark hair away from his forehead. "Yes, this is your uncle Forest's house. You were sound asleep when we arrived last night."

Julie looked around, surprised to see their suitcases lined up just inside the door. She frowned. How had they gotten there? It was obvious Forest had retrieved them from the car, but when had he put them in here?

"Bobby, your bedroom is through that doorway." Julie pointed to the smaller, connecting room. "Why don't you take your suitcase and unpack your things?"

"Okay." He bounded from the bed with the enthusiastic energy of a seven-year-old. It was an encouraging change from his recent listlessness. He grabbed his suitcase and lugged it across the floor and into the next bedroom. Julie smiled when she heard his exclamation of delight as he entered the little room. It sounded good. He'd been too sober, too quiet since Jeffrey's accident and death.

She flopped back on the bed, her mind whirling with

the events of the night before. After making his startling announcement about the ghost of Kingsdon Hill, Forest had turned and gone back into his room, leaving her stunned and frightened in the dark hallway.

With the light of morning streaming through the windows, chasing away the lingering shadows of night, his words about a ghost seemed ridiculous. More than likely what she had heard was Bobby. It wouldn't be the first time the little boy had moaned or cried out in his sleep.

She stretched, feeling surprisingly rested despite the interruption of her sleep in the middle of the night. She was suddenly anxious to get up and explore the house—acquaint herself with the place that had been Jeffrey's home.

It was nearly an hour later when she and Bobby made their way down the wide staircase, both showered and hungry. They followed the scent of fresh-brewed coffee and fried bacon through the living room and into a large kitchen, where a slender old woman stood at the stove with her back to them.

"Good morning," Julie said.

The woman whirled around, her wrinkled face wreathed in a huge smile. "Ah, there you are! Forest told me we had guests." She moved closer to Bobby and bent down, her smile warm and welcoming. "My, you're the spitting image of your father."

"You knew my daddy?" Bobby asked in surprise.

"Indeed I did. I'm Lottie Currothers, and I raised your father from the time he was a baby, spanked his butt more times than I care to admit."

Bobby smiled shyly, and Julie realized that perhaps this woman held the answers to the thousands of questions that plagued her.

"Here, sit down." She gestured to a round oak table

where two place settings awaited them. "If you're anything like your father was, you'll eat at least a dozen of my hotcakes." She placed a plate of golden pancakes on the table, then looked at them both expectantly. "Eat," she commanded.

Julie helped Bobby fill his plate and pour syrup, watching as the old woman busied herself at the stove. "You've been here a long time, Mrs. Currothers?" she asked.

"Please, call me Lottie. Everyone does." She poured Julie a cup of coffee, then joined them at the table. "I lived here for thirty years...until Jeffrey left. In the last ten years I've come in and done the cooking and a little housework, although Forest is pretty self-reliant."

"I'm sure he is," Julie replied dryly, thinking of Jeffrey's brother. "Where is Forest this morning?"

"He's a very early riser. He already had his breakfast and left for his morning walk." Lottie turned her attention to Bobby, who was in the process of polishing off his pancakes. "That's what I like to see, a boy with a healthy appetite."

"These pancakes are good," Bobby said, a glob of syrup dripping from his chin. Julie used her napkin to wipe it off, smiling when he squirmed away from her and resumed eating.

"If you like those, wait until you get a taste of my homemade cinnamon rolls. They were always your daddy's favorite," Lottie said.

"Then they'll be my favorite, too!" Bobby proclaimed. For a moment his bottom lip quivered ominously, and Julie feared tears for the loss of his father would follow. However, he looked at Lottie, drew in a deep breath and smiled bravely at his mother, then focused his attention back on the last of his pancakes.

Julie realized the questions she wanted to ask the older woman about Jeffrey would have to be posed later, at a time when Bobby wasn't present. His grief over his father's tragic death was still too raw, too painful.

"I didn't get to see much last night when we arrived, but from what I did see, this is a marvelous house," Julie said to Lottie.

The old woman's brown eyes sparkled and she nodded, a soft smile easing the deep wrinkles on her face. "Ah, yes, it's a wonderful house. It was built almost a hundred years ago by Gabriel Kingsdon." She looked at Bobby and her smile deepened. "That would have been your great-grandfather. They say he was a brilliant, ambitious man. He came here and built this house. He opened a sawmill down in the valley. The town of Kingsdon grew up around the mill."

"Wow," Bobby said, obviously impressed that there was a town named after not only his great-grand-father, but himself as well. Julie knew at that moment that this trip had been worthwhile. Bobby needed to know his roots, and she had none of her own to offer him. "Can we go see the sawmill, Mom?" he asked, showing the boyish eagerness that had been sadly lacking in recent months.

"I don't know, honey. We'll see."

"Next week there's the fall festival, a big celebration down at the mill. You'll want to go to that. Everyone attends," Lottie said. Again her gaze fell on Bobby. "There's all kinds of races and contests for kids, and enough food to feed the people in four counties."

"Ah, Mom, we've got to go to that," Bobby exclaimed.

"We'll see, Bobby," Julie said again absently. "Whatever made Jeffrey leave all this behind and move to New York City?" she asked.

The friendly sparkle in Lottie's eyes was immediately doused. "I wouldn't know nothing about that," she said stiffly as she turned back to the stove.

A ripple of unease crawled up Julie's spine.

"Mom?" Bobby looked at her uncertainly, as if he sensed her disquiet.

She patted his arm and smiled reassuringly. "When did you say this festival was?"

"Next Saturday." Lottie turned back around and smiled, although her face had a remoteness that hadn't been there moments ago. "It's a whole day of fun for young and old alike."

"We gotta go, Mom."

"Go where?" Forest Kingsdon appeared in the doorway.

Both Julie and Bobby jumped at the unexpected sound of the deep voice. "Land's sakes," Lottie exclaimed with a hand over her heart. "I ought to box your ears, sneaking up on us like that." She began clearing the dishes from the table. Julie rose automatically to help. "Just sit yourself back down," Lottie protested firmly. "I reckon if I can cook it, I can clean it up." Julie hesitated with her plate in her hand, then finally sat again.

Forest walked across the kitchen, filling the room with his sheer masculinity. He was dressed in a pair of worn jeans and a red flannel shirt that emphasized the width of his shoulders. In the bright sunshine that filled the kitchen, Julie wondered how she'd thought for a single moment that he looked anything like Jeffrey. Forest was bigger, more vital, more primal than Jeffrey had ever been.

Forest poured himself a cup of coffee, then leaned

against the cabinet, a smile curling one corner of his mouth. "Lottie is quite territorial about her kitchen," he observed.

Julie said nothing, thinking that the old woman had probably learned about being territorial from him. He'd certainly been unfriendly last night about sharing his domain. For an instant her mind filled with a vision of him standing naked before his bedroom window. Heat swept into her cheeks and she cleared her throat self-consciously. "Lottie was just telling us some of the history of the house," she said. "From what I saw last night, it's quite a beautiful place."

"Are you my uncle?" Bobby asked, apparently unable to contain his curiosity as he stared up at the tall man.

"I suppose I am." He sipped his coffee. His gaze landed on Bobby, then immediately moved back to Julie. "You're welcome to explore the house. However, I'd prefer that you stay away from the basement. That's my workroom, and it wouldn't be safe for the boy."

"His name is Bobby," Julie returned tightly.

He drained his coffee and handed the cup to Lottie. "I've got to get to the mill." He strode out of the kitchen.

Julie immediately jumped up. "You stay here and finish your milk," she said to Bobby. Then she followed Forest, catching up with him as he reached the wide staircase. "Forest?"

He turned and stared at her. He'd thought she'd looked young the night before, but this morning in the full sunshine he noted the lines that radiated out from the corners of her eyes, lines that proclaimed her to be older...and a woman who smiled often. However, she wasn't smiling now. Her lips were compressed in a tight line and her brown eyes sparked with yellow flecks of angry fire.

"You asked me last night to give you one good reason

why I'd come here. That boy in there is my good reason." Her words were clipped, filled with suppressed emotion and an unconcealed dislike. "Nine months ago he lost his father in a tragic car accident. He's frightened and lonely, and right now he needs more than I can give him. I don't know what happened years ago between you and Jeffrey, but that doesn't matter. I don't want your money. I'm not here to interfere in your life. We just need some time, and Bobby needs a connection to his father's brother. He desperately needs you."

Each one of her words bit into him like the ferocious teeth of a vicious dog, reminding him of another time, another boy…a boy whose cries now tormented his dreams, twisted his soul, haunted this house. Forest knew Julie was attempting to appeal to his heart. What she didn't know was that he had no heart. Inside his chest was a ball of bitterness that ate at him day and night, and a misery of guilt that weighed him down like a mountain.

He looked down at her, reluctantly admiring the steely strength in her eyes, the determination that stiffened her shoulders. "I'm sorry. I have nothing to give to him." Without waiting for her to speak again, he turned and went upstairs.

Minutes later he left the house, walking out into the cool morning air and heading for the path that led through the woods, eventually winding its way to the back entrance of the sawmill.

As he walked along the dirt trail, the sky disappeared behind huge tree limbs and leafy canopies. A chill permeated him, the natural crispness of the forest in autumn, the unnatural cold that had been with him for ten long years. He could have driven his car to the mill, but walking through the woods was his penance, a self-imposed punishment for past transgressions.

Had he been a stronger man, he would have taken his own life long ago, ended the nightmares, the inner turmoil that afflicted him. However, part of him would not allow such an escape. Death would be too easy, would be far too good for him.

As always when he reached a certain fallen tree, he paused and allowed his mind to skip back to a distant time. He sat down on the thick trunk and covered his face with his hands.

The woods suddenly came alive with the sounds of boyish laughter, childish mirth that momentarily filled Forest's soul. "Come find me! I'm hiding!" The child's voice expanded in his head, followed by giggles that drew an answering smile to his lips. He allowed the auditory memory to play through him, like a healing balm on deep wounds.

A bird overhead crowed raucously and the memory faded, leaving him empty, bereft. He groaned and tore his hands from his face, looking around wildly, as if he could make the memory become reality by sheer willpower alone. But of course, he couldn't.

"Come on, Mom," Bobby clambered up the narrow stairs that led to the third floor of the old house.

"Bobby, wait up, I don't think we should—"

"Aw, Mom, you heard Uncle Forest. He said we could explore." Bobby paused and turned to look at her impatiently. "He said we shouldn't go down to his workroom, but he didn't say nothing about upstairs."

"Anything." Julie automatically corrected her son, who sighed in exasperation.

"Whatever," he answered. He danced from one foot to the other, waiting for her to catch up with him.

They had been exploring the house most of the day.

After Forest had left for the mill, Julie had silently seethed a good part of the morning. Lottie's sudden unfriendliness when she'd asked about Jeffrey and Forest's coldness had left her confused and upset.

She and Bobby had finished their unpacking, then had begun the adventure of investigating the nooks and crannies of the house. It had taken them the entire morning just to explore the first floor, which included the large living room, the kitchen, a library, a formal dining room and a small office. They'd eaten lunch, then moved to the second floor, where they'd discovered six bedrooms and three baths. It was nearing suppertime now, and Bobby was determined that they finish their exploration of the third floor before it was time to eat. Julie was pleased by his curiosity, the enthusiasm he seemed to draw from merely being in these surroundings.

"Wow, look at all of this stuff," Bobby exclaimed when he opened the door at the top of the stairs and walked into a large room. Shrouded furniture, antique trunks, unmarked boxes—remnants of lifetimes were contained here. Julie batted at a cobweb as she followed her son, who blazed a trail through the room, stopping here and there to exclaim over a particular item.

She climbed over a stack of boxes and found Bobby staring at his reflection in an antique mirror, the glass distorted and warped. "See how funny I look?" he said with a giggle, pointing to the squat, fat image before him. His giggles increased when she stood next to him.

A moment later he was off again, exploring further. His footsteps stirred the fine layer of dust and sent it floating in the air.

"Come on, Bobby," Julie said, stifling a cough. "It's too dusty up here." She walked back toward the doorway.

"Mom, come and look at this."

"Bobby, I don't think we should be up here," she said. There was something sad about this room of boxes and castoffs. She wondered if any of Jeffrey's things were here. When he had left this house, had the items he'd left behind been boxed up and relegated to dust and cobwebs? A chill suddenly touched her as she realized the attic held a definite unnatural iciness. "Come on, Bobby."

"Mom, please! Just come and look at this. You gotta see it!" There was awe in Bobby's voice, and with a sigh, Julie wove her way to where he stood. Before him was a rocking horse. Not an ordinary rocking horse. This one was quite large, and obviously hand carved. It was breathtaking. A wild stallion with flaring nostrils and powerful haunches, it looked as if it might snort and bolt across the room at any moment.

"Oh, it's beautiful," Julie breathed softly. She ran her hand lightly across the flowing wooden mane, her fingers disturbing the sheen of dust.

"Who do you think it belongs to?" Bobby asked.

"I don't know. Perhaps it was your uncle's, or your father's." It was impossible to tell the age of the piece. It might have been a hundred years old, or it could have been carved more recently. The dust that coated it was the only visible sign of age.

"You think Uncle Forest would let me use it?" Bobby asked.

"You're too old for rocking horses," Julie said, guiding him away from the horse and back toward the stairs.

"Not that one. Did you see how big it was?"

"Ah, there you are." Lottie greeted them as they descended the staircase. "I thought you might like to know supper will be ready in about fifteen minutes."

"Oh, thank you, Lottie. We'll wash up and be right down." Julie hesitated, noticing the necklace around the older woman's neck. "What a beautiful piece of jewelry," she said as she stepped forward to get a closer look.

"I've had it for years and years," Lottie said, holding out the filigreed-gold heart. "It used to have a heart-shaped ruby hanging from the bottom, but it fell off somewhere years ago. I never found it."

"That's a shame, but it's still a beautiful necklace." Julie touched Bobby's shoulder. "Come on, sport. Let's go wash the dust off before we go downstairs to eat."

"You might use the bathroom at the far end of the hall on the right. Forest came in just a few minutes ago and he always heads right to the shower," Lottie said.

Julie thanked her for the warning and then led Bobby down the hallway. Thank goodness Lottie had told her Forest was home. All she needed was to walk in on the man while he was in the shower. One unexpected encounter with his naked body had been quite enough.

Minutes later, they went down to the kitchen, where Lottie was busy setting platters of hot food on the table. "Sit down, sit down," she instructed them. "Forest should be here in just a minute."

"Hmm, everything looks wonderful," Julie said, sliding into the chair the housekeeper indicated.

"Old Mr. Kingsdon used to say that in another life I must have been head cook for the gods," Lottie replied proudly.

"You mean Forest and Jeffrey's father?" Julie asked.

Lottie nodded. "Richard Kingsdon." Her eyes dimmed with sadness. "He died too young."

"Who?" Forest stepped into the kitchen, his body almost vibrating with tension as he looked first at Lottie, then at Julie.

"Your daddy," Lottie replied, and Forest visibly relaxed.

"How did he die?" Julie asked.

"There was an accident at the mill." Forest walked over to the table and held out a book to Julie. "I found this at the mill today and thought the boy might like to look through it. It's the history of the town of Kingsdon and the family."

"Thank you," Julie said, surprised and touched at the gesture. Perhaps there was some hope here after all, she thought. As Forest took the seat next to her, she was vividly aware of his scent, the fresh smell of the timberland mingling with the clean odor of minty soap.

For the next few minutes they filled their plates and ate in silence. Bobby's wide-eyed gaze went from his food to his uncle, and Julie knew her son was intimidated by Forest's forbidding ambience. Julie could relate to his feelings. In truth, she was rather intimidated by the tall, dark man with the deep, haunted eyes herself.

He didn't offer any conversation, but gave his full attention to his food. With his eyes focused on his plate, she took the opportunity to note the sinful length of his black lashes, the angular harshness of his jaw, the sensual fullness of his lower lip.

He looked up suddenly, his gaze locking with hers. The corner of his mouth curved upward in a mocking smile, letting her know he was aware of her intense perusal. She flushed and broke the connection, staring back down at her own plate.

What was wrong with her? Why was she so drawn to him? What was it about him that made her so physically aware of him? It had been nine long months since Jef-

frey's death, and for the year before that the physical side
of their marriage had been nonexistent. As always when
she thought of Jeffrey, an arrow of guilt pierced through
her and she consciously shoved away thoughts of him.

"Did you have a good day today?" she asked Forest,
determined to have a normal conversation with the silent
man.

He looked at her in surprise, as if her question was
completely alien to him. "Yeah, fine." He hesitated a
moment, then added. "What about you?"

"We explored the whole house. Don't worry, we
steered clear of the basement," she replied.

"We found a really cool rocking horse in a room upstairs," Bobby blurted out.

"Bobby," Julie admonished her son. "Eat your green
beans."

Bobby lowered his head, obviously disappointed at his
mother's intervention in what had been most likely going
to be an impassioned plea for the wooden horse.

The meal ended in silence, then Forest excused himself
and disappeared. Julie sat waiting while Bobby finished
eating.

"What that man needs is a wife and children of his
own," Lottie observed as she cleared away Forest's plate.
"He's lived here too long by himself."

"He's never been married?" Julie asked.

Lottie shook her head. "I've told him time and time
again he should be filling this place with little children
of his own. But he doesn't listen to me. Forest doesn't
listen to anyone." She pressed her lips together, as if
regretting what she'd said.

Julie had no problem believing that. Forest definitely
seemed to be a man who lived by his own rules.

"Mom, I'm stuffed," Bobby said, patting his slender tummy with a contented sigh.

"Okay, you did a pretty good job cleaning your plate." For a moment Julie stared at her son, her mind whirling. She had to decide what they were going to do. If they were going to remain here, she needed to get him into school as soon as possible. Between packing and traveling, he'd missed a week of second grade. She didn't want him falling too far behind. Sometime this evening she needed to sit down and talk to Forest about her plans.

"What's the matter? What are you staring at? Do I have a glob of mashed potatoes on my nose or something?" Bobby asked, making Julie realize she'd been gazing intently at him.

"Nope, no mashed potatoes." She grinned at him. "I was just thinking that you look like a kid who needs a good beating at checkers."

"Ha, fat chance I'll take a beating!"

As mother and son scooted away from the table, Julie smiled at Lottie. "Thank you for a lovely dinner," she said.

Lottie waved her hands in dismissal. "Don't thank me. It's my job."

"Well, it was all delicious," Julie added, then she and Bobby went upstairs to their rooms. "You go get the checkerboard and we'll play in here on the floor," she said.

Bobby zoomed toward his bedroom, stopping in the doorway. "Wow!" he exclaimed.

Julie joined him there, shocked to see the wooden rocking horse standing in the corner by the window. Forest must have carried it down. "Why don't you get a damp washcloth from the bathroom so we can wipe the dust off him?"

"All right!" Bobby raced away in the direction of the bathroom. He returned a moment later with the requested washcloth. The game of checkers was forgotten as the two worked to clean the rich wood. Again Julie marveled at the workmanship of the piece, the exquisite attention to detail. Bobby's face flushed with excitement as he climbed up on the gleaming horse's back. As he rocked, the horse creaked rhythmically, a dull thump following each creak.

"Do I look like a cowboy?" Bobby asked.

Julie laughed. "Like a rootin' tootin' rodeo rider," she agreed, knowing that until the novelty wore off, the horse would be a big addition to Bobby's games of make-believe.

The evening passed quickly, consumed with a dozen games of checkers interspersed with Bobby "riding the range." By nine o'clock, the excitement of the day had worn out the little boy. Julie tucked him into bed, then went in search of Forest.

She found him in the living room, in the chair in front of the fire where he had sat the night before. For a moment she stood in the doorway, hesitant to disturb his obvious introspection. However, he must have sensed her presence. He turned and looked at her, his eyes momentarily revealing a pain beyond enduring, a torment too deep to bear. It was there only a moment, then gone, shuttered beneath a mocking smile. "Something you need?" he asked.

"I'd like to talk to you." She entered the room and sat in the chair across from him. "First of all, thank you...for letting Bobby use the horse."

He shrugged. "It was just sitting upstairs gathering dust." He focused his gaze back on the dancing flames in the stone fireplace. "It was made to be ridden."

"I appreciate your letting Bobby enjoy it." She sat for a moment. "I'm assuming you've resigned yourself to the fact that we're going to be here for a while?"

He looked at her darkly. "Do I have a choice?"

"No." She sighed and folded her hands together in her lap. "Forest, I know you don't want us here. But I have to be brutally honest." She felt a flush sweep into her cheeks. "We have nowhere else to go. We're broke, and we need to stay here long enough to get back on our feet."

"How long?" he asked.

She shrugged. "I don't know. A couple of months. We'd stay out of your way. Bobby would go to school, and I'll get a job. Within a couple of months we should be able to scrape together enough money to leave and start again someplace else."

"Jeffrey left you broke?" There was little surprise in Forest's voice. He shook his head and sighed ruefully. "Jeffrey never had a head for finances."

"We lived quite well. I had no idea what a horrible state our finances were in until his death. Jeffrey took care of those things—" Julie broke off, for a moment remembering the horror of having their home sold out from under them, their second car repossessed, even most of their furniture taken away by collectors who couldn't be paid. It had been a nightmare. "Bobby and I tried to hang on, but I realized all we had left was his inheritance here, and even that isn't worth anything as far as cash flow goes."

Forest leaned back in his chair and closed his eyes, one hand rising to rub his forehead. "You can't make us leave," Julie added with a touch of bravado. "We have a legal right to be here."

He opened his eyes and stared at her, his gaze moving

slowly, insolently down the length of her. She felt the heat from his eyes and couldn't control the flush that warmed her cheeks. "You're right," he said. "I can't force you to leave. But I think you'll find Kingsdon Manor an inhospitable place."

"Certainly no more inhospitable than you are," she said with a touch of dry humor, perversely wanting to get a rise out of him, a flicker of emotion of any kind.

He laughed, showing a flash of pearl white teeth, and Julie felt her breath catch in her throat as she saw how attractive he looked with a genuine smile curving his lips. "I have a feeling with or without Kingsdon Manor you'd be fine."

"Probably, but Bobby needs to be here right now. He and Jeffrey were very close. He needs to see where his father grew up, needs this connection." Julie stared into the fire, remembering the horror of Jeffrey's death. There was a part of her that felt so guilty...guilty because in some small corner of her heart, his death had almost been a relief. Knowing how important it was for a boy to be with his father, she would have never divorced Jeffrey, even though their marriage wasn't an especially happy one. She'd believed in the sanctity of family and would have done nothing to break hers apart. Fate had done that for her.

"So, what kind of a job are you going to try to find?" Forest asked, pulling her from her painful thoughts.

She shrugged. "Whatever there is. I don't have many skills. I was in college when I met Jeffrey and he never wanted me to work."

"There aren't many opportunities for work in Kingsdon."

"I'll find something," she said with an assurance she didn't feel. She stared into the fire for a long moment, then looked at him curiously. "Jeffrey didn't talk much about his life here. He didn't talk much about you. What happened between the two of you?"

Again his mocking dark eyes swept over her. "I'll open up this house to you, Julie. But leave the past alone. What happened between me and my brother is really none of your business." He stood up. "Good night." Without a backward glance, he left her alone to the warmth of the fire and the questions that remained unanswered.

None of her business? He was wrong about that. The past that had shaped Jeffrey, caused his dark depressions and the emotional distance and disturbances that had made their marriage fall apart, was very much her business.

At least Forest seemed somewhat resigned to the fact that she and Bobby would be here for a while. First thing in the morning she would check into enrolling Bobby in the local school, then she would start the torturous task of job hunting.

She stifled a yawn with the back of one hand and decided to go to bed. Entertaining Bobby all day had taken its toll and a good night's sleep sounded blissful.

The minute she turned on the light in her bedroom, she heard the familiar creak and groan of the rocking horse. "Bobby," she said sharply as she strode across the room. "You should have been asleep an hour ago." She flipped on his light and stared at her son, sound asleep in his bed. In the corner by the window the rocking horse careened wildly back and forth, as if it were being ridden by a phantom cowboy.

CHAPTER THREE

"Come on, Bobby, you don't want to be late for your first day of school." Julie verbally prodded her son, who had been in his room for the past ten minutes, supposedly putting on his shoes. The early morning sunshine streaked in through the window, promising another beautiful day. Bobby giggled and said something too low for her to hear, then giggled again.

"Bobby?" Julie pulled the brush through her hair a final time, then went into the smaller room to see what her son found so entertaining. He sat cross-legged on the floor, looking at the empty chair next to the bed.

"Oh, it's cold in here. Do you have the window open?" He didn't answer for a moment. "Bobby?"

He started and smiled at her. "No, the window isn't open."

She looked at him curiously. "Are you ready to go?"

"I'm guess I'm ready." He stood up reluctantly, his smile gone.

Julie knew the emotions going through him and gave him a quick, reassuring hug. "You wait and see, it won't be so bad. You'll like the new school and you'll make lots of new friends today." She gave his thick hair a final combing with her fingertips. "Come on, we'd better go if we don't want you to be late."

"I don't care if I am," he replied.

"Well, I do," Julie answered. Before they left the room, she opened the curtains, hoping the sun shining in would chase away the chill.

Moments later they were in the car and driving toward Kingsdon Elementary School. As they entered the small community of Kingsdon, Julie looked around with interest.

It was a pleasant little town nestled against the foot of the hills. Brilliant autumn hues lent spectacular color to the tree-lined streets and manicured lawns. They passed the sawmill and advanced to Main Street.

Kingsdon's business district was laid out around the town square, a large park that had the county courthouse in the center. A sign at the entrance to the park announced the fall festival that weekend.

"Mom?" Bobby looked at her expectantly as she pulled up in front of the brick school building.

"What?" Julie parked the car and turned off the engine, then faced her son.

"Uncle Forest doesn't like me much, does he?"

Surprise winged through her at his words. "Oh, honey, I don't think it's that your uncle Forest doesn't like you..." She struggled for an explanation of Forest's distance, realizing she simply didn't have one, especially not one a little boy would understand. "Maybe it's just that he's not accustomed to having a kid around."

"I think he's sad," Bobby replied.

Again Julie was surprised. Sad? Perhaps. Certainly she'd caught a glimpse of deep shadows in Forest's eyes, shadows that seemed to radiate up from his heart, his soul. She shoved away thoughts of Forest and smiled at her son. "I'll tell you what would be sad...if we sat here in the car and talked for so long that you were late." She opened her door. "Come on, sport."

It took nearly half an hour to get Bobby squared away in his new second-grade class. She signed the papers that would allow his school in New York to transfer his records and discovered that, unlike the bus service in a bigger district, the school bus would, starting the next day, pick Bobby up and drop him off at his front door.

With him taken care of, Julie turned her energy to the task of job hunting. She drove back to the city square and found a parking place, then looked around, surveying the stores and offices that made up the business district.

She looked at her wristwatch, realizing it was still too early for most of the places to open. Instead of driving back up the hill to the house, she spied a café and decided to have a cup of coffee while she waited.

Pushing open the door to the café, she stepped inside and was instantly embraced by warm, moist air and the scent of cholesterol-laden cooking. It smelled wonderful. The pleasant smile on her lips wavered as she realized everyone in the place was looking at her. It was as if the whole scene in front of her was frozen, and the silence was deafening. She had the distinct feeling conversations had stopped midsentence the moment she'd walked in the door.

"Order up!" a voice yelled from the back, and that broke the curious spell, although Julie felt furtive glances directed at her as she slid onto a stool at the counter. She smiled uncertainly at a table of burly men who sat together toward the back of the café.

The waitress, a gray-haired, plump woman, approached her with a friendly smile. "Morning," she said as she handed Julie a menu.

"Good morning. Just coffee, please," Julie said, giving her back the menu.

The name tag the woman wore read Betty. "So, how you finding things up on the hill?" she asked as she poured the coffee.

"Fine," Julie replied, unable to hide her surprise.

Betty grinned. "We don't get many strangers in town. Heard Jeffrey's widow was staying up at Kingsdon Hill. I figure that's you."

Julie nodded, feeling the curious prickle on the back of her neck that told her she was still an object of interest for the others in the café. "I'm looking for a job. Do you know of anyone who needs any help?"

Betty leaned against the counter and shook her head. "Nope. Other than the mill, there aren't a whole lot of jobs to be had here."

"It seems like a nice little town."

Betty poured another cup of coffee. "It's all right, I suppose. We don't get a lot of new folks moving in. Most find us too small, too provincial, too gossipy for their liking."

She wiped a dribble of coffee from the pristine countertop. "I heard through the grapevine you've got a little boy."

Julie nodded. "Bobby. I just got him enrolled in the elementary school."

Betty leaned across the counter, so close that Julie could smell the rose scent of her perfume. "You keep an eye on that boy of yours, you hear?"

Something in her voice, a whispered urgency, caused Julie's heart to lurch in response. "What do you mean?"

"Betty?" A squat, chubby bald man stepped out from the kitchen area. "I'm not paying you to gossip, I'm paying you to work." He frowned at the waitress, then at Julie.

"You watch that boy of yours," Betty warned again, then carried the coffee to the table of men in the back.

Again an unnatural silence gripped the occupants of the café and as Julie heard the sound of the door swinging open, she turned to see Forest walking in. His eyes flared in surprise at the sight of her.

"Morning, Forest," Betty said as she set a mug on the counter next to where Julie sat.

"Betty," he returned, and he nodded at the men at the back table. Julie was acutely aware of him as he eased himself onto the counter stool next to hers. He usurped all the space, his firmly muscled leg pressing warmly against her own.

His scent surrounded her—the wild smell of timber, the clean scent of fresh wood shavings and sawdust. It was a pleasant, intensely masculine smell, one she found extremely attractive.

She wanted to move her leg away from his, but didn't want him to think he made her uncomfortable. Besides, she didn't find the intimate contact uncomfortable, she found it decidedly provocative.

She hadn't seen him that morning. He'd left before she and Bobby had gone down to breakfast. She now turned to him, as always noting the aura of darkness that seemed to cling to him no matter what he wore, no matter what his expression. "You come here often?" she asked, more to begin a conversation than for any other reason.

"Every morning for my coffee break." His large hands curled around his coffee cup. He fixed his gaze on it, as if ignoring her would make her go away.

"I decided to come in for a quick cup of coffee before I start job hunting." She willed him to look at her, converse with her. "You are the most taciturn man I think I've ever met," she finally exclaimed irritably. "You can't even make a stab at the pretense of sociable conversation."

He turned on his stool, the movement causing his leg to press more forcefully again her own. He eyed her, his dark brows raised mockingly. "Nice weather we're having, isn't it?"

"Yes, it is," she answered easily, as if she didn't notice the sarcasm in his voice and didn't want to wring his thickly muscled neck. "I hope it stays nice for the fall festival this weekend."

"It's supposed to rain," he said, turning back and staring into his cup.

"Ah well, a little rain won't keep Bobby and me away. I'm anxious to meet all the people Jeffrey grew up with and learn a little about his past." She wanted to say that she sensed secrets here—secrets about Jeffrey and what had driven him away from Kingsdon Hill. She'd sensed secrets in Lottie's eyes, too, and again in Betty's strange words.

If possible, Forest's countenance darkened, but he didn't say anything. Instead he turned on his stool and nodded again to the men at the table in the back.

"I'm fixing twelve of my famous rhubarb pies for the festival," Betty said.

"Rhubarb pie. That sounds wonderful," Julie observed.

"You ain't tasted *Betty's* rhubarb pie," a burly man at the back table replied teasingly.

Betty snorted. "It wasn't leafy salads that gave you that belly." The rest of the men laughed, but it was a hollow sound.

Julie looked at her wristwatch, oddly relieved to realize it was time for her to start hitting the business establishments. Something wasn't right here, and she had no idea what it was. There was tension in the air, a palpable tension that seemed to radiate from Betty, from the men at the table and most especially from Forest.

Murmuring a quick goodbye to Betty, then nodding to Forest, she put a dollar on the counter and left the café.

She'd gone only a few steps when her arm was grabbed from behind. She whirled around to see Forest. "What are you doing?" she asked, jerking her arm from his grasp.

"I want to talk to you."

"So talk," she replied, chilled despite the warmth of the sunshine overhead.

"The festival is supposed to be a day of fun. It's a day to visit with neighbors, laugh with co-workers." His eyes narrowed as they bore into hers. "It's not a day to dig into the past." In the black of his eyes she saw the spectral presence of inner demons, the forlorn darkness of hell. "Just leave it alone, Julie." His voice was slightly hoarse with suppressed emotion. "Jeffrey is dead and nothing can be served by rooting around in what happened long ago. Just leave it the hell alone."

"What are you so afraid of?" Julie asked softly.

His face blanched and for a moment she was afraid she'd gone too far. "I'm not afraid of anything but mouthy women asking too many questions, digging into business that has nothing to do with them." He turned and strode away from her as she stared wordlessly after him. When he had turned out of sight, the sun suddenly seemed brighter, warmer. She frowned thoughtfully. There were secrets here, secrets that for some reason Forest didn't want discovered. What had happened in the past that he didn't want her to know?

Despite her feeling that Bobby needed to be here, had seemed to react positively to these new surroundings, Julie couldn't help but feel that the best thing she could do for all of them was get together some money and get the hell away from Kingsdon Hill.

* * *

"Oh boy, this looks like fun!" Bobby exclaimed as he and Julie walked through the entrance to the town park. On a bandstand in front of the courthouse musicians played a raucous rendition of a Sousa march, and the air was redolent with the smoky scent of barbecue. There was a festive excitement in the air as throngs of people milled around, obviously enjoying the mild autumn weather. The rain that Forest had predicted hadn't materialized, and it was a perfect day for outdoor activities.

"There's Jimmy." Bobby pointed to a young boy standing near the barbecue pit. "Hey, Jimmy!" he yelled, then he looked at his mother in silent appeal.

"Go on," she said, and smiled as he immediately shot off to join his little friend. She moved over to a picnic bench near a huge oak tree and sat down, enjoying the warmth of the sun on her back. She watched as Bobby and Jimmy giggled and shoved each other in the eternal bonding process of young males.

Bobby had settled into school with surprising ease. He liked his teacher, Mrs. Watkins, who he said smelled like roses and always talked nice. The week of school he had missed while they traveled didn't seem to have put him behind, and he'd even managed to make half a dozen new friends. Bobby's relatively easy adjustment was about all that was perfect with her life at the moment.

Julie had spent the last week job hunting to no avail. Each day she'd come back to the house a little more dispirited than when she'd left. If she didn't know better she would swear it was a conspiracy and everyone had been warned not to give her a job. She sighed. She'd been in Kingsdon a week and still had no prospects. Nor was she any closer to a relationship with her husband's brother than she'd been when she'd lived a thousand miles away.

As thoughts of Forest entered her mind, she looked around, knowing that he'd left the house early that morning to help ready things for the festival. She spotted him standing beneath a large tree, the colored leaves above him casting shadows on his face and shoulders.

He stood alone, surveying the crowd like a despot overlooking his empire. As always, he was dressed informally, in a checkered flannel shirt that stretched across the broadness of his chest, and a pair of jeans that had long ago conformed to the muscled contours of his buttocks and legs. He looked primitive, like a frontiersman come to town to spend his hard-earned money on women and whiskey.

There was something about the man that hit her in an intensely physical way. He'd been rude, almost threatening toward her since the moment she'd arrived at his house, but that didn't dispel her fascination with him. She'd seen very little of him through the last week, consciously staying out of his way. However, whenever they had encountered each other the tension rippled between them, a tension that made it difficult for her to draw a full breath when in his presence.

Why hadn't he married? He should be considered the catch of the town. He was relatively wealthy, single and attractive…and he had dark shadows in his eyes that proclaimed loudly Do Not Trespass. Julie sighed, realizing she'd answered her own question of why he wasn't married. He didn't invite closeness from anyone. It was like he kept an invisible shield around himself to keep others away. What she couldn't figure out was why she felt so compelled to breach that shield and draw to the surface the obscure secrets she sensed he held within.

It was obvious that something horrible had happened between Forest and Jeffrey, something causing a deep turmoil that still affected Forest. He refused to talk about Jeffrey, refused to give her any clue as to what had happened between the two brothers. She had a feeling that if she could solve that particular mystery, she would be much closer to understanding the severe depressions that had assaulted Jeffrey, the nightmares that had often caused him to weep in his sleep.

She felt her breath tightening in her chest as he sauntered toward her. As always when his eyes played over her, she had the disturbing impression that he could see through her clothing. She felt naked and vulnerable beneath the heat of his gaze. She was also aware of other people watching them, as if expecting some sort of high drama.

"Afternoon, Julie," he said, his voice mockingly pleasant.

"Good afternoon, Forest. It's a beautiful day for the festival, isn't it?"

He nodded, dark amusement darting in his eyes. "Why is it we seem to always discuss the weather?"

She shrugged. "I was just making an idle observation." She cast a furtive look around and noted again that she and Forest held the attention of the people around them. "Why is everyone looking at us?" she asked.

Forest looked around in turn, his amusement more obvious now as it curled the corners of his lips. "This is a small town, Julie. A small town that thrives on gossip. I'm the boss man, the king of the castle, so to speak." His dark eyes drew her in, and without conscious thought she leaned closer to him. "You know what they'll be saying?" He reached out and touched a strand of her hair, his touch sending shock waves through her. "They'll say we're lovers."

She gasped and stepped back. "That's ridiculous," she scoffed.

"Idle gossip usually is." He hesitated a moment, as if he wanted to say more. Then his eyes darkened, and with a curt nod he moved away and left her standing alone.

"He's a handsome hunk, isn't he?"

Julie jumped at the sound of the friendly voice coming from just behind her. She turned to see an attractive, ash blond woman grinning at her knowingly. "I'm Lorna Richards, ace reporter, editor and owner of the *Kingsdon Gazette*."

"Hi, I'm Julie Kingsdon."

"Oh, I know who you are...the gossip mill in this community is the most healthy thing about it." She grinned candidly, displaying a chipped front tooth that only added to her charm. "I know you have a little boy who started school this past week, and I know you've been pounding the pavement looking for a job. Any luck?"

Julie shook her head. "I think I've knocked on every door of every establishment in this town, and nobody needs any help."

"You didn't knock on mine."

Julie smiled at Lorna. "You're right. But I'm fairly unskilled and definitely don't have a degree in journalism. I figured it would be a waste of your time and mine."

"Can you type? Answer a phone?"

"Well, sure, but—"

"Then you're hired. You can start Monday morning." Lorna laughed at Julie's expression of surprise. "My secretary quit two weeks ago because she had a baby."

"But I don't know anything about reporting or newspapers," Julie protested.

"You don't have to. I do all that stuff. I just need somebody to be my girl Friday." She held out her hand to Julie. "Deal?"

"Deal." Julie shook her hand, feeling a renewed burst of optimism. She had no idea what Lorna intended to pay her, had no idea what hours she would work or exactly what she would do, but it didn't matter. She'd taken the first step in getting on with her life.

"Now, let's get to the good stuff...the gossip." Lorna grinned irreverently. "How are you finding things up on the hill?"

Julie looked over at Forest. "Rather chilly. I showed up uninvited, and Forest hasn't been thrilled," she answered, then bit her tongue. After all, she was speaking to a reporter.

Lorna laughed, then sobered as she nodded her head toward the tall man. "I can imagine. He's always been sort of a loner with a chip on his shoulder."

Julie turned to Lorna with interest. "You've known him a long time?"

"He's the one who chipped my tooth when we were in junior high school. We all went to school together, and my parents were friends with Richard Kingsdon. I was two years older than Forest and several years younger than Jeffrey. We were at their house visiting and a fight broke out between the two boys. Forest went to hit Jeffrey with a tin can and got me instead. By the way, I was sorry to hear about Jeffrey's death."

Julie nodded, then looked back to where Forest was now standing, near the barbecue pit. "So the two brothers weren't close?"

"Half brothers," Lorna replied, and Julie turned to her in shock. She winced. "You didn't know that Jeffrey and Forest were half brothers?"

"No, I had no idea."

"Jeffrey's mother died when he was two, after a long illness. The speculation is that Forest was the product of a brief fling Richard had with a woman who worked as his secretary for a couple of years. When Forest was born, she left town, and nobody knows what happened to her."

Julie silently digested this new information. "Jeffrey rarely spoke of Forest, but when he did he never mentioned Forest being a half brother."

"That's odd. He loved to torment Forest when they were younger."

Julie looked at Lorna curiously. Finally...finally she was getting some answers. "Torment how?"

"Oh, you know...hateful kid stuff, like throwing it in Forest's face that his mother didn't want him and that his birth was just an unfortunate accident. Jeffrey could be pretty mean, and Forest would take it for so long, then he'd have a fearsome explosion of anger." Lorna's face colored slightly. "Sorry, I shouldn't be talking ill of the dead, and Jeffrey was your husband."

Julie smiled. "He was my husband, but I'm aware he wasn't a saint." She had occasionally seen glimpses of Jeffrey's cruelty in the years they had been married.

"No man I've ever known was a saint." Lorna shook her head and laughed ruefully. "Me, I've been married and divorced three times, and believe me, none of them were saints." She grinned saucily. "I've got the getting-married part down pat...it's staying married that gives me trouble."

Julie laughed, feeling an instant liking for the woman.

"Come on," Lorna said suddenly. "Let's go get a cold beer."

Julie looked around for Bobby and found him playing

on the jungle gym with a number of other boys. Seeing that he was occupied and having fun, she nodded to Lorna and stood up. Together the two of them walked over to where beer kegs were set up.

"Two, Charlie," Lorna said to the man working the keg.

"Coming right up." He filled two plastic glasses with the foamy brew and handed them to the women. "You're looking mighty fine today, Lorna," he said with a flirtatious grin.

"So's your wife, Charlie Maxwell, and she's bigger and meaner than both of us, so you'd do well to watch yourself." Lorna laughed as the big man looked sheepish. "Let's go over there in the shade." She pointed to another picnic table near the playground equipment where Bobby was playing.

Once the two were settled at the table, Julie took a sip of the cold beer. "It's been years since I've had a beer," she said. "Jeffrey wasn't much of a drinker, even socially."

"He never did much drinking when he was younger, either. Now Forest, he was a horse of a different color. When he was a teenager he was a real wild child."

Julie looked to where Forest now stood with a small group of men. He was speaking and his face was lit with an animation she hadn't seen before. Again she felt a curious pull toward him, an attraction stronger than anything she'd ever felt before. She looked back at Lorna, disturbed by her own emotions where Forest was concerned.

"You've got a cute kid," Lorna observed.

Julie smiled. "Thanks. He's a good kid, but he really misses his daddy."

"It's tough to lose a parent when you're so young."

Lorna shook her head sadly. "It's tough to lose anyone you love. But time heals some of the hurt. A lot of people in this town thought Jeffrey would never marry again after he lost his first wife."

"His first wife?" Julie stared at Lorna in confusion. "What do you mean?"

This time it was Lorna's turn to look at Julie incredulously. "You didn't know that Jeffrey had been married before?" Julie shook her head, for a moment feeling like she'd been punched in the stomach. Lorna sighed and withdrew a pack of cigarettes from her purse. "Wow, I had no idea you didn't know." She lit a cigarette and inhaled deeply. "If smoking doesn't kill me one of these days, my big mouth will." She looked back at Julie. "I suppose if you don't know about his first wife, then you don't know about his son, either."

"His son?" The words choked in Julie's throat, and for a moment she felt like she was swimming in a sea of unreality. "Jeffrey had a son?" She thought of Bobby. Did he have a half brother running around somewhere in the town of Kingsdon? *Oh, Jeffrey, what does all this mean? Why didn't you tell me?* What else didn't she know about the man she had been married to for eight years? "Where...do they live here in Kingsdon?" she finally managed to ask, through the constriction of her throat.

Lorna shook her head. "His wife, MaryAnn, died from complications right after childbirth. Jeffrey hardly had time to mourn her, what with a newborn to care for. Those three Kingsdon men doted on that baby. Little Christopher ruled that roost, and a special bond seemed to develop between Forest and the little fellow."

"So what happened? Where is Christopher now?" A curious sense of dread accompanied Julie's question.

"He's, uh, dead."

"Oh, how sad. What happened to him?" Julie asked, trying to fight her way through a myriad of emotions.

Lorna looked over at Forest, who now appeared to be watching them. She compressed her lips tightly. "Look, I've said far more than I should have." Nervously she ran a hand through her short blond hair.

"You can't stop now," Julie protested. Her head spun dizzily with the information she'd received. "What happened to Christopher? How did he die?"

Again Lorna shot a look at Forest. Julie followed her gaze. His eyes suddenly met hers, a heated glimpse that whispered of suppressed anger, dark secrets and haunting guilt. For a moment time seemed suspended and she felt herself falling into the black hole of his gaze, falling into an abyss so devoid of life, so devoid of love that it frightened her. She averted her head, breaking the visual contact with him as she looked back at Lorna.

"Lorna, please. Tell me what happened to Christopher." Julie continued pressing, her need to know exploding inside her. She reached out and grabbed the reporter's hand in hers. It was cold, lifeless, and she suddenly realized Lorna was afraid. "Tell me," she whispered urgently.

Lorna shook her head and gently freed her hand from Julie's grasp. "If you really want to know what happened to little Christopher…ask Forest."

Julie looked back at Forest. Despite the distance that separated them, she could feel his tension, see the darkness of his eyes. Suddenly she, too, was afraid.

CHAPTER FOUR

Darkness filled the bedroom. The moon was hidden behind black clouds that had moved in near dusk. Bobby lay on his back in bed, knowing he should be asleep, but sleep was the farthest thing from his mind.

It had been an awesome day…the best that he could remember in a long time. He'd watched a log-splitting contest and had run in a three-legged race with Jimmy as his partner. They hadn't won, but they'd laughed so hard Bobby's tummy still hurt.

Of course, his tummy might hurt because he'd eaten three hot dogs, a bunch of spicy ribs, two cotton candies and a big plate of beans. He and Jimmy had also shared a glass of beer, which Jimmy had managed to sneak from one of the kegs. Bobby was glad his mom hadn't found out about the beer. She would have had a fit, and that would have made his tummy hurt even more. Besides, he hadn't liked it very much, although he had told Jimmy it tasted great.

He turned over on his side, staring out the window into the darkness of the night. The wind had picked up and tree branches scratched against the windowpane. He pulled the blanket closer around him. The branches sounded kind of creepy.

He missed his daddy. There had been times when his dad hadn't been nice, when he'd screamed and yelled, then cried. Those times had scared Bobby. But then there had been times when his dad had cuddled him close and held him so tightly it had stolen his breath. It had felt good. Missing his dad was a hurt inside him that never went away. He felt it now, stabbing in his heart, causing tears to burn in his eyes. He wiped them away, refusing to be a baby and give in to them.

He wished his uncle Forest was nicer. There were times when he looked at him and Bobby had the feeling he wanted to be friends. But then there were other times when his uncle Forest's eyes scared him. He shivered, thinking of when his uncle stared at him and looked mean.

A whisper of cold air suddenly sailed over him, cold enough to penetrate the blanket he was under. A faint, boyish giggle followed. Bobby rolled over and sat up, peering into the inky darkness of his room with excitement. "Hi. Where are you?"

Another soft giggle filled the room, first coming from the rocking horse, then from the opposite direction. Bobby smiled, knowing his new friend was playing games. He waited impatiently, his gaze skittering around the dark room. Then he saw him. A faint glow appeared, a glow in the form of a small figure sitting on the back of the rocking horse. As Bobby watched, the glow grew dimmer and the figure took a more solid form. He was about Bobby's age, and dark-haired like him. He was dressed the same as he'd been the last time Bobby had seen him, in a pair of worn jeans and a bright red sweatshirt.

"I wondered if you'd come back to see me again," Bobby said softly.

I'm back. He didn't speak aloud, but rather talked in Bobby's head. It was as clear to Bobby as if he said the words out loud.

"How do you do that?" he whispered.

How do I do what?

"How do you talk in my head?"

The little boy grinned. *I just do it,* he replied. *I can do lots of things.*

"Like what?" Bobby pulled his legs up against his chest and wrapped his arms around them, enthralled with his new companion.

I can fly.

"Show me," Bobby replied. He gasped and clapped his hands in glee as his friend floated up above the rocking horse, then moved to hover directly above where Bobby sat on his bed. He laughed as his friend floated down to sit next to him on the mattress.

"Bobby?" At the sound of his mother's voice, Bobby's friend vanished.

Julie turned on the bedroom light and frowned at her son. "You're supposed to be asleep. What are you doing in here?"

"I was talking to my new friend, but he disappeared when you came in."

"A new friend?" Julie entered the room, immediately shivering as a draft of icy air enveloped her. "Why is this room so cold? Do you have the window open?" She looked toward the closed window, then checked to make certain the heat vent was open. Maybe she should speak to Forest about the drafts in this room.

Sitting on the edge of Bobby's bed, she pulled the blankets up tightly around his neck. "Now, what's this about a new friend?"

"I don't know his name, but he's come to visit me twice."

"And he disappeared when I came in here?" Julie asked, and Bobby nodded. An imaginary friend. For some reason this new development didn't particularly worry her. Bobby had always been an imaginative child, and when he was five he'd had a make-believe friend named Gifford who he insisted was a furry rabbit. Every night for a month Gifford had eaten dinner with them and had slept with Bobby. Then, as mysteriously as he'd appeared, Gifford had vanished.

With Jeffrey's death still so painful to Bobby, Julie wasn't surprised that a new fanciful friend had come into her son's life. "And is your new friend a bunny rabbit, or a fat, ugly toad?" she teased.

Bobby looked at her with disgust and rolled his eyes. "Mom, he's not an animal. He's a little boy like me, and he can fly all around the room. He makes me laugh."

Julie lightly touched the end of his nose. "That's the best kind of friend to have, the kind who makes you laugh." She smoothed his hair away from his forehead, then kissed him soundly. "But I don't like new friends who keep my son up past his bedtime, and your bedtime was long ago." She gave him a final smile. "Now go to sleep."

She blew him a kiss from the doorway, then shut off the light and left the room. She went through her own bedroom and down the stairs. Ever since she and Bobby had come home from the festival earlier in the evening, she'd been waiting for Forest to return. She wanted to talk to him about Christopher. She needed to talk to him.

After she'd spoken to Lorna, the rest of the day had passed in a haze for Julie. The woman's words had whirled around and around in her head, creating a dizzying affect she couldn't seem to shake off. She'd met a hundred people during the afternoon, but she couldn't remember a single name...except the name Christopher.

She curled up on the sofa, grateful that Lottie had built a fire before she'd left the house for the night. The warmth radiated outward and comforted her. She'd been cold all day, enclosed in a chill of half madness as she realized her relationship with Jeffrey had been built on lies of omission.

How could he have not told her about his first wife? His child? How could he have kept such an important piece of himself, his past, a secret? It was no wonder they had never achieved the kind of closeness she'd longed for, needed; he'd kept a large portion of himself private and unattainable.

She jumped as a flash of lightning flickered outside the window, followed by a low rumble of thunder a moment later. Oh, good, she thought irritably. A storm seemed a perfect ending to an emotionally tumultuous day.

She'd thought the darkness of night would bring Forest home, but it had been dark for nearly two hours, and he hadn't returned. Surely if it began to rain, he would come back.

She didn't know how long the festival would last, didn't know if it was still going on. If it was, surely the rain would put an abrupt end to the festivities.

Julie was aware of the wind picking up, slapping tree limbs against the windows in the living room, creating a mournful whistle as it blew around the corners of the huge house. Above its siren call, the low sound of sobbing drifted to her.

She sat up, tilting her head with a frown, unsure if it was somehow connected to the wind or something entirely different. It rose and fell, and she finally recognized it as the eerie, pitiful sobbing of a child.

She jumped up and headed for the stairs. Bobby had always been afraid of storms. He'd always been afraid of thunder. She turned on the light that lit the stairwell, then climbed upward, pausing midway as the electricity flickered off, then came back on. She continued her ascent,

anxious to get to Bobby and ease his fear. When she got
to her room, she moved through the darkness and stood
in the doorway that led to Bobby's smaller room. She
could hear his breathing...the deep, regular rhythm of
sleep. Above that, the crying persisted. A flash of lightning revealed Bobby in his bed, sound asleep.

Julie's mouth suddenly went dry and her breathing
grew shallow with fear. Calm down, she told herself as
she retraced her steps back to the hallway. Lightning
slashed the sky again, spilling erratic light into the long
hall. Thunder rumbled closer and the crying seemed to
intensify in volume. Cold chills danced up her arms, then
down her spine in response to the childlike weeping.

The house suddenly felt cold around her, unnaturally
cold. She hesitated, the haunting noise louder now, as if
she were closer to the source. She followed it down the
hallway, past Forest's bedroom, past the spare rooms and
the second bath. Then it stopped. Julie could hear the
moaning of the wind, but the weeping stopped as suddenly as it had started.

She stood unmoving at the end of the hallway, her
heart pounding with abnormal rapidity. Had it been real?
Had the sound of a child crying been genuine or had she
imagined it? God knew, her mind was filled with
thoughts that would be conducive to imagining something like this. All day long her head had been full of
old mysteries, haunting secrets and the mysterious death
of a poor little boy. It wouldn't surprise her to discover
the crying had been part of her overly active imagination.

She started back down the stairs, stifling a scream as
the electricity once again flickered off...on...then it
stayed off. She stood still in the middle of the stairs,
waiting for the light to come back on. After several mo-

ments she realized the storm had intensified outside and the electricity might remain off indefinitely.

Grabbing the banister, blinded by the profound darkness, she eased her way down the remaining steps. When she reached the bottom, she bumped headfirst into a solid wall of flesh. A scream rose to her throat and spilled out of her. She started to fall backward, but her shoulders were grabbed by large hands.

"What the hell are you doing running around in the dark?" Forest demanded.

"I didn't start running around in the dark. I was half-way down the stairs when the lights went off." She shrugged away from him and bumped into the ornate umbrella stand, which she couldn't see. She stifled a protest as he grasped her arm and led her out of the darkness to the living room, where the fire provided reassuring illumination. "I didn't know you were home," she said as she breathed a sigh of relief and sat down on the sofa.

"I've been here for hours. I've been downstairs in my workroom." He eased himself into the chair she had begun to think of as his. It was the huge wing chair closest to the fire. She'd never seen him sit anyplace else in the room.

"What do you do down there?" Julie asked curiously.

His gaze was dark and enigmatic. "Whatever I want to do."

Julie nodded, trying to figure out the best way to broach the subject she most wanted to talk about. "I have a job," she said, deciding to talk about the easy things first.

His dark eyebrows rose curiously. "Where?"

"At the newspaper. I'm going to be Lorna Richards's girl Friday."

A flicker of humor danced in the darkness of his eyes,

and the corner of his lips curved upward. "You'll find Lorna colorful, to say the least."

"She seems very nice."

"Oh, she is. Lorna is a jewel to everyone but the man who finds himself her husband." A genuine smile lit his features. "Lorna has a tendency to suck the lifeblood out of her husbands."

Julie smiled, easily able to see Lorna doing that. "I'm just grateful she's giving me a chance at a job." She hesitated, wanting to speak to Forest about Jeffrey's first wife, his little boy. She wanted to find out what had happened to Christopher. But she was reluctant to bring up a topic she knew would make him angry.

For the first time since she'd arrived, Forest appeared relatively at ease. The lines on his face were relaxed and the tension that usually radiated from him was gone. For the first time he seemed open, less guarded, and she didn't want to do or say anything to disturb the tenuous peace of the moment.

"Everyone seemed to have a good time today," she observed.

He nodded. "I started the fall festivals ten years ago as a way to bring together the community and thank the people who work for me at the mill. I tried it the first year, and it was such a rousing success, I decided it should be an annual town event."

Lightning slashed the semidarkness of the room and a clap of thunder sounded directly overhead. "It's a good thing the storm held off until now," Julie observed. "How long do you think the electricity will be off?"

"Who knows? It almost always goes out when we have a storm." He stood up and put another log on the fire. Squatting on his haunches, he took the poker and jabbed at the wood on the grate, a shower of sparks engulfing the new piece. He put the poker back, then stood up and looked at her. "I think I'll call it a night. It's been a long day." He headed toward the doorway.

"Forest…wait. I need to talk to you." Julie stood up, knowing that if she wanted some answers, she needed to ask questions now. He turned and looked at her curiously. "I know about Jeffrey's first wife. I know about Christopher."

The name hung in the air between them. Forest's mouth compressed into a tight line and his eyes blackened with suppressed emotions. "If you know all about it, then you don't need to talk to me."

"I don't know everything, and I do need to talk to you," she protested, moving to stand directly in front of him. "I have to know what happened. You might claim the past as belonging only to you, but that's not true. Whatever happened years ago had a significant affect on my life as well."

"What are you talking about?" he asked, his sentence punctuated by another clap of thunder.

"I married a man who suffered deep depressions, a man who was incapable of achieving the kind of emotional intimacy I wanted and needed." Tears burned in Julie's eyes, tears of regret, guilt and a deep sorrow she knew would follow her for years to come. "Whatever happened had a profound affect on Jeffrey, and that had an equally profound affect on my life. I need to know what happened."

His eyes were cold, emotionless. "You've had a week to ask your questions around town, hear all the rumors about what happened to Christopher."

"Nobody has told me anything. It's like everyone is afraid to talk about it. I know Christopher is dead, but I don't want to listen to rumors. I want the truth. Lorna told me that if I want to know what happened to Christopher, I should ask you." She held his gaze, not flinching beneath the fiery anger that burned there.

He seemed to grow with his rage. His shoulders expanded as he drew in a deep breath. "What makes you so certain I'll tell you the truth?"

She shrugged. "I guess I'll just have to trust you."

He laughed, a harsh, bitter sound that echoed the thunder rumbling overhead. "Trusting me would be your first mistake." Beneath the rancor of his words was an ache of anguish that pierced through her. She suddenly realized that whatever had happened, it had left an indelible mark on this man, a scar every bit as deep as the one left on Jeffrey. She also realized his rage masked pain, an enormous pain of such proportion it momentarily stole her breath away.

"Trusting you is all I have," she finally said softly. She reached out and took one of his hands, marveling at the warmth of his flesh against her own chilled skin. He tried for a moment to yank away, then with a deep sigh allowed her to lead him over to the sofa. She sat down next to him, intensely aware of the heat of his body so close to hers.

"Please, tell me what happened. Tell me about Christopher." She gently squeezed his hand, then released it, uncomfortable by the warmth the physical contact provoked inside her.

Forest winced, as if hearing the child's name was physically painful. He leaned forward and buried his face in his hands, the firelight etching him in golden tones that did nothing to soften his obvious agony.

When he finally lifted his head, his eyes were still filled with torment. "I can't," he said faintly.

"You have to," Julie persisted. "If you can't talk

about it for yourself, then do it for me. I have to know what happened to him."

He leaned back in the chair and released a weary sigh of resignation, his fight unexpectedly gone. "Christopher was the brightest, most loving child I've ever known." His voice was low, so soft she had to lean forward to hear him. "From the moment he was a toddler, he loved me as nobody else had in my entire life—unconditionally, eternally, absolutely. He greeted me every day with a good-morning kiss and insisted I be the one who tucked him in each night." He closed his eyes for a moment, as if savoring those precious memories from the past.

He opened his eyes and looked at Julie curiously. "Jeffrey never said anything to you about MaryAnn or Christopher?"

"Nothing." This time Julie heard the hollowness in her own voice as she realized Jeffrey's refusal to talk about his past was indicative of all that had been wrong with their marriage. "I always sensed there was something in his past…something that had hurt him, scarred him."

"Hatred. That's what did it. The kind of hatred that twists in your guts and tears out your heart." Again his voice was soft, and she could see his own grief weighing heavily in the slump of his shoulders, the weary expression on his face.

She leaned closer to him, wanting to wrap her arms around him and ease the shadows from his eyes, assuage the pain that radiated from him as strongly as his prominent, masculine scent. "Tell me," she urged softly. "Tell me what happened to Christopher."

"It was a long time ago. I don't remember all the specifics." He drew himself up defensively. Outside, the storm seemed to reach its zenith, creating a spastic light show complete with thunderous booms.

Julie studied his features, so handsome, yet so racked with a soul-deep affliction. "I know he's dead. How did he die? An accident?"

He stared into the fire, as if lost for a moment in the blazing flame. Time seemed suspended as Julie waited for him to speak. "It happened a couple weeks after the accident at the mill that killed my father. I was injured in the same accident, hit in the temple with a load of wood." His voice was flat, as if he'd successfully removed himself emotionally from the painful events. "I'd been off work recuperating, and during the days I babysat Christopher, while Jeffrey went to the mill." His voice was hoarse, as if the mere act of remembering stole most of his breath. "I remember giving him cereal for breakfast. He was mad because he wanted me to fix him pancakes, and I didn't want the mess."

A winsome smile suddenly crossed his features and Julie drew her own breath in sharply at the beauty it brought to his face. "Christopher was more than a little spoiled. He threw temper tantrums when he didn't get his way. He had one that morning, stamping his feet and telling me he hated me." His voice caught in his throat and he looked up at her, his dark eyes liquid with unshed tears. "I should have let him have his way that morning. I should have made him pancakes. I should have given him anything he wanted."

This time Julie didn't fight her impulse. She reached out again and took his hand. For a moment it remained slack, then he curled his fingers through hers, gripping tightly. "We spent the morning playing hide-and-seek," he continued. "Christopher loved to play that game." His voice was tense, as if his throat had constricted. "After lunch I insisted we have some quiet time. I sat right here and Christopher stretched out in front of the fire on the floor.''

Forest dropped her hand and stood up. When he turned back to face her, his eyes reflected the red of the fire's glow, an unearthly light of damnation. "I fell asleep." He whispered the words, as if he'd just confessed to a mortal sin. "I fell asleep, and when I woke up I was standing in the middle of the forest and Christopher was gone.''

Julie frowned, unable to comprehend exactly what he was saying. "You were asleep and he just disappeared? I don't understand.''

He drew himself up, and it was as if the storm had moved inside, into the room…into him. Tension vibrated in the air and a clap of thunder caused Julie to jump half out of her seat.

Forest rubbed a hand over his face, and when he looked back at her, his features again displayed anger. "You shouldn't have made me go through this all over again. I don't know what happened to Christopher. Damn it, I don't know." The rage slowly left his face and he gazed at her coldly, dispassionately. "But I can tell you what Jeffrey thought happened.''

"And what's that?'' she asked.

He hesitated a moment, his eyes not leaving hers. "Jeffrey thought I killed Christopher. He thought I took him out in the woods and killed him, then buried the body where nobody would ever find it. To this day it hasn't been found.''

Julie's heart thumped in an unsteady rhythm and for a moment she was sorry she'd asked, sorry she'd pried. She'd had no idea it was such an ugly past. "And what do you think happened?'' she asked in a subdued whisper.

Again the light of the damned shone from his eyes and his mouth twisted in a bitter smile. "I think the same thing, Julie. I think I took that little boy out into the woods and killed him."

CHAPTER FIVE

Julie stared at him, unsure what to believe, what to think. His words pulsated in the air, as if with a life force and energy of their own.

Forest slumped back in the chair, his internal storm apparently spent with the confession.

"I...I don't understand. If you killed Christopher, then why aren't you in jail?" she finally asked incredulously. She sank down on the sofa again and continued to stare at him. "Surely there was some sort of an investigation?"

Forest laughed bitterly, the weathered lines of his face deepening. "If that's what you want to call it. Sheriff Wolvertine asked me some questions, then released me."

"If the sheriff thought you were responsible for Christopher's disappearance, he would have arrested you," she protested. Nothing made sense, especially his confession of sorts. Why would Forest kill a child he'd obviously loved with all his heart? And how was it possible to kill somebody while you slept? It made no sense. Nothing made sense.

"Hell, Sheriff Wolvertine wasn't about to arrest me for anything," Forest scoffed. "He's got three sons who work for me at the mill, as do most of the men in this town. Families depend on the mill—this whole town depends on it. With me in prison and Jeffrey on the verge of an emotional breakdown, the whole operation would have folded, and all those men would have lost their livelihoods."

"If he'd thought you were guilty, he wouldn't have let you go," Julie repeated firmly.

Forest stared at her long and hard. "Are you really that naive, or just a damned fool?"

Julie flushed and raised her chin a notch. "I guess I'm just a damned fool, because none of this makes any kind of sense to me. You say that you don't know what happened between the time you went to sleep and the moment you woke up in the woods, and yet you're so certain you killed Christopher. Why?"

Forest's look was baleful, and a tic moved erratically in the lean muscle under his cheekbone. "That's what I said." He raked a hand through his hair, his features creased in aggravation. "Look, I went through all this ten years ago, and I don't intend to rehash it now. It's done, it's over and nothing can ever change what happened that day." He stood up once again, and there was a sardonic lift to his sooty eyebrows. "You wanted to know all the deep, dark secrets of the past. Well, now you know them." He turned, obviously intending to leave the room.

"Forest...wait." Julie jumped up out of her chair, still feeling that the tragedy remained as much a puzzle as ever. She couldn't leave it at this, with so many questions still whirling around in her head, so many pieces not fitting together. "How do you know Christopher is dead? If his body was never found, then how do you know he wasn't kidnapped, taken by somebody?"

Again his shoulders slumped and despair washed over his features. He suddenly looked achingly young, devoid of hope, vulnerable as a child who found himself alone and abandoned. "I know he's dead. I knew it the moment I woke up in the woods." He placed a hand over his heart. "I knew it here. I felt his absence."

And Julie felt Forest's pain. It radiated out from him, engulfing her in its depths. Despite the irrationality of it all, she believed him. If something ever happened to Bobby, she'd always thought she would instantly know— that someplace in her heart, she would feel it immediately.

"There's one thing you haven't mentioned, one question you haven't answered," she said softly. He waited, looking at her impassively. "Why?" she asked softly. "Why would you have harmed Christopher?"

For a moment his shoulders remained slumped in defeat and his eyes reflected a grief so deep it sent a resounding ache through her. "I don't know," he finally said, and from the emptiness of his voice, she realized that that fact more than anything haunted his every moment. "I loved Christopher, but I hated Jeffrey. Jeffrey tormented me from the time I was small. He hated me with all his heart, all his soul, and I responded in kind." He shrugged and straightened his shoulders, the vulnerability vanquished along with his expression of grief. "Jeffrey maintained that in a moment of madness, my hatred of him overcame my love for Christopher. And I think that's exactly what happened." He didn't wait for her to reply, but instead turned and went up the stairs to his bedroom.

He moved across the darkened room to stand at the window, a lingering taste of bitterness in his mouth. Oh, God, it had been agony, reliving those moments.

He closed his eyes and went back...back to that day, that instant in time when his life had been ripped apart forever. After their morning of playing hide-and-seek, and a lunch of bologna sandwiches, Forest had sat down in the chair in front of the fire, and Christopher had stretched out on the floor. They had talked for a little while. Man talk, Christopher had always called it. He'd asked Forest why birds chirped, why girls giggled and if his mother was up in heaven looking down on him.

Christopher had finally drifted off to sleep. For a long time Forest had stared at the sleeping boy, his heart filled with a kind of love he'd never felt before. The loneliness he'd known as a child, with only a brother who hated him and a demanding, critical father, was eased by Christopher's love. It filled him so completely it frightened him at times. Then Forest must have fallen asleep, also.

Next thing he knew, he'd been alone in the woods, the sound of Christopher's screams echoing in his brain. What had happened? How had he gotten here? And where was Christopher? Heart pounding, terror tasting sour in his mouth, Forest had run for the house. He'd burst into the living room and stared at the place in front of the fire—the place where Christopher had been. Gone. He was gone.

Forest had run back outside, his head filled with Christopher's screams—screams of horror, screams of pain, screams that made Forest's blood run cold. Why had Christopher screamed? What had Forest done? Dear God, what had he done?

He'd called Jeffrey, who'd arrived moments later, and together they had searched the woods, looking for the little boy. Finally, the two had called the sheriff for help. While they'd waited for him to arrive, Jeffrey had exploded.

"What did you do to him?" he had screamed, wrapping his hands around Forest's neck. Forest had defended himself against the attack, wrestling out of his brother's grip and dodging wild blows.

"I don't know what happened," he had exclaimed.

"I—I was asleep and he—he just disappeared." The words sounded weak even to his own ears.

"Liar," Jeffrey cried, the chords of his neck bulging. "You killed him, didn't you? You brought him out in the woods and killed him, then hid his little body."

"No!" Forest backed away from Jeffrey, horrified, yet filled with a weighty dread. "No! I love Christopher." Confusion swirled in his head. The screams... Christopher's screams.

"You bastard," Jeffrey spat. "You don't love him as much as you hate me. You've always hated me. I'm the real Kingsdon, I married MaryAnn and Christopher belongs to me. You couldn't stand it that he was mine. He was the only thing that mattered to me, and you killed him."

Forest's mouth had worked to form a denial, but no words had come. What Jeffrey'd said was true. There had been times when his hatred of his brother had been all-consuming. And why had he found himself standing in the forest, with Christopher's cries still echoing in his head?

He now opened his eyes. Outside, the storm had moved away, the lightning appearing halfhearted and tired. Each distant flash displayed the thick brush, the tangled undergrowth of the woods.

For the past ten years, every morning when he awakened and each night before he went to bed, Forest stood here at the window, staring into the woods. He had a feeling that if he stared long enough, concentrated hard enough, he would finally be able to remember exactly what had happened on that autumn afternoon so long ago.

He'd lied to Julie. He hadn't been asleep when Christopher disappeared. He'd experienced a blackout. That had been the first time it had happened. He didn't know how long it had lasted, or what he'd done while in the bizarre state of fugue. The only thing he knew for sure was that when he'd come to, he'd been standing in the woods, and somewhere in the dark recesses of his mind, Christopher's screams echoed. As Forest replayed those horrifying moments, he'd feared Jeffrey might be right.

The week following Christopher's disappearance had passed in a haze. Groups of townspeople had searched the woods, and Forest had talked to Orville Wolvertine, confessing what he feared, what Jeffrey had accused him of. "Hell, Forest, don't talk nonsense," the sheriff had protested. "Everyone in town knows how much you love that little tyke. The boy just wandered off, got lost. Don't worry, we'll find him."

But they hadn't, and after a month, everyone came to the conclusion that Christopher was probably dead. Jeffrey had left town a broken man, and Forest lived with a haunting guilt that ate at him day and night. As much as he wanted to deny it, he feared Jeffrey was right. In some sort of hate-induced fugue, he'd killed Christopher.

He turned away from the window, logically knowing that no matter how long he stood here and stared, Christopher wasn't going to magically walk out of the woods and make everything right. There was no way to go back and fix the past. Christopher's death had destroyed what little connection had existed between Forest and his brother. It had caused Forest to doubt his own sanity, to close himself off from everyone, to spend the last ten years hating himself more than anyone else could ever possibly hate a man.

He knew with certainty that Christopher's body remained in the woods. Someplace out there amid the tangled underbrush was the little boy he had loved, and Forest would never rest until he finally found him. He walked the woods each day, searching, looking, needing to find Christopher and give the child a proper burial. It was the least he could do. He'd spent the last ten years trying to figure out how to atone for a mortal sin he didn't remember committing but knew he had.

He stripped off his clothes and got into bed. He threw an arm across his eyes, shielding his gaze from the distant lightning. Sleep, he knew would be elusive, just as he knew that if he did manage to fall asleep, his dreams would be haunted ones.

It still bothered him that Julie had been able to hear the ghostly cries that for so long he had thought only he could hear. He'd always believed the cries were his own personal torment, the internal echo of his guilt. But if Julie could hear them, then the ghost was real, not just a figment of his tormented imagination.

He was afraid…not of the ghost, but of the blackouts, which he feared might cause another tragedy. He was afraid of what he might do to Julie, to Bobby. He was afraid that there was a murderer inside him, and that when he blacked out, that evil entity exploded in a killing rage. With Jeffrey's family once again in the house, Forest was deathly afraid.

Julie sat at the kitchen table, staring thoughtfully into a cup of coffee. Dawn was just breaking outside, but despite the early hour, Lottie had told her that Forest had already left for the mill.

"On Sunday?" Julie had asked in surprise.

"He goes in half days on Sundays, says it's the only time he can catch up on all the paperwork," Lottie had explained. The old woman had poured Julie a cup of coffee, then disappeared into the laundry room.

Julie stifled a yawn, then took a sip of her coffee. She

hadn't slept well after her conversation with Forest.
When she finally had fallen asleep, her dreams had been
filled with the spectral vision of a little boy, thick woods
and Forest.

The images of Forest had been as tangled as the woods
that had surrounded her in the nightmarish landscape.
One moment he had beckoned to her, his expression one
of exquisite tenderness and eternal love. The next his face
had been twisted with a murderous black rage, an overwhelming insanity, and his footsteps had crashed through
the undergrowth as he'd chased her. In her dream, she
was no longer Julie, but had somehow been transformed
into Christopher, and she didn't know if she was running
for her life, or merely playing a game of hide-and-seek.

She knew the dreams had been her unconscious attempt to work through the inconsistencies and lingering
questions surrounding Christopher's disappearance and
Forest's part in that tragedy.

She'd awakened no closer to having any answers. Her
restless night had made her tired and cranky, and certain
that Forest hadn't told her everything. She couldn't seem
to get past the idea that somehow he believed that, while
asleep, he had harmed Christopher.

People didn't kill while sleeping. Did they? She'd
heard crazy stories of people on diets who wandered in
the night, eating Twinkies and Moon Pies while deep in
the throes of slumber. But she'd never heard of anyone
killing somebody.

What had happened that day? What had happened to
little Christopher? And what had happened to Forest that
had made him so certain he'd killed the child? What was
he hiding from her? What was he not telling her?

Julie got up from the table and poured herself another
cup of coffee, the questions nagging insistently. Lottie

bustled in with a laundry basket full of freshly dried clothes. The lemony scent of fabric softener filled the kitchen. The housekeeper placed the basket on one end of the table, then sat down and began folding the garments.

Julie sat down across from her and reached for one of the articles of clothing. "Now, now, missy. This is my job," Lottie protested.

"Please, let me help," Julie replied. "I'm not accustomed to spending my days doing nothing." She carefully folded one of Bobby's T-shirts. "Besides," she continued, "I'd like to talk to you."

"About what?" Lottie asked in surprise.

"About Christopher."

An expression of sadness pulled at Lottie's features. "Ah, the day he disappeared is the day the very life went out of this house." She took another T-shirt from the basket and meticulously folded it. "It destroyed what little relationship was left between Forest and Jeffrey."

"I've heard the two brothers weren't very close," Julie observed.

Lottie snorted. "That's the understatement of the century." She leaned back in her chair, laundry apparently forgotten for the moment. "Jeffrey was six years old when Richard brought Forest home. He didn't prepare Jeffrey in any way, just sprang a new baby brother on him. Jeffrey was used to being the king of the castle, so to speak, and he didn't cotton to sharing anything with Forest." Lottie paused a moment, her faded blue eyes distant with memories. "That Jeffrey, he was spoiled rotten, and he had a mean streak in him that often got him into trouble. There were times I feared he'd kill Forest before the youngster got big enough to defend himself. Still, I blame Richard for the way the boys got along."

"Their father? Why?" Julie asked, her hands reaching for another piece of clothing to fold.

"Richard liked competition, and he encouraged it between Forest and Jeffrey. As they got older, he often played them one against the other." Lottie sighed and ran a hand through her gray hair. "I think if left alone, those boys would have been fine together. For a long time Forest idolized Jeffrey, and if their father hadn't interfered, those two would have been as close as any two real brothers could be." Lottie raised her chin, a flash of fire in her eyes. "I told Richard once, told him he was ruining the both of them, the way he pitted them against each other, but he just laughed and said competition was healthy, good. He insisted it would make them both fighters and winners."

"How sad," Julie said, her heart expanding for the little boys who'd been conditioned to compete with each other, to hate each other. It scared her sometimes, what damage parents could do to their children in the name of love.

"I don't think Forest ever really forgave Jeffrey for marrying MaryAnn. She'd been Forest's sweetheart for over a year when Jeffrey managed to woo her away and marry her, lickety-split. Of course, in Jeffrey's defense, I think he loved MaryAnn, but I think he loved her more because Forest did, too. When she died, I thought Forest and Jeffrey would finally be able to put their differences behind them for the sake of that little boy. And for a while, they did."

"But it didn't last."

Lottie shook her head. "No, it didn't last. As Christopher got older, he adored Forest, and Jeffrey resented their closeness. Forest had a playfulness, a gentleness that Jeffrey didn't have, and it drew Christopher to his uncle like a bug to a light.'' She sighed, a heavy, sad exhalation of breath. ''Then Richard died and things between Forest and Jeffrey got worse. They were fighting about the mill, fighting over Christopher. Usually I baby-sat the lad while Jeffrey was at work, but that particular week my sister was sick with a fearsome case of the flu, and I spent my time nursing her. Forest had been home since the accident that killed Richard. He'd taken a bad blow to the head and suffered a little dizziness. He wasn't well enough to be back at work, but he insisted he could watch Christopher while I was away.''

''What do you think happened?'' Julie asked, the laundry forgotten as she leaned forward. While she waited for Lottie to answer, she was aware of the ticking of the clock on the oven, the slight hum of the refrigerator.

Lottie frowned, and when she reached for another piece of the laundry, her hand trembled slightly. ''I don't know, and I don't care to know. Jeffrey was crazy that day, saying all kinds of horrid things, and Forest was half-crazed as well.'' She sighed and pressed two fingers against her forehead, as if to ease a headache. ''I like to think Christopher just wandered off. Christopher had a fascination with the woods. He'd gotten his butt whipped more than once for going off by himself.''

Julie frowned. ''But Forest seems to think he did something to hurt Christopher in some way.''

Lottie shrugged her shoulders and busied herself folding the last of the clothes, but Julie saw that the old woman's eyes were haunted with a tinge of fear. ''That's between the man and his maker. It's true enough that there was bad blood between the brothers, but nobody really knows what happened that day.''

Again Julie felt her head spinning. The discussion of the relationship between Forest and Jeffrey had only added fuel to the fire. Jeffrey had stolen Forest's girlfriend. Had that betrayal been the final straw, setting alight a seething rage that had festered for years? In a moment of explosive madness, had Forest harmed the one thing he knew Jeffrey held dear?

Lottie stood up, the basket of clothes neatly folded. "I'll put Bobby's things on your bed so I won't wake him," she said.

"Lottie, do you think Forest harmed Christopher?" Julie asked.

The old woman's face blanched and for a moment she didn't speak. "I'll tell you what I think. I think there's evil in this house." Before Julie could respond, she turned and disappeared out the door.

Julie expelled a deep breath and got up to pour herself a third cup of coffee. At this rate she'd suffer caffeine overdose before the sun was completely up in the eastern sky. Sipping the brew, she remained at the window, staring out into the woods.

Evil in the house? Was there evil in the house or in the man? What about the ghost? She suddenly thought of the eerie sobbing she'd heard. In all the drama of Forest's confession the night before, she had forgotten to tell him that she'd heard the pitiful crying just before he'd come up from the basement.

Was it possible that what she'd heard was the ghost of Christopher? Julie had certainly never thought much about ghosts, though she supposed that, someplace in the back of her mind, she didn't completely discount the possibility of such a thing. She had a very open mind when it came to things paranormal. She knew there was much that science couldn't explain, might never be able to explain.

If there really was a ghost, and the ghost was indeed

Christopher, then why was he here? Didn't ghosts usually haunt because they were troubled souls not at rest? Was Christopher haunting this house because of Forest's presence? Was he haunting the man who had murdered him so long ago?

She shivered and curled her fingers around the warmth of her cup. That's all I need, she thought ruefully, to discover that Bobby and I are caught between a crazed murderer and a vengeful ghost.

She smiled, the shiver receding as she realized she was letting her overactive imagination sweep her away. There was absolutely no proof that Forest had murdered Christopher, and there was no proof that what she'd heard the night before had been the ghost of the little boy. And there's no proof that Forest is innocent, a tiny voice reminded her, only confusing the issue more deeply.

Leaning back in the chair, she replayed last night's conversation with Forest in her head. Why did he believe with such vehemence that he'd harmed Christopher? She knew there was something he wasn't telling, some secret that would make sense of all the madness. But what?

Sighing in disgust, she got up and poured the remainder of her coffee into the sink. She rinsed the cup and set it in the dishwasher, then left the kitchen.

She paused just outside the doorway that led down to the basement. Forest's workroom. He spent most of his time at home down there. What did he do? *Anything I want.* She remembered his answer. She wrapped her fingers around the doorknob, the cool metal reassuring as it turned easily beneath her grip.

Before she could think, before she could dissuade herself with good old common sense and caution, she opened the door and peered down the stairs.

The stairway was dark, the steps themselves narrow

and steep, disappearing into utter blackness. She turned on the light switch and illuminated the stairs, walking down the first couple before she could change her mind. She needed to know. She needed to see exactly what was down here.

As she crept cautiously downward, her heart beat a rapid tattoo, resounding eerily in her ears. It made it seem like the basement had a heartbeat, and the heartbeat was in her head.

She reached the bottom of the staircase and stared at the door in front of her. She hesitated, feeling odd about invading Forest's privacy. But she had to know if there was something down here that would attest to his guilt…something that might be indicative of a monster inside him. Was there some kind of clue to his crime in this room? Some piece of evidence that made him soul-certain that he'd hurt Christopher? She had to know for herself. But more, she had to know for her son. Bobby was Jeffrey's child also, and if Forest was some kind of a monster who had hated Jeffrey with such passion, might Bobby be in danger?

Her heart was still thudding as she opened the door and stepped into the dark. She fumbled on the wall until she found a switch. Turning it on, she realized she stood in a large room. A workbench ran along one wall, a peg-board above it. There were electric saws, and tools she didn't recognize both on the bench and hanging on the wall. The floor was covered with wood chips and shavings, and the entire room smelled clean and fresh like Forest.

"What did you expect? Heads in jars? A freezer full of body parts?" she muttered in relief. Whatever she'd expected, it hadn't been the normal woodworking shop where she now stood.

Against one wall was metal, floor-to-ceiling shelving, and on those shelves was an array of carved items. Julie walked closer, marveling over the exquisite detail of each piece.

She picked up a figurine of a fox, the detail of the rich wood breathtaking. It was crouched as if ready to spring on its prey, its ears at attention. It looked so real, she half expected the woodland animal to sniff her hand. She carefully set the piece back and picked up another one, this one a wolf. As she ran a finger over the delicate carving, admiration swept through her...admiration for the obvious talent, the overwhelming patience and pure genius that had created each line.

She set the wolf down, her attention captured by a figurine that was separate from the others. It was a little boy on a rocking horse. The same rocking horse that now sat in Bobby's bedroom.

The boy on the horse looked to be about five years old. His hair was shaggy, as if he were between haircuts, and his mouth was open in what was obviously a burst of laughter. A dimple indented his left cheek and thick lashes enhanced his lively eyes.

Carefully Julie took the figure off the shelf, feeling the love that had gone into the carving. It flowed in the lines, radiated from the detail. A man who created such miracles with his hands couldn't destroy a human life. It wasn't possible that Forest could have carved this piece and been responsible for Christopher's death.

As Julie's hands reverently stroked the little statue, she knew with a gut-deep certainty that Forest did not have the capacity to harm anyone.

"What in the hell are you doing down here?"

Julie gasped in shock and whirled around to face Forest, whose features were twisted in anger. The certainty she'd felt only a moment before fled beneath the rage that emanated from him.

"I—I'm sorry." Julie felt a flush of heat stain her cheeks. "I—I shouldn't have come down here, but I was curious."

Forest didn't say anything for a moment, then he sighed resignedly. "Yes, that definitely seems to be one of your more-irritating character traits," he replied tightly. A muscle worked in his jaw. He walked over to where she stood and took the figurine out of her hands. He carefully placed it back on the shelf, then looked at her once again.

Julie took a step backward, away from his commanding presence. "I didn't know I had more than one irritating character trait," she said, trying to ease the uncomfortable tension that vibrated in the air.

"You have several." He took another step and stopped so close to her that she could feel the heat emanating from his body, see the gray flecks softening the darkness of his eyes. His lower jaw was shaded slightly with a growth of whiskers that only intensified his overt masculinity. Her breath was suddenly trapped in her chest, held captive by the heat of his gaze.

"Like what?" she finally asked breathlessly, aware that the anger that had pulled his features taut only moments ago was gone. Suddenly she realized it wasn't anger at all that she saw stirring in the depths of his eyes. It was something else, something that frightened her more than his rage. It beckoned to an answering emotion in her.

"Your hair looks so soft, so touchable, and I find that fact most irritating." He reached out and wrapped a strand of it around his thumb.

She knew she should turn and run...run as fast as she could away from the flaming warmth of his body, the hypnotic gaze of his eyes. And yet she found herself not wanting to escape. From the moment she had accidently stumbled upon him naked in his bedroom, she had fought the flicker of sexual desire that sparked in the pit of her very being. Now that flicker burst into an inferno, sweeping over her. Her body tingled from head to toe and made it impossible for her to turn and run. Impossible for her to do anything but stand and wait for him to take what he wanted from her.

He released the tendril of hair and with a single fingertip traced the line of her jaw. "And damn you, your skin looks soft as silk, and I find that irritating as hell," he whispered. The pad of his finger was slightly rough, and she wondered what it would feel like caressing her breasts, running across a turgid nipple. She gasped softly as his fingers stroked across her lips. Back and forth they moved, the tip of one delving slightly into the wetness of her mouth.

It was madness, pure craziness. This man had only last night confessed to possibly being a murderer. But Julie didn't want to think about that. Not here. Not now.

She closed her eyes and heard his desire in the way his breath quickened as he touched her mouth, caressed the curve of her jaw. Then his mouth was on hers, his lips demanding as his arms enfolded her against the length of him.

It was not a gentle kiss. It was a kiss of hunger, of urgency. It tasted of tortured loneliness and voracious need. Julie didn't fight against it. Instead she gave in to the wildness of the moment, realizing this was what she had wanted from the moment she had first met him.

His mouth was hot, his tongue dueling with hers as his arms pressed her closer to the contours of his body. She was aware of his arousal hot and hard against her abdomen, but it only fed the intensity of her own response to him. The force of his loneliness wrapped around her, called on the isolation she had felt not only in the past year, but all her life. She felt a completeness, as if in mating their feelings of loneliness, they banished them.

With a guttural groan, he tore his lips from hers and pushed her away. For a moment neither of them spoke. The room was filled with the sounds of their ragged breathing.

"I... Why did you do that?" she finally asked. She reached up to touch her mouth, aware that her lips were slightly swollen and throbbing from his kiss. And worse...she wanted him to repeat it. She wanted him to kiss her again and again and again.

His gaze made it impossible to guess what he was thinking. Black, obscured by the power of his own will, his eyes told her nothing. "Let's just say I decided to indulge my own brand of curiosity," he finally said. "You wanted to see my room. I wanted to taste you." His eyes blazed once again with a hungry fire that caused her heart to jump erratically. "I want you, Julie. I wanted you from the moment I opened my door and saw you standing on my porch."

She gasped as he pulled her to him again. She could feel him, hot and rigid as he cupped her buttocks and drew her intimately against him. A bitter smile played over his sensual lips and he moved her body back and forth against his, the friction creating an urgent heat inside her. "How would you feel about making love to a murderer? There are some women who would find the very idea titillating. Are you one of those, Julie?'' He released her once again and stepped away, his features taut with anger.

Beneath the brutality of his words, she heard the forlorn tones of confusion, the emptiness of the abandoned. ''What is this, Forest? Just another technique to try to make me run away? Leave here?'' She ached with a need she couldn't define, the emptiness back inside her, too. ''You can't make me leave, Forest. You can't make me leave with your anger, and you can't make me leave with your sexual advances.''

''Get out of here, Julie. Leave me alone.'' He turned away, as if he couldn't stand the sight of her.

''Forest?'' She placed a hand on his broad back, realizing his anger wasn't directed at her. Self-loathing rolled off him in waves, washing over her and making her heart ache for him. ''Forest, I can't believe that you did anything to hurt Christopher. You couldn't. A man who creates such magic with his hands doesn't kill.''

He whirled around, his face twisted with the self-hatred she'd felt only moments before. ''Magic? I'll show you magic.'' He grabbed her hand in a painful grip and pulled her across the room. He yanked open a cabinet door and pushed her closer.

Inside were more figurines. These weren't like the ones on the open shelves. These demanded the dark recesses of a closed cabinet. They were nightmarish figures carved by the dark side of the artist. Despite her abhorrence, Julie studied the pieces, repelled yet drawn to the beautiful horror of each one. Trees twisted and gnarled, with faces of demons on the trunks; a wolf with teeth bared, feral and dangerous—each and every piece reflected nature at its most perverse, an ominous slant to the world.

He turned her around to face him, his eyes flaming with a soulless intensity that frightened her. He pulled her close to him, so close she could feel the heat of his breath on her face. "This isn't magic, Julie. It's madness. Sheer madness." He laughed, and the madness rang in his voice, radiated from his eyes.

With a small cry she pulled out of his arms and ran up the stairs. His laughter followed her—the laughter of the damned.

Julie's perfume lingered in the air long after she had run out of the room. The light floral scent wrapped itself around him, penetrating his senses, piercing his soul.

Forest sank down on the stool in front of the workbench, his head dizzy, his body trembling from the aftermath of the kiss. He shouldn't have kissed her. Dear God, he shouldn't have tasted the honeyed heat of her lips.

He'd forgotten. He'd forgotten the sweetness of holding a woman. He'd forgotten the feel of a woman's softness against his body, the hot mystery of a woman's mouth beneath his. Not any woman...Julie.

Her name exploded inside him, and he lowered his head into the cradle of his arms on the bench. The anticipation of that kiss had been building inside him since the moment she'd appeared on his doorstep. That night she'd looked so tired, so beaten, yet she'd had a hint of irrepressible pride sparking in her caramel-colored eyes. He'd felt an immediate ignition of attraction, an instantaneous burst of desire that had grown rather than diminished over the course of the week.

For the past ten years he'd been isolated from everyone. Initially, it had been his tremendous grief that had kept people at bay, then it had been the misery of his guilt, the rumors and whispers that had kept him distant, separated from everyone in town. It hadn't taken long for loneliness and detachment from others to become a habit, a way of life.

But in a heartbeat Julie had changed all that. She'd made him remember the human need for love, the tactile pleasure of skin touching skin, mouths seeking heat, bodies moving in unison to the ancient rhythm of passion. She'd made him remember all the things he could never again have, all the things he no longer deserved. He remembered...and he wept.

"The only thing I really need you for is to answer the phones," Lorna explained to Julie on Monday morning. "I'm out of the office a lot and people are always calling in with items they think will make good stories. Just take their name and number and get an idea of what they're calling about."

Julie nodded and sat down at the desk in the small front room of the newspaper office. Lorna had already explained to her that the *Kingsdon Gazette* was a weekly, with a strictly local slant. She'd given Julie the official tour of the premises, which consisted of a large storage room with file cabinets from floor to ceiling. A portion of the room, partitioned off with more cabinets, was Lorna's office. The actual press resided in the basement.

"Oh, you should be getting a call sometime this morning from Edith Windslow. Just pretend like you're taking her name and number." Lorna grinned. "She calls every Monday to relate her experiences over the weekend in a UFO." Lorna leaned a hip against the desk. "According to Edith, the aliens pick her up every Friday night, spend the weekend conducting all kinds of examinations on her, then deposit her back in her bed Sunday night."

"Do you believe her?"

Lorna laughed. "I believe Edith is a lonely ninety-year-old woman who needs some excitement in her life. But no, I don't believe she's spending her weekends in a spaceship." She looked at her watch and stood up. "I've got to get out of here. I have an appointment in ten minutes with a lady who says she has a pumpkin that's shaped like Abraham Lincoln's head." She grinned. "It's a rough job, but somebody's got to do it." She grabbed a camera off a shelf. "I should be back before noon." With a wiggle of her fingers, she left the office.

Julie sat at the desk and looked around. Outside the large expanse of glass that formed the front of the office, the autumn sunshine cast a golden glow on Main Street. Up and down the street she could see signs of businesses being readied for a new day. An old woman swept the sidewalk in front of the grocery store. Shades across the windows of the hardware store moved upward, as if at the orchestration of an invisible hand.

Kingsdon was a nice town. The kind of place where Julie might have considered putting down roots. She didn't miss living in the city. She had often tried to convince Jeffrey to move out of New York City to a smaller community upstate.

Bobby was thriving here. He'd done more emotional healing in the week they'd been here than he had in the entire nine months since his father's death. If things were different, she would stay here. She and Bobby would become part of Kingsdon and revel in belonging. But things weren't different, and she knew she would eventually have to leave. Forest's kiss had changed everything.

Heat rose up inside her as she remembered his mouth

on hers, the hardness of his body pressed intimately against her own. The kiss had rocked her to the core, evoked a heat of passion inside her she'd never before experienced.

Her and Jeffrey's physical relationship had always been rather tame. Although Julie had come into their marriage expecting passion and desire and the kind of physical intimacy only lovers could attain, it didn't take her long to realize Jeffrey wasn't a particularly passionate man. It didn't take her long to bury the passionate side of her own nature and settle for something less.

But Forest's kiss had reawakened that hunger, dormant for so long. She instinctively knew that Forest would never be satisfied with a woman who settled for less. He would demand response, expect the same kind of breathless passion he gave.

She jumped as the telephone rang, grateful for the interruption of her disturbing thoughts.

"*Kingsdon Gazette*," she said into the receiver, pen and paper ready to take a message. She put the pen down and smiled as Edith Windslow introduced herself and proceeded to relate her latest adventure aboard a martian spaceship.

The morning passed quickly. Surprisingly, there were a number of phone calls from citizens who had something they wanted announced. Mrs. Johnson, principal at the elementary school, called about a school carnival coming up in two weeks. Burt Simpkins wanted to put an ad in the paper for his dry-cleaning establishment. Several people called and left their names, with instructions for Lorna to call them back.

Lorna returned to the office just before noon. "Grab your purse and let's go get some lunch," she said as she breezed in.

"Shouldn't one of us stay here through the lunch hour?" Julie asked.

Lorna shook her head. "I always close up for an hour at noon. Everyone knows that if they have something that can't wait, they can find me at the café." She put the camera away and looked at Julie expectantly. "Come on, as a first-day-on-the-job treat, I'll buy your lunch."

"You don't have to do that," Julie protested as she followed Lorna out of the office into the noonday sunshine.

"You're right, I don't." Lorna grinned. "I'll just do it this once, and only if you order the special."

Julie laughed. "It's a deal."

The café was packed. Most tables were filled with burly men in flannel shirts who smelled of wholesome sweat and fresh-cut wood. Julie wasn't surprised. This was the only restaurant in a town too small to boast more than one fast-food place, a pizza parlor that delivered.

Julie and Lorna found a table in the corner and both ordered the meat loaf special from Betty.

"So, how was your morning?" Lorna asked, propping her elbows on the table as her gaze darted around the room, making flirtatious contact with several of the men.

"Actually, it was busier than I expected. I took several messages for you."

"Hmm, Monday mornings are always the same. The phone lines burn up with people wanting to get their names in the paper." Lorna wiggled her fingers at one particularly attractive blond man. "Martin Baylor," she said beneath her breath. "I have a date with him this Friday night."

"He looks nice," Julie observed.

"You should see him in a pair of cotton sweatpants and without a shirt."

Julie laughed as Lorna rolled her eyes and fanned herself with her napkin. Then she sobered slightly and took a sip of her water. "How long has the paper been in existence?"

"Forever," Lorna answered, giving Julie her full attention as Martin Baylor and his buddies paid for their lunches and left. "I've run it for the last five years. I bought it from Old Man Canterfield. He'd been editor and owner for the past twenty-five years."

"Are there copies of back issues anywhere? On microfilm?"

Lorna laughed. "You won't find any microfilm in this town, but I do have most of the old issues filed in those cabinets in the back room. Why?"

"Just curious," Julie said. "Would you mind if I looked through them in my spare time?"

Lorna shrugged. "Help yourself. Anything particular you're looking for?"

Julie shook her head, reluctant to tell Lorna exactly why she wanted to look at the old papers. "No, I just thought it might be a good way to really get to know the town and its people."

"Sure, you're welcome to look through whatever you want," Lorna replied.

The waitress brought their food, and they'd just begun to eat when another group of men walked in from the mill. Julie felt her breath tighten in her chest as she saw Forest among them. He nodded at the two women, then joined the men at a table nearby.

"You know, I had a massive crush on Forest when we were in high school," Lorna confessed as she smothered her meat loaf with catsup. "He was one of the heartbreakers of the school. Sinfully handsome but coolly aloof."

"Did you ever date him?" Julie asked, carefully keeping her gaze averted from him. Even the sight of him disturbed her, reminding her of the way his mouth had tasted, the feel of him so bold, so intimate against her.

"Nah, Forest was always too much man for me." Lorna grinned. "I like mine a little more agreeable, more malleable."

Julie laughed. "I can't imagine anyone being too much man for you."

Lorna's gaze went back to Forest and she frowned thoughtfully. "I don't want a man with a lot of angst. Forest is just too intense for my taste. If anyone is going to have emotional baggage in my relationships, it's going to be me!"

Again Julie laughed. There was something very likable about Lorna's irreverence toward herself and her love life. Julie wished she could be more like her boss and not take herself quite so seriously, but she couldn't.

Raised in a series of foster homes, she'd found the most important thing in her life when she'd been growing up was her dream of having a husband and a family. Unfortunately, her marriage had not fulfilled many of her expectations. She now realized that Jeffrey, having lost a family once before, had probably been afraid of the degree of intimacy Julie had desperately needed out of the relationship. Their marriage had likely been doomed from the very start.

Julie looked back at Forest, once again replaying his kiss in her mind. It had held nothing back, had demanded that she relinquish all of herself, and for those few moments when his lips had claimed hers, she had.

She had a feeling that Forest would expect and demand total acquiescence of body, mind and soul, and there was a part of her that hungered for that. Another part was frightened by the thought of such total surrender.

"So are you and Bobby planning on staying permanently in Kingsdon?" Lorna asked, pouring another huge dollop of catsup over the remaining piece of her meat loaf.

"I'm not sure," Julie answered truthfully. "Right now I'm just kind of taking things one day at a time. To be perfectly honest, part of what brought us here was the fact that Jeffrey left us completely broke." She felt a flush of embarrassment sweep over her face. "I didn't realize how far in debt we were until bill collectors came and took nearly everything we owned."

"Oh, hon," Lorna said sympathetically. "Bad enough to find yourself a young widow, but a broke widow at that…"

"Things could be worse," Julie said. "At least we had a place to come to, and now I have a job, and before long Bobby and I will be firmly back on our feet."

"And I hope you'll stay here in Kingsdon for a very long time." Lorna toyed with her fork for a moment, then looked at Julie once again. "Although I have to admit, I'd feel better if you could find another place to live." She leaned over the table. "There have always been whispers about that house, and Forest."

"You mean because of Christopher?"

Lorna nodded. "Did you ask Forest about him?"

"Yes, although he was reluctant to talk about it," Julie admitted.

Lorna shook her head. "It was such a tragedy. It really split the town apart. The men at the mill were already divided into two camps, those who followed Jeffrey and those who followed Forest." She twirled her fork and looked at Julie once again. "There were some who believe Forest did something horrible to Christopher, that he wanted to break Jeffrey completely.''

"That's ridiculous," Julie exclaimed uneasily. She still didn't know what to believe, but she wasn't about to discuss the issue with the woman who owned the local paper. She wasn't going to be the one to feed the Kingsdon grapevine. Lorna seemed to get the hint and concentrated on her food.

They ate for a few more minutes in a companionable silence. Julie was acutely conscious of Forest's presence in the room. It was as if her eyes were magnets and he were a sheet of metal. No matter where she tried to look, her gaze was drawn back to him.

She knew he felt her, too. Each time her gaze was pulled to him, his eyes looked at her. It was like a childish game of peekaboo, with first one, then the other quickly looking away.

Julie was almost grateful when she and Lorna finished eating. As they got up to leave, Julie was aware of Forest's gaze once again. She could feel it lingering on her, hot and hungry, as she walked out of the cafe.

"Lorna, do you believe in ghosts?" she asked as they walked back to the newspaper office.

"Ghosts?" Lorna looked at her in surprise. "You mean like spirits who rattle chains and haunt cemeteries?" She shook her head. "Nah, not me. I don't believe in any kind of supernatural garbage. Why?"

"Oh, just curious, that's all."

Lorna looked at her skeptically. "Just curious, huh? You'd better lie to me better than that. I'm a newspaper woman, remember? I've got a nose for stories, and my nose is definitely twitching at the moment."

Julie laughed uncomfortably, somehow sorry she had brought the subject up. "It's probably nothing."

"Come on…give," Lorna demanded.

"Twice since being in Kingsdon Manor, I've heard a strange sound."

"What kind of a sound?" Lorna unlocked the office door and they went inside. Julie sat down behind her desk and Lorna pulled up a chair in front of her. "What kind of noise did you hear?" she repeated.

"Crying. The sound of a child crying." Julie smiled self-consciously. "I know it sounds crazy, but I think it might have been the ghost of Christopher Kingsdon."

Lorna stared at her wordlessly for a long moment, then threw back her head and laughed. "Oh, Julie, you don't really believe that, do you?"

Julie flushed hotly. "I know what I heard," she protested. "I heard a child crying. It wasn't Bobby and it sounded eerie, otherworldly…like a ghost."

"But I got the impression that Forest wasn't too thrilled when you showed up on his doorstep."

"That's true, but what does that have to do with anything?" Julie asked with a frown.

Lorna smiled patiently. "Have you considered the fact that those noises might have been made on purpose, so that you'd think you'd heard a ghost and would hightail it right out of that house?"

Julie opened her mouth to protest, then frowned again. Was that possible? When she'd written Forest to see if it would be okay for her and Bobby to come here, he'd never answered her. She knew how disagreeable he had been when she'd first shown up at the house. It had been he who had first planted the idea of a ghost in her head. Was it possible that he manufactured those eerie noises to frighten them away? Had she heard the ghost of Kingsdon Hill, or had she heard the madman of Kingsdon Hill?

CHAPTER SEVEN

Forest sat at his workbench, trying to focus on the carving he held in his hands instead of on the woman who seemed to invade his every thought. Julie. Her very name was a litany of torment that caused fire in his veins. She'd stirred a hunger in him, a hunger that had been denied for far too long.

He frowned and ran his hand over the piece of wood, then picked up a sheet of fine sandpaper and began working it back and forth across the surface.

He hesitated as he heard the whisper of a footstep on the stairs, smelled the scent of sun-warmed hair and bubble gum. He felt a prickling at the small of his back and knew somebody was watching him. He knew immediately it was the boy. Bobby.

He swiveled around on the stool and saw him peeking around the corner of the door. "What are you doing there?"

Bobby stepped into the room hesitantly, his gaze darting about with curiosity. He shrugged and kept his eyes averted from Forest's. "Mom told me you made stuff down here." He took a step closer to the shelves. "Wow, did you make this stuff?"

Forest fought his initial impulse to bellow at the boy to get out. Since the moment Julie had arrived at the house with Bobby, he'd kept himself distant from him, not wanting to care, not wanting another child to get into his heart.

Still, as he looked at Bobby, he realized he didn't want

to send him away. The little-boy scent filled the room like a haunting memory from the past and he could feel the unbridled energy coming from the child. ''Does your mother know you're down here?'' he asked.

Bobby shook his head and frowned. ''She told me to stay away from here.'' The frown disappeared as he looked again at the wood carvings on the shelves. ''Did you make the big rocking horse that's in my room, too?''

Forest nodded. ''A long time ago.''

Bobby moved closer to where Forest sat. ''Could you teach me how to carve stuff?''

Forest looked at him in surprise. Christopher had often liked to play down here while Forest worked, but he'd never expressed any interest in learning how to carve.

''I'd like to learn how to carve a fox like that.'' Bobby pointed to the wooden fox on the shelf.

''Before you can carve a fox, you should be able to draw one.'' Forest knew he was taking a chance, knew he shouldn't be anywhere near the boy, but at the moment his need was greater than his fear. He needed to go back to that time years ago, when he'd found the magic of childhood with a special little boy.

He pulled another chair up to the bench and motioned Bobby into it. He then withdrew some paper from a drawer and set it and a pencil before Bobby. ''You draw me a picture of a fox and we'll see what we have to work with.''

''Okay,'' Bobby agreed enthusiastically. He immediately began sketching, pausing occasionally to scratch the end of his nose or erase an errant mark. ''Did my dad know how to carve?'' he asked.

At the thought of Jeffrey, Forest's stomach clenched as if a tight vise gripped it. No, your father only knew how to hurt, how to taunt, how to hate. And he taught me to do the same. "No, your father didn't carve," he answered.

"Who taught you how to do it?" Bobby asked, his attention still absorbed in the picture he was drawing.

"Nobody. I just taught myself."

"Cool." Bobby looked up and smiled at Forest, an open, wonderful smile.

Forest began working the sandpaper back and forth on the chunk of wood in his hand, his thoughts whirling. Were all kids so open, so automatically accepting? That was one of the things that had always amazed him about Christopher. Children were naturally nonjudgmental, naturally giving. What had happened to Jeffrey and him? How had their childhoods been so twisted, their characters so perverted? How had hate become such a constant thing between them?

He looked back at Bobby, noting how, when the boy concentrated, he caught his tongue between his teeth. Forest did that, too. It must be a Kingsdon trait. Ah…family. This child was part of Forest's family; his own blood ran through him. Forest's heart ached at the loss of another boy…and with the knowledge that he could never allow himself to be close to this child. He couldn't put another son of Jeffrey's in danger. He couldn't put his own heart at risk again.

"What do ya think?" Bobby held up his completed picture. Forest took it from him and looked at it critically, surprised that the boy displayed a natural talent.

"Not bad. Here, let me show you something." Forest grabbed another pencil and erased the ears that Bobby had sketched. "You've drawn him ready to pounce, but the ears are wrong. They need to be more alert…like this." Forest quickly began redoing them. He'd completed one when he felt it—the sensation of cold air on the back of his neck. His nose became filled with the scent of the woods, the smell of thick vegetation and slightly rancid mulch.

Alarm swam through him. He knew what was about to happen. It was always the same. He shoved away from the bench, his stool crashing to the floor behind him. "Get out of here, Bobby."

He was vaguely aware of the little boy staring at him in frozen fear. He was also conscious of a seeping darkness at the fringes of his vision, a darkness attempting to swallow his consciousness. "Run, Bobby, run!" he gasped desperately, and breathed a ragged sob of relief when the boy's momentary paralysis broke and he scampered up the stairs.

Forest sank down on the floor, head in hands, hoping the child had run fast enough, far enough. Then the blackness descended completely, and he knew no more.

"Whoa!" Julie exclaimed as Bobby ran into her in the kitchen. "Hey, what's your hurry?" She held him by the shoulders. His eyes were huge as he looked up at her. "Bobby? Is something wrong?"

"Uh, no, nothing's wrong." He squirmed in her firm grip. "I've just got to go to the bathroom."

She eyed him sharply, with the natural instinct of a mother.

"Mom, really. I've got to go." He wiggled out of her grasp and darted away from her, up the stairs.

Julie stared after him. She didn't know what was wrong, but she knew what Bobby's bathroom look was, and that hadn't been it. She suddenly realized that he had come from the direction of the basement stairs. Had he been downstairs in Forest's workroom? She'd told him time after time not to go down there, not to bother his uncle.

She decided to get to the bottom of things and went in search of Bobby. She caught him by the shoulders as he barreled out of the bathroom. "Were you downstairs with Uncle Forest?"

Bobby's face grew pale with guilt. He hesitated, then nodded his head. "I just wanted to see what he did down there all the time."

"I told you not to go down there, young man."

"Don't worry, I won't again," Bobby assured her in a way that was distinctly unreassuring.

"Why? What happened?"

Bobby's eyes widened and his bottom lip jutted out slightly. "It was okay at first. He was kinda nice and told me to draw him a picture. Then all of a sudden he changed, and he yelled and told me to run away. His face was all mean and I ran. I won't go down there anymore, Mom. I promise."

Julie didn't know whether to spank him or hug him. She opted for a hug and held him close for a moment. "Didn't you tell me you had some math homework tonight?"

"Aw, Mom," Bobby protested.

She pointed in the direction of his room. "Go on. Do your homework, then clean up that room." She watched until he disappeared through the doorway of her bedroom, then she turned and went back downstairs to the kitchen. She walked over the window, disturbed by what Bobby had told her.

Forest had been nice, then had suddenly changed. His face had turned mean looking. What Bobby had said replayed in her mind. Was it merely a case of a man being impatient with a little boy's snooping? Or was it something darker, more sinister? She shivered and stepped away from the window, suddenly terribly afraid.

"See you Monday," Julie said to Lorna as she left the newspaper office on Friday afternoon. She walked outside into the waning autumn sunshine, moving in the direction of her car.

It had been a good week but a tiring one. She'd forgotten how hectic life could be when working at a full-time job and dealing with a seven-year-old. Still, it was a good kind of tired. For the first time in a long while, she felt like she was actively working at her life, not just letting it roll her along like a tumbling rock.

She climbed into her car and cranked down the window, for a moment just sitting and relaxing as she contemplated the last five days. Not only was she answering the phones, but Lorna now had her writing some of the news stories and laying out ads. She and Lorna were quickly developing a nice friendship despite their differences in philosophy and experience. They often spent their lunch hours indulging in lively discussions and arguments about men, marriage and politics.

Julie was enjoying every aspect of her new job, and at noon that day had opened a bank account and deposited most of her first paycheck. She now sighed with satisfaction and started the engine of the car.

The thought of the evening ahead filled her with anticipation. Bobby was spending the night with one of his new friends, and Julie was looking forward to a long soak in a bubble bath and an early bedtime to recuperate from the long week.

As she drove through town, her thoughts turned, as they often did, to Forest. She'd scarcely seen him all week, but that didn't matter. Out of sight was definitely not out of mind where he was concerned. Since their kiss, he had occupied far too much of her thoughts during the day, and at night he possessed her dreams. They were erotic dreams that reached into the core of her being and lingered for several long, exquisite moments after she awakened.

True to his word, Bobby hadn't ventured down to the basement workshop again, and Julie had decided that Forest had merely exhibited the irascibility of a man who didn't want to be bothered.

Despite the fact that everything seemed to be going well, Julie felt like she was functioning with her breath held. She went to bed with an air of expectation and awoke with the same sense of weighty anxiety. She wasn't sure what she expected to happen, but knew that the house itself seemed to radiate a tension that filled her with a curious sense of dread. She felt as if she were waiting for a shoe to drop and had already been warned that it was going to land directly on her head.

At least there had been no more ghost sounds during the last week. She still didn't have any idea if what she'd heard had really been the ghost of Christopher Kingsdon, or an orchestrated attempt to scare her off. It didn't matter either way. For the moment she wasn't going anywhere. Until she had enough money to finance a new start someplace else, she and Bobby were stuck right where they were.

She pulled her car up in front of the house, struck as always by the darkness that shrouded the dwelling. Despite the golden glow of twilight, which painted the tops of the trees in lush tones, the saffron light did nothing to alleviate the shadows that possessed the place. It was as if the house itself repelled the light, preferring the nighttime.

It seemed a reflection of Forest. The house, like the man, appeared lifeless, without hope, devoid of a soul. There was an emptiness of spirit both in the man and in the house where he lived. "Silly woman," she muttered to herself as she parked the car and got out. She definitely needed a restful night...a night without dreams.

When she went inside, she found Lottie in the kitchen preparing the evening meal. "It's going to be an hour or so before we eat," the older woman said. "The roast is taking longer than I expected it to," she explained.

"That's all right with me," Julie replied. "We had a late lunch today, and I'll use the hour to unwind a little bit." She went upstairs, anxious to get out of her panty hose and skirt and into a comfortable pair of jeans.

Once changed, she decided to sit on the back patio for a while and enjoy the last gasp of fall. The trees that last week had been bedecked in splendid autumn dress had begun their yearly striptease, shedding colorful leaves and baring stark limbs.

The patio consisted of a small area of brick and cracked concrete that held rusted, wrought-iron furniture. She assumed it hadn't been used in years. Julie moved one of the chairs so that it faced the woods, which loomed dark and primal at the edge of the overgrown lawn.

She spotted the break in the undergrowth that she knew was the beginning of the path Forest took on his way to work each morning. Funny, she'd been here two weeks and had yet to explore any of the surrounding, wooded territory. And soon winter would grip the area, making a walk in the woods much less desirable.

She got up from her chair, suddenly wanting to follow the path that Forest walked every day. Why did he walk

to work? Why didn't he drive down the hill to the mill?
What lure did the woods hold for him?

She went back to the kitchen door and called to Lottie.
"I'm going to take a walk. I'll be back in a little while."

"If you're walking in the timber, don't you go off that
path. There're deep ravines and fallen trees all over the
place."

"Don't worry," Julie assured her. "I have no intention
of going off the beaten path."

Julie quickly discovered that the beaten path was difficult enough. Although it started out fairly wide and lit
with the pale golden hues of the evening sun, it soon
narrowed. The trees crowded together, their limbs forming barriers overhead that blocked out the sun and muted
all sound. Here no wind rustled the leaves, no wild animals scurried. There was nothing but forest, black and
impenetrable.

The air was cooler, and even though Julie knew that
colors had no odor, it smelled *green*...like tangled vines
and slippery moss and thick weeds. As she walked, she
passed some of the ravines Lottie had warned her
about—steep ditches that appeared to plunge into dark
nothingness. She shivered and moved to sit on a fallen
tree trunk along the path.

Christopher. She still found it difficult to realize Jeffrey
had once had another wife, another son—a family and a
life he'd lost through tragic events. It was no wonder
she'd always sensed a certain amount of emotional detachment from him. She realized now that he'd probably
been afraid to care too deeply, afraid to love too much,
afraid that he would lose again. Christopher's death had
taken its toll on her as well as Forest and Jeffrey. Her
failed marriage had been a victim of the past and its
tragic circumstances.

She frowned, aware of the sound of footsteps drifting to her from someplace up ahead. Unsure exactly what it was she heard, she stood up and moved forward cautiously, trying to be as quiet as possible. She stopped again and listened intently. Yes, it was definitely the sound of footsteps crunching the flooring of dead leaves and grass. It seemed to be coming from an area just to the left of the path where she stood.

She parted the thick brush, startled to see Forest pacing back and forth in a small clearing. She started to call his name and move forward to greet him, then hesitated. Something was wrong. She stepped back amid the brush, frowning as she stared. Something was wrong with Forest. His gait was slow, almost dreamlike as he paced back and forth.

But it was his face that captured her attention. It was completely unlined, unnaturally devoid of expression...empty of any emotion. As he turned back to face her once again, he looked right at her, yet there was no indication that he saw her. His face remained passive, untroubled, and in that instant she saw the beauty that his features could possess without the torment, the haunted look that was always there.

Still, it disturbed her, the utter passivity, the strange jerkiness, the repetitive motions. It wasn't normal. It was the same thing she'd seen briefly that day in the kitchen. As she watched, he suddenly stopped pacing. He looked around the clearing, his gaze wild, the torment back in his eyes, twisting his features.

Instinctively Julie melted deeper into the brush, not wanting him to see her, knowing he wouldn't want to find her watching him. He looked down at his wristwatch, then hissed a curse, the sound exploding the silence and causing Julie to stumble backward. She turned and ran silently back up the path.

It didn't take her long to get to the house, where she threw herself into the wrought-iron chair on the patio and tried to catch her breath. What had she just witnessed? What had he been doing? Why had he looked like he was on drugs or in a strange trance?

Thoughts whirled in her head as she watched the entrance to the path, expecting him to emerge at any moment. He'd looked so peculiar, like a malfunctioning robot. *The porch light is on, but nobody is home.* The old adage came to mind and she realized it fit perfectly. For a moment, as he'd paced back and forth, he'd been nothing more than a vacant shell, absolutely empty inside.

She remembered a night long ago when she and Jeffrey had gone to a club and watched the stage show of a hypnotist performing on volunteers from the audience. She'd watched with interest as he'd worked his magic on the six people who had come forward. When they were hypnotized, they had all worn the same expression Forest had, as if all the emotions had been emptied out of them.

But there had been no hypnotist in the woods. So what had Forest been doing? What had caused the strange blankness that had momentarily gripped him?

She jumped as he emerged from the path, a dark scowl on his face. The scowl seemed to intensify as his gaze fell on her. "What are you doing out here?" he asked.

"It was such a beautiful evening I decided to take advantage of it." She was glad her voice sounded normal and didn't reflect the turmoil of her inner thoughts.

To her surprise, he grabbed a chair and pulled it up near hers, then sat down. For a moment he didn't speak, and his gaze lingered on the woods. The last golden light spilled down on the tops of the trees, and the sky had filled with deeper oranges and purples.

She watched him, trying to summon the nerve to confess that she'd seen him in the woods, that she'd noticed something odd. But as always, his expression invited no entry into his personal thoughts. Besides, she reasoned, perhaps it had been nothing more than the fact that he'd been deep in thought. Maybe she'd only imagined the utterly empty expression on his face.

"It won't be long before the snow falls," he said.

"I'll bet it's beautiful when all the trees are covered with snow." Julie looked back at the woods, trying to imagine it frosted with snow and gleaming with ice crystals.

He turned and looked at her. "Beautiful?" He sighed and gazed back at the woods. "I suppose some would find it beautiful." His features pulled tight again. "For me it's never beautiful. It's harsh and lonely and—" He broke off and stood up. "I'm sure Lottie has dinner ready."

Julie nodded and followed him inside. They ate in silence. Normally Bobby filled in the blanks in the mealtime conversation, telling Julie about his day at school and his friends. Forest rarely added anything to the conversation, although he never seemed to mind Bobby's childish prattle.

They'd almost finished eating when, to Julie's surprise, Forest asked about Bobby. "Where's the boy?"

Julie frowned irritably. "Why do you have so much trouble with his name? He isn't just some boy, he's your nephew, and he's spending the night with a school friend." She sliced into her roast beef more viciously than necessary, her anger rising too quickly to control. "I find exceedingly irritating the way you keep your distance from him by refusing to even speak his name. It's one of the many things I find irritating about you," she added.

His dark eyebrows rose and a mocking smile curved his sensual lips. "You mean I have more than one irritating characteristic?"

She blushed hotly, suddenly remembering that a very similar conversation had preceded the explosive kiss they'd shared. He seemed to remember the same thing, for his arrogant smile faded and he frowned down at his plate. "So who is his school friend?"

"Roger Courtland. Lottie told me the Courtlands are a very nice family, and I spoke with Mrs. Courtland this morning to make sure she was aware of the boys' plans."

He nodded. "The Courtlands are a nice family. Bill is one of my foremen at the mill, and his wife works part-time at the library."

"I'd like to visit the mill sometime. I'd like Bobby to see it," Julie said.

"Why?" He gazed at her dispassionately.

Julie shrugged. "I don't know. I've never seen a mill before, and it's part of the Kingsdon heritage."

"Don't you have any heritage of your own?" he asked brusquely.

"As a matter of fact, I don't." Julie's stomach knotted as childhood memories swept through her. Memories of loneliness, and the feeling of not belonging to anything or anyone. She took a sip of her water, then continued, "I have no idea who my father was, and my mother died when I was two years old. I don't remember her at all. My heritage is a series of foster homes, some good, some bad."

"You had no other family?" Forest asked.

Julie shook her head. She wanted to tell him that that

was probably why she'd jumped almost immediately into marriage with Jeffrey. She'd had an enormous need to create a family for herself, and it was only now that she understood the distance Jeffrey had maintained would have eventually destroyed their marriage, had he lived. She'd needed more from him than he could give.

She picked up her water glass and took another sip, then looked at Forest, needing him to understand why he and his background was so important to her, and to Bobby. "I know the emptiness I've always felt. Like a drifting boat with no anchor, no port. I don't want Bobby to feel that. I want him to know his roots, understand his heritage."

Forest shoved his empty plate away, the darkness back in the depths of his eyes. "His grandfather was a philanderer, his father was a ruined man and his uncle is a madman." He stood up. "Some heritage the kid is getting." He stalked out of the room, leaving Julie alone in the sudden, overwhelming silence of the house.

CHAPTER EIGHT

Although it was not quite eight o'clock when Julie finished her bath, she pulled on her nightgown and crawled into bed. The hot bubble bath had relaxed her and she knew sleep was only a blink away. She yawned and turned out the bedside lamp, then snuggled into the sheets and closed her eyes.

A knock sounded on the door. "Just a minute," she called out. She stumbled from the bed and turned on the lamp, then answered the door. Forest was there.

"I'm sorry, I didn't realize you were ready for bed." His gaze flickered darkly as it played over the length of her. Bold and hot, it lingered here, caressed there. Her nightgown suddenly felt like molten silk, as if the heat of his eyes caused it to smolder and adhere to every curve of her body.

"What do you want?" She licked her lips, her mouth suddenly dry as her body vibrated with expectation, anticipation...of what, she didn't know.

"This is Bobby's." He held out a sheet of paper, a drawing of some sort. As she took it from him, their fingers touched, and Julie felt a jolt of electrical current sizzle through her.

She looked down at the picture blankly. "What is it?" she asked, trying to forget the fact that they were all alone in the big house, that her flesh was on fire with a hunger she knew only he could satisfy.

"Bobby drew it, and he had the ears all wrong. I fixed them." His voice sounded strange, husky with suppressed emotion. She knew the memory of their kiss burned in him as hotly as it did in her. That kiss had stoked a fire so intense she knew there was no way to put it out. The only solution was to let it flame freely until eventually it burned itself out entirely. "I ran across it in my workroom just a little while ago and thought Bobby might want it back."

She nodded. She knew that a single touch from him would cause her to spiral out of control. She wanted to lose herself in the shadows of his eyes, surrender to the frenzied need inside her.

He backed away, as if he saw the fire inside her and was unwilling to commit himself to the flames. "Good night," he said tersely, then disappeared down the long, dark hallway.

She released a shaky sigh and closed the door. Her heart ached with the intensity of desire that pounded through her. What was she going to do with this flood of wanting? How on earth was she supposed to survive this gnawing need? She'd never wanted a man like she wanted Forest.

It wasn't until she got back into bed that she realized Forest hadn't called Bobby "that boy," but instead had referred to him by name. Surely that was a good sign, a sign that he was starting to accept his nephew.

She turned out her lamp and rubbed her forehead tiredly. God, things were so confusing. She didn't know whether to be glad or afraid that Forest might get closer to Bobby. She didn't know whether she was putting herself and her son in jeopardy by being here or not. She only knew that at the moment there were too many questions and not enough answers to satisfy her.

The air around her suddenly seemed too warm. She kicked off the blankets and tried to keep her thoughts away from Forest. Damn the man for being so attractive, for possessing eyes that promised exquisite sins. Damn the man for giving her that soul-searing kiss.

She tossed and turned until nearly midnight, by which time she was so frustrated she wanted to scream. She'd been exhausted when she'd gotten into bed, but Forest's brief visit had chased all sleep away.

She sighed again and sat up, realizing it was ridiculous to lie in the dark and wait for sleep to claim her. Turning on the lamp, she reached for the paperback book she'd bought during her lunch hour that day. Surely if she read for a little while, she'd finally be able to shove away all thoughts of Forest and fall asleep.

Plumping her pillow up behind her back, she opened the murder mystery and began to read. She'd read only a few pages when the lamp next to the bed flickered off, then back on. She leaned over and checked the bulb, making certain it was screwed in tightly. At the same moment she became aware of a chill that gripped the room. It was more than a chill. The room was icy cold, and the premonition of dread that had filled her for the last week returned, this time exploding inside her as she sat unmoving on the bed.

Her chest rose and fell with each labored breath. She felt her heartbeat increase in rhythm, and the palms of her hands were suddenly sweaty.

A frigid finger of air stirred along her bare arms, raised the hairs on the nape of her neck and rippled across her face. As it swept over her she filled with immeasurable loneliness. Sadness overwhelmed her, swallowed her.

She was consumed with an ache of such loss. Alone...she was so alone. She gasped as the lamp flickered off and on once again, and she realized tears were spilling down her cheeks, tears she didn't understand but couldn't stop. She only knew that she was lost, abandoned and frightened by the intense, hollow desolation that swept through her in wave after agonizing wave.

As quickly as it began, it ended. The loneliness immediately dissipated, although her body still shook with uncontrollable tremors.

She pulled the blanket up closer around her, her fingers shaking as she placed the book she'd been reading on the table next to the bed. What had just happened? She rubbed her hands over her eyes, finding remnants of her tears still wet on her cheeks. Had she fallen asleep for a moment and merely dreamed it all?

"No," she whispered in answer to her own question. She hadn't been asleep. The flickering lamp had been real. The cold air that had drifted over her like the horrifying caress of the dead...it had all been real. In fact, the room was still unnaturally cold. So cold.

The lamp blinked off again, plunging the room into darkness, and she tensed, unsure what to expect, but knowing to expect something.

An enormous boom resounded. Julie screamed and jumped from the bed, terror riveting through her. The noise erupted once again, and a picture crashed to the floor as the walls shook from the roar. Without waiting another moment, afraid that the walls themselves were tumbling down, she ran out into the dark hallway, where she met Forest. "What is it?" she asked breathlessly. "What's going on?"

"I—I don't know." His voice sounded strained, tense. He grabbed one of her hands. "Come on, I've got a flashlight in my room." Together they moved down the dark hallway and into his bedroom, where moonlight spilled in through the windows, painting the masculine furniture in ghostly illumination.

He led her to the bedside table, where he released her
hand, opened the drawer and withdrew a large flashlight.
He clicked on the high-power beam and, absurdly, Julie
felt better, safer. Surely a powerful flashlight and Forest
could protect her from things that went bump in the night.
"I'm going downstairs to look around," he said softly.

"I'll come with you," Julie exclaimed, not about to
be left alone in the dark.

Together they crept down the stairs. Julie clung to Forest's arm as the flashlight pierced the blackness before
them. They had gone halfway down the stairs when the
booming began again. It reverberated through the house,
seeming to come from nowhere and everywhere. It surrounded them, engulfed them.

Julie flew into Forest's arms, clutching him as the
walls, the roof, the house around them exploded in sound.
Cold air enveloped them. Their breaths were expelled in
vaporous mists that swirled like frantic spirits in front of
them. The stairway vibrated beneath their feet, as if
threatening to blow apart and cast them to the ground
below.

Julie hid her head against his chest. She squeezed her
eyes closed, afraid of what she might see, horrified by
the thunderous booms that ripped the air around them.
They came in patterns of five. Five booms, then a moment of silence, then five more.

"What is it? What is it?" Julie screamed, wanting to
press the palms of her hands against her ears to block out
the noise, but afraid to release the death grip she had on
Forest.

"I don't know," Forest said again, his voice strained
and nearly inaudible amid the deafening pandemonium.
Wave after wave of sound assaulted them, as frosty air
embraced them.

Julie didn't know how long they stood there. Time lost all meaning. She kept her head tucked against Forest's chest, focusing only on the feel of his beating heart and the fresh, minty scent of soap and masculinity. Those were the only normal things in a world gone mad. Around them reality had stopped and horror reigned, and Forest was a warm, safe center.

The very air surrounding them was oppressive, filled with an unnatural pressure that made her want to scream again. Her sanity was slipping and she hugged Forest more tightly. She wanted to crawl inside him and hide there.

"It's over."

Julie didn't move, but whimpered into the hollow of his neck, her eyes still tightly closed.

"Julie." He gently moved her away from him. "It's over."

"Are you sure?"

"Can't you tell?" He stepped back.

Yes, whatever it was, it was over. The air around them was warm again. Normal. She could see the light of her bedside lamp spilling from the doorway into the hall. The pressure, the tension she'd felt surrounding them was gone. Yes, at least for the moment she knew he was right. It was over.

"Let's go downstairs and see what we can find." Forest clicked off the flashlight as he turned on the hall light. They cautiously descended the rest of the stairs, both expecting to find complete destruction in the rooms below.

Nothing. They searched each and every room, but found no aftermath, no evidence of anything amiss. Despite the thundering noise that had crashed through the house, they found nothing broken in any of the rooms.

"I don't understand," Julie said as she sank down onto

the sofa. "We weren't hallucinating. Those noises were real. It sounded like the house was falling down...like a wrecking ball was slamming into the roof, the walls."

"I don't know what to think," Forest admitted. He sat in his chair before the fireplace and leaned forward with his head in his hands. A muscle in his jaw worked like a misplaced heartbeat, letting Julie know he was more disturbed than he acted.

"Has anything like this happened before?"

He shook his head. "Never."

Julie frowned, searching for rational explanations for the strange phenomena they had just experienced. "There isn't some sort of military base nearby, is there? Or an airport? Maybe they were sonic booms." She flushed as he raised his head and eyed her wryly. "Is there some sort of a fault line under the house? Or an underground river?" Her flush deepened. "Well, I'm trying to think of rational explanations," she said defensively.

"Don't waste your time," he said softly. He leaned back in the chair and closed his eyes. He remained that way for a long time.

Julie stared at him, Lorna's words suddenly coming back to her. When she had told her boss about the crying sounds, Lorna had suggested that perhaps Forest was responsible and the whole thing was an attempt to drive her away. But as Julie stared at his face, she knew there was no way he was responsible for this. She'd felt his heartbeat racing as fast as her own. He'd been frightened, too.

He didn't look frightened anymore; he merely looked weary, beaten. She fought her impulse to go sit on the floor next to him, to lay her head in his lap, to comfort him by letting him know that in some strange, perverse fashion she cared.

He opened his eyes and sighed. "We might as well go on back to bed. I think it's all over for the night."

He stood up and Julie followed. Frustration gnawed at her, along with a lingering whisper of fear. She followed close behind him as they went up the stairs. She dreaded the moment when he would go into his room and she would be left all alone. "Forest," she said as they stopped in front of his bedroom door. "What do you think the noise was?"

"It wasn't any sonic boom or earthquake." He hesitated a moment. "It was Christopher."

Julie sucked in her breath. Somehow she'd known he was going to say that. She'd thought the same thing herself. But hearing it spoken aloud caused her mind to rebel at the thought of a dead child causing such terror. "That's crazy. Christopher is dead."

Forest's eyes glittered darkly. "Julie, you've heard him crying. Didn't you feel his cold breath on us while we stood on the stairs? It's Christopher, I know it is."

"But...but why is he here? What does he want from us?"

"From me," Forest corrected her. "He wants retribution from me."

"Aren't you afraid?"

He tilted his head thoughtfully. "No. You have to be alive to be afraid, and I've been dead since the day Christopher disappeared."

His words, so empty, again filled with such loneliness and despair, touched a chord deep inside Julie. Without thinking, she reached up and gently stroked the furrow in his brow, allowing her finger to linger, to stroke down the side of his strong face.

She'd meant to comfort him in some way, but instantly knew she brought him no comfort. His eyes flared, and she knew that her touch had whipped up the wild winds of tension that had whirled between them since the night of their kiss, the same wanton winds that had blown through her earlier when he'd come to her room. And as she gazed into the depths of his eyes, she felt that wind blowing hot and wild around her, through her. She knew immediately what the tension was—desire, pure and unadulterated.

He jerked her hand away from his face and pulled her tight against the heat of his bare chest. A faint groan escaped from him as his hands slid over her nightgown, burning her with heat through the silky material. He cupped her buttocks and eased her closer, against the hardness of his arousal.

She gasped at the intimacy and tilted her head back to look at him. His mouth instantly claimed hers in a ravenous kiss. His tongue invaded her, seeking, demanding, refusing to accept anything but total surrender. And without a second of hesitation, she surrendered.

Forest stepped away from her for only a moment, to give her enough time to protest, to stop the craziness of where they were headed. But she didn't want to stop. He could see the heated lust in her eyes, see the pulse that ticked erratically in the hollow of her throat.

He willed her to find the strength to turn away, to run back into the safety of her own bedroom, for he had no strength of his own. He was tired of being strong. He was sick of being alone. He wanted her, but knew he had nothing to give her except his passion, and his soul-sickness.

Run. Get away from me. He tried to mentally communicate this to her, tried to ignore the way the swell of her breasts pressed invitingly against the silk of her gown, the nipples erect as if seeking the heat of his own chest. He tried to ignore that damnable pulse in the hollow of her throat, wanting nothing more than to press his lips against it, taste the sweetness of her skin, sweep his tongue against the heat of her flesh.

She gasped softly, as if able to read his mind. For a moment their gazes locked, and in her eyes he saw the same desire that swept through him, the desire to take, to fill a need, to abandon all common sense.

As he watched her, willing her away from him, she straightened her shoulders and swept past him, into the moonlit, silvery hues of his bedroom. With a curious sense of dread and exhilaration, he followed her.

He paused just inside the doorway, his breath catching painfully in his chest. She stood by the side of his bed, bathed in the moonlight spilling in the window. As he watched, she reached up and pushed the straps of her gown from her shoulders. It slid down the length of her body and pooled like a puddle of milk on the floor, leaving her clad only in a pair of wispy panties. Her breasts gleamed in the moonlight, small but perfectly formed, the dark erect nipples stirring his blood as nothing had in years.

Still he remained unmoving, trapped by his mixed emotions—the heady desire that soared through him and the knowledge that if he took her, he would awaken a need inside that he had denied for years.

"Forest." Even her voice sounded hot to him, throaty with passion, sultry with promise. She moved to lie down on the bed and opened her arms to him, beckoning him to join her in this moment of madness.

In that instant his inertia broke, and with a muttered curse, he tore off his jeans and approached the bed. He hesitated, the edge of the mattress pressing into his thighs, surprised to realize his body was trembling. For a single moment he was gripped with incredible fear. His mouth went dry as he tried to identify the source of his sudden, overwhelming anxiety. He shouldn't be here with her. He didn't deserve her passion.

She rose to her knees and reached for him. She wound her arms around his waist, her hands caressing the broadness of his back. Her breasts pressed intimately against his chest as her mouth found the hollow of his neck. The flick of her tongue against the heat of his throat caused his fear to fade away and be replaced with a frenzied need to possess her.

The fear that had momentarily gripped him was banished beneath the assault of her nearness, her almost-total nakedness. With a groan, he lowered her onto the bed and joined her in the tangle of sheets and moonbeams.

His mouth founds hers, drinking in liquid fire that warmed him through, and he realized it would be easy to drown in this woman. It would be easy to let go of all control and take her quickly, savagely. It would be easy to immerse himself in sating his own hunger. But he didn't want it that way. He didn't want it to be quick. He clung to control, wanting this moment, this night with her, to last forever.

As he kissed her, his hands sought the fullness of her breasts and he rubbed his fingertips across the turgid nipples, felt them swell and become harder at his touch. ''Julie. Julie.'' He whispered her name as his lips left hers. Her skin smelled clean and feminine, like soap and springtime and woman. He wanted to lose himself in her, crawl into her and away from the pain and loss that had been his companion for so long. He wanted to drown himself in her scent, in the silkiness of her skin, in the heat that radiated from her and warmed places inside him that had been cold...so cold for so long.

He moved one hand down the flat of her stomach and cupped his palm against the silky panties. Her damp heat enticed the fire inside him and he pressed his palm against her as she arched to meet his intimate touch. She sighed in pleasure as his fingers crept beneath the nylon material, finding her moist and open.

Her response, her obvious pleasure, fed his own, his need painful as he struggled to maintain control. "Please," she whispered urgently, and he knew she wanted more. Her eyes were glazed and her skin flushed with her response to his touch, but he wasn't ready to complete what they had begun.

"Not yet," he replied, dipping his head forward so his tongue could flick erotically over the tip of one of her breasts. At the same time he swept her panties down past her hips, to a point where she impatiently kicked them the rest of the way off.

As his fingers once again sought her moist heat, her hips rocked against his hand in a sexual rhythm that caused his blood to surge. His fingers slid in and out, his thumb circling the sensitive area and causing her to gasp, to increase her movements against him.

He knew she was climbing to her peak, could feel the tension that built and rippled through her, and he watched her intently, coveting the expression on her face, her violent response to his touch.

She cried out suddenly and stiffened against him, her body trembling uncontrollably with the force of her climax, and as she melted beneath him, his own control snapped.

He moved on top of her and buried himself in her, gasping as she enveloped him in hot velvet. Then he was lost—lost in the need he'd suppressed for far too long. Lost in Julie.

Julie was lost as well. She had been from the moment she'd stepped into his room, smelled the scent of him that lingered on the sheets, permeated the very air. He surrounded her, his heart beating against hers as he moved inside her. She responded to him in mindless wonder. He filled her as she'd never been filled before, demanded that she meet his thrusts with matching ones of her own.

Somewhere in the back of her mind she knew their lovemaking had absolutely nothing to do with love and everything to do with need. And it was more than a physical need. As he stroked deep within her, he captured her face with his hands, commanding her to look at him, connecting with her in a way that had little to do with what their bodies were experiencing.

She felt his need, shimmering in the air around them, shining from his eyes, which glowed silvery in the moonlight. She felt it echoing inside her and pulled his head down so their lips could meet in a kiss of hunger, of rapture.

And then she couldn't think anymore. She could only feel…accept…and surrender to Forest.

When it was over, he rolled off her so that no part of his body touched hers. She felt his physical distance, but not as acutely as she felt his emotional withdrawal. She leaned up on one elbow and stared at him, searching for words to bridge the distance between them.

He had one arm flung across his eyes, his expression hidden from her. The moonlight caressed his body, and the sight of his masculinity, the memory of what they'd just shared, stirred desire once again. She fought the impulse to reach out and stroke him, watch as arousal overtook him, force him again to take her to the heights where he'd just swept her.

"Forest?"

He didn't answer, didn't move.

"Forest?" She placed a hand on his arm and felt him flinch beneath her touch. "That was...beautiful." She smiled, realizing how inadequate words were to describe what they'd just shared. He didn't answer, didn't move. "Forest? Don't you think we should talk about what just happened?"

He moved his arm away from his face and looked at her. His eyes glittered dark and hard. "No, I don't think we should talk about it. I think you should go back to your room and forget this ever happened."

"I can't do that." She leaned closer to him, watching as shadows overtook his eyes, shadows that had been momentarily banished while they'd made love. "I don't want to forget what went on between us." She placed her hand on his chest and felt the thundering of his heart. "I want to do it again." She leaned over and flicked the tip of her tongue across his flat male nipple. She was shameless and she knew it, reveled in it. "I want to do it again right now."

His eyes flared, the pupils dilating, and with a thick groan he pulled her on top of him. This time the need, the urgency was gone, but the hunger was still there. And this time it was she who caressed, who stroked, tormenting him until he cried out hoarsely, his harsh face revealing all the emotions he normally guarded so closely.

"Damn you," he whispered as she stroked him to full arousal.

"Yes," she answered heatedly. "Damn me." She'd rather have his damnation than his cool disdain. She'd rather have his anger than the unnatural facade he presented to the world. She wanted to break through the shield he'd placed around himself for the past ten years, shatter it and find the heart of the man.

She hovered over him, her hands touching, lingering, caressing, and her lips did the same. And with each touch, each caress, he cursed her passionately, and she reveled in his rich emotion.

With a low moan that vibrated deep in his chest, he rolled over, taking her with him and placing her beneath him once again. As he buried himself in her she lost all rational thought and allowed herself to be swept to the place he took her, a place of mystery and magic and the exquisite wonder of Forest.

Silence. Again. Only this time they remained entangled, too exhausted to pull away from each other. Time passed, minutes expanded. She matched her breathing to his, relaxing in the slow, steady rhythm.

The moon had moved behind the clouds, casting the bedroom in darkness. Julie didn't think, was afraid to. She didn't have the energy to deal with the regret she knew would come with the dawn. She didn't want to analyze what force, what winds of fate had brought them to this place at this time. She wanted only to savor the sensations that still coursed through her, to relish the state of utter fulfillment that embodied her. With a sigh, she closed her eyes and allowed herself to fall into a dreamless sleep.

CHAPTER NINE

Forest knew the instant sleep claimed her. He felt the energy leave Julie's body and knew she'd given herself up to him completely, trusting him enough to fall asleep.

There had been very little tenderness between them. Their lovemaking had been primal, fueled by need and executed with lust. Only now, while she slept, did he allow his heart to feel what his body had experienced.

It had been so breathtaking to accept what was offered freely, and to respond in kind. She had given not only with her body, but with her heart as well. She'd held nothing back from him and he'd found a soul-soothing magic in her arms. If only it could be this way always. If only the demons that raged inside him could be soothed so easily. If only…

This should never have happened. He'd been a fool to allow Julie and her son into this house, an even bigger fool to allow her into his bed. He'd sworn to himself that he'd never let anyone get close to him again. He would never put another person in jeopardy by allowing himself to care. He couldn't afford to care for Julie, and he definitely couldn't allow her to care about him. He didn't deserve that. He was the worst kind of person…a murderer who'd killed a child he loved.

He eased himself up and away from her and went to the window, where he stood and stared out at the woods. It was a more-profound, deeper-black area in the darkness of the night, but he'd looked out so often he could easily imagine every tree, every twisted vine.

Christopher! his heart cried out. The name brought with it such pain that it twisted his gut. He knew with certainty that the forces that filled this house—the cold spots, the booming, the child's eerie wailing—were all his nephew demanding a pound of flesh from the man who had taken his life. Unfortunately, he couldn't appease him when he didn't know exactly what it was the spirit wanted. Did Christopher want him dead? Was that the only way to give his restless soul the peace it needed? He ripped a hand through his hair and leaned his forehead against the windowpane. "What do you want from me?" he whispered. He couldn't undo what had been done so long ago. Hell, he couldn't even remember what had been done.

Julie. His heart cried out a second time. Damn him for the weakness that had allowed him to make love to her. He couldn't care again. He couldn't take the chance of loving her. He was afraid—afraid of what he was capable of, afraid of what he might do during one of the blackouts that had already ruined his life and stolen the life of another. He had to get her away from here. He had to force them to leave. He had to get them to go before another blackout occurred, before another tragedy happened.

He stood at the window for hours. Dawn was just starting to creep over the tops of the trees when he heard Julie stir. He turned and watched her. The golden morning hues glimmered in through the window and found her, painting her sweet skin with a luminous glow. Her eyes were still closed and he could see her lashes, thick and gold tipped. The bed sheets were twisted around her waist and hips, exposing her breasts and the tantalizing length of her shapely legs.

He was surprised to feel desire rocket through him once again. And the desire brought with it anger—anger at himself for wanting her and anger at her for wanting him. He grabbed his jeans and pulled them on, then moved to the side of the bed and touched her shoulder, ignoring the satin texture beneath his fingers.

"Julie." He spoke her name harshly, needing his anger to guard him, to keep her away.

Her eyelids fluttered, then opened. As she looked up at him, a soft smile curved her lips. It was the smile of a woman sated, heavy with slumber and filled with promise. It was an arrow through his heart, a piercing pain of dreams lost and hope abandoned.

Her smile slowly faded when she saw his expression. She frowned and sat up, reaching for the sheet, as if it would provide shelter from his hard gaze.

"The sun's coming up. You should go back to your own room." He heard the coldness in his voice, and she must have felt it, for she pulled the sheet more closely around her.

She frowned and shoved her hair away from her face, obviously fighting off the last lingering vestige of sleep. "Forest...I...don't you think we need to talk about what happened?"

"There's nothing to talk about. It was a stupid mistake."

"Perhaps," she agreed. "But it happened, and I think it fulfilled a need we both had."

He looked at her in surprise, unsure what he'd expected from her. Certainly not this. "Strictly physical," he added.

She hesitated, as if she was going to contradict him, then nodded grudgingly. "Okay, if that's what you need to think."

For some reason her answer made his anger rise once again. He saw only acceptance in her eyes, an acceptance of him that was threatening because he wanted it so badly and knew he didn't deserve it. He deserved her loathing, her hatred. He needed it to preserve the barrier that would keep her safe from the murderer he feared resided within.

He leaned toward her, close enough to see the golden specks that flamed in her brown eyes. "Actually, you're right." He reached out a finger and stroked the side of her cheek, noting how she unconsciously leaned toward his touch. "I did have a need…an incredible need." He cupped her face in his hands. "I had an incredible need to make love to Jeffrey's wife."

She drew in a sharp breath and jerked away. "You don't mean that," she said faintly, her eyes staring into his as if trying to see into his soul. "That's a despicable thing to say."

He shrugged, noting how the spark in her eyes had intensified, how her lips quivered. His intentional cruelty had wounded her, but he couldn't stop now. He must push her away. "You want to talk about what happened? That's what happened. That's what pulled me to you from the moment you arrived on my doorstep. Jeffrey tormented me from the time I was born. He took from me every chance he got. And even though he's dead now, I'm not finished taking from him."

She stumbled from the bed and grabbed her nightgown from the floor. Her jerky movements were uncoordinated and she gasped for air like somebody who'd been punched in the stomach. He hardened his heart against the tears that glimmered in her eyes as she faced him once again. "I don't believe you," she said, her chest heaving. "This had nothing to do with Jeffrey. There weren't three of us in that bed, there was only you and me."

He narrowed his eyes and swept them down her body,

slowly, insolently. "I have to admit, once things got started, I forgot exactly why I wanted you. You're a good lover, Julie. Jeffrey was a very lucky man."

He watched the anger build inside her. It flushed her cheeks a becoming pink and caused her spine to stiffen regally. God, she was beautiful, and her anger fed his desire as intensely as her earlier eagerness had done. "You lied to me before," she said, her voice quivering slightly. "Just a little while ago you told me you weren't afraid of the ghost of Christopher because you were dead, and dead men don't feel fear." Her entire body now trembled with the force of her anger. "You aren't dead, Forest. I know, because dead men aren't bastards." Without waiting for his reply, she turned and left the room.

Forest released a deep sigh and turned back to stare out the window. She was right; he was a bastard. The worse kind of bastard. The bleak emptiness was back, surrounding him, engulfing him. She was right: he wasn't dead. He hurt too damned much to be a dead man.

"I'm out of here," Lorna said at two o'clock the next Friday afternoon. "I've got a couple of leads to check out on a hot new story, then I'm heading home to get ready for my date with Martin." She handed Julie a couple of sheets of paper. "If you could just type these up for me, then you can go ahead on home."

"Sure, no problem," Julie agreed, then added with a sly grin, "Hmm, that makes two weeks in a row you've gone out with Martin. Getting serious?"

Lorna laughed. "It's still a bit too early to tell. I like the way he looks in and out of his jeans, and he makes a terrific homemade pizza, but marriage is not based on sex and food alone. Time will tell if he has other attributes that make him marriage material." She headed for the front door. "Don't forget to lock up," she said, then disappeared into the afternoon sunshine.

It took Julie only a few minutes to type up the letters Lorna had left, then she locked the front door and went into the back room. She'd been waiting all week for an opportunity to look through the old newspapers and see what had been written at the time of Christopher's disappearance.

She quickly discovered that there didn't seem to be any discernible order to the way the papers were filed. As she worked, looking for the time period she wanted, her thoughts whizzed through the events of the past week.

The few times she and Forest had run into each other, they'd circled each other like two wary animals. She was still incredibly angry with him, but oddly enough, her anger was tempered with sadness. She didn't believe the horrible things he'd said to her after they had made love. There was no way she would ever believe that the only reason he had wanted her was because she had been Jeffrey's wife.

She'd felt the loneliness inside him, a deep, abiding loneliness that had reached out to her, and despite his assessment that what they'd shared had been strictly physical, she knew it had been much more than that. She'd felt his soul reaching out, stroking hers. His body had made love to her, and no matter how he tried to deny it, his heart had, too.

More than ever she was determined to find out exactly what had happened on the day Christopher disappeared. No matter how often and how loudly Forest announced his guilt regarding his nephew's death, she simply couldn't believe it. She'd lain in his arms, felt his heart beating next to hers, felt the torment that encased his soul. He wasn't a murderer; he couldn't be. A man who was capable of murder wouldn't be capable of evoking such emotion in her. Something didn't ring true about Christopher's disappearance. She was determined to discover the truth of what had happened ten years ago, determined to break the bonds of self-hatred that kept Forest an emotional prisoner. As long as he believed he'd murdered Christopher, his heart would forever be encased in ice.

She focused her attention on the task at hand, moving to a second file cabinet when the first didn't yield what she sought.

It was nearly five o'clock when she finally found what she'd been looking for. She pulled out an old, yellowed newspaper with a headline that read Kingsdon Heir Disappears.

Unfolding the fragile paper, she spread it out on the floor, then sat down cross-legged and stared at the photographs on the front page. There were two, one of Jeffrey and Forest, the other a snapshot of Christopher.

She studied the picture of the two half brothers first. It had apparently been taken long before the death of Christopher. The body language of the two men displayed the subtle animosity between them. Jeffrey commanded attention first, looking young and arrogant in the center of the frame. Forest was a step behind him, his body turned slightly away, as if he hadn't particularly wanted to be in the picture in the first place. Julie's heart ached for the young men, whose lives had been torn apart, their happiness destroyed, by the disappearance of a little boy.

She turned her attention to the photo of Christopher, vaguely surprised at his likeness to Bobby. Christopher had the same hair, the same lively dark eyes. Even the shape of their faces proclaimed them to be related by more than mere boyhood.

She scanned the article quickly, disappointed to discover that it told no more than what she already knew—sketchy facts that neither confirmed Forest's guilt nor vindicated him. Looking at the picture of Christopher once again, she sighed and traced a fingertip over the yellowed paper. "What happened to you?"

She leaned back against one of the file cabinets, her thoughts whirling in her head. Was it possible to hate somebody so much you would kill his child? Was it possible for hate to be so intense it could override all love?

In truth, she didn't know. Hatred had never had any place in her life. But she knew it was an emotion that twisted people's guts, perverted their souls, transformed them into monsters. Newspapers were filled with stories of normal, rational people shoved over the edge by hatred.

She didn't believe Forest had killed Christopher. She couldn't believe it. Even in sleep his social conscience surely wouldn't have allowed him to take the life of another. The story Forest had told her simply didn't wash.

She sighed again, refolded the newspaper and placed it back in the file where she'd gotten it. No questions had been answered. Looking at several more papers, she found several follow-up stories, but no new information, no answers to her questions.

As she remembered the fearsome banging that had resounded through the house on the night she and Forest had made love, a shiver raced up her spine. Had it been what Forest said it was? Had the ghost of Christopher Kingsdon made the walls vibrate and sound like they were falling down? If he was a ghost, then he was a very angry one. Why else would he be haunting the house, unless it was to avenge his death...and demand retribution from the man who had murdered him?

Julie screamed as a loud booming suddenly resounded. Then she shook her head ruefully as she realized somebody was pounding on the door of the office. Leaving the back room, she hurried toward the door, where a petite, white-haired woman was using her tiny fist as a battering ram.

"It's about time," she said, bristling as Julie unlocked and opened the door.

"I'm sorry, we're closed for the day," Julie explained.

"News don't just happen between nine and five on weekdays." The old woman swept past Julie regally and planted herself in the chair in front of her desk. She motioned Julie into the opposite chair. "Well, park yourself if you want a story better than who grew the latest fruit in the shape of some historical figure."

Julie hid a smile as she sat down. She had a strong feeling she knew who sat across from her. "What kind of story do you have for me, Mrs. Windslow?" She ventured the guess and was awarded a wide smile displaying ill-fitting dentures.

Edith Windslow leaned forward, her vivid blue eyes sparking with ancient mysteries and perhaps a tinge of dementia. "You've heard of those encounters of the third kind? Well, I've had better than that." She frowned. "You'd better get paper and pencil ready. You young people don't have memories the length of my nose. Me, I remember everything that's happened in this town for the last eighty years." Her frown deepened and she tilted her head quizzically. "Memory is a perverse sort of thing, ain't it? I can remember what my mama served for my fifth birthday party, but I don't remember what I had this morning for breakfast.'' She waved her hands, her frown disappearing.

For the next twenty minutes, Julie listened to Edith's latest tale of alien abduction. What the woman lacked in facts, she more than made up for in creativity. Julie dutifully took notes. Even though she knew Lorna would never use the story, she didn't want to hurt Edith's feelings, and in truth found her story fascinating. Besides, the old woman seemed harmless enough despite her wild imagination.

''I know most folks think I'm nuts,'' Edith said as she rose from the chair at the end of her tale. ''But there are some of us who are more in touch with the other side of reality.'' She hesitated at the door and tilted her head, and her keen blue eyes seemed to peer into Julie. ''You know what I'm talking about. You've been touched by the other side, haven't you?''

''No, I don't know what you're talking about.'' Julie took a step backward, away from the suddenly insightful gleam in the old woman's eyes. What had appeared as dementia before now seemed to be aged wisdom.

''Sure you do. The scent of the spirit world clings to you.'' Edith reached out a bony hand and placed it on Julie's arm. Her touch was cold and caused a shiver to creep up Julie's spine. ''You have a son, don't you?''

Fear clutched at Julie. ''Yes,'' she answered hesitantly.

Edith closed her eyes for a moment, her head nodding as if she were receiving a secret communication. Her eyes snapped open again, wide and startled. ''Watch him. Guard your boy closely.'' The old woman snatched her hand away, as if having contact with Julie's skin was somehow abhorrent. ''Danger. Danger.'' The madness was back in the bright blue eyes.

She nodded curtly to Julie, then turned and hurried

down the sidewalk, muttering under her breath as her head bobbed up and down.

Bobby. The name reverberated through Julie with a sense of urgency. She looked down at her wristwatch and gasped. It was nearly six o'clock. She had never been this late. Julie had arranged her hours so that she would always be home by four, when the school bus dropped Bobby off at the house.

Grabbing her purse, she quickly locked up and ran for her car. As she drove, she fought the panic that threatened. Had Lottie already left for the day? Was Bobby all alone with Forest?

"Forest would never harm Bobby," she said aloud, as if speaking the words would make them so. Whatever had happened ten years ago was a tragic accident. Forest couldn't have killed Christopher and he would never do anything to hurt Bobby.

Still, as she remembered the way Forest had looked when she'd stumbled upon him in the woods, fear constricted her throat. No, Forest would never harm Bobby if he was in his right mind. But what if he didn't know what he was doing? What if he had been in the same strange state she'd seen him in in the woods, and had led little Christopher out of the house and killed him?

"Stop it. Just stop it," she commanded herself firmly as she stepped on the gas. She was allowing the ramblings of an old woman to affect her mind. After all, Edith declared that she was whisked away to martianland every Friday night. What did she know about anything?

Still, she had known Julie had a son. She'd known about Bobby, and she'd said he was in danger. The car skidded to a stop before the house, and Julie flew out and through the front door. "Bobby?" she yelled. She paused in the entry hall, listening for a reply. "Bobby? Are you here?'' When there still was no answer, she hurried into the kitchen. Empty. No sign of Lottie. No sign of Bobby.

Her heart pounded with such intensity that her chest ached. She left the kitchen and took the stairs two at a time. She raced into her bedroom, then into the smaller, attached room. Bobby's schoolbag was on his bed, his good slacks tossed on the floor. So he'd come home from school and changed clothes. Where was he? Dear God, where could he be?

She gazed out the window, staring toward the woods, afraid she would see Forest leading Bobby down the path toward the dark center of the tangled growth. More frightening was the possibility of seeing Forest walking out of the woods…alone. Her hand covered her mouth in horror at the very thought. Would the crime of ten years ago be reenacted now, with Bobby the innocent victim? Did Forest have a dark side, one he didn't know about, one that thrived on hatred and murder? Oh, God, would Bobby just disappear, as Christopher had done?

Then she saw them. Together. Not on the path that led to the woods, but rather on the patio below her. Forest was helping Bobby to flip hamburgers on a small gas grill.

She leaned her forehead against the windowpane and expelled a small sob of relief. Oh, God, for a moment she had thought…she had feared… Shame flooded through her. She'd allowed a silly old woman to stir horrid thoughts about a man her heart told her was innocent. Was her belief in Forest so fragile?

She watched Forest and Bobby, waiting for her pulse to regain its normal rhythm, waiting for the lingering fear inside her to recede. As she stood there, Lottie bustled out of the kitchen and set a large bowl on the wrought-iron table. She must have been out back when Julie came in a few minutes earlier.

Julie released another sigh, her gaze captured once again by Forest and Bobby. They could easily be mistaken for father and son. Their hair shone with the same dark, rich highlights, and both could use a visit to the local barbershop. If she were closer she'd see that their eyes were shaped the same, although she knew her son's would never reveal the dark torture that deepened Forest's.

At that moment Bobby looked up and caught sight of her. A huge grin lit his face and he gestured for her to come down. She nodded and waved back at him. Her hand froze in the air as Forest looked up, and their gazes locked. Everything she had tried not to think about, tried not to remember since the night they had made love, was there in the heat of his eyes. Unfortunately, the taste of fear still lingered in her mouth like the aftermath of a bad dream. It reminded her that he was an enigma, a man whose inner darkness taunted her with whispers of danger. She wanted so desperately to believe him innocent, but there was a little bit of doubt there, one that had exploded inside her when she'd thought Bobby might be alone with him.

She turned away from the window and quickly changed clothes, then went down to join the people on the patio—the two men closest to her heart.

"I don't know who thought of it, but eating outside was a fine idea," Julie said an hour later as she and Forest sat on the patio. For a change, dinner had been pleasant. It was as if she and Forest had silently agreed to a truce. The tension that had been so thick, so uncomfortable between them since the night of their lovemaking was momentarily put aside. They'd finished eating, and Lottie had whisked the plates away, then left for the night. Bobby was on the back lawn, tossing a football up in the air, then catching it.

"It was Bobby's idea," Forest said. "Actually, he wanted a picnic on the grass, but he agreed to compromise and eat outside. There won't be many more warm evenings."

"Hmm, all I know is it feels nice to be outside."

Forest nodded and looked over at Bobby, his expression rather wistful. "I should take pity on him and play a little catch with him. A football was meant to be thrown back and forth."

"Why don't you?" Julie urged. "I'm sure he'd love it."

He hesitated another moment, then bounded out of the chair and ran across the yard toward Bobby. Within minutes the two were playing catch. Julie relaxed in her chair and watched them as the evening shadows deepened.

There was something wonderful about watching them play together. As Forest chased after Bobby's errant passes, stretched to catch the ones he could, he displayed a natural athletic ability and grace and reawakened in Julie the desire she had spent the last week tamping down. He was so breathtakingly masculine, and just looking at him made her feel so distinctly feminine. She pushed away these disturbing thoughts, not wanting to dwell on the splendor of being held in his strong arms.

Forest was infinitely patient with Bobby, cheering him when he threw a good pass, encouraging him to work harder when he didn't.

The first time Forest laughed out loud a thrill raced through Julie. She'd never seen him laugh before, had never heard the rich tones, watched his eyes crinkle in merriment. It was beautiful, bewitching, magically transforming his features with inner illumination.

It's not fair, she thought sadly. It wasn't fair that Forest needed the joy of having a child in his life, and Bobby needed the role model of a man in his, yet fate had conspired to make it impossible for the two to give to each other.

This moment together, sharing, bonding, was an anomaly, one Forest would not allow to be repeated. As long as he believed himself to be a murderer, he would forever keep himself isolated, allowing her only a painful glimpse of what might have been.

"Whew, that kid has some energy," Forest exclaimed as he rejoined her at the table. He picked up his glass of tea and took a long, deep swallow.

Never had he looked so attractive to Julie as now, with a sheen of sweat across his brow and a flush of color on his cheeks. She wanted to see him laugh again. She wanted to make love to him again. She averted her gaze and looked back at her son, who was once again tossing the ball up in the air and catching it.

"He's a good kid," Forest said softly.

"You like children," Julie observed.

He hesitated a moment, then nodded. "I never had any interest in children or having a family until Christopher was born." He smiled softly, and again Julie caught a glimpse of the man Forest might have been if tragedy hadn't permanently scarred his soul. "Oh, I suppose someplace in the back of my mind I assumed that, when the time was right, I'd get married and have kids. But Christopher made it all seem so much more real, so much more desirable. I wanted to fill this house with children's laughter." He gazed up at the structure that loomed behind them. "It's never been filled with much of anything but hatred."

"It's not too late," Julie said. "You could still fill the house with love, with children."

He shook his head, and it was as if the dark shadows of the evening emanated from his eyes. "You still don't get it, do you, Julie?" He stood up. "I don't have children...I kill them."

CHAPTER TEN

"Bobby, it's time to head inside," Julie called as the purple hues of dusk deepened and spread fingers of darkness around them. The night brought with it a cool breeze that rustled the last leaves on the trees and reminded her that winter was just around the corner.

Would she and Bobby still be here when the snow flew? Lorna had told her that winters here could be harsh, with frigid temperatures and deep snow. But surely the winter chill could not compete with the chill Forest's parting words had placed around her heart.

He didn't have children, he killed them. His pronouncement, so stark, so blatant had shocked her. Was she a fool to remain here in this house with a man who believed himself guilty of a heinous crime? If she truly thought Forest was a threat to Bobby's safety, then no financial crisis would keep her here. If she had to, she would live in her car along the side of the road to keep Bobby safe.

But her heart simply refused to believe in Forest's guilt. She realized that watching Forest play catch with Bobby, seeing his features free from guilt and bathed in the glow of happiness, had caused the last of her doubts to fade away. She knew he was innocent as surely as if she'd been there on that day, as if she actually knew what events had led up to Christopher's disappearance. Forest was not a killer, and she was gambling her life and her son's on her gut instinct.

Still, she hadn't been there and she didn't know exactly

what had happened. Forest had said he'd fallen asleep, had insisted he'd killed in his sleep. But that couldn't possibly ring true. Something else had happened that day, something he hadn't told her.

All she had to do was figure out why he felt so adamant about his own guilt. He'd fallen asleep; the child had wandered off and gotten lost. It was probably as simple, as tragic as that. So why on earth did he believe he'd done something terrible? What secret did he hold? What else had happened that day that made him so certain of his own guilt?

She rubbed her forehead tiredly, aware that the night was growing colder. "Bobby, come on now. It's getting too cool and dark for us to be out here." She stood up and looked across the yard to where Bobby appeared to be talking to himself. He had his hands on his hips, and although she was too far away to hear what he was saying, his face was twisted in a frown. It looks like Bobby and his imaginary friend are having a fallout, she thought.

She frowned, wondering if she should be worried about the appearance of this new imaginary friend. Surely not. Surely it was just a harmless manifestation of a lonely little boy.

Once he was more adjusted in school, and as he made more plans with his new friends, this newest imagined playmate would just disappear, like Gifford the Rabbit had years ago.

"Bobby," she called again, the tone of her voice letting him know she was losing patience.

"I'm coming," he yelled. He picked up his football and ran toward her. As he drew closer, she could see his troubled expression.

"Honey, is anything wrong?" she asked.

"Nah, my friend just doesn't want me to go inside yet. He's mad at me."

Julie smiled. "Perhaps your friend doesn't catch colds as easily as you." She met him at the edge of the patio and threw an arm around his shoulder. "Besides, the nice things about imaginary friends are that they don't stay mad for long."

"But he's not...oh, never mind." Bobby's foot caught on one of the concrete patio bricks, displacing it and nearly tumbling him on his face. He regained his balance and leaned down to replace the brick, but paused. "Hey, Mom, there's something down here." He reached down into the space the errant brick had revealed and withdrew a small, metal strongbox. "Wow, I wonder what it is. Maybe it's a treasure chest. Pirate's gold or something cool like that."

Curious, Julie took the box from him. "Come on, let's go inside and see what you found."

They went into the kitchen. Bobby danced around the table with excitement as Julie tried to decide if they should open the box or take it directly to Forest. When she saw the initials etched in the metal, however, she knew she wasn't going to fetch Forest, at least not until she'd looked inside.

Whatever the box held would only add to his pain. With one finger she traced the indented letters *CK*. Christopher Kingsdon. Besides, perhaps there was a clue of some kind inside, a clue to what had happened to the little boy. "Come on, Mom. Open it," Bobby encouraged eagerly.

"Yes, yes, all right." Julie fought down a slight tinge of guilt as she unhooked the latch and opened the box. Inside there was no pirate's gold, no splendid treasure, but something even more valuable. Polished rocks, a tattered bird's nest, old photographs, a rabbit's foot—the treasures of boyhood all safely preserved in a metal box. Her heart ached as she thought of the little boy who had tucked these treasures inside, a little boy who had met a mysterious, tragic end.

"Wow, who do you think this all belonged to?" Bobby asked curiously. He took the white rabbit's foot and rubbed its furry softness against his cheek.

"I'm not sure," Julie answered. She wasn't ready to talk to Bobby about Christopher, although eventually she knew she would have to tell him about his half brother. Still, she knew right now he would only find it confusing to discover that his daddy had had another wife, another son, a full life before he'd been in their lives. "Maybe we should just give this to Uncle Forest," she finally said. "He'll know what to do with it."

Bobby replaced the rabbit's foot with a sigh. "I wish it would have been pirate's gold. That would have been so cool."

"It's time you wished yourself right up into a bath. Go on," she said, stilling the protest she knew was coming.

"If I was a pirate I'd never have to take a bath," Bobby grumbled as he left the room.

Julie sat down at the table and pulled one of the photos out of the box. It was a picture of Forest and Christopher. The little boy was no older than three, and his arms were wrapped tightly around Forest's neck. Forest looked so young, with no torment, no torture in his eyes. There was such joy, such love emanating from their faces that it was like a knife twisting in Julie's heart.

It was time she talked to him again. When he'd told her about Christopher's disappearance, she'd had the suspicion he was holding something back...that there was a piece of evidence or something he'd refused to divulge. It was time she pressed him.

She looked at the picture once again and realized why she was so determined to prove Forest innocent. The stakes were suddenly enormously high. She was falling in love with him.

"Oh, no," she gasped softly as she allowed the full intensity of this new discovery to sweep through her. She hadn't intended this to happen, had fought against it since the moment she'd arrived. But somehow, some way, Forest had managed to touch her in a place she felt had never been touched before...right in the center of her heart.

She could stop it all now—stuff the feelings she had for Forest into the darkest recesses of her mind and not allow them to go any further, not allow them full bloom. If he never touched her again, if she refused to allow the memories of their lovemaking to enter her thoughts, then perhaps the crazy feelings would pass like a painful, but harmless case of the flu.

She stood up and relatched the catch on the box, wishing she could lock her emotions away as easily. As it was, she knew she would have to lock them into her heart and not allow them any escape. There was no hope here. There was no future with a man like Forest. He was tainted with the bitter relics of his tortured past, condemned to spend his life alone...in the rancor of his own self-hatred.

Realizing Bobby was probably finished with his bath, she took the box and went upstairs. Later, after he was tucked in bed for the night, she would give the box to Forest. After all, it wasn't right for her to keep these pieces of Christopher from him. She wasn't in the position to make a decision like that.

It was nearly two hours later that Julie finally got

Bobby into bed and worked up the nerve to go down to the workshop, where she assumed Forest had been since he'd left them in the backyard.

She crept down the stairs to the basement, reluctance slowing her pace, the box tucked under one arm. She could hear him in his room, the sounds of sandpaper rubbing against wood. She hesitated outside the door, realizing this place had become his sanctuary. This was his asylum from the town, where his exalted position as mill owner made him not quite belong. From a past he couldn't forget and an offense he couldn't forgive.

Julie knocked on the door, trying not to remember that the last time she'd been inside the workroom they'd shared an explosive kiss that had rocked her very senses. She tried to forget that she now carried a part of his painful past under her arm.

He opened the door. "Something wrong?" he asked curtly. He moved back across the room and sat down at the bench. He picked up a figurine and began sanding it once again, not looking at her.

"No. Nothing's wrong. I'm sorry to bother you...." She felt a flush heat her face as he paused in his work and gazed at her.

"You've done nothing but bother me since the minute you arrived here." For a moment he looked at her objectively, as if he had successfully removed himself from her, as if she was nothing but a stranger who had mistakenly wandered in here.

Her flush intensified. She would have to work very hard to achieve the same detachment. "That was never my intention," she said softly. She moved closer to where he sat, her attention caught by the figurine he was working on. "Oh, that's beautiful." She took another step nearer, to see more clearly the wooden bird Forest held.

"It's a falcon," he said softly. "Do you really like it?"

The bird's wings were bent in midstroke, giving an immediate impression of flight, of freedom. The hooked beak gave the raptor a proud nobility. It looked beautifully savage, like the man who had crafted it. She nodded in answer to his question.

He looked at the bird dispassionately. "Did you know that falcons are often trained to kill crows?"

She shook her head, unsure what he was talking about. He gave one wing a final brush with the sandpaper, then held it out to her. "It's finished. You can have it."

"Oh, no, I couldn't...." And yet her hand reached out, as if of its own volition. When she took it, she was still able to feel the warmth of his hand in the wood. She held it for a long moment, then set it down on the table, suddenly remembering why she had come down here in the first place. "I have something for you." She took the box from beneath her arm.

His eyes widened, first with recognition, then with pain. "Where did you get that?" His voice was husky, filled with the emotions he normally kept so tightly capped. He reached out a hand, then withdrew it, as if both drawn and repelled at the same time.

"Bobby tripped over one of the bricks in the patio. This was hidden underneath it."

Forest inhaled deeply, then took the box from her. His hands trembled slightly as he ran his fingertips across the etched initials. "I gave this to him when he was five. He was such a collector of stuff and always had things shoved in his pockets. We decided he needed a treasure

chest, a special place to store all the good stuff a boy
could find.''

He placed the box before him on the worktable and
stared at it, as it afraid to open it up, see what remnants
of Christopher lay within. ''I etched his initials here on
the morning of his fifth birthday.''

Julie moved to stand directly behind him, knowing
how difficult this would be, wanting to comfort him but
not knowing how. She felt the tension rolling off him in
waves and wondered how many times in the last ten years
he had faced painful relics of the past alone.

She watched as he opened the box. A small, almost
inaudible groan escaped him as he began to pull out the
items one by one, holding each for a long moment, then
laying it aside. Julie placed a hand on his shoulder, needing to connect with him, wanting him to know she shared
his pain.

He gasped softly as he withdrew a heart-shaped ruby
from the very bottom of the box. He held it up and shook
his head ruefully.

''That's from Lottie's necklace,'' Julie exclaimed, remembering when the housekeeper had told her about it.

He nodded, holding it so that the bright light overhead
danced in the cut of the stone. ''That little scamp. I always suspected Christopher had found this someplace
around the house and had kept it. I used to call him the
Little Crow. From the time he was a baby he loved
bright, sparkly things.'' His hand closed around the
jewel, clutching it so tightly his knuckles turned white.

''Forest?'' Julie spoke softly.

He spun around on the stool and caught her by the
waist, pressing his head against her heart. Although his
face was turned into her, so she couldn't see his expression, she felt the sobs that suddenly ripped through his

body, and she held him tightly. She stroked his hair, trying to absorb some of his pain, make it more manageable for him.

And as she held him, she realized she couldn't ignore her feelings for him. She couldn't avoid what her heart told her—that she was helplessly, irrevocably in love with Forest Kingsdon. And as the utter hopelessness of that love swept through her, she held him closer and allowed her own silent tears to fall.

She didn't know how long she remained there with Forest's tears staining her blouse and her own tracking, one after another, down her face.

Finally, the sobs that had racked his body diminished, then stopped altogether. Still he held on to her waist, as if she was his only salvation, and she held him, too, wishing she could be his redemption.

With a low moan, he finally released his hold on her and sat up. Julie's heart ached at the emptiness revealed in his face. He looked as if all he'd had inside were tears, and with them gone, he had nothing left within.

"Please," he said, turning his face away from her, obviously embarrassed. "Please…just get out. Leave me alone. I need to be alone."

"Forest, you've had the last ten years to deal with this alone. Isn't that long enough?"

He looked up at her, his eyes black as night and as empty as death. "Christopher is gone forever, and that's how long I'll be dealing with what I've done. Now, please, leave me." He turned back around and buried his head in his arms. The overhead light caused the ruby heart beside him to glitter as if mocking her, mocking her love.

Again hopelessness overwhelmed her. The past had an unyielding hold on Forest, a hold she didn't know how to break. She couldn't fight the spirit of a little ghost boy, couldn't break the bonds that would keep Forest captive forever.

She picked up the wooden falcon, then turned and walked out of the room, granting Forest his wish to be alone. Climbing the stairs slowly, she felt her heart ache with her newly discovered love, a love doomed by the mysterious events that had happened ten years ago. Never had she felt so helpless, and her helplessness stirred an anger at the Fates who had cast her here, with another man incapable of love.

"What do you want from him?" she whispered as she walked through the living room. "Let him go, Christopher." She talked to the walls, to the ceiling, feeling foolish and yet compelled to beg a spirit to release his possessive hold on the man she loved.

Climbing the stairs to her room, she felt old, ancient, beaten by things she didn't understand, couldn't comprehend. She knew there was an enormous capacity for love in Forest, a capacity he refused to entertain because of the crime he thought he'd committed. As long as he believed he'd murdered Christopher, he would never allow himself to reach out to her or anyone else. He would forever refuse to seek happiness.

She sat down on the edge of her bed, overwhelmed by the hopelessness that seemed to permeate the very walls of the house. Sighing, she quickly changed into her nightgown, then peeked into Bobby's room to check on him before retiring herself.

Moonlight spilling in the window showed that Bobby's bed was empty. "Bobby?" She turned on the light to make sure her eyes weren't deceiving her. He was nowhere in the room.

The bathroom, she thought immediately. Quickly she

went down the hall, the first niggle of worry sweeping over her as she realized the bathroom was dark and empty. "Bobby?" She ran down the hallway to the second bathroom. It, too, was empty. The fear that had only been a whisper inside her now exploded. Where was Bobby? He'd been in bed, sound asleep, when she'd gone downstairs to talk to Forest, but that had been almost an hour ago. He almost never got up in the middle of the night for anything. Where had he gone? Where could he be?

She pounded down the stairs, her heart thundering erratically as she remembered the odd look in Edith Windslow's eyes. "Danger. Danger," the old woman had said when she'd spoken of Bobby. And now the feeling of imminent danger was horribly real.

"Don't panic," Julie warned herself. Maybe he was in the kitchen getting a late-night snack. That thought reassured her as she raced toward the kitchen. Bobby wasn't there...but the back door was wide open, letting in the cold night air. She hurried to the door and peered out. The moon was brilliant overhead, sending down a luminous light that painted the landscape in ghostly fashion. Toward the back of the yard, heading toward the woods, was her son.

His pale blue pajamas shone starkly in the moon's glow, silhouetting him against the deeper darkness of the looming woods. For just a moment those very woods seemed to breathe, seethe as if with a life force of their own. The thick grove of trees appeared to move with ominous intent, and she imagined she could feel a nearly imperceptible pull directed at her son.

"Bobby!" she screamed, terrified at the sight of him heading toward the black growth of the woods. His feet stopped and he hesitated. "Bobby," she yelled again, and he turned to look in her direction.

The cold night air surrounded her as she stepped out the door. "Bobby, get in here," she cried, her fear mingling with the first stirring of anger. What on earth was he doing outside at this time of night? He knew better. She'd often told him of the dangers of wandering in the woods. She was vaguely aware of Forest's footsteps hurrying up the stairs from the basement.

"What's going on?" he asked, coming to stand behind her. "What's he doing out there?"

"That's what I intend to find out," Julie replied, not taking her eyes off her son. He was still turned toward her, but he wasn't moving. It was as if he was torn, trying to decide whether to follow whatever impulse had led him out into the darkness of the night, or listen to his mother, who called him back.

Again Bobby turned and looked toward the woods, his body poised as if to run away from his mother, away from safety.

"What in the hell is he doing?" Forest asked tersely.

Julie didn't know if the fear that surrounded her was her own or Forest's. All she knew was that her body thrummed with a pulsating rhythm of imminent tragedy.

"Doesn't he know it's dangerous out there in the dark?" Forest said angrily. "I'll go get him." He shouldered his way past her, but at that moment, whatever had kept Bobby stationary snapped, and he ran toward Julie and Forest.

When he reached them, Julie grabbed him by the shoulders, her fear momentarily displaced by anger. "What on earth are you doing out here?" she asked. Hysteria rose up inside her and she fought against it. "I should spank the living daylights out of you."

Bobby's eyes were huge as he gazed first at his mother, then at Forest. "I'm sorry, but I had to, Mom. I had to come out here. He wanted me to, and I couldn't make him mad."

"What are you talking about?" Julie asked. Without waiting for an answer, she led him back into the warmth of the house, aware that his little body was quivering with a chill.

She didn't say another word until she had him in front of the fire in the living room, where the warmth of the flames effectively battled the chilliness of the night.

Forest walked over to the bar and held up a bottle of brandy. When Julie shook her head, he poured himself a glass and sat down in his wing chair.

"Now, talk to me, Bobby. You've been told time and time again not to go near those woods, yet here you are in the dark of night heading right toward them." Julie's shiver dispelled the worst of her terror.

Bobby sat down on the floor, refusing to meet her gaze. "I knew you'd be mad. I told him you'd be really mad. But I couldn't help it. I told you, he wanted me to go. He told me I had to."

"Who, Bobby?" Forest asked. "Who told you to go out into the woods?"

"My new friend," Bobby answered, then looked defiantly at his mother. "And he's not imaginary. He's as real as me, and he's magic."

"Oh, Bobby." Julie sighed in frustration. "You're old enough to know the difference between what's real and what's imagined, and you know that you're never supposed to go into the woods. Now I don't want to hear any more nonsense about this new friend."

Bobby stood up, his little face twisted with his own frustration. "Mom, he's real! He's as real as you and me!

He wanted me to go into the woods, and I couldn't help it. He made me go. He made me do it!'' Tears spilled down Bobby's face. "He's as real as I am, and he's got dark hair like me and his name is Christopher... Christopher the Crow.''

Bobby sobbed and ran from the room just as Forest gasped and stood up. His brandy glass fell from his hands, shattering against the hardwood floor, and his gaze sought Julie's. Terror drenched her once more as the implication of what Bobby had said swept through her. It wasn't an imaginary friend that had called him into the woods in the middle of the night. It had been the ghost of a dead boy.

CHAPTER ELEVEN

For a long moment neither Forest nor Julie spoke. The air around them vibrated with the lingering aftermath of Bobby's shocking words. The fire snapped, shooting sparks that caused Julie to jump. Forest bent down to pick up the shards of his broken glass.

Julie watched as he moved with wooden footsteps to the bar, where he grabbed a towel, then cleaned up the last of the mess from the dropped glass of brandy. It was impossible! Her mind rebelled with protests as she replayed Bobby's words in her head. And yet she knew it wasn't impossible, and the thought that a dead little boy was communicating with her son filled her with a kind of horror she'd never before experienced.

When he finished cleaning up the mess on the floor, Forest stood up and met her gaze. "Julie, there has to be a logical explanation," he protested. She knew he was wrestling with the same doubts that assailed her. "Surely Bobby heard us talking about Christopher and borrowed the name for his imaginary friend."

For a moment uncertainty swept through her. Yes, surely that must be the answer, she thought. But it didn't make sense, and she quickly shoved the idea away and shook her head vehemently. "No, Forest. Bobby didn't hear us talking, and his friend isn't imaginary." She should have known it was more than her son's imagination. She'd seen him talking to his "friend," had watched him only that evening in the yard having an argument with him. She should have known it was something more than just a lonely little boy playing let's pretend.

She shivered and wrapped her arms around herself, trying not to remember the terrifying moment when she'd been afraid Bobby would ignore her call and run into the darkness of the woods. She'd felt the magnetic pull emanating from the trees, an otherwordly energy drawing Bobby away from her, away from safety.

"The spirit of Christopher tried to lure him into the woods. Why?" Hysteria rose up inside her once more. "Why, Forest?" She moved forward until she stood in front of him, her eyes pleading for answers. "What does he want with Bobby? Dear God, what's going on?" Her voice rose a full octave with the last question, and he grabbed her by the shoulders as if to keep her from falling apart.

"Julie." He said her name sharply, but she barely heard him. All she could hear was Edith Windslow's words of warning: *Danger. Danger.* The old woman had seen Bobby at risk. What did Christopher want with him? Why had he wanted Bobby to go into the woods in the middle of the night? Did Christopher want Bobby dead? Oh, God, did he want her baby dead like him?

Numbly she allowed Forest to lead her to the sofa and pull her down next to him. Her thoughts spun around and around in her head as she tried to separate a little boy's fantasy from reality. Maybe Forest was right, she thought wildly once again. Perhaps Bobby had heard them mention Christopher and had simply borrowed the name for his imaginary friend. Yet even as she thought this, she knew it wasn't true. In an instant, she remembered the chilling air that often filled Bobby's bedroom, the night that the rocking horse had been wildly moving by itself.

Christopher had been in Bobby's room. This wasn't a

case of Bobby's imagination; it was a case of a true paranormal occurrence. "Forest, what's happening? What does Christopher want with Bobby?" she asked.

He placed an arm around her shoulder and drew her against his warmth. As she rested there she realized for the first time that she was trembling uncontrollably. "I don't know," he finally answered helplessly. "Are you sure there isn't any way that Bobby might have heard us talking about Christopher?"

"He called him Christopher the Crow. Forest, you told me just this evening that that's what you used to call Christopher. There's just no way Bobby could have heard that or made it up." She shivered again. "I've seen him talking to Christopher. I've felt Christopher's presence in Bobby's bedroom." She pulled out of Forest's embrace and looked at him. "You have to tell me again exactly what happened the day Christopher disappeared. You have to tell me everything."

He looked at her in surprise, his jaw tightening. "But I've already done that," he protested.

She stared at him, seeing once again the haunting secret that always seemed to linger just at the edges of his dark eyes when he spoke about that day. "You have to tell me every detail that you can remember."

He reacted with anger. "What good will that do? I've already told you everything that happened. There's no point in going over it all again."

"You didn't tell me everything, did you?" she asked softly. She looked at him expectantly. He hesitated. "Damn it, Forest, this isn't just about you anymore. This is about Bobby being in danger, and in order to know what we're up against, I need to know the truth...the whole truth."

He sighed and raked a hand through his hair, and

something seemed to absorb all the light in his eyes. "I told you that I fell asleep and ..and I must have killed him while I was sleeping." She nodded and he exhaled deeply. "That's not the whole truth."

Julie felt a shiver of fear spiral up her spine. She had a sudden desire to place her finger over his mouth, stop him before he said whatever he was about to say. She wasn't at all sure she really wanted to know the whole truth. Then she thought of Bobby, and the fear that had lit his eyes, the horror that had suffused her as he'd walked toward those dark woods. "Then tell me the whole truth. Tell me what happened."

He didn't look at her. Instead he stared into the fireplace, as if his greatest wish was to jump in and let the flames consume him. "I was sleeping, dreaming peaceful dreams, but something woke me." His voice was low, without emotion and she realized he'd once again removed himself far from the events of that tragic day.

"Go on," she said. She placed a hand on his arm and squeezed lightly.

"It was the click of the back door opening that woke me. I knew Christopher must be leaving the house. He loved the woods, and even though he'd been warned many times not to go near them alone, he often went exploring. I remember standing up, intending to stop him before he got out of the house. I reached the back door and looked outside, but he'd already disappeared into the woods. That boy could run like the wind. Anyway, that's when everything went blank. I blacked out."

Julie frowned. "What do you mean, you blacked out?"

He turned and looked at her, his face yielding a helpless horror that caused the fear inside her to intensify. "I remember standing there, and the next thing I knew I stood in the middle of a small clearing in the woods and

I could hear a scream, his scream still lingering in my mind." His hand trembled slightly as he rubbed it across his lower jaw. "I knew immediately that something horrible had happened…that *I* must have done something horrible. Why else would I be standing in the woods? Why else would Christopher's scream be so loud, so vivid in my mind?"

Julie stared at him. "Had you ever had that kind of blackout before?"

He shook his head. "That was the first time."

"But it wasn't the last," she observed knowingly. He looked at her in shocked surprise. "I saw you, Forest," she admitted. "I saw you when you were in one of those blackouts," she said.

"What are you talking about?" he asked hoarsely.

"You were in the woods. It was—I don't know—about a week ago." Julie remembered that moment when she had spied him through the branches. She's been struck by his slow, almost dreamlike movements, the utter passivity of his face. It all made sense now. It hadn't been drugs. It had been some kind of a blackout.

Forest grabbed her hand, his grip almost painfully tight. "Wha-what was I doing?" he asked.

"Ouch. Forest, you're hurting my hand." He immediately released his hold, but the tension rolled off him as he leaned toward her, his features twisted with inner torture. She realized at that moment what Forest's greatest fear was what haunted him day and night. He was afraid that in a blackout, he turned into some kind of a monster. "Oh, Forest, you weren't doing anything." She took his hand once again. "You looked like a sleep-walker. If that's the state you were in when Christopher disappeared, you didn't kill him. You couldn't have."

Oh, God, how he wanted to believe that. He'd been

afraid…so afraid of what happened to him in those blank moments he experienced from time to time. It was always the same—the scent of the woods, thick and oppressive, then nothing. He always came to in the same clearing, Christopher's favorite place, always in fear of what he'd done.

It wasn't until this very moment that he realized how much Julie's denials of his guilt soothed his soul, and he longed to let her hold on to her belief in his innocence, despite his fear to the contrary.

The fact that she hadn't believed he was a killer, refused to accept that he was capable of such an act, had been the first comfort he'd allowed himself in years. But he couldn't allow it. He couldn't let her believe in him. He couldn't let her obscure what he knew: that he'd done something to Christopher, and now Christopher's spirit wanted revenge.

"Julie, you've got to take Bobby and leave here," he said. "I'm afraid for you, for him."

"I don't intend to do anything until I talk to him some more and find out exactly what's been happening with this little friend of his. If it really is the ghost of Christopher talking to him, contacting him, then maybe we can figure out why, what it is that Christopher wants from all of us."

Forest looked at her. "I know what Christopher wants. He wants retribution. He wants me dead, too."

"Have you been to the doctor about your blackouts?" Julie asked, as if she hadn't heard what he'd said.

He nodded. "After that first one, after Christopher disappeared, I thought maybe it had something to do with the accident at the mill, the bang on the head I'd gotten. I went to doctor after doctor, had every test ever created. Nothing." Bitterness rang in his voice, a bitterness he couldn't control as he remembered the tests, the doctors, the futility of seeking answers nobody had. "I went to the best specialists money could buy and they all told me there is absolutely nothing physically wrong with me."

"That's ridiculous," Julie scoffed. "There has to be something that's causing them."

"I even went to a couple of psychiatrists, certain that I was a multiple personality or was just plain insane, but they sent me home, said the fugues were probably stress related or figments of my imagination." He laughed bitterly, then sighed and looked at Julie again. "They didn't think I'm crazy, but I know I am. There's no other explanation for the blackouts, and what I did to Christopher."

"Come on, let's go talk to Bobby." She stood up and took his hand. "Maybe we can find some answers."

"Julie, I was serious. I think you and Bobby should leave here." It suddenly seemed extremely important to him that he know they were safe....out of harm's way, out of the reach of the evil that was happening here. "I'll pay to get you relocated someplace else."

"We'll talk about that later. First we need to talk to Bobby and see what he knows about our angry little ghost."

Forest hesitated, touched by the fact that she simply refused to run away from this house, from him. "Julie, I said I'd pay for you and Bobby to leave here. You can pick wherever you want to live in the whole country."

She shook her head. "I can't leave."

"Why not?" he asked.

She smiled softly. "You told me once that one of my most irritating characteristics was my curiosity, and at the moment it's raging completely out of control. I'm not leaving here until I get some answers." Her smile faded.

"Besides, we don't know what Christopher wants with Bobby. It's possible that no matter where we go, no matter how far we run, he'll still haunt my son until he gets it." He saw the fear that glimmered in her eyes at this thought, but then it vanished and strength shone through. She held out her hand to him. "Come on, Forest. Maybe together we can make some sort of sense out of all this craziness."

He looked at her hand, stretched toward him. How he wanted to take it, feel the warmth of her support as her fingers clasped his. But no matter what questions still needed to be answered, there remained one irrefutable fact—Christopher was dead and he had been there, had heard the boy's last scream, had probably caused that scream. Ignoring Julie's hand, he stuffed his own in his back pockets and followed her up the stairs.

Bobby was in his room, although he wasn't asleep. His light was on and he lay on his back, as if waiting for them to join him. When they walked in he sat up and looked at his mother anxiously. "Am I still in trouble?" he asked, then caught his lower lip between his teeth.

"No, honey, you aren't in trouble," Julie said, sitting down on the edge of his bed. "But we need to talk about Christopher."

Bobby nodded, glancing at Forest, then back to his mother. "Mom, Christopher isn't imaginary, but he isn't real like me, either."

"What does he say to you?" Forest asked.

Bobby shrugged. "Different stuff. We play together. He likes to play hide-and-seek."

Forest gasped and leaned weakly against the doorframe. He wasn't sure he'd believed it until this very moment, but he knew now with certainty that Bobby was in touch with Christopher. Somehow Christopher had managed to breach the veil that separated the physical plane and the spiritual one. What were Christopher's intentions? What did he want from Bobby? Forest could understand Christopher's haunting of him. He'd always assumed Christopher's cries were intended to drive him over the edge of sanity or into a guilt-induced suicide. So why was Christopher manifesting to Bobby?

"When did you first see him?" Julie asked.

Bobby frowned thoughtfully. "It was right after we moved here. At first I'd just see him standing at the edge of the woods. Then one night he came to my room and talked to me, and we became friends."

"When does he talk to you?" Julie asked.

Bobby shrugged. "Different times. Sometimes he comes during the day, but mostly at night right before I go to sleep. He talked to me in school one time and got me in trouble with the teacher."

Julie looked at Forest, and he knew what she was thinking. If Christopher talked to Bobby in school, that meant the spirit wasn't tied to this house or the woods. It meant it was possible that Christopher might appear to Bobby no matter where they went.

"Bobby, honey, we believe Christopher is the ghost of a little boy who died a long time ago," Julie explained. Forest could see Julie's care in choosing her words and knew she was trying to decide how much to tell her son about his half brother. "He got lost in the woods and died, and we don't know why he's come back. We don't know what he wants."

"I knew he was a ghost," Bobby said. "I knew because he can fly and turn invisible and do all kinds of cool things." The excitement that lightened his voice faded and he frowned once again. "I knew you'd get mad

if I went into the woods, but Christopher wanted me to
go. He told me I had to, and I couldn't help it.''

"Did he say why he wanted you there?'' Forest asked.

Bobby shook his head. ''No, he just wanted me to go.''

"You mustn't go into the woods, ever again,'' Julie
said firmly. ''It doesn't matter what Christopher tells you
or how much he wants you to. The woods are dangerous,
and you must never go there again.''

Bobby nodded and yawned sleepily. Julie stood up.
''That's enough for tonight. We'll talk more in the morning.'' She bent over and kissed Bobby good-night, then
she and Forest went back down the stairs and into the
living room.

Forest headed directly to the bar and poured himself a
second glass of brandy, hoping he could drink this one.
He needed it. He needed to warm the chill that had taken
up residency deep inside him.

"I'd like one of those, too,'' Julie said as she sat at
the edge of the sofa closest to the fire. Apparently she
had an inner chill as well, Forest thought. He carried the
drinks over to where she sat and handed her one, then
sat down beside her.

As she stared into the fire, he looked at her. The hysteria that had played on her features earlier was gone,
replaced by a wrinkled brow that indicated deep thought.

She was clad in the nightgown she'd worn on the night
they'd made love. It was a silky, long white gown that
emphasized the perfect swell of her breasts and the slender curve of her hips. He was vaguely conscious of her
scent, sweet and floral, surrounding him.

She leaned back and the wrinkle in her brow smoothed,
as if she was finding a certain peace as she stared into
the fire. But under her soft exterior was a will of iron,
he knew. She'd survived what he suspected had been a

rather unhappy marriage. She'd managed to overcome Jeffrey's tragic death and financial ruin. She was strong, but he had a feeling she was now up against more than she could handle.

He remembered the night they had made love, the feel of her breath against the hollow of his neck, the way her body had yielded to his as if they'd been made specifically to fit together. It was a tantalizing memory, one he'd tried to keep out of his mind, away from his heart since the night it had happened. But now he allowed the memory to play through him, rich and full, every nuance of it an exquisite torture.

He could love her if he let himself, but he couldn't allow himself that luxury. He still didn't know what happened to him in his blackouts. He still didn't know what he was capable of during one of them.

He frowned as he remembered the harsh words he'd said to her on that night they'd made love. The hurt that had radiated from her eyes haunted him as effectively as did Christopher's mournful sobs. "Julie?"

She turned and looked at him, her gaze soft, accepting. He stared into his brandy, unable to look at her and speak of that night without revealing the fact that he wanted her again. And he didn't want to complicate things between them.

"Forest, what is it?" she asked softly.

"I just wanted to apologize for the things I said to you...those things about Jeffrey. What we did was a mistake, but what I said to you afterward was unforgivable."

Her fingers touched his arm, then reached up and stroked the side of his face. Fire. Her touch was like fire against his skin, evoking the familiar heat of desire inside. It was a fire that burned twofold, lighting the flames of passion and burning him with the fact that he couldn't accept the warmth. He grabbed her hand and removed it from his face.

"Julie, you and Bobby should leave here, leave me." He forced himself to look at her. "It isn't safe for you any longer. You have to face the fact that there's no way to fight Christopher. He wants revenge against me, and perhaps what he's doing is using Bobby to get to me. There's danger here." He stood up angrily. "And there's no guarantee that I'm harmless. There's no guarantee that in one of my blackouts I won't take Bobby out in those woods and make *him* disappear."

She took a sip of her brandy and set it down on the coffee table, then stood up and approached him. "Forest, somehow, some way we're going to figure this all out. At least Christopher is talking to Bobby. Perhaps we can communicate with him through my son. We can find out exactly what happened the day he disappeared, and we can find out why he's still here, haunting this house, these woods."

Forest opened his mouth to protest, to tell her that he knew why Christopher was doing what he was, but she placed a finger against his lips. "Forest, there's no guarantee that Christopher won't continue to communicate with Bobby no matter how far we run. You heard what Bobby said—that he's come to him in school. That means he has the power to manifest outside this house and the place where he died."

She removed her finger from his lips, the strength he loved back in her eyes. "This has become our home, and I'm not about to let the ghost of a seven-year-old run me out." She reached up and touched her lips to his. "I'm going to bed now, and tomorrow maybe we can figure out how to give Christopher whatever he needs to finally rest in peace." She looked at him for another long moment. "Perhaps we can find a way to finally give you the peace you need."

For a moment, as she gazed into his eyes, he saw the reflection of the man he would have been without this tragedy. He saw the man she thought him to be, and the vision, the need to be that man, ached inside him. She touched his face one last time, then turned and left the room.

Forest sank down on the sofa. The taste of Julie's lips still lingered on his mouth. Her scent remained in the air, rich and intoxicating. How easy it would be to open his heart entirely to her. She was so sure of his innocence, and that certainty was a balm to his soul. Unfortunately, it was a belief he couldn't share.

Peace. Oh, God, if he could only find peace. He knew what Christopher wanted. He wanted revenge, retribution; he wanted Forest dead. And before Forest would allow himself to harm Bobby, or allow Christopher to harm either Julie or her son, he would grant Christopher his wish. If he had to, he'd kill himself first.

CHAPTER TWELVE

Julie was already up and in the kitchen when Forest came down the next morning. He looked at her in surprise. "What are you doing up so early?" he asked.

"Waiting for you." She smiled and gestured toward a chair at the table, then poured him a cup of coffee and set it before him.

"Where's Lottie?" he asked, looking at his watch. "She's usually here by now."

"She's already been and gone. I sent her home," she said and his dark eyebrows lifted quizzically. "She took Bobby to spend the day at her house as a favor to me."

"Why?"

Julie drew in a deep breath, unsure how Forest would react to her next words. "Because I didn't want to have to worry about Bobby while you and I go ghost hunting."

"Ghost hunting? What are you talking about?" He stared at her blankly. "I've got to go to work."

"The mill can't run for a day without you?"

He frowned. "Well, I suppose it could, but..."

"Call in sick." She hurried on before he could protest. "Forest, I thought about this all night long. Maybe the reason Christopher is talking to Bobby is because Bobby is a child and open to the experience. I'm sure it never occurred to Bobby to fight against Christopher's spirit. His childish innocence, his untainted mind allowed the communication to happen."

"So what does that have to do with my going to the mill today?"

"I just thought that maybe you and I could go into the woods, into that clearing where you awoke after your blackout on the day Christopher disappeared. Maybe if we open ourselves up, call to Christopher, he'll come and talk to us." She flushed at his obvious skepticism. "I know it sounds crazy, but do you have any better ideas?"

"Only one." He looked at her, his eyes dark and foreboding.

"What?" Julie asked, a strange apprehension sending cold fingers up her spine. "Forest, what are you talking about?" There was something in his tone, a glint in his eyes that somehow frightened her.

He shook his head. "Never mind. I'll call the mill and tell them I won't be in today." He stood up, then hesitated, his hand on the wall phone. "We'll try it your way first."

"And then?" Julie asked, still apprehensive. What was he thinking? What dark thoughts flitted in his mind and caused his eyes to blacken in despair?

He shrugged. Instead of answering her question, he turned, picked up the phone and dialed the mill. As he spoke to one of the foremen, Julie went to the window that provided a view of the woods.

She took a sip of her coffee, her gaze lingering on the spot where Bobby had stood in the darkness the night before. Why had Christopher called him there? Why did he want him to go into the woods? The question had kept her awake most of the night. Was Forest right? Was the ghost avenging itself on Forest through Bobby? Anything could have happened to Bobby out there in the darkness. He might have gotten lost; he could have been hurt. He might have died…was that what Christopher wanted? She shivered and took another sip of the hot coffee.

She looked back at Forest. She'd sat through the wee

hours of the night, holding the wooden falcon that Forest had given to her, and she'd realized her love for him was all tangled up with her unshakable belief in his innocence. There was no way to separate the two. She loved him, and that love refused to accept the possibility of his guilt. But if he hadn't killed his nephew, then why had Christopher come back? Why was he haunting them?

Forest's blackouts frightened her because she didn't know what they implied. What caused his loss of consciousness? If there was no medical basis for the condition, then what? Did he suffer some sort of mental aberration?

Forest hung up the telephone and turned back to Julie. "Okay, I'm free for a day of spirit hunting."

"You have to take this seriously or it won't work," Julie exclaimed, then added, "although it might not work anyway." She sighed. "All I know is I refuse to just sit idly by and be terrorized by a ghost child." She looked at him and her eyes flashed defiantly. "And I still refuse to believe that you killed that little boy."

"And I keep telling you that I believe I did," he answered dully.

For a long moment they simply looked at each other. She knew her unshakable belief in him shone from her eyes just as strongly as his agonizing doubt gleamed from his. "I guess all we can hope for is that Christopher will be able to tell us which one of us is right."

He nodded curtly. "You'd better get a jacket. It will be cool in the woods." He grabbed a denim jacket that hung from a hook just inside the back door. "We might as well get this show on the road."

"Forest, it is worth a try, isn't it?" Her gaze searched his face, loving the strength of his jaw, the shadowy depths of his eyes.

He hesitated, then nodded slowly. "At this point I'm willing to try anything to finally discover some answers." His voice was weary. "This has to end, Julie. I'm tired of living like I have for the last ten years. I'm tired of the guilt. One way or another this all has to come to an end soon."

Again apprehension snaked up her spine at the resigned tone of his voice. Where before he'd always exhibited self-loathing and a crippling guilt, sometime in the last couple of weeks he'd moved beyond that, she realized, into a weary kind of acceptance that for some reason scared her.

"Forest, it will be all right," she said softly. She went to get her coat from upstairs.

Forest turned and stared out the window where Julie had stood while he'd spoken on the phone. The sky above was gray. It was as if the sun knew what journey he and Julie were about to take and hid in fear of their dabbling into the spirit world of ghosts. It was a crazy idea, but at this point he was willing to try anything. He sensed danger moving closer, not only to him, but to Julie and Bobby as well. There was a strange sort of energy, like an electrical current resonating in the air. He had the feeling that somehow psychic energy was gathering, gaining strength and substance for some malevolent reason.

"Ready," she said from behind him.

He turned to see her bundled in a cranberry jacket, which managed to match the color of her cheeks. For a moment he felt breathless from her beauty. Wildly, irrationally, he fought the impulse to grab her up and whisk her far away from this house. However, he knew no matter how far they ran, no matter what distance they trav-

eled, they couldn't escape the madness they'd been dealing with...for he feared that madness was inside himself.

"Julie." He took her by the shoulders, his hands caressing the cotton jacket beneath his fingertips. "Before
we leave here, before we go out into those woods, you
have to promise me something."

"What?" Her eyes searched his, the tone of his voice
apparently frightening her. Good; he wanted her frightened. He needed her frightened to assure her safety. "If
we get into the woods and I feel a blackout coming on,
I'll tell you to run. Do it. Don't wait, don't question me.
Run like the devil himself is after you." For he just might
be, Forest thought to himself.

"Forest, I'm not afraid of you."

He tightened his hold on her shoulders. "You have to
promise me, or I won't go. You should be afraid of me.
I'm afraid, and besides, I couldn't live with another...another accident..." His voice trailed off.

She placed the palms of her hands on either side of
his face, her eyes gazing into his. "Okay, I promise."

He relaxed, realizing belatedly how tense he'd been,
how frightened he'd been of going into the woods alone
with her. "Okay, then let's go."

Together they went out the back door and into the crisp
morning air. "Looks like rain," Julie observed, glancing
up at the overcast skies.

"Perfect haunting weather," Forest said with a wry
smile.

Julie gazed at him thoughtfully, her stride matching
his as they walked across the overgrown yard. "I wish I
had known you before." She flushed slightly and looked
down at the ground.

"Why?"

She looked at him again, her eyes so clear, so devoid

of guile. "Every once in a while you exhibit just the hint of a wonderful sense of humor."

Forest nodded and breathed in deeply. "It's been a very long time since I've found anything remotely humorous." He looked up at the overcast sky, then back at her. "I lost my sense of humor the day Christopher disappeared." He focused his attention on the woods they were approaching. He'd lost his soul on that day so long ago. *Oh, Christopher, I'm sorry. Whatever part I played in this...I didn't mean it. I loved you.* Forest felt the anguish, the despair that was never very far from the surface rising up inside him as the tangled growth and dense trees drew closer and closer.

Julie sensed the darkness rising up inside him. She saw his features grow tense, the muscle in his jaw jump and clench ominously. It was as if the shadowy aura of the woods suddenly grew within him, muffling his light.

They didn't speak as they entered the woods and followed the path Julie had taken on the evening she'd seen Forest in his odd state of fugue. She walked behind him, wishing for sunshine to banish the deep shadows that filled the narrow path. She stifled a squeal as some unseen animal scurried away from them, rustling dead leaves as it ran to safety. Forest turned and looked at her, his eyes as black as night. "Okay?"

She nodded and wrapped her arms around herself, as if her own embrace could bring her comfort. He turned and continued walking. She wanted to spin around, run back to the house. She hadn't quite anticipated the oppressive quality in the air. She wasn't ready for the ominous shadows, the scent of death that hid in the thicket surrounding them. She hadn't expected Forest's absolute withdrawal into himself and whatever darkness resided inside him.

Maybe she was wrong about him. Maybe her belief in his innocence was only the naiveté of a woman blinded by love. She'd seen women like that on television talk shows, women in love with mass murderers, blinded to the evil by their sick love. Maybe he really did have a dark side, one she had never seen, but one that had reared up on a day long ago and had culminated in the death of a little boy.

Maybe that dark side was only released out here, in the woods where there were no laws or social mores, where nature was at its most wild and savagery was the only rule. Panic knotted in her chest, a raw panic that made breathing difficult, almost impossible. Her eyes widened as he suddenly spun around again to face her, his eyes black orbs that radiated no light, no hint of his inner thoughts.

"Julie." His voice was hoarse and he held out his hand to her. In that instant Julie realized that it was grief that blackened his eyes, guilt that twisted his features, and all her doubts faded in the knowledge of her love for him. She took his hand and squeezed it, reassured by his touch. He led her into the same small clearing where she'd seen him before. "This is where I came to consciousness after Christopher disappeared," he said softly. "This is where I heard his last scream."

"This is where I saw you when you were in a blackout," she replied. "Something draws you here, so this is where we'll sit." Julie sank down onto the leaf-covered ground and patted the spot next to her. He sat down and they were immediately surrounded by a thick, heavy silence. Not an insect buzzed, not a single bird called, not a breath of air stirred. It was as if they were in a strange sort of vacuum.

"I've been back to this same clearing a thousand times in the past ten years," he said, breaking the stillness.

"Probably more times than you are aware of," Julie said. "I would guess you come here every time you black out. When I saw you, you were walking back and forth like you were in some sort of a dreamworld. Your face…" She hesitated, unsure how to describe the beauty of his face without his worries darkening his features. "You just looked like you were in a dreamworld," she finished inadequately.

"More like a nightmare," he said starkly.

"Tell me about Jeffrey and you," Julie said.

He shrugged. "What's to tell? We hated each other."

"Always?"

He frowned thoughtfully and stretched out on his side. A leaf clung to his hair and she reached over and picked it off, refusing to allow her fingers to linger in the thick locks she loved. "There was a time I thought the sun rose and set in Jeffrey," he finally said reflectively. "He was my big brother, strong and confident, and more than anything, I wanted us to be friends." He rolled over on his back and folded his arms beneath his head. "But Jeffrey didn't want to be friends. I was a baby when my mother left town and Richard brought me here. From the time I can first remember, Jeffrey was angry at my very presence. I think he hated me because he was afraid that somehow I'd take all our father's love and leave nothing for him. He was accustomed to being alone, being the little king. He was afraid I'd somehow usurp his position."

He closed his eyes, and for a moment Julie wondered if he'd fallen asleep. But his eyelids flickered and she realized he was entertaining memories of his painful past. He opened his eyes suddenly and in them she saw the

light of revelation. "I didn't hate him, not really. I—I
think I loved him. And in Christopher I got the chance
to love him all over again. It was like having Jeffrey
without his hate, without his fear. In Christopher I saw
all the good that might have been."

Julie smiled, pleased that at least in this, he had found
a certain amount of peace. Her smile faded as another
thought came to mind. "But Forest, if you really didn't
hate Jeffrey, then why would you have killed Christopher?"

The peace he'd momentarily found was fragile and de-
teriorated beneath the weight of her question. "I don't
know," he whispered hopelessly. "Perhaps I really am a
monster," he added, closing his eyes once again. He remained that way only a moment, then sat up, anger tugging at his features. "This was a stupid idea," he said
irritably. "I can't believe I actually let you talk me into
this."

"As I recall, you didn't have any better suggestions,"
she answered dryly.

"Well, this is stupid," he returned.

"Forest..." Julie sat perfectly still, her heart thudding
in a rapid rhythm of expectation. Cold air flowed over
her, frigid air that had nothing to do with the weather or
lack of sunshine. "Don't you feel it?" she whispered
urgently. "He's here. Christopher is here."

Forest tensed. "Julie...run," he said, his teeth
clenched tightly together. "Run."

But she couldn't. She couldn't move. Faint, childish
sobs drifted over her, penetrated her, evoking tears. Loneliness and despair overwhelmed her. The crying was eerie, rising and falling on the wind, but there was no wind.
Julie felt as if all humanity's suffering was contained

within the sobbing, and it pierced her heart, the very depth of her soul.

It was as if she lost all sense of self and knew only the deepest, darkest anguish. It filled her, consumed her, and she sobbed beneath the weight of it.

"Julie, for God's sake," Forest yelled frantically, his face taut with the last vestige of control. "I'm losing it. I'm blacking out. Get out of here! Run!"

The crying stopped at the same moment that Forest's eyes went completely blank and the paralysis that had held Julie captive snapped. She jumped up, poised to run, but hesitated, her attention arrested by Forest.

He stood up, his face completely devoid of emotion, his eyes open but unseeing. He walked slowly, hesitantly back and forth in a small area. He paused occasionally and tilted his head as if listening to some inner voice. He whispered something, a single word so soft she couldn't hear it.

Julie felt no threat of physical danger from him. It was as if his life force had disappeared, or turned so far inward it couldn't be detected. The cold still encircled them, along with a pulsating energy.

She stepped closer to him, needing to hear what word it was he kept repeating over and over. "Forest?" She said his name softly, experimentally, unsure what his reaction would be.

He paused and turned toward her, but she knew he didn't actually see her. Once again he tilted his head. "Five," he whispered.

"Five what?" she asked.

He frowned, as if the question were far too difficult to answer. "Five," he repeated, then the blackout passed. His eyes filled with emotion and instantly she felt his energy once again radiating from him. He sank down to the ground, his body trembling violently.

"You didn't run," he accused harshly.

"I couldn't." She searched his face, which looked achingly weary. "Are you all right?"

He hesitated, then nodded. "Just tired. I'm always exhausted after a blackout." He looked at her again, this time with a touch of fear. "What did I do?"

"Just paced back and forth, and you said one word—*five.*"

"Five?" He frowned. "Why would I say that?"

Julie smiled in frustration. "I was hoping you'd be able to tell me what it means."

He shook his head. "I have no idea."

"Come on, let's go home and warm up."

He stood, and she went to his side to support him. Together they made their way out of the clearing and back to the house. Once inside, they shrugged out of their jackets, and Forest set about making a fire in the living room.

When the flames danced warmly, he and Julie sat down on the floor before them, as if they needed the proximity of the fire to chase away a bone-shivering chill.

Forest stared into the blaze, wishing he could jump into it and put a finish to all this madness. When would it all end? When would Christopher's cries for justice be answered? God, he was tired of living with the burden of his guilt.

"Forest?"

He turned to look at Julie. The fire's glow painted her features in lush golds, and he wanted her, wanted her fire to ease his pain, wanted her energy and passion to surround him. He wanted her to keep him from feeling the hopelessness that had become an all-too-familiar companion. He wanted to reach out to her, to take her in his arms and make love to her. But he couldn't. He wouldn't use her in that way. It wasn't fair. It wasn't right.

"What do you feel just before you black out?" she asked, her brow wrinkled in thought. "You were able to warn me that you were losing it, so you must feel something."

He nodded, gazing back at the fire, unable to look at her without wanting her. "Just before I black out I always smell the woods and feel a horrible cold, and I'm overwhelmed by anguish. Then it happens."

Julie leaned closer to him, so close he could smell her heady fragrance. "Forest, those are the same things I feel when Christopher is present. The cold, the despair... somehow your blackouts and Christopher's spirit have to be tied together."

He sighed. "But that's not possible. I had the first blackout on the day Christopher disappeared." He stared at her, wanting to defuse his need for her. "I killed Christopher in that blackout," he reminded her harshly.

"We don't know that, and I don't believe it," she returned evenly. "Oh, Forest!" She sighed softly and put her arms around him, in what he knew was an attempt to comfort him. But it didn't help. Instead it enticed him, evoking emotion so strong, so intense that he couldn't fight against it, and in truth didn't want to.

He pulled her onto his lap and found her lips, already parted and eager, as if this was what she'd intended all along. He found the fire he'd wanted in her mouth and jumped in, needing it to sweep away his despair, his guilt, the loneliness of his life.

Her mouth gave to him, with nothing held back. Her tongue met his boldly, echoing the hunger that raged inside him. As the kiss continued, his hands crept up beneath the fleece of her sweatshirt, drawn to the warmth of her bare skin.

He pushed her bra up to free her breasts, and she moaned softly into his mouth, further heightening his desire. It took only moments before he was frustrated with the excess material of her clothing. With her help, he pulled the sweatshirt over her head, then removed her bra.

Then it was her turn to help him take off his shirt. Immediately he pressed her against him, loving the friction of her soft breasts against his muscular chest. By mutual consent, with no words spoken, they both stood up and took off their jeans, baring themselves completely to the warmth and light of the fire and each other.

Somewhere in the back of his mind, Forest knew they were about to do what he'd sworn he wouldn't do again. Somewhere in the back of his mind he knew it was wrong—all wrong, for he was a damaged man who had nothing to offer her except this moment in time, this passion so intense.

She stood hesitantly, the glow of the fire playing on the sleek length of her legs, the sweet swell of her breasts, the lovely lines of her face. She didn't cringe at her nakedness, despite the hot gaze he cast on her. Rather, she stood proudly, as if she were a gift to him. And she was—a gift of light, of goodness after too many years of being alone.

He approached her and reached out and caressed her face. She closed her eyes and tilted her head into his hand. He remembered the last time they'd made love. It had been all lust, primal and frenzied. He didn't want that now. He wanted soft sighs and sweet exploration. He wanted to take all the time left in eternity. He wanted forever.

His heart thundered as he reached out to touch the swollen bud of her breast. He realized his anticipation was almost as sweet as actual consummation. He bent his head and flicked his tongue over the pebbly hardness of her nipple. She moaned again and sagged slightly. Together they sank to their knees on the floor, their mouths seeking and finding each other once again.

Julie. His head was filled with her. Julie. His heart overflowed with her. There was no room for any other thought but her. As they kissed, her hands stroked languidly up the muscles of his back, then tangled in the hair at the nape of his neck. Her body moved against his in a sensual dance of tactile pleasure. He could feel the heat of her, smell the feminine scent of desire, and he wanted to drown in her forever.

Her hands worked their way down his back once again, the feather-light caresses sending him spiraling up to a higher plane of desire. A gasp escaped him as her fingers encircled his hardness. Their lips parted and he looked into her eyes, saw the glazed brightness there.

He eased her down onto the rug in front of the fire, the heat of the flames equal to the heat that came from her. "Julie, Julie," he whispered against the sweet hollow of her neck.

She moaned in response as his fingers found the source of her heat, delved into her velvety softness. He watched her face in the fire's glow, coveting the waves of pleasure that swept over her features as his fingers stroked within.

They took turns pleasuring each other with silken strokes, exploring the nuances of passion, finding hidden points of exquisite pleasure as part of their intimate discovery. He marveled in the marbled smoothness of her skin and in the honeyed taste of her. He felt as if he'd known her forever, perhaps in a million lifetimes before.

She offered the comfort of an old love, the frenzied excitement of a new one.

When he finally possessed her, easing deep within her, he felt complete, connected as he'd never before been in his life. As she accepted him, opening beneath him like a flower to the sun, moaning his name over and over, he knew this was to be his true torture. He looked deep into the depths of Julie's eyes and knew the memory of this moment would stay with him long after she and Bobby had moved on, long after she realized there was no future here with him. This he would remember forever. This would be his torment.

As they rode the crest of passion together, he realized that this—the memory of loving Julie—would be the true haunting that would eventually break him.

CHAPTER THIRTEEN

Julie remained in his arms for a long time after they finished making love. Slowly their heartbeats fell into sync, finding the rhythm of complete fulfillment. Still she remained, reluctant to break their union.

It wasn't until she realized he'd fallen asleep that she finally eased up and out of his arms. She grabbed her clothes from the floor and went upstairs. She took a quick shower, redressed, then went back down the stairs to where Forest lay sleeping in front of the fire. She curled up in the chair where he normally sat and watched him.

It was a pleasure to indulge herself in watching him sleep. He looked younger, the lines of his face nearly invisible in repose. She'd wanted to tell him, she'd wanted to speak of her love while they had made love, but she'd been afraid. He'd done very little to make her believe that his feelings for her were anything but desire. He'd never indicated to her in any fashion that he might be falling in love with her.

Still, as she watched him sleep, she allowed her love for him to flood over her, warm her from within. The fire played on his body, casting warm golden hues on his splendid nakedness. He was so beautiful. Surely a man so beautiful couldn't be evil. Shoving this thought aside, she stared at him once again.

She could see the sinful length of his lashes, sooty black against his paler skin, the whisper of whiskers that darkened his lower jaw. The lips that were normally held

so tightly, so tautly, were relaxed into a becoming fullness as he breathed softly in and out.

Oh, Forest, she thought wistfully. If only there was
some way to ease your torment. If only there was some
way to prove to you that you aren't guilty of killing
Christopher. If only I had the ability to make you whole
again.

She stared into the fire, knowing she wished for the
impossible. How could she prove to him something that
she couldn't even prove to herself? Her belief in his innocence was simply a gut instinct.

She straightened in the chair as Forest stirred, looking
like an awakening golden giant as he stretched and eased
himself up to a sitting position. "What time is it?" he
asked, still groggy with sleep.

"Not late. You didn't sleep very long."

He raked a hand through his tousled hair, then looked
at her for a long moment.

She tensed. "Please don't say it," she begged softly.

"Don't say what?" He frowned and stood up. He
scanned the floor, spying his jeans, then grabbed them
and pulled them on.

"Please don't tell me it was all a mistake." She
couldn't stand it if he said that.

He sank down on the sofa and ran a hand across his
jaw, then sighed. "No, I won't tell you that," he finally
said. "I can only tell you that this is all there is. Julie, I
have nothing to offer you. No promise of a future, no
promise of tomorrow."

"I'm not asking you for any promises," she said
evenly, although her heart wanted more, cried out for
more.

He closed his eyes, as if pained by her words. "If you
refuse to leave here, if you intend to continue to live in

this house, there is something you have to promise me.''
The torment was back on his face, wild and savage as he
gazed at her.

"What?" she asked. At this moment she was almost
willing to promise him anything.

"You have to promise me that you will never allow
Bobby to be alone with me. Never."

"Forest...I—"

"Promise me," he thundered angrily.

"I promise," she instantly agreed, wondering at his
intensity.

"It's a promise you cannot break," he added, then
slumped back against the cushions of the sofa, his eyes
closed once again.

"Forest?" She was frightened, not so much by him as
for him. She moved from the chair to the sofa and sat
down next to him. "Forest, what is it?" She searched his
face. "Talk to me. Tell me what you're thinking."

"I don't know." He rubbed his jaw, then looked at
her once again. "I just feel like things are reaching a
crisis. Can't you sense it in the air? An energy, a horrible
kind of pressure?"

"I...yes, I feel it," she admitted reluctantly. She'd
hoped it was just her. She'd hoped the pressure, the heavy
anxiety, was just her imagination.

"What if it's inside me? What if it's me who's about
to explode? God, I'm so frightened for you and Bobby."
His eyes seemed like soulless, dark orbs. "If I killed
Christopher, then there's no guarantee that I won't kill
again, and Bobby is the most vulnerable." His gaze
turned hard. "You have to make certain he's never alone
with me in the house."

She took his hand and held it tightly, wishing she could
sweep his fears away, but knowing she couldn't. All they

could do was wait and see what Christopher had in store for them. ''I promise,'' she said, knowing that, in at least this, she could offer him some comfort. ''I promise,'' she repeated, and leaned her head against his thigh.

Bobby changed out of his clothes and into his pajamas. He was pooped. At first, when his mother had wakened him early and told him he was going to spend the day with Lottie, he'd been upset. Lottie was old, and even though she was nice, he didn't want to spend his whole Saturday with her. But he could tell his mom was in no mood for him to argue with her, so he'd gone with Lottie.

But surprisingly, it had been a fun day. Lottie had taken him to her little house, and the first thing she'd done was fix him the best cinnamon rolls he'd ever tasted in his life. He'd eaten four, then she had talked him into helping her rake leaves in her yard.

They'd spent the afternoon at the movie theater, eating hot, buttered popcorn and licorice sticks. Bobby decided if he could choose a grandma, he'd pick somebody like Lottie, who laughed at all the funny spots and didn't hide her eyes when the movie was bloody.

After that he'd helped Lottie cook supper, and she'd entertained him with stories about when his dad and his uncle Forest were little. All in all, it had been a surprisingly good day.

''Bobby?'' His mom knocked on the door, then came into the bedroom. ''All ready for me to tuck you in?''

He nodded and climbed beneath the sheets. As his head hit the pillow, he yawned tiredly. His mom smiled and sat down on the edge of the mattress. ''Tired?'' she asked.

''Yeah. Lottie might be old, but she wore me out.''

His mom laughed. "I have a feeling Lottie could wear out anyone," she said.

Bobby nodded thoughtfully. "Mom?"

"What, honey?"

"Do you think it would be okay if I sort of pretended that she's my grandmother?" He looked at his mother to see her reaction.

For a moment she didn't answer, then she smiled— one of the smiles that told him she was happy. "I think Lottie would be proud if you wanted to pretend she's your grandmother." She leaned forward and kissed him soundly on his forehead. "Now, my little man, it's time to close your eyes and go to sleep."

"'Night, mom," he said as she rose from the bed and turned off his light.

"Good night, Bobby," she said, then left the room.

Almost immediately Bobby felt the coldness that always signaled his friend's arrival. He remained still, knowing that Christopher would show himself when he was ready. He could smell the odor of the woods, as if his room were suddenly filled with trees and brush and mossy rocks. He grinned in anticipation.

Hi.

Bobby sat up and instantly saw Christopher sitting on the back of the large rocking horse. He wore the same jeans and sweatshirt that he always wore, and the horse creaked and groaned beneath his weight. "Hi, yourself," Bobby replied.

Where were you all day? I was lonely.

"I spent the day with Lottie," Bobby answered. "We went to the movies." He smiled shyly. "I wish you could have gone with us."

I don't like it when you leave here.

Bobby shrugged. "I had to go. My mom made me."

Let's play a game.

"Sure," Bobby agreed enthusiastically. "What do you want to play?"

Let's play hide-and-seek.

Bobby frowned. "We can't play hide-and-seek in here. The room is too small. There aren't enough places to hide."

Let's go outside and play. There's lots of places to hide out there.

Bobby shook his head vehemently. "I can't. I got in trouble last time I went out to play with you."

But you have to. I want to play and you're my friend. You're my only friend in the whole world.

Bobby hesitated. It was nice to have a friend that would come to his bedroom at night. He didn't want to make Christopher mad, but he didn't want to make his mom mad again, either. He shook his head. "I'm sorry, I can't, Christopher. I'd probably get a real good spanking if I go outside. My mom was really mad at me the last time I went outside in the dark."

Christopher rocked the horse faster, the smile fading into a petulant frown. *I thought you were my friend.*

"I am your friend," Bobby protested. He wrapped his arms around himself, aware that the room was growing colder. A weird pressure was affecting his eardrums—that and an unpleasant humming sound.

If you're really my friend, you'll come with me outside. Come to the woods with me, Bobby. Please. I need you to come with me.

Bobby hesitated, and in that instant Christopher disappeared. Bobby scrambled from the bed and looked out the window. The night was black, but standing at the edge of the woods was Christopher. His form shimmered, as if he had swallowed the moon, and he raised a hand, beckoning for Bobby to come with him.

Come on, Bobby. The desire to follow Christopher was nearly overwhelming. Bobby felt Christopher's need, intense and almost physically painful. He wanted to go with him, but his mother's warnings about the danger of the woods rang in his ears.

"No," Bobby whispered fervently. He climbed back into bed and pressed his palms against his ears, frightened as he felt Christopher's rage sweep over him. Cold...it was so cold. "Don't be mad, Christopher. I can't," he whispered, squeezing his eyes shut.

After tucking Bobby safely into bed, Julie went downstairs and found Forest in the kitchen, fixing himself a sandwich of leftover ham from their evening meal. "Want one?" he asked.

She shook her head and sat down at the table. "Bobby must have had a wonderful day today with Lottie. He asked me if he could pretend that she's his grandmother."

Forest grabbed his sandwich and joined her at the table, a smile curving the corners of his mouth. "Lottie would be thrilled by that. She should have married and had a dozen kids and grandkids of her own."

"She never married?"

Forest shook his head. "She has a sister, but other than that, we were always her family." He leaned back in the chair. "Lottie was as near a mother to me as anyone," he said reflectively. "My father's love was conditional, but Lottie's was always there, no matter what." He took a bite of his sandwich and chewed thoughtfully. "Even though she thought there was a possibility that I might have done something terrible to Christopher, she never stopped caring about me.''

"I guess that's what family is supposed to do...believe in you even when the odds aren't in your favor.''

He smiled ruefully. "Not the Kingsdon family. There was never any doubt in Jeffrey's mind that I was guilty.''

Julie felt his pain as swiftly, as sharply as if it were her own. "When tragedy happens, people always look for somebody to blame. You were the most convenient scapegoat. That doesn't mean Jeffrey was right.''

Forest's smile faded. "I just wish I knew what I could do to give Christopher peace.''

And I wish I could give you some peace, Julie thought. Before she could speak, the lights overhead flickered off, then on again. "Ah, speaking of the devil," Forest said softly when the lights flickered once again.

"Forest!" As the lights went off and stayed off, Julie sought his hand across the expanse of the table. Before she could find it, however, his fingers closed securely around her wrist. The darkness of the kitchen was impenetrable. "Forest?" she whispered as he pulled her up from the table. His grip was tight as he led her toward the back door.

She heard the click of the door opening, felt a cold breeze sweep over her face, smelled the night air reaching out for her. She tried to break loose from his grasp, afraid as he pulled her closer and closer to the doorway. "Forest, what—what are you doing? Where are we going?" She planted her feet, his hand pulling her with incredible force.

At that moment a glow lit up the doorway between the kitchen and the living room. She turned and saw Forest across the room, standing there with a candle in his hand. Whose hand...whose hand was holding hers? In the dim illumination of the candle glow she looked down and saw nothing...nothing around her wrist. She emitted a single scream, then sank to the floor in a dead faint.

When she came to she was lying on the sofa and the lights were back on. Forest hovered over her, his face gaunt with worry. "Are you all right?" he asked anxiously as she slowly eased herself into a sitting position. She winced and gripped the side of her head, which palpitated like a bass drum. "You hit your head on the floor when you fainted. Are you sure you're all right?"

She nodded, her fingers examining the side of her head, where a lump was forming. "How long was I out?"

"Only a minute or two. Here, put this on your head." He handed her a damp washcloth. She did as he said, holding the cool cloth against her brow. She sighed as the pain ebbed to a dull throb.

"Julie, I didn't mean to frighten you," he said apologetically. "As soon as the lights went out I went into the living room to get a candle."

She shivered. "And while you were gone, somebody took my hand and pulled me toward the back door. I—I thought it was you. Then I saw you and—" She broke off and stared down at her hand. "It was Christopher. He wanted me to go outside, into the woods."

Before Forest could answer, the lights flickered off, then on, and once again the air grew cold. "He's coming again!" Julie exclaimed. She stood up and reached for Forest. He grabbed her, held her tightly against the length of him. Then the lights went out and the booming began.

"Mommy!" Bobby's terrified cry came from upstairs and shot through Julie like a fierce electrical shock. Not Bobby, she prayed. Don't hurt Bobby.

"Bobby!" she yelled back, and together she and For-

est ran up the stairs. She sobbed as they stumbled and
her shin banged painfully into one of the steps. Forest
helped her up and they hurried on. "Bobby!" she
screamed again, her fear for her son racing through her.
They met him in the hallway. He lunged into them in the
darkness.

"He's mad," Bobby sobbed. He burrowed his head
against Julie's midsection. "He's mad 'cause I won't go
with him outside."

"It's all right," she said, hugging him tightly against
her as Forest embraced them both. "It's all right," she
repeated mindlessly. The three of them stood together in
the hall as the house around them exploded in sound.

Boom. Boom. Boom. Boom. Boom. Silence. Then the
same. Over and over again it came, always the same pat-
tern. Five, Julie thought. Five. That's what Forest had
said while he was in his trancelike state. Five. She wanted
to tell Forest. It was important. Christopher was trying to
tell them something. But she couldn't compete with the
noise that surrounded them, and so she clung to Bobby,
clung to Forest and waited for Christopher to finish his
tantrum.

"But what does it mean?" Forest asked, his voice
harsh with frustration.

"I don't know," Julie answered softly, not wanting to
waken Bobby, who slept on the sofa nearby. She and
Forest sat on the floor in front of the fireplace, trying to
figure out what it was Christopher was trying to tell them.
"Five," she repeated. "It has to mean something. First
you said it when you were in your blackout, then the
booms came in series of five. He's trying to tell us something, but what does it mean?" She shivered and picked
up the poker to stir the embers of the dying fire.

"Here, let me." Forest added another log, then took the poker from her.

Julie frowned thoughtfully. "What is he trying to tell us? I should have gone with him when he was pulling me outside."

The poker hit the floor and Forest grabbed her by the shoulders, his eyes blazing as hotly as the flames. "Don't be a fool. You can't trust him. He might have been luring you to your death."

"But he's just a little boy," she gasped softly.

"A dead little boy." Forest released her shoulders and picked up the poker once again, his gaze fixed on the fire. "If I killed him and he wants revenge, the greatest pain he could cause me would be to harm you and Bobby."

It was the closest he'd ever come to admitting that he cared about them, and Julie cherished the words. She hugged her knees to her chest and stared into the fire. The house itself still radiated a strained sense of expectation, as if it was holding its breath, waiting for the next explosion of spirit energy.

Julie shivered, wondering what the next occurrence would bring. There was no way to prepare, no way to defend against this kind of intruder. Locked doors, closed windows—nothing worked against an apparition who wanted inside. "So, what do we do now?"

Forest put the poker away. "I guess we wait and hope that somehow Christopher will let us know what he wants, hope that we figure out what 'five' means."

"He's getting bolder, more desperate." Julie shivered again as she remembered that moment in the kitchen when she'd felt that hand wrapped around her wrist. It had felt so real and had pulled her toward the door with such intent. "What we need here is an official Ghost-buster," she said.

He smiled tightly. "I checked the yellow pages. Un-fortunately, the town of Kingsdon seems to be curiously lacking that particular kind of business establishment."

"Hmm, too bad." She grinned. "Maybe when this is all over we could start a business. Kingsdon and Kings-don, Ghostbusters Are Us. Let us clean your house of all unwanted ghosts and goblins." She giggled, knowing her punchy mood was due to a mixture of exhaustion and stress, but unable to stifle it.

Forest grinned, too, as if her laughter were infectious. She clapped a hand over her mouth, not wanting to waken Bobby, but unable to control the giggles that bub-bled up inside her. "We can hire Edith Windslow as our public-relations woman. She can advertise for us not only here, but on Mars as well. I wonder if martians have ghosts?"

Laughter rumbled out of Forest. "I don't know," he said. "But I'll bet Edith does." They laughed uproari-ously, and when they finally calmed down, Julie looked at him helplessly, hopelessly. "This is going to be over soon, isn't it, Forest?" She heard the desperation in her own voice.

The pain was back in his eyes. "Yes," he said softly. "One way or the other, this is going to end soon." He scooted over next to her and placed an arm around her shoulder.

She leaned her head against him, needing his warmth to take away the chill pervading her bones. She released an exhausted sigh, wondering what Christopher had in store for them.

CHAPTER FOURTEEN

When Julie awakened the next morning, she knew what she needed to do. She woke up in front of the fireplace, to find Bobby still sleeping on the sofa and Forest nowhere in the room.

By the time she'd showered and changed clothes, Lottie had arrived and the scent of fresh coffee wafted through the air. Julie got Bobby up and told him to get dressed, then went into the kitchen.

"That coffee smells heavenly."

Lottie smiled, poured her a cup and set it before her at the table. "You want some breakfast? I could whip you up some eggs."

Julie shook her head. "No, thanks. I've got an errand to run. Have you seen Forest?"

Lottie nodded. "He's downstairs." She shook her head in bewilderment. "Said he's not going to the mill today. I asked him if he was sick, but he said he wasn't."

But, Julie knew he was sick, sick with the haunting of a little boy and afraid to leave her and Bobby alone, afraid that Christopher would somehow manage to lure them out into the woods.

By the time Julie had finished her coffee, Bobby appeared in the kitchen, dressed but still sleepy. "If Forest comes up before we get back, tell him we're running errands and should be home in an hour or so," Julie told Lottie. Lottie nodded.

Minutes later, Julie and Bobby were in the car heading toward town. Julie hadn't wanted to tell Forest where she was going because she knew he'd think she'd lost her

mind. And she probably had. But she couldn't sit idly by
and wait for Christopher to reveal to them what he
wanted. She didn't intend to endure another psychic battle like the one they had gone through the night before.

There was nothing more frightening in this world than
knowing you had been touched by someone from the
spirit world. Every time she thought of that moment in
the kitchen when she'd felt those fingers encircle her
wrist, she wanted to scream. Never in her life had she
been so frightened.

It took her several minutes to find the address she
sought, but she finally did. The house was nestled at the
base of Kingsdon Hill. The house was small, but neat,
with cream-colored shutters against pale blue aluminum
siding. The front yard was oversized, the grass yellowed.
She looked over at Bobby, who had fallen back asleep,
and decided to leave him in the car.

She got out and locked Bobby in, then walked up to
the front door. The place looked deserted. She hesitated
before knocking, suddenly feeling enormously foolish for
coming here. She could almost hear Lorna's laughter:
"You needed help so you asked the town loon?" Julie
pulled up the collar of her jacket, a chill of apprehension
cooling the back of her neck.

Taking a deep breath, she knocked loudly. The door
was instantly opened by Edith. "Good morning, dear.
I've been expecting you," the old woman said, ushering
her inside. "Told my friends I couldn't go with them this
weekend because I was needed here."

Julie sat down in a chair next to the window, where
she could look out and see Bobby. For a moment words
failed her; she didn't even know where to begin. Why
on earth had she come here?

"Well, spit it out, girl!" Edith exclaimed.

She took a deep breath. "You told me the other day

that you sensed my son was in danger, that you knew I've been touched by the other side.''

Edith nodded and eased herself down in a chair next to Julie. "Give me your hand," she demanded. Julie did as she asked. "Now tell me everything.''

Julie did. She told the old woman about Christopher and Jeffrey and Forest. She held nothing back. She told of Forest's fears that he'd killed the child, of Christopher luring first Bobby, then her into the woods. She told Edith about Forest's blackouts, about him whispering the word *five*. Finally, with a trembling voice she scarcely recognized as her own, she told the old woman about the fingers clamping around her wrist and tugging her toward the back door.

When she was finished, Edith released her hand and leaned back in her chair, her brow deeply wrinkled in thought. She looked at Julie sharply. "You love Forest." It wasn't a question. It was a statement of fact, and Julie merely nodded.

"Did you come here today to see if I could tell you if he's innocent of the crime?''

"No." Julie felt a flush warm her face. "I know he isn't guilty. I—I know it in my heart.''

Edith nodded, as if satisfied with her answer. "Well, it's easy to figure out why Christopher talks to Bobby. There's a blood connection there, and a strong psychic bond. But he's trying to communicate something... something important." Edith frowned once again. "It's odd. I don't sense any anger from the spirit of Christopher. I sense an aching loneliness. He's scared and so lonely.''

"And that's what I've sensed from him," Julie agreed, remembering the deep, abiding loneliness that evoked tears in her each time she felt it. "But Forest thinks he wants revenge, that he is dangerous.''

"Forest is blinded to everything but his own feelings of guilt. He's a danger only to himself," Edith replied without hesitation. "Forest haunts himself much more than Christopher does. His feelings of guilt will destroy him long before Christopher will."

Fear suddenly shot through Julie as she remembered Forest's promise that this would all be over soon. She'd seen the black despair that obscured all else in his eyes. Somewhere inside, she'd feared the choices he'd make in order to appease what he thought was Christopher's hunger for revenge.

"I've got to go," she said, rising from the chair with a sense of urgency. "I've got to get back home. I've got to get back to him."

Edith walked her to the door, sorrow etched in her lined face. "It's a sad, sad thing," she said, shaking her head. "A man in torment and a little boy whose body has never been properly buried. That poor little boy, so lost, so alone in the woods. Such a sad, sad thing." She gave Julie a quick hug. "You come back if you need me again. Just don't forget—most weekends I'm with my friends on the mother ship."

Julie thanked the woman, then raced to her car, her heart pounding with dread as Edith's words whirled around and around in her head. Forest was in danger from himself. She knew exactly what Edith meant. Would Forest take his own life in an effort to appease the ghostly demands of Christopher?

"Oh, please, no," she said softly. Surely he wouldn't do anything so drastic, so final. And yet, as she remembered his desperation, his resignation when he'd promised it would all be over soon, her heart lurched in fear.

"Mom?" Bobby awoke as they pulled up in front of the house.

"Bobby, I want you to go into the kitchen and stay

with Lottie,'' Julie said, trying to keep the panic out of her voice. ''She'll fix you some breakfast.''

''What are you gonna do?'' Bobby asked, obviously feeling the tension coming from her.

''I need to have a talk with Uncle Forest.''

Minutes later Julie walked down the stairs to the basement, relieved to hear the sounds of Forest working. Without knocking, she walked into the room. He turned around, a smile lifting his lips. ''Good morning,'' he said.

''I love you.'' The words slipped out of her mouth before she knew they were even in her mind. He stared at her blankly. She flushed hotly, but realized she'd already thrown caution to the wind. ''I don't expect a reply. I don't expect you to reciprocate. I just need you to know that I love you.'' Her voice shook with a sudden flare of anger. ''Forest Kingsdon, if you ever do anything to hurt yourself, I'll find you, either in heaven or hell. I'll hunt you down, and I'll haunt you like you've never been haunted before.'' She drew in a deep breath and released it with a shudder, emotionally spent by her outburst. ''I— I just wanted you to know that,'' she finally said, then turned to leave.

Forest watched her go. She loved him. Her words should have granted him enormous joy, for he realized now that he loved her, too. He loved her as he'd never before loved a woman—with his heart, with his soul. But it was a murderer's heart and a blackened soul, and it was a love that had no future.

He sat down on the stool in front of the workbench, staring blankly at the carving he still held in his hand. So, she'd guessed about his final, ultimate option to quiet the ghost of Christopher. A whisper of a smile touched the corners of his mouth. She'd hunt him down in heaven or hell. Didn't she realize he was already in hell?

He sighed and set the chunk of wood down on the

bench, his thoughts, his heart still consumed with Julie. She and Bobby had brought life back into this house, something that had been missing for a long time. But no amount of love could bring life back to him. He was damned, damned by evil blackouts that had already caused the death of one child. How long would Julie's love for him last if he had another blackout and Bobby disappeared just like Christopher? How long before Christopher's demand for justice really did drive him over the edge and into complete insanity?

"She'll find another man to love," he whispered to himself, the words causing an arrow of pain to stab him in the chest. She was young and attractive and had the kind of passion that demanded the same in return. Eventually she would find a man, a whole man who could give her the kind of love she needed. Julie was a survivor, and she would survive this heartache and eventually move on.

He didn't know how long he'd been sitting at the bench when he felt it…the familiar cold. It brought with it the smell of fallen trees and shadowy brush. Christopher.

"No." Forest tensed as he felt the well-known darkness reaching out for him. He gripped the edge of the workbench. As always, he fought against it, trying desperately to cling to consciousness. The cold intensified, surrounded him, crawled inside him. "No," he whispered again, fighting with all his mental capabilities. But the darkness grew, expanded and swallowed him whole.

Julie went from the basement to her bedroom, leaving instructions for Bobby, who was eating breakfast, to come up when he finished his meal.

In the bedroom, she picked up the wooden falcon, tears

blurring her vision. She sank down on the bed, her fingers stroking the lines of the carved bird, her heart aching with her love for Forest.

It was tragic, all of it—Christopher's death, Forest's guilt, her love for him. Tragic that there seemed to be no answers, no resolution. How long could they exist in this house, being bombarded by a little ghost? How long could she stay, loving Forest and knowing there was no future, no hope?

She placed the falcon back on the dresser, her mind replaying her conversation with Edith. She didn't know what she had expected from the old woman. She'd hoped for answers, but should have known Edith would have no more answers than they did. *A little boy whose body has never been properly buried...* Edith's last words lingered in her mind and she frowned. The loneliness, the feeling of abandonment—those weren't the emotions of a ghost wanting revenge. They were the emotions of a little boy whose body had never been found, a little boy who was lost in the woods.

"My God," she gasped softly. Christopher wasn't trying to avenge his murder. He was trying to help them find him. As soon as she thought it, she knew it was true. It felt intrinsically right. Five. Five. What did it mean? Five yards? Five miles? Five what? She had to tell Forest. Damn it, why hadn't she realized it before?

She left the bedroom and hurried down the stairs. As she entered the kitchen, she paused and looked curiously at Lottie. "Where's Bobby?" she asked.

Lottie shrugged. "I went into the laundry room, and when I came back, he was gone. I assumed he'd gone upstairs with you."

Julie's breath caught painfully in her chest. "No, he didn't." She fought against the dread that lodged in her throat. Maybe he'd gone upstairs to the bathroom and she'd just missed him when she'd come down. Don't panic, she told herself calmly. She went to the bottom of the stairs and called his name. No reply. The silence was deafening. Where was Bobby? The dread that had lodged in her throat exploded into full-blown panic. Running back to the kitchen, she went to the stairs that led down to the basement. "Forest?" she cried. Again the silence screamed at her, and she knew with gut certainty that Forest was no longer in the basement. Where was he? Where was Bobby?

She dashed back into the kitchen and to the back door, icy terror gripping her. She stared at the woods and knew they were there…someplace in the dark woods with Christopher.

Without thought, she ran toward the woods, sobs of terror ripping through her. She crashed through the brush, unmindful of the thorns and brambles that reached for her, scratched at her. She knew only the need to find Bobby, find Forest.

"Julie?"

She broke into the clearing and fell toward Forest. He caught her by the shoulders. "Julie, what's wrong?" he asked urgently.

"It's Bobby. He's gone."

Forest dropped his hands from her, a look of dawning horror suffusing his features. "Oh, God…oh, please, no." He stared at Julie in abject panic. "I—I just had a blackout." He grabbed his head with both hands, his eyes wild with torment. "Oh, my God, what have I done? What in God's name have I done?"

Julie stared at him. Her heart thundered so loudly it seemed to fill the clearing. Forest had had a blackout and Bobby had disappeared. Ten years before he'd had a blackout when Christopher disappeared. Her head screamed with the implications, but her heart couldn't accept it. "No," she whispered. She'd seen what he did in his blackouts. He didn't turn into an evil monster. There was no evil inside him. "Forest, you haven't done anything. What we have to do right now is find Bobby."

"It's just like before," Forest said tonelessly. "It's just like when Christopher disappeared. It's all happening again."

She grabbed his arm and jerked it impatiently. "That doesn't matter right now. What's important is Bobby. We have to find him."

Forest looked at her, and slowly some of the horror in his eyes dissipated. "Yes...yes, we've got to find him. We've got to find him."

Together they left the clearing, stomping through the woods and calling his name over and over again. Lottie joined them in the search until she tired, then she went back to the house in case Bobby should show up there.

As the minutes passed and they walked deeper and deeper into the woods, Julie fought against hysteria. Forest was like a man possessed, calling Bobby's name over and over again until his voice was hoarse. She felt his torment but could do nothing to assuage it. She couldn't do anything but pray for Bobby. Where was he? Where was her baby?

They'd searched for over an hour when despair finally gained possession of Julie. She sank down onto a fallen log and sobbed. "The woods are too big. There's too much timber," she cried. Forest sat down beside her, her despair echoed in the hollowness of his eyes.

"Maybe he's not out here," Forest offered without conviction.

Julie shook her head. "He's here. I feel him." She squeezed her eyes shut. "He's someplace in these woods and he's scared and alone...just like Christopher." Her eyes flew open as she remembered what had brought her out of her bedroom in the first place. "We need to go back to the clearing," she said with conviction. "Christopher has been trying to tell us something, and that's the place you always go when you're in one of your blackouts."

They backtracked to the clearing. Once there Julie stood and looked around. "Five," she said softly. "Five is what he wanted us to know. But five what?" She looked at Forest in frustration. "Forest, Christopher doesn't want revenge. He wants to be found. He's been lost in these woods for ten years. He wants us to find him."

Forest gazed at her helplessly. "But how?"

"Listen." Julie tilted her head, then froze. Drifting on the air was the sound of pitiful sobbing. "Bobby!" she cried, all other thoughts fleeing from her mind. "Bobby, where are you?"

"Julie." Forest grabbed her upper arms and held her in a viselike grip. "Julie, that's not Bobby. Listen, it's Christopher."

She hesitated and knew he was right. Cold air encased her, sweeping over her with the icy breath of an open grave. The childish sobbing ripped at her heart, ached deep inside her, and tears began to fall from her eyes. "I—I have to go," she said, struggling to free herself from his grasp. "I have to...I need to go." She stumbled free from him.

"No, don't." Forest's fear deepened his voice and he grabbed her arm once again. "It could be a trick. He could be luring you to your death."

She shook her head vehemently. She reached up and touched the side of Forest's face. "We've been so frightened by him. We've been fighting against him all along. The thing we've forgotten is that he's just a little boy. He's a scared little boy who is lost." She broke away from Forest and headed down the path, toward the sound of the cries.

"Julie, come back," Forest called from behind her, but she couldn't stop now. The crying possessed her completely. She was surrounded by it and succumbed to it, allowing it to lead her where it wanted her to go.

The whimpers pulled her down an unfamiliar path, one that was narrow and steep, with deep ravines on either side. There was no sunlight on this path, only dark shadows and the scent of rich earth and green vines. As she passed each crevasse, she subconsciously kept count.

The cries grew louder, more intense, like the wind howling mournfully about the eaves of a house. Only this wind was inside her, its sorrow deep in her heart. She not only heard the cries, she felt them, around her, inside her. She was vaguely aware of Forest just behind her, finding the narrow path difficult to maneuver because of his bigger size. And still the cries drew her onward.

It was as she reached the fifth ravine that the cries seemed to explode in her head. She stopped, her heart thudding anxiously, and looked over the side. The sides plunged steeply downward, the bottom too dark to see.

She took a step closer and screamed as she felt the moist earth lip give way beneath her feet. Flailing her arms wildly, she fought for balance. Feeling only empty air, she heard Forest's impotent cry as she fell.

She plunged down the hillside, her body gaining momentum as she rolled, sticks and brush flattening beneath her. She finally came to rest at the bottom. For a moment she remained perfectly still, waiting for the pain of broken bones and bruises to assault her. There was no immediate ache, so she cautiously sat up.

"Julie?" Forest cried from above, his voice tortured beyond comprehension. "Julie?" he sobbed.

"I'm all right," she yelled back. "It's okay."

"Mom?" The small voice came from her left, and in the murky darkness that surrounded her, she saw Bobby sitting on the ground.

"Oh, baby," she cried, hurrying over to him and pulling him into her arms. "Are you all right?"

"I fell. I hurt my ankle. I can't walk on it." Bobby sobbed and held on to her. "I couldn't get up. I was so scared."

"Shh, it's all right now," Julie said, hugging him close.

"Julie?" Forest yelled again, his tone frantic. She realized he couldn't see what she was doing, didn't know that Bobby was with her.

"It's okay, Forest. Bobby's here."

"Is he all right?"

"I think so. He's fine. We're going to come up." Julie stood and helped Bobby to his feet. He cried out as his right foot touched the ground. She leaned forward and raised his pant leg. His ankle was already swollen. It was either broken or badly sprained. "Put your arm around my waist and lean against me," she instructed.

They took a step forward, but stopped as Julie's foot stumbled over something. She started to kick whatever it was out of her way, then stopped, horror sweeping through her. Beside her foot, half-covered with leaves, was what looked to be a bone. She swept the leaves away and realized there was an entire skeleton.

"Forest, you'd better come down here," she said with unnatural calm.

"What's wrong?"

She took a deep breath, then answered, "I think we just found Christopher."

CHAPTER FIFTEEN

"Okay?" Julie asked Bobby. He was resting on the sofa, his sprained ankle professionally taped by the doctor who had just left.

It had been a crazy afternoon. Forest had descended into the ravine and helped her carry Bobby out. They'd come right back to the house and had called the sheriff and the doctor. Within minutes the driveway had been filled with cars, and Forest took the sheriff, his men and the county coroner to the ravine where Christopher's body was.

"Mom?"

"What, honey?" Julie asked, stroking a strand of Bobby's dark hair away from his forehead.

"Are you mad at me?" The boy's eyes filled with tears. "I didn't mean to go, but Christopher was crying and I just wanted to help him."

"Oh, honey, I'm not mad." She gathered him into her arms and held him close, tears filling her eyes as she realized again how very close she'd come to losing him. "I was scared when we couldn't find you."

"I was afraid you wouldn't be able to find me, but Christopher said he'd bring you to me. He did, didn't he?"

Julie thought of the child's cries that had led her through the twisted undergrowth, down that narrow path. "Yes, Christopher led me right to where you were. He wanted you to be okay, and he wanted us to find him."

She released Bobby and stood up as Forest came into

the room. "They just took him away," he said. He sank down on the chair, a look of bewilderment on his face.

"Forest?"

"They've ruled his death accidental. It appears that he must have fallen off the trail and into the ravine. When he fell, he hit his head on a rock and that's what killed him. The rock was still there, under his head."

"I told you," she said softly, a rush of relief sweeping through her. "I told you that you couldn't be responsible." She searched his face, looking for some sign of inner peace, some elation at the knowledge that he hadn't been responsible for Christopher's death. But his eyes were dark, enigmatic.

"Uncle Forest?"

Forest looked at Bobby.

"You don't have to be sad anymore. Christopher is happy now. He told me so," Bobby explained.

Forest frowned and stepped closer. "What did he tell you?"

"He told me he just wanted us to find him. He didn't like it in the woods all by himself. He just wanted to play hide-and-seek, but he fell off the trail." Bobby hesitated. "He said something else, too, but it didn't make any sense."

"What?" Forest asked, his voice edged with tension.

"He said to tell the falcon that the crow loves him."

Forest's face crumbled and tears filled his eyes. With a curt nod, he left the living room.

"Did I say something wrong?" Bobby asked worriedly.

"No, honey, you said something very right," Julie assured him. Leaning down, she quickly kissed his forehead. "I'll be right back." She hurried into the kitchen, where Forest sat at the table, his head buried in his arms.

Julie sat down beside him, touching his head so he'd

know she was there. He cried, and Julie understood that, for the first time, he wasn't crying for Christopher, he wasn't crying from guilt. This time his tears were for himself, and for the ten years he'd spent hating himself. He cried for the man he might have been, the things he might have done, the people he might have loved except for the burden of his guilt. She knew they were tears that would finally heal him.

He didn't cry for long, and when he finally raised his head, she saw that the haunted look gone from his eyes. "It's really over, isn't it?" he asked hoarsely.

She nodded. "Yes, I think it's finally over."

He rubbed a hand across his forehead. "There's no way Bobby would know that Christopher used to call me Falcon. It was a game between us—the falcon and the crow." He rubbed his forehead again. "There's something I still don't understand. The blackouts."

"I think I do. I think every time you blacked out it was because Christopher was trying to contact you—and you felt overwhelmed by your worry, your concern for him, your love, your guilt. The feelings on both sides were so powerful that they sort of short-circuited your nervous system and you couldn't respond normally."

He frowned. "But what about that first time…the day Christopher disappeared?"

She reached across the table and took his hand. "Forest, I think when you had that first blackout Christopher was already dead. It would take only a moment for an energetic little boy to reach that ravine and fall, and you told me he could run like the wind. He died instantly and tried to contact you at once."

Forest nodded, accepting her explanation. It made as much sense as anything. He looked at her hand enclosed in his, felt her love radiating toward him. It stunned him, the total realization of her love. But it was too soon. His head was filled with the overwhelming events of the day.

He gently removed his hand from hers. "I—I think I need some time alone."

Julie nodded and watched as he disappeared down the stairs to his workroom. She didn't know what she had expected, what she'd anticipated. All she knew was what she'd wanted—to see the haunted look gone from his eyes. For him to take her in his arms and tell her he loved her. But perhaps he didn't.

She closed her eyes, fighting against the heartache that thought brought with it. At least his pain was finally over, and perhaps that alone could be enough for her. Perhaps...but she didn't think so.

Julie watched Forest as he leaned over and placed a hand on the newly erected headstone. Christopher now rested not only beside his mother, but with Richard and Jeffrey as well. Forest had paid to have Jeffrey's body moved here, to the Kingsdon Cemetery, where the family could rest together.

It had been two weeks since Julie had fallen into the ravine and found Christopher. It was amazing how quickly everything had returned to normal. Bobby had gone back to school with tales of a ghost boy who'd needed to be found. His story, along with his bandaged ankle, had made him something of a hero with his classmates.

Forest had gone back to working long hours at the mill, then closing himself off in his workroom. He kept himself distant, detached from everything and everyone. And Julie went back to work at the newspaper office and tried to forget that she loved him.

Now, as she watched him saying his final goodbyes to the little boy he had loved and lost, her love for him was a physical pain in her chest. He'd never made any promises, but she had so hoped...

"Mom?" Bobby tugged lightly on her coat.

"What, honey?" She turned to him and pulled his collar up more tightly around his neck. It was a raw day, with the promise of snow in the air.

"Are we going to live here forever?"

Julie hesitated and looked back at Forest. He'd been so distant, had kept himself so isolated the last two weeks. She wondered now if his passion for her, the desire that had burned so hotly and drawn him to her, had just been a result of the strange experiences they had shared. Perhaps it had been only his desperation that had caused him to reach out to her. Desperation, not love.

"Mom?"

Bobby pulled her from her thoughts, reminding her that he was waiting for an answer. "I don't know, Bobby. Forever is a long time," she finally answered. "Would you like to stay here in Kingsdon?"

He nodded vigorously. "I want to stay right where we are." He looked over to where Forest still remained by the graves. "We've got family here, Mom. We've got roots."

She smiled, remembering how on the drive from New York she'd kept telling him that—that they were going to Kingsdon because they had roots there...family. No matter how her heart ached for Forest, she couldn't be sorry they'd come. Bobby had found what he needed here, and no matter where they went, Bobby would have those roots.

Forest stood up and walked back to where she and Bobby stood, his face radiating a peace that soothed her aching heart. To Julie's surprise, Bobby immediately reached for his hand. "It's okay now, Uncle Forest.

Christopher is happy now. And we can all be happy, too.''

Forest nodded, his gaze on Julie. ''Yes, I think it's time we all find some happiness now.''

''Hey, it's snowing,'' Bobby announced. Sure enough large flakes were drifting down from the overcast sky.

''Come on, we'd better get back up the hill before the roads get slick,'' Forest said. Together they got into the car and drove back up the hill to Kingsdon Manor.

An hour later Julie stood at her bedroom window, staring out at the swirling snow, which now covered the ground and was rapidly piling up. Lorna had warned her that winters here could be harsh, and she had a feeling this would be the harshest one she'd ever known. The thought of being snowed in with Forest, of having to hide her love, endure his distance, was devastating.

''Julie?''

She turned at the sound of Forest's deep voice. He stood in the doorway, his gaze dark and enigmatic. ''Can I talk to you for a minute?''

''Of course.'' She hoped her emotions weren't there on her face to be seen. He'd been burdened with unnecessary guilt for so long. She didn't want to burden him now with her love. He'd probably come to ask her how much longer they were going to stay. He'd never wanted them here in the first place, she reminded herself.

''Where's Bobby?'' he asked curiously as he stepped into the room.

''He's downstairs in the kitchen with Lottie. They were going to make some hot chocolate.''

He nodded and walked over to where she stood, his eyes still not revealing anything of his inner thoughts. ''They say we might get a foot of snow by morning.''

''Lorna told me the winters could be long here.'' Julie's mouth was dry. He stood too close to her and offered her nothing. "Did you come here to talk about the weather?"

He smiled. "No, actually, I came here to talk about heaven and hell."

She frowned. "Heaven and hell?"

He nodded and took another step toward her. She stepped back, feeling the cold panes of the window behind her.

"You really would have hunted me down in heaven or hell?" he asked.

She realized what he was talking about and felt a hot flush sweep over her face. "I was frightened for you when I said that."

"And what about the other part?" He stood so close to her that his heat warmed her front as efficiently as the window cooled her back. "Did you say you loved me only because you were frightened for me?"

"No. I said it because I meant it." Her heart thundered in her chest, so loud she was certain he must hear it.

He tilted his head, his gaze soft as it rested on her face. "How...how could you love me?" he asked incredulously.

She sighed, her heart aching with her love. She reached up and placed a hand on his cheek. "Oh, Forest, how could I not?" She removed her hand and turned to stare out the window, unsure what he wanted from her, what he was willing to give in return. "It's funny, Jeffrey was charming and so easy to fall in love with, but it was so difficult to stay in love with him. You...you were difficult to fall in love with, but..." She turned and looked at him once again, this time knowing her feelings were in her eyes, knowing she was unable to hide the intensity of her love for him. "I think I will always love you."

He groaned and pulled her to him, his lips capturing hers in a kiss that stole her breath, banished the cold of the window and surrounded her with heat. "Oh, Julie, I love you," he said when their kiss ended. "I love you so much it frightens me."

Tears trembled on her lashes as she clung to him. "I've been so afraid. You've been so distant, so aloof since we found Christopher."

He led her over to the bed and they sat down. "I had to be sure," he said softly. He touched a strand of her hair, then cupped her chin. "I had to be sure the black-outs were really gone, that all this was truly over." He released her face, his eyes still warm and tender as he gazed at her. "It wasn't until today, at the cemetery, that I knew it really was over. I know it sounds crazy, but I felt Christopher's peace and knew it was all going to be okay. But it won't be okay without you."

Julie's heart exploded with happiness and tears once again sparkled in her eyes. "I was afraid I'd have to leave here, leave you. I couldn't have stayed here, loving you silently."

"If you ever leave me I'll hunt you down, whether in heaven or hell. I'll hunt you down and haunt you like you've never been haunted before."

Julie laughed with abandon. "I think one haunting is quite enough for me." Her laughter died and her love once again surged up within her. "I'll never leave you, Forest. You're part of my heart, my soul. I wouldn't be alive without you."

"Then you'll marry me?" he asked, his body tense, his eyes momentarily dark with anxiety. "Julie, I want to marry you and be a father to Bobby. I want us to fill this house with laughter and love."

"Oh, yes, Forest. Yes." Again his lips met hers, and in his kiss she heard his promise of tomorrow, the promise of forever.

When their kiss ended, he pulled her up. "Come on,

let's go tell Lottie and Bobby.'' He frowned for a moment, his gaze going out the window, where the snow obscured any view. ''We might have to wait until spring for a honeymoon.''

''No, we won't,'' Julie said with an impish smile. ''I'm sure if we talked to Edith she could get us booked on one of her weekend flights.''

Forest laughed, the rich, full sound embracing Julie. ''Or we could just stay here and be snowed in for the winter.'' His eyes burned hotly and a shiver of delight raced up her spine.

''I suddenly have a feeling that winter won't be long enough,'' she said. As she looked at him, saw the beauty of his features freed from torment, the promise of his love so bold, so pure in his eyes, she knew he was finally the man she'd always known he could be. A good, loving, gentle man. And she knew their love would last through good times and bad...through heaven and hell.

* * * * *

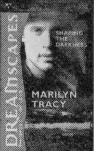